THICKER
THAN
WATER

THICKER
THAN
WATER

A Laurel Highlands Mystery

LIZ MILLIRON

LEVEL
BEST BOOKS

Author Photo Credit: Holly Tonini

First edition

ISBN: 978-1-68512-440-3

Cover art by Level Best Designs

This book was professionally typeset on Reedsy.
Find out more at reedsy.com

To Annette Dashofy, Jeff Boarts, and Peter Hayes, the best critique buddies an author can ask for.

Praise for Thicker Than Water

"A pitch-perfect procedural with excellent pacing, and crisp dialogue. It's the relationships that had me speeding through the pages. This is one where I didn't see the ending, and where a crime was a crime, but I sympathized with the motivation. Brava!" — Gabriel Valjan, Agatha, Anthony and Shamus-nominated author of the Shane Cleary Mysteries series

Chapter One

Defense attorney Sally Castle hefted a box from the tottering pile in the middle of the room. She pulled open the neatly folded flaps. "This appears to be your junk." She looked up.

Her partner, Tanelsa Parson, stood by the window, engrossed in her phone, her thumbs flying, completely oblivious to anything else.

Sally straightened and brushed a lock of hair out of her eyes. "Hey, T. You going to help unpack, or am I interrupting something?"

Tanelsa looked up with a jolt and stuffed the phone in her back pocket. "Nah, it's just Lisa."

"Something wrong?" Lisa was Tanelsa's wife, a small Asian woman with a personality much bigger than her five-foot-three frame. She normally didn't communicate with Tanelsa while at work.

"No, forget it." Tanelsa strode over to the box and looked inside. "You're right, that's my shit." She lugged the box over to a dark wood desk in the corner and thumped it on the surface.

A box of accessories didn't warrant such treatment. "Seriously, are you okay? You're not fighting with Lisa, are you?"

"No, we're cool." Tanelsa pulled items from the box. "Nobody told me I'd be packing and unpacking twice within two months when I accepted this gig."

"Well, nobody told me there was a leak in the roof that would result in a cascade to rival Cucumber Falls, and the landlord would boot everyone out, either." The downpour of water didn't quite match the size of the popular Laurel Highlands natural attraction, but indoors, the effect was much the same. At the time, Sally had a vision of visitors to southwestern Pennsylvania showing up to dance around in their bathing suits. She hadn't stuck around long enough to see it happen. She'd found this place within days of starting her search and, thankfully, it had been empty, allowing them to sign the lease and start the moving process. All the big items and boxes were delivered yesterday, and today, Tuesday, they began the process of unpacking boxes. With any luck, they'd finish by tomorrow and be open for business. She figured she and Tanelsa had set a record for packing, moving, and unpacking in slightly more than two weeks.

Tanelsa emptied the box and tossed it in the pile by the door. "At least the rent on this place is lower."

"Yeah, but it's farther away from the courthouse. What we gain in savings, we lose in visibility."

"True. We get any new clients since we moved?" Tanelsa peeked in another box. "Hanging files. Where'd we decide to put the filing cabinet?"

Sally waved at the opposite corner. "Over there. To answer your question, no. I'm still irritated that our former landlord wouldn't let us hang a bigger *We've Moved* sign on the door. With all the construction work, I'm afraid no one will see it."

"We'll have to think of creative ways to spread the word. You posted it on our social media, right?"

"I did. Cross your fingers it works."

They worked until noon. The only conversation between them concerned ownership of box contents, how they wanted to arrange furniture, and where to put the all-important coffee pot. Sally glanced at her watch. "What do you say we break for lunch?"

"I was hoping you'd say that. Do we order in or go grab a sandwich from the place down the street?"

Before Sally could answer, a soft cough sounded behind her. "Excuse me, are you the lawyers who used to have an office by the courthouse?"

Sally turned to see their visitor. She was a redhead, not older than her early twenties. Designer clothing could not disguise a body that would make a Playboy model weep with envy. Her makeup and skin were flawless, with sooty eyelashes framing deep brown eyes. This was a girl who would draw attention in any room she walked into, but at the moment, a hesitancy hung over her like a heavy cloak. "That's us," Sally said. "I'm Sally Castle. This is my partner, Tanelsa Parson. What's your name?"

"Madison Tilgher." The girl's voice was low-pitched, and it was easy to imagine her talking in sultry tones. "People call me Maddie."

"Nice to meet you, Maddie. How can we help?"

She took in the half-unpacked room. "I'm interrupting. I'm sorry." She turned to go.

"No, wait. We were only talking about lunch." Sally glanced at Tanelsa.

Her partner waved her on and held her hand to her head, fingers mimicking a phone. *What do you want?* she mouthed.

Sally nodded. "Get me a turkey on rye, with Swiss, brown mustard, lettuce, onion, and tomato." She darted after Maddie. "Hey, hold on."

The girl had reached the door. "I don't want to keep you."

"It's okay. It'll take a while for food to arrive. Why don't we go in here?" Sally gestured to the small conference room designated for client meetings. A long rectangular table took up most of the space. Sally removed two chairs from the stack in the corner. "Please, have a seat."

Maddie hesitated, then sat and held a purse with the Michael Kors logo in her lap. "I'm sorry to bust in on you like this. You must have just moved in."

"This morning, to tell the truth. We signed the lease on Monday. You're our first visitor in this space." Sally wished she could go grab a legal pad and pen, but she was afraid Maddie would disappear. "Did you see our sign?"

"Yeah." The young woman clutched the handbag. Her manicure, like her makeup, was perfect. "I'm not even sure you *can* help me."

"Why don't you explain your situation, and I'll be the judge of that?" Sally was used to the hesitant type of client who wanted help, but either didn't know how to ask or didn't believe they deserved attention.

Maddie bit a plump lower lip. "There's this guy."

"Friend, boyfriend, co-worker?"

"None of the above?" Maddie gave a weak laugh. "He's...it's complicated."

"Okay, don't worry about that now. What's he done?"

"I want him to go away. But he insists on hounding me. He calls at all hours, when I'm in class, when I'm at the dorm, or even the library."

Sally leaned on the table. "You're a student?"

"Yes, a senior at St. Vincent College." Maddie paused. "I've told him to beat it, but..."

"He doesn't follow instructions. I get it." Maddie had a stalker. It didn't matter the role in her life, at least not right now. "Is he also a student?"

"No."

"Has he hurt you?"

"Oh, gosh, no. But he says things, you know? I wouldn't be surprised if I came out of class one day and he was waiting for me."

"I see." Now Sally really wanted that pad. "Have you tried contacting the police?"

"No." Maddie sent her deep-red hair flying with her head shake. "I don't think the cops could do anything. Like I said, he hasn't hurt me."

"You'd be surprised. Wait here. Let me get some paper so I can take some notes. I'll be right back." Sally got up and went to her desk. Of course, that box hadn't been unpacked yet. She yanked open ones containing books, files, and printer materials. Where were the office supplies?

As she found the one she was looking for, slit through the tape on the flaps, and pulled out a pad, she heard the front door open and shut. Maybe it was Tanelsa, but Sally suspected she knew what had happened. Sure enough, when she returned to the conference room, it was empty.

Chapter Two

Two days later, around one in the afternoon, Trooper Jim Duncan sped down New Salem Road, heading west from the Uniontown State Police barracks. "What road are we looking for again?"

His partner, Trooper Jenny Cavendish, sat in the passenger seat of the unmarked state Ford and consulted the sticky note in her hand. "Stoney Point. Tell me again why we're doing this?"

"Because I trust Aislyn McAllister. If she thinks something's off, it is." He slowed and made the turn. "This is probably a pretty place in the summer and early fall. Lots of trees."

"Uh-huh. This is it. We're looking for 29787." Cavendish brushed ash blonde hair out of her eyes. "A missing person is not a crime, you know."

The left side of the road was open grass, brown and withered in the November chill typical of southwestern Pennsylvania. Leafless trees clawed toward a frosty blue sky on the right. "Just keep your eyes open."

Less than two minutes later, Cavendish pointed. "Right here."

"Thanks for the warning." Duncan stomped on the brake just as he was about to drive past his destination and slewed the car into a finely-graveled driveway that ended at a farmhouse with an imposing wrap-around front porch, fresh white paint, and windows flanked by deep red shutters. He parked near a marked Ford Interceptor at the front of the house and got out. A big rhododendron bush, leaves tightly curled against the cold resided at the far end of the porch. Wilted hostas and the remains of the summer annuals dotted the black mulch of the front garden. He mounted the steps and noted the eye-hooks for a porch swing. The furniture was gone, but

5

marks on the wood floor gave evidence of the chairs that must take up the space during the warmer months.

Cavendish followed. "What has Trooper McAllister done to earn your trust?"

"She was my last trainee as an FTO when I worked patrol." Duncan used a shiny brass knocker attached to the dark red door to announce their presence.

"You trust her because you trained her?"

Duncan heard both skepticism and mirth in his partner's voice. He didn't turn. "No, I trust her because she's good."

The door opened, and Aislyn McAllister stood before him in a neatly pressed gray uniform. She'd taken off her campaign hat, and her blonde curls, still not recovered from their summer-sun bleaching, were pulled back into a knot at the back of her head. McAllister stood only about five-foot-three, but had the compact build of an athlete. Anyone who underestimated her because of her size would be in for a rude awakening. "Thank God, you made it." She waved them in.

Duncan made the introductions between the two women. "What's the problem?" He watched as his partner and his protégé eyed each other, no doubt making whatever judgments women do when meeting each other.

"If Sally didn't have brown hair, I'd say you had a thing for blondes," Cavendish said.

"Can we stay on topic and off the hair color of my women friends?" The only way this situation could be worse was if his girlfriend, Sally Castle, were here. He could easily imagine her, Cavendish, and McAllister bonding together and discussing him.

McAllister snorted. "If you insist." She pulled out her notebook. "Let me catch you up before you meet the homeowner. At about ten o'clock this morning, Susan Hepworth, that's the woman who lives here, reported her son, Noah Freeman, missing. He ate breakfast at seven-thirty, she saw him at the table at eight, but she'd been doing laundry and assumed he was playing video games, based on the noise from the living room television. When she checked, the game controller was on the floor, the game still on, and Noah was gone. She checked the surrounding houses before calling us."

Cavendish hooked her thumbs in her belt loops. "Two hours, that's not a long time. How old is this kid?"

McAllister looked up from her notes. "He's nineteen, but he's also autistic. High-functioning, according to Ms. Hepworth, but still a risk if he's out on his own. Plus Dunlap Creek Lake is not far from here, and Noah doesn't know how to swim."

Cavendish gave a low whistle. "That changes things."

"Yes, it does."

Duncan immediately thought of all the possible places such a person could hide and the potential tragic outcomes. "You made all the usual calls? Got the right people involved?"

"Of course." McAllister flipped a page in her book. "Searchers found him a little before noon, hiding in a shelter at Dunlap Creek Park. He was in full meltdown, kept flapping his hands, and showed a lot of the signs of distress common in autistic individuals. No one could get near him until Ms. Hepworth arrived. He appeared to be unharmed, a few scratches that could be attributed to crashing through the underbrush, but nothing serious. However, when we got him home, he kept talking about a sleeping lady. No one could get much sense out of him, not where he'd seen her or who this woman was. He just kept repeating 'She's sleeping, She's sleeping, and she's blue' over and over again. When Ms. Hepworth suggested maybe it had all been his imagination, he got quite agitated."

"Did you look for this sleeping lady?"

"I did, but nothing. Nobody else has seen anything like that. Ms. Hepworth seemed pretty confident that he'd imagined things."

"Don't get me wrong, I'm glad he was found," Cavendish said. "But I don't understand why you called us."

McAllister's eyes glinted, and she fixed Cavendish with an icy stare. "He's too insistent. Yeah, I get it. He's not the best witness. But what if he's right? Who in their right mind takes a nap, outside, in early November? Especially around here? There was a hard frost last night and there's another warning on for tonight."

Duncan interceded. "You're suspicious."

"That might be a little strong, but I'm concerned." McAllister flipped her notebook so it closed. "I'd sent the K9 unit away, as well as everyone else, the first time we found him because all I had was the word of an unreliable witness about the woman. I couldn't justify sending them out, especially when K9 got a call about a missing kid in Washington County. But if this other woman exists, based on Noah's description, she's dead or in serious trouble. Blue could be blue skin or lips. If she's alive, it's hypothermia for sure, and she's in danger. If it's because she's dead, well, I think we ought to find her, don't you?"

"Absolutely."

"I did the best I could, but I didn't see anything. No one I spoke to saw anyone like that. Noah was no help. Every time his mother or I mentioned it, he became agitated."

Duncan adjusted his jacket. "I know you've tried, but I think the first step is to talk to Noah again. Maybe we'll be able to coax some more information out of him."

McAllister shook her head. "And there's the problem."

"The mother won't let us?" Cavendish asked.

"No." McAllister slipped the notebook back into her pocket. "Noah is missing. Again."

Chapter Three

Duncan exchanged a look with his partner before speaking. "What do you mean *again?*"

"Exactly what I said." McAllister didn't sound happy. From the sour expression on her face, she'd already had this conversation and wasn't looking forward to doing it a second time.

Cavendish crossed her arms. "How do you lose a nineteen-year-old autistic boy twice in one day?"

"Turns out it's not that hard, and Ms. Hepworth says it's not normal for him, but not unusual, either." McAllister shrugged. "We brought Noah home after finding him the first time. Ms. Hepworth left him in the kitchen with a cheese sandwich, some chips, and a glass of milk. Then she walked me to the door, said thank you. I told her I was glad he was safe, blah, blah. I was in my car writing up the call report and trying to decide what to do next about this phantom woman when she came pelting out of the house, white as a sheet. Instead of eating his lunch, Noah had left via the sliding glass doors in the kitchen and was nowhere to be found. He moves fast, I'll tell you that. There are several fields around here. I checked them out, but I didn't see anything. I also did a quick search of the nearest woods, nothing. I went back to the shelter near the lake where we found him the first time. Abandoned. So I gave up and called you."

Cavendish turned to Duncan. "Not a great situation, but I repeat. A missing person is not a crime. We don't know if this woman exists. It sounds harsh, but until and unless her body is found, there's nothing for us to do here. It's a job for search and rescue, not Criminal Investigation."

"Time out." The mutinous look on McAllister's face made Duncan step between the two women. "McAllister, what exactly do you need?"

She shot one last look at Cavendish. "Ideas. Am I missing something?"

Cavendish looked back at the younger woman. "What about calling someone in search and rescue to help you find both people? Maybe the local fire department?"

Duncan rubbed his chin. "Let's go talk to the mother."

Sue Hepworth sat at a butcher-block island, clutching a sodden tissue. Strands of her light-gray hair were plastered to her forehead, and her brown eyes red-rimmed. She looked to be in her mid-fifties. Her face had a few lines, and her figure was far from willowy, but it was obvious she'd been a good-looking woman in her youth. "Did you find him?"

"No, ma'am." McAllister yanked a fresh Kleenex from a paisley-patterned box on the counter. "I'd like to introduce you to Troopers Duncan and Cavendish. They're from our Criminal Investigation Section."

"Are you detectives? Have you come to search for my son?"

The instant hope in her face cut Duncan's heart. "No, the state police doesn't have that title, and we don't usually conduct missing person searches. I've worked with Trooper McAllister in the past, and she asked me for advice." He pulled out a stool and sat next to Sue. "Tell me what happened this morning, the first time Noah disappeared."

Sue dabbed her eyes and took a steadying breath. "We had breakfast like we always do. I left Noah in the TV room, playing video games, while I went and started the laundry. He normally doesn't move, but when I checked on him about half an hour later, he was gone. This was around nine-thirty. The front door was open. I called the neighbors, but no one had seen him. I searched for another hour or so, and then I called 911." Tears traced down her cheeks. "I know he's nineteen, and maybe it's silly, but you don't understand. He needs help. I can't imagine the trouble he'd get in to if left on his own."

"It's not silly at all." Duncan glanced at McAllister. "How'd you find him the first time?"

"Pure luck," she said. "The K9 unit was in the woods and had led us to a ratty old cabin. It was locked up tight, but then I noticed a path. I followed it down to a little boat dock, and he was sitting there, staring at the water and talking to himself. We coaxed him back to the house. I dismissed everyone who was there and got ready to leave."

"Autistic people often seek water when they are upset. I remember that from a training session we had a couple years ago." Duncan refocused on Sue. "The second time, tell me what happened."

"I shouldn't have left him alone." She closed her eyes. "I left him here in the kitchen. Watching TV. One of his favorite shows. I swear I locked the door. I went out into the driveway to talk to Trooper McAllister and thank her. We talked, oh, ten minutes? No more than fifteen. I came back into the house and heard the TV, so I assumed he was there." She pounded the wood. "I should have checked! I went to move around some loads of laundry. It took less than five minutes. But when I looked into the kitchen, he was gone. Thank God Trooper McAllister hadn't left yet."

"Is it normal for Noah to run off like this?" asked Cavendish.

Sue shrugged. "It's hard to define *normal*. In general, he stays put. But if he gets bored, he'll wander off. Or if he's obsessed with something."

Like the sleeping lady. Noah wasn't at the dock. "Did you check the lake shore?"

McAllister spread her hands. "Only around the dock. I figured I needed backup for a thorough search."

"What are we going to do?" Sue asked. She buried her face in her hands. "This is all my fault."

"No, it's not." Duncan looked at his partner. "Cavendish, call Uniontown police. See if they have a K9 unit free since ours is out on another call."

She lifted her eyebrows. "We aren't in the city limits."

"No, but in a case like this, I'm sure they'll be happy to help. Then I want you to stay here with Ms. Hepworth in case Noah returns." He stood and pointed at McAllister. "You're with me. Show me this dock."

They walked from the house, through the woods across the street. Duncan picked his way through the trees, painfully aware that his wingtips were not the best footwear for the situation. "Remind me to always carry a pair of boots with me."

"Yeah, you're not dressed for this kind of foray." McAllister grinned. "What's wrong with your partner? She always this uptight?"

He pushed a bare tree branch out of his way. "She doesn't think this is a case for Criminal Investigation, that's all. She's right and we do have things to do back at the office. But I'm not gonna stand on formality when an at-risk teenager is MIA."

"Thank God." McAllister pointed. "That's the dock."

The wood planking was well-aged and faded from the sun. Small gaps between the boards allowed the water to be seen. Duncan eyed the jagged wood of the handrail. An invitation for a splinter if he'd ever seen one. A dilapidated shack was next to the dock, and a pile of rope showed where a boat could be tied up, but this late in the season, it was gone. "You said he was sitting on the dock?"

"Yep." She ran a hand over her head. "Staring at the water, mumbling to himself. It was not easy to convince him to go with me. That's the first time I heard he was talking about the sleeping lady."

"Too bad he didn't give you a location on her." Duncan scanned the horizon. No sign of life or watercraft. "That cabin, did you try the door?"

"No, there's a padlock on it."

He nodded. "Is there an inlet to this lake?"

"Not sure." McAllister did her own visual survey. "Over there, maybe? It's pretty obscured, but there might be a small stream or something."

"Let's take a look. Keep your eyes peeled for footprints, broken branches, anything that would indicate a human passed through the area." He headed for the spot, careful to stay away from the shore, which looked fairly marshy. "Yep, it's not much this time of year, but it's a trickle. Let's see where it leads."

The water traced back into the woods. They followed it for about ten yards before McAllister pointed. "There he is."

Noah Freeman sat on a boulder, arms tightly crossed against his chest. His eyes were closed, and his hair flopped over his forehead. A beam of sunlight glinted on the reddish locks. His lips moved in silent speech.

"Stay here," Duncan said. He moved slowly, deliberately toward the boy.

He hadn't had a lot of interaction with autistic people, but he knew he had to be calm. "Hey, Noah."

The teenager's eyes flew open. "No, no, no." He flapped his hands in clear distress.

Duncan stopped at least five feet away. "No need to get excited. I'm a friend of your mom's. She's worried about you."

"No, no, no."

Duncan looked around. There wasn't anything to sit on, but he squatted so he was at Noah's eye level. "It's okay. What are you doing out here?"

Noah's hands still fluttered, but he stopped speaking. He fixed Duncan with a suspicious stare.

"How about this? Let's go back where it's warm. I bet your mom will have a good snack for you."

"I gotta help her."

"Okay, we can do that." Duncan shifted on the leaf mold, releasing a scent of decay. "Who?"

"My friend, Maddie. She's sleeping. I saw her before, but I didn't recognize her. But now I did, and I can't wake her up. I knocked on the window, but she didn't hear me."

"Where is she? I'll see if I can help her."

Noah hesitated. "Over there." He waved in the direction of the locked cabin.

"Are you sure? I think that might be shut up for the season, Noah." Duncan pivoted. He could just see the building through the trees. "The door is locked."

"No, no, no." Noah shook his head, sending his hair flying. "Maddie is sleeping. I can't wake her up."

"All right." Duncan stood and beckoned to McAllister. "Here's what we're going to do. You stay with my friend Aislyn. I'm going to go see if I can help Maddie. Does that sound good?"

Noah didn't answer. He stared at Duncan with eyes the size of saucers.

McAllister turned so her back was to Noah. She pitched her voice low to prevent him from hearing. "It's locked, Boss."

"No harm in me checking it out. Stay with him and be calm." Duncan moved off toward the little cabin. It was more of a shack, really. He doubted there was more than one room inside. A battered metal chimney protruded from the roof, which was covered in shingles that had seen better days. A new-looking padlock adorned the door. He slipped on a pair of nitrile gloves and tugged, but it didn't give. On instinct, he took out his phone, snapped a picture, and slipped it back in his pocket.

He circled the cabin. A few windows, no more doors. He was about to decide McAllister was right when he noticed a small gap at the bottom of a window. He took a shot of it, then tugged. The pane slid up, mostly noiselessly, with only one sticking point. Not what he would have expected from a place that looked as though no one had been there in decades. There was no screen. "Hello, Maddie? This is Trooper Jim Duncan from the State Police. Anyone in there?"

No answer, but a familiar scent wafted out. More than leaves were decaying inside.

It didn't take much effort to hoist himself through the window. He waited for his eyes to adjust. Once they did, he made out a pale figure, tousled dark red hair across her face, but it didn't obscure the scarf tied around her throat. She was practically naked, only a g-string and a bra on her curvaceous young body. Out of habit, he checked for a carotid pulse, but the waxy blue tinge to the skin and the chill of the touch meant it didn't surprise him when he found nothing.

Duncan went to the front door. A couple of strong shoves broke apart the aged and rotted wood. "McAllister, you got your radio on you?"

"Always," she called back. "Why? Did you find Maddie?"

"I think so." He turned back toward the body. "She's blue all right, but she isn't sleeping."

Chapter Four

Duncan stood outside the crime scene while techs worked over the building. Inside, Fayette County deputy coroner Tom Burns examined the body. Duncan fired off a quick text to Sally, letting her know he'd be working late.

McAllister came up beside him. "You took pictures of the door, right?"

"Yeah. And the window I used for entry." He tapped the breast pocket of his jacket. "Did you talk to Cavendish?"

"I did. Told her to call off the request for the K9 unit. She's with Ms. Hepworth, trying to find out more about this Maddie. Last name Tilgher, by the way. I stayed just long enough to learn she was a student at St. Vincent College. She was supposed to graduate in the spring." McAllister pointed toward the road. "You want me to canvass the houses nearby?"

"Please. You know the drill. I'm particularly interested in how recently this place has been used."

"Who says it's been in regular use?"

"The window I shimmied in barely stuck and didn't make a sound. It's been greased. And that lock isn't rusty, either."

She nodded. "Got it. Tommy-boy inside?"

"I'm gonna talk to him next. Call me if you come across anything interesting."

"Will do. Tell him we'll get pizza when this mess is cleaned up, okay?" She moved off through the trees.

Duncan grinned. McAllister and Burns had not been together much longer than he and Sally had been dating, but they acted like an old married couple. He tugged on a new pair of nitrile gloves. Before going inside, he examined the outside of the cabin. Aside from the window he'd used to gain entry and the splintered front door frame, the cabin appeared to be exactly what it was. A rundown shack. The dry, cracked wood walls were the veterans of at least a dozen southwestern Pennsylvania winters. The other window showed a lot more grime. Unlike its partner, it didn't move when tugged. Moss hung off the roof, and dry, crackly leaves piled against the walls.

A tech dropped numbered tent cards on the ground near the open window. "Stay clear, please."

Duncan held up his hands. "What've you got?"

"Boot prints there and there." The tech pointed. "Nice impression. Someone came through here with a heavy-tread shoe, either large for a woman or medium-size for a man. The heel of the left foot is worn down a little on the outside. You got lucky. It's been warmer the last couple of days, so the ground was softer, but then we had a freeze last night. There's quite a bit of the pattern left."

"Could it have been from today?"

"I doubt it. Here in the shade, the ground is still pretty hard. Your wingtips didn't even dent it."

Which meant the crime scene could be twenty-four hours old, if not older. The cabin had been locked up tight, except for the one window. That might prevent too much evidence from decaying and being lost. "Anything else? I entered through there. I hope I didn't leave anything behind."

"You didn't, and neither did the owner of the boots. I'm pretty sure these are at least a day old." The tech led Duncan over. "This is greased pretty well. No snagged fibers. No fingerprints. The actor was gloved or wiped everything down."

"Or entered through the door and is the one who locked it."

"There is that. But we didn't find anything there."

Duncan had half-expected the news about the prints. The weather had been cold the last couple of days. It wouldn't have been unusual for people to be wearing gloves. The boot print made up for the lack of other physical evidence. "Nice job. Is the deputy coroner still inside?"

"I think so. I saw the van pull up, and it's still parked in the same spot."

Duncan made a wide circle so as not to interfere with the tech's work and headed for the front door.

Inside, Burns, his facial expression mask-like, knelt by the young woman's body. "Duncan."

"Hey. You holding up all right?" The two had met in a similar situation once before. Duncan knew that scene conjured up bad memories for his young friend. This couldn't be much better.

"As good as I can be given the situation." He examined the victim's nails and carefully placed paper bags over her hands, closing them with rubber bands.

"Is there any sign of sexual assault?"

"No." Burn's moved his finger in the air down the girl's scantily-clad form. "Her clothing, such as it is, is all intact. I see no traces of semen, so either he used a condom, or nothing happened."

"She must have been up to something. She's only wearing a bra and panties. Very fancy ones, too. Even I can see that, and I'm not an expert."

"Which puzzles the hell out of me. Look at this place." Burns gestured around the room. "No furniture except this old cot with a ragged wool blanket. It's freezing, even with the sun up. No heat. Hardly what I'd call a romantic getaway."

Duncan conceded the point. "What else?"

"Bruising on her neck, petechial hemorrhaging in her eyes. And there's a big-ass circular bruise on her thigh." He lifted the girl's head. "There's a contusion back here, but I don't know how serious it is. My guess is it might have dazed her, but not fatal."

"Her attacker knelt on her to hold her down and strangled her?"

"Possibly. We'll be able to tell if the hyoid was fractured when we autopsy. It usually isn't when you have a ligature, like the scarf. I'll tell you something else." He tapped one of the paper bags. "She was a fighter. There's skin under several of her nails. I'm willing to bet that whoever did this has some nice scrapes on their hands or arms."

"Which will be conveniently covered by long sleeves and gloves, given our chilly temperatures lately. But maybe we'll get DNA." Boot prints and skin. Not bad, actually. He'd handled scenes that yielded a lot less.

Burns muttered something under his breath.

"What was that?"

"Nothing." The young man returned to examining the victim's head. "She was a good-looking girl. Got a name for her?"

"I have a name, but it's from a nineteen-year-old autistic boy. I'd like something more definitive."

Burns shook his head.

"Has anyone found her ID, maybe a purse and the rest of her clothes? She didn't get here in her skivvies."

"Check with the techs outside," Burns said and nodded toward the door. "They took a couple bags of stuff out not long ago. Might have been clothes."

"Thanks. When do you think you'll do the autopsy?"

"It's Thursday." Burns sat back on his heels. "Tomorrow afternoon, maybe? Call me."

"Will do." Duncan clapped his hand on his friend's shoulder. Normally, Burns was full of mordant humor. He hadn't made a single off-color comment during the whole conversation, which said volumes about where his head was.

Outside, the late-afternoon November sun was low in the sky, the light further hidden by a bank of clouds that showed up. If the surrounding trees had been in full leaf, it would have looked like early evening instead of late afternoon. Duncan hailed another tech. "Are you the one who processed the inside?"

The tech paused in her work. "That was me."

"The deputy coroner said you took out a bunch of things. Can I see them?"

"Over here." She led him to a pile of evidence bags. "Cashmere sweater, size small, high-end designer. One dark-wash pair of jeans, also high-fashion. One pair of Prada boots, chocolate brown leather. Those look almost new and not knock-offs. And one of those puffer coats, Patagonia. Also genuine. I don't want to think about how much this girl spent on clothes if the rest of her closet looks like this."

The victim had money, or a generous friend. "What about a purse?"

The tech grabbed a bag. "Michael Kors with a Gucci wallet. It had several credit cards, her license, and fifty dollars in cash."

"Name?"

The tech peered through the bag. "Madison Tilgher. There's also a student ID from St. Vincent."

Noah's identification had been accurate. "Thanks." Duncan scribbled down Maddie's address. "What about a phone?"

"Haven't found one yet. But we're still looking."

He doubted any young person these days went anywhere without her phone. "Keep me posted." He walked away and checked the time. Just past four-thirty. McAllister had taken Noah home before heading out on her canvass of the neighborhood. She hadn't reported back, and he didn't want to interrupt her. She'd contact him when she was done, or if she learned something important. He'd left Cavendish with Noah's mother. Noah had been too distraught to talk before. Maybe the presence of his parent would change that.

* * *

Sally stretched out on the couch and rested her feet on a tufted stool. Since the moving was complete and there was nothing on the schedule, she'd left work early and gone over to her sister's house in response to a plea for help in completing some school projects. She swirled the wine in a glass held in her right hand and stared at the gas fireplace flames on the opposite wall.

Noreen Kennedy, the eldest of the Castle siblings, entered and took a seat in the chair. "Well, that's done." She poured herself a glass of wine. "The boob tube should give us at least thirty minutes of peace. How do you feel about pizza for dinner? Craig's out of town, so it's just you, me, and the kids."

"I'm up for anything that means food appears on the table with the least amount of effort from me." Sally sipped, savoring the rich, velvety, smoky taste of the wine. "What is this? It's got a nice plum flavor."

"You like it? It's Barbera 2011 from Greendance Winery out in Mount Pleasant." Noreen tapped her phone and thumbed the screen. "I have a new mission. To sample every wine from every winery in the area."

"I approve." Sally studied the light as it illuminated the rich red liquid. "Tell me. When did school projects start involving parents so much? I don't remember you or Jonathan or I needing that much help from Mom or Dad."

"Oh, don't get me started." Noreen held up a finger. "Hi, I'd like to order a medium pizza with pepperoni, sausage, onions, and olives." She sent a quizzical look at her sister.

Sally gave a thumbs up.

"Yes, delivery, please." Noreen rattled off a credit card number, her phone number, and address. "Forty-five minutes. Got it. Thanks." She tapped the end button and tossed aside the phone.

"Do the kids like all that?"

"They can have pizza rolls." Noreen let her hair out of its clip and shook her head. "While I've got you here, let's talk about Thanksgiving. You've been dragging your feet giving me a straight answer about your plans and now the holiday is only two weeks away. Mom doesn't want to cook. If I do the turkey, can you bring a pie, maybe a green bean casserole?"

"I'm having dinner at Jim's. His parents are coming in from Arizona." Sally didn't look at Noreen. *Maybe if I avoid eye contact, she'll let it slide.*

No such luck. "Ooo, sounds serious. What's going on with you two anyway?"

"What kind of wine did you say this is? It's unique."

"Don't change the subject, sis. You really like this guy. I can tell."

So much for avoiding the subject. "I do. That's why I don't want to screw it up. I'm going to let it develop."

"A relationship is not 35mm film, Sally." Noreen sniggered. "You've never had a problem cutting men loose before because you knew immediately it wasn't going to work. Anyone can see Jim is different. You've been together for what, six months? When are you going to take the next step?"

"We're enjoying the relationship. Whatever happens will do so naturally."

"Aren't you both a little old for that?" Noreen clasped her hands around her knee.

"What does that mean?"

"Well, you're thirty-five. He's what, thirty-seven? You aren't kids, Sally. You're mature adults who should know what they want. Personally, I can't believe you said *no* when he asked you to move in."

Sally swirled the wine. "I didn't say *no*. I said *not yet*. I had just quit my job, and I was starting my own firm. One major life change at a time."

Noreen's expression betrayed her disbelief. "Isn't your dog living with him?"

"Yes, Jim is taking care of Pixel." The retired racing greyhound she'd adopted in October needed space. Even if Sally's current apartment allowed animals, Jim's fenced back yard was a far better option. Plus, this way, Pixel could spend the day hanging out with Rizzo, Jim's Golden Retriever, instead of being alone for eight hours. And she saved the cost of doggie daycare.

"Don't you think his owner should join him? You spend most of your time in Confluence anyway."

Sally sighed and set down her glass. "Why are you pushing me, Reen? You and I have always wanted different things out of life. This has never been an issue before."

"Mom called me last night." Noreen had the grace to look guilty. "You know how she gets. She wants more grandchildren, specifically from her youngest child. She's taken to buying bridal magazines, did you know that?"

Sally groaned. She should have known. "Tell her to relax and stop nagging you. Or else I'm going to elope and save everyone the stress."

Noreen threw a pillow at her sister. "Don't you dare. I'd never hear the end of it."

It was a half-empty threat. Louise Castle would be devastated if her baby eloped, and Sally would never subject her sister to bearing the brunt of the fallout. Passive-aggressive Louise would never complain to Sally, but she'd talk Noreen's ear off. Besides, she was pretty sure Jim would never agree to such a scheme. "Fine. Do me a favor, though. Don't tell her Jim's invited me to meet his folks. That'll just add fuel to her fire. She'll have me halfway down the aisle before I can turn around."

Noreen got up to refill her glass, then returned to the couch. "Only if you do me a favor in return."

"What?"

"Tell me what's holding you back. You love this guy, he loves you, What's the holdup?"

"Argh." Sally finished off her drink and looked around for the bottle. "There is no holdup. Jim and I are happy with how things are. There's no rush. And if you make a crack about a ticking biological clock, I'm leaving."

"I wouldn't dream of it." Noreen sipped. "Tell me the truth. If I had this conversation with Jim, would he think the same?"

"Yes." But deep down, Sally wasn't sure that was true. Jim would happily get married again. He always said he wanted kids. There was just one little problem.

Sally had never seen that future for herself.

Chapter Five

When Duncan returned to the Hepworth house, a car was backing out. He watched the sleek compact with the name of one of the newer food-delivery services speed off. *Pizza delivery guys have better rides than when I was young, that's for sure.*

Inside, he heard the muted sound of the television and smelled tomato sauce, Italian herbs, and garlic. He found Sue Hepworth and Cavendish seated at the table in the kitchen, takeout containers scattered on the top. Noah was nowhere to be seen. "Is your son okay?"

"He's fine. I ordered him a pizza, and he's watching TV." She dumped pasta with shrimp from one of the containers into a wide-rimmed bowl. "I'm sorry to eat in front of you, but I'm starving. I missed lunch in all the excitement. If I don't do something normal, I'll lose it completely. Your partner refused food. Do you want anything? I have plenty. It's shrimp and linguine in garlic sauce."

"Stress reaction." His stomach grumbled, and he hoped the woman didn't hear it. "Thank you. I'm not hungry." He took a seat next to Cavendish. "Noah seemed pretty upset when I found him earlier. Did he tell you anything?" he asked his partner.

"Not a word," she said. "Ms. Hepworth got him calmed down, but the second I mentioned the girl's body, he became agitated again. All that hand flapping."

"I'm sorry about that," said Sue. "It's not uncommon, the repetitive gestures and words. Noah is fairly high-functioning, as long as I'm around to guide him. This afternoon definitely put him off his game."

"Are you sure he won't run again?" asked Cavendish.

"That's why I'm eating here, so I can watch the back door. I'll hear the front if he tries to go that way, and I'll stop him."

"I've had a little training," Duncan said. "I tried to be gentle, I assure you."

"Oh, that's not a criticism. You seem like a nice man, and I'm sure you did your best." She stabbed her fork through a shrimp. "But if he did see that Tilgher girl's body, and judging from his reactions, I think he did, it would be very upsetting. That's why he left the second time, to go back to her."

"The door to the cabin was locked when I arrived," Duncan said. "Tell me, would Noah have the presence of mind to lock it?"

Next to him, Cavendish took out a notepad and pen.

Sue paused. "I doubt it. He either would have broken down on the spot or run away. You said you found him sitting on a rock near the stream?"

"Yes." He knew his partner was capturing the essentials, so he focused on his subject.

"Then it was the latter." She raised the laden fork to her mouth, then lowered it. "Although, if the door was locked, how did he see the body?"

"The windows were uncovered. They're pretty dirty, but you could see through them, and one had a clear view of the victim. He could easily have spotted her if he got curious and looked inside. Would he recognize her in such a situation? Low light and through dirty glass?"

"Oh, absolutely." Sue ate the pasta and paused to chew and swallow. "He's not stupid or slow, Trooper. That's a stereotype, but autistic people are often quite intelligent. Their little tics prevent others from understanding that."

Duncan sat back. "How does Noah know Maddie? We found her ID, by the way. It's definitely her."

Sue took her time answering. "She volunteered at the center where Noah goes for daily social activity. He's...fond of her. She was a very lively, engaging person, from what I understand."

Cavendish looked up. "Did he have a crush on her? Noah?"

Sue sniffed. "It was nothing like that, I assure you. Noah doesn't look at relationships the way we do. I doubt a single romantic or sexual thought crossed his mind. She was a girl who spent time with him once a week, that's all."

The dismissive note in her voice put Duncan on alert. Noah's mother might not think her son could consider a woman that way, but he wasn't so sure. "You didn't care for her."

The fork clanged against the bowl. "I never said that."

"You might as well have. Your tone of voice and expression are enough. Why didn't you like Maddie Tilgher?"

Sue gripped the utensil. "I didn't have much of an opinion about her, to be honest. I may have thought she was a little, how would you say it? Free around the people who visit the center, but trust me, I didn't know her well enough to dislike her." She busied herself with her dinner.

He changed tack. "She was wearing very expensive underwear, and the clothing we removed from the scene was all high-end fashion. Did she come from money?"

"I haven't the faintest idea," Sue said. She ground some black pepper on her meal. The rasping sounded a bit ferocious. "I didn't speak to her much, just 'hi, how are you' when I picked Noah up."

"Did you know she was a student at St. Vincent?"

"She mentioned once how expensive college was. I figured she was in school somewhere. It had to be local, because she volunteered every week, no breaks."

"Even over the summer?"

"Yes."

Interesting. "Was her volunteer work related to her studies?"

Sue's voice turned snappy. "I said I barely knew her. How would I know what her major was?"

Cavendish paused in her writing. "What do you mean she was free with the center members?"

"Just what I said." Sue didn't look up. "Sometimes she'd make what I thought were inappropriate comments, especially if she saw two people of the opposite sex being friendly. 'Is this your girlfriend?' They are developmentally handicapped. Teasing them about love isn't what I consider good behavior. They aren't sexual like that. Then again, what would someone studying business know?"

"You just said you didn't know what Maddie's field of study was."

Sue glared. "It was an example. Many of the volunteers at the center aren't in education or a related field."

"I don't think what you said is true." Cavendish's voice was mild, but her expression indicated to Duncan she was intrigued. "People are people. Sex is a natural urge, and I don't see why Noah, or those like him, should be any different. I'm sure they're curious about what goes on between a boy and a girl behind closed doors. They just don't talk to you about it."

"How would you know?" Sue stabbed the pasta. "My son is an innocent child who has never thought of a woman like that in his life. How many autistic people do you know? How can you be so confident?"

Cavendish held up her hands. "None. I'm sure you know better. You never argued with her, then? Told her how you felt?"

"For the last time, I barely spoke to her." Sue tossed her head. "She was someone who took care of my son, that's all. She did her job well enough. Yes, I thought she could be a little more restrained, but it was never bad enough I had to speak to the center director."

Duncan looked at the woman in front of him. She wore a cardigan over a turtleneck so he couldn't see any scratches. Her hands were unblemished. Nothing she'd said or done indicated she'd wish harm on Maddie Tilgher.

So why did Duncan suspect she was lying?

* * *

Maddie had lived in Pittsburgh with her parents in the Regent Square neighborhood. Duncan called the Pittsburgh Bureau of Police and arranged for one of their officers to go over to the house to make the death notification and let Mr. and Mrs. Tilgher know two troopers were on their way.

They left the Parkway at the Squirrel Hill exit right after coming out of the tunnel and made their way into the city. "Where are we heading?" Duncan asked.

"East End Avenue." Cavendish checked the map on her phone. "Keep heading up South Braddock. I'll tell you when to turn. Looks like if we get to the Frick Park baseball fields, we've gone too far."

"Got it." Typical of Pittsburgh, cars lined both sides of South Braddock. Duncan drove carefully, watching for random pedestrians.

"The Hepworth woman is wrong, by the way."

"About what?"

"My next-door neighbor's son when I was growing up was autistic. I don't think they called it that back then, but I'm pretty sure he'd get the diagnosis now. Anyway, my dad caught him looking through my bedroom window when I was sixteen, and he was seventeen." She smirked. "Teenage boys are all the same."

"You think Noah felt that way about Maddie?"

"I'm saying it's possible, that's all." She glanced at the houses along the street. "Just like it's *possible* she didn't appreciate it."

Duncan had little experience, but he was inclined to agree with his partner. Mental disability didn't mean a lack of physical desire. "Any particular way you want to handle the Tilgher interview??"

"The Pittsburgh cops have already done the notification, right?"

"Yeah. I didn't want to traumatize these poor people any more than necessary. Hearing your daughter isn't going to be home for Thanksgiving is bad enough. Learning it's because she was murdered is awful. At least this way, the Pittsburgh cops can get a family liaison officer on site quickly."

"Good. I hate that part of the job." She checked her phone again. "Turn right at the next street. Then make the second left."

He didn't know anyone who did enjoy it. He'd made that visit more than once, and it was never easy, no matter how the person died.

East End Avenue looked like a suburban street, even though it was squarely nestled in the Pittsburgh city limits. Houses huddled next to each other, most of them made of red brick. They all appeared to be similar in structure, two stories with an attic dormer window. Porches were bare or held summer furniture stripped of the cushions. On a Friday evening, cars lined the leaf-strewn street, the mature trees long bereft of their autumn finery. Duncan had to drive a few houses past his destination to find a free spot. Once outside the car, he could hear passing traffic on South Braddock. The air smelled dusty, and the crisp brown leaves skittered along the sidewalk.

"Nice neighborhood," said Cavendish as she came up beside him.

"For a city, sure." Duncan looked over his shoulder. "We need to go back that way."

"I forgot. You're a small-town boy."

"I prefer more room between me and my neighbors, that's all."

They approached the Tilgher residence. A decal from St. Vincent College adorned the window of the front door. Duncan knocked.

A young Black woman in a Pittsburgh Bureau of Police uniform answered and stepped out on to the porch. "Evening. You the troopers from the PSP?"

"Jim Duncan, Jenny Cavendish."

The officer held out a hand. "Marcy Bellows. I'm the family liaison officer. Mr. and Mrs. Tilgher are in the living room. Needless to say, they're more than a little shook up."

"I can believe it." Duncan pulled out a notebook. "Have they said anything?"

"Not much. Maddie is their youngest child and only daughter. They have two older boys, both out of the house. Lots of pictures. Maddie graduated from Oakland Catholic. Good grades, got a good scholarship to St. Vincent. In high school, she swam and played softball, although she didn't continue either sport in college."

"She get up to any shenanigans at school?" Cavendish asked.

"Not as far as her parents knew," said Bellows. "Oh, they figured she was up to the usual undergrad drinking and partying, but Mr. Tilgher said her grades were good. She expected to graduate next spring magna cum laude."

Duncan noted that. "Anything else we should know?"

"They haven't said much. Come on, I'll introduce you."

Inside, the temperature of the house had been dialed up so high that Duncan felt beads of sweat form between his shoulder blades within thirty seconds of entering. The Tilghers huddled together on an overstuffed suede couch. An untouched cup of tea rested on the end table. Colorful knitted Afghans covered two matching chairs, both of which appeared to be recliners. A flat-screen television took up one wall. A montage of framed photographs littered the other, leaving only small gaps of cream-colored paint between them.

"Mr. and Mrs. Tilgher, this is Trooper Duncan and Trooper Cavendish from the Pennsylvania State Police." Bellows picked up the tea. "They need to ask you some questions about your daughter. I'm going to take this to the kitchen, but if you need me to stay, I'll be right back."

Mrs. Tilgher didn't move. Her gray hair showed touches of red, the color much like Maddie's. Red-rimmed eyes, only a shade darker than her daughter's, stared zombie-like into space. It was hard to guess her age. The ravages of grief had left their mark. But if she'd stood, Duncan was sure she'd be within half an inch of Maddie's height.

Mr. Tilgher, on the other hand, was a mountain of a man. Standing, he'd easily match Duncan's six-three and maybe an inch more. The eyes in his weather-beaten face were dark blue, the hair a healthy mix of black and gray. His gaze flickered up. "I wish I could say it was a pleasure to meet you."

Duncan indicated the chairs. "May we sit?"

Tilgher nodded, a jerky movement.

The troopers took their places. "First," Duncan continued, "our sincerest condolences on your loss. It's an insufficient statement, but we can't imagine what you are going through, and we're truly sorry." How many interviews had he started with the same trite but well-intentioned words? Too many.

Cavendish leaned forward in the other chair. "Conversations like this are the worst part of any police officer's job."

Tilgher's Adam's apple bobbed as he swallowed. "Thank you. Elise and I," he squeezed his wife's shoulders, "are pretty torn up. Maddie is...she was my little girl. To think of her dead like that...."

"We understand." Duncan shot a look at Cavendish, who correctly read the telegraphic message and took out her notebook. "Officer Bellows tells me Maddie was a senior at St. Vincent."

"She was a finance major." Tilgher took a Kleenex from a nearby box and handed it to his wife. "On track to graduate with high honors."

"You must have been very proud." Sue Hepworth's sneering comment about business majors floated through his mind.

"She was a damn good student in high school, too." Tilgher's eyes gleamed fierce and proud. "Smartest of all my three kids. Put her brothers to shame. Good athlete to boot. She was a member of the National Honor Society and volunteered with her high school's environmental club."

"Busy girl." Duncan clasped his hands on his knee. "What about at college? Was she involved in any groups there?"

"She didn't talk much about extracurriculars on campus." Tilgher dashed a massive hand across his eyes.

Mrs. Tilgher finally spoke, albeit in a toneless voice. "Her freshman year, she did a few things. She wrote for the school paper, and I think she tutored local high school kids. But she said she'd gotten too busy with her own studies to continue."

Duncan took in the modest furnishings and considered the nature of the house and the people in front of him. The car parked outside, which he assumed belonged to them, was an older model Chevy. "How was Maddie paying for college? I don't have kids, but I know it can be expensive."

A proud expression formed on Tilgher's face. "She had a merit scholarship for twenty-thousand dollars. She also had loans. What that didn't cover, she worked to pay for, including books and stuff. She never asked us for a cent."

"What kind of job did she have?"

"She worked at a local coffee shop right before college and her freshman summer. But then she got a job down near school. Something in the arts, as I understood it. Films advertising the area to tourists."

Cavendish looked up. "She worked for the Laurel Highlands Visitors Bureau?"

"Nah, I think it was an independent outfit." Tilgher stroked his wife's hair. "Same kind of thing, though."

"Such a pretty girl," Mrs. Tilgher murmured. "She was so friendly and outgoing, always has been. All the boys liked my baby."

Duncan rubbed his chin. "You said she got along with boys. Did she have a boyfriend?"

Tilgher bristled. "She wasn't a tramp."

"I'm not suggesting that," Duncan responded, voice mild. "But in situations like these, it's important to know all the relationships in her life. Most of the time, victims have a personal connection to their attackers. Truly random incidents are the minority."

"There was someone," Mrs. Tilgher said, voice faint.

"Do you know his name?"

"No." She pressed her lips together. "She'd gone out with him a couple of times. She met him through one of those apps young people use for dating. I warned her to be careful, but she said it wasn't serious."

"I don't suppose you know the name of the app."

Mrs. Tilgher shut her eyes and gave a quick headshake.

Cavendish took up the questioning. "What about other people in her life? Did she ever mention any other men?"

Tilgher's face reddened. "Why are you carping on guys? Couldn't it be something else?"

Duncan kept his face still, but his gut ached for this man. Hadn't Bellows explained the situation? "Mr. Tilgher, do you know where and in what state Maddie was found?"

"Officer Bellows said my baby was in a cabin somewhere. In her underwear."

"Then you must understand that the circumstances make us focus on any men she might have known. It is certainly possible the killer was a woman, but to be honest, that's not our first line of thought."

Tilgher paled. His mouth worked, like he was chewing his tongue, fighting with himself on whether to say something. The words burst from him. "Was she raped?"

"There is no evidence of sexual assault," Duncan said in his most compassionate tone.

Maddie's father closed his eyes. "My daughter didn't talk much about school, Trooper. When she did, it was usually nothing serious. Oh, she'd gripe about a professor or a grade. To her, a B was tough to swallow. But I don't recall her mentioning anyone who was giving her grief, nothing that could end in murder anyway."

Mrs. Tilgher maintained her trance-like stare. "My girl got along with everybody. She was very friendly."

Duncan thought a moment. "What about friends on campus? Did she have a roommate?"

"Maddie's lived with the same girl since freshman year," Tilgher said. "They're in a suite now, but Maddie and Evie have been friends from the beginning."

"What's Evie's last name?"

Tilgher's forehead puckered. "Martin, I think."

"Do you have a phone number for her?"

"No, but they live in Room 219, Rooney Hall. I'm sure you can find her there."

Duncan stood. "I'm going to leave you my business card." He passed it over. "So is Trooper Cavendish. If you think of anything, even if it seems trivial, please do not hesitate to call one of us. Once again, I'm sorry for your loss. No need to get up. We can see ourselves out."

Chapter Six

S
ally curled up on the couch at Jim's, book in her hand. She'd made it through dinner at Noreen's without further discussion of her marital future. She had gotten back to Jim's in plenty of time to feed Rizzo and Pixel, build a fire, and set some beef stew to warming. Now, the dogs were sacked out in front of the fireplace, Pixel's tongue lolling out of his mouth as it often did when he was content. The rich smell of meat, gravy, vegetables, and herbs spread through the house.

At the sound of tires on gravel, both dogs leapt up and sprinted to the door, tails wagging furiously. Sally had learned early to stay out of the way when they were enthusiastic like this. Pixel's tail, in particular, should be classified as a deadly weapon.

A minute later, Jim entered. "All right, guys. I'm home. Yes, I'm glad to see you, too. Come on, make a hole."

Sally laid aside her book and watched as he gave both canines a vigorous ear rub. "Someone is happy to see you. Two someones, actually."

"I hope they aren't the only ones." He came over and kissed her. "That stew better taste as good as it smells. I'm famished."

"Go change, and I'll get a bowl ready."

He went upstairs. The dogs started to trot after him, but decided the stew was more interesting and followed their noses to the kitchen. Sally ladled out a generous helping, cut off some thick slices of sourdough bread, and set the food on the table. She brought out butter and an Edmund Fitzgerald porter, which she opened, but didn't pour into a glass.

Jim appeared a few minutes later, dressed in his favorite ratty PSP sweatpants and a t-shirt, hair tousled. He kissed her again. "Thank you." He picked up the beer, took a swig, and sat.

The dogs took up sentry duty next to him, one on each side, alert for the tiniest bit of gravy that might drop their way.

"What was the emergency?" She got herself a glass of Merlot and sat at the end of the table.

"First a missing boy, then a dead young woman." He recapped his day.

Sally set her glass down with care. "What did you say the victim's name was?" It couldn't be the same person.

"Madison Tilgher. Goes by Maddie." Jim reached for the butter, but stopped. "Why does that shock you?"

"Because she was in my office two days ago."

He blinked. "Was she a client?"

"No, I think she might have become one, but the conversation never got that far. She left. But not before she hinted at trouble she was having with a man."

"What is his name? How does she know him?"

Sally spread her hands. "Your guess is as good as mine."

"Damn it." He thought a moment, then returned to buttering his sourdough. "But she definitely said she had an issue with a guy? Wait, you're not breaking the rules, are you?"

"I told you, she's not a client." She rubbed Pixel's velvety ears, but the dog only had eyes for the stew. If only she'd been able to get Maddie to say more or not been so careless as to let her walk out, the young woman might be alive. Tanelsa could have brought the damn legal pad. "When I saw her, she was dressed in awfully expensive clothes for a college student."

"All of the items at the scene were pretty high-end, too. Don't think we won't be following up on that. She got money from somewhere, and it wasn't her family."

Pixel shook his head, and Sally took her hand away. "You said she's a friend of the boy who found her, Noah? He must be devastated."

"I think he is. At least, from what I know of people on the autistic spectrum, he acted fairly upset. We couldn't get anything out of him besides Maddie's name, that she was blue, and she was sleeping."

"How did he know? You said he didn't go in the cabin." Could Noah be the guy Maddie had been talking about? That idea didn't fit. Surely Maddie would not have sought legal help to deal with an autistic teenager two years her junior. She'd have gone to the parents. *Unless they weren't inclined to reprimand their son.*

Jim dragged a piece of bread around the edge of the bowl to wipe up some gravy. "My guess is he saw her through the window. Maybe he called out to her. I don't know because he wouldn't tell me, and after we got him home, his mother insisted he was too upset to talk to us."

"That seems unlikely."

He shrugged. "It could be she was protecting her son. Can you blame her?"

"No." She took a sip of wine. "Why do they have different last names?"

"I didn't get a chance to ask. The interview with the mother turned pretty frosty, and she ushered us out. Cavendish thinks Freeman is the father's name; he ran out on them, and although Ms. Hepworth didn't change Noah's last name, she either changed hers or never took it in the first place."

"If they were married."

Jim nodded. "Cavendish is of the opinion they weren't. There aren't any pictures in the home. Not even one of Noah and his dad when Noah was a little kid. It's almost as if Noah appeared one day, and she took him in."

"Hmm." Sally rolled the thoughts around. "She could have had Noah keep his father's last name for child support purposes or to make sure he got death benefits. Something."

"I'll see when I run a background check on Sue Hepworth tomorrow. It was too late to do it today."

"What did the neighbors say? You must have talked to them."

"I sent McAllister to do the canvass." He took another bite and washed it down with some beer. "Nada. They all know Noah, think he's a good kid, despite his disability. Only one had ever seen the victim, and no one knew her name. None of them know about Noah's father or any family background. The boy and his mother only moved in last year, and she hasn't encouraged curiosity on that point."

Sally rested her chin in the palm of her hand. "What do you think?"

"She's holding back on something. She got very testy when Cavendish suggested her son might have sexual thoughts about a woman. Hepworth admits to not liking Maddie very much, but denies it went beyond not approving of some of her comments."

"Which, of course, you find suspicious."

"Not necessarily. Definitely curious." He buttered another slice of bread. "I'll know more eventually. Oh, I might have to attend the victim's autopsy tomorrow. I don't know if that will make me late. Burns said to call him."

"No problem. Tanelsa got all the stuff set up today, but we decided to bail on tomorrow. We figure we've already lost a week of productivity. What's one more day? I'll hang out here with the boys." She looked at Rizzo and Pixel, who could have participated in one of those living statue exhibits. They were so still, eyes locked on Jim as he ate. She considered her next words. "What do you think of Noah?"

"You mean, do I think he could be a murderer?" Jim arched an eyebrow. "I think anybody could fill that role. But if you're asking where he stands on the list, honestly, I don't know enough yet."

"Fair enough."

He paused. "Enough shop talk. Did you have a good day with your sister?"

"It was okay." She made a face. "School projects sure have changed since I was a kid. I don't ever remember my mom and dad being so involved. It was 'here's the paper, scissors, and glue, have at it.' But Noreen said today was an easy one."

He chuckled. "Any word on an apartment?"

She avoided his gaze. She hadn't been looking very hard. She also suspected Jim knew it, but he was too tactful to push the issue of her moving in. "A few nibbles, but I haven't found anything acceptable. Not for a dog the size of mine. I hate to keep asking you to house him, though." *Liar.*

"It's not an issue. Pixel and Rizzo get along great." He pushed aside his bowl, now nearly wiped clean. "Let's talk about Thanksgiving."

"A major American holiday involving the celebration of the arrival of people who decimated the Native American population and gives us the excuse to overindulge and watch football all day."

"Smart ass." He grinned. "My parents are looking forward to meeting you. Assuming you haven't changed your plans."

"I haven't."

He leaned his arms on the table. "I know that look. That's your 'I really wish this would all go away' expression. What's wrong?"

"Reen asked me about the state of our relationship. I guess my mother wants to start planning a wedding." She huffed. "Why can't everybody take a chill pill? What's the rush?"

He laughed. "I've met your mom, remember? I understand. But what does this have to do with my parents coming for Thanksgiving?"

"I don't want to spend the holiday fielding questions about when we plan to get married and have kids."

"They won't do that."

"How can you be sure?"

He reached out and covered her hand. "Listen. I'm happy. Are you?"

"Of course."

"Then don't worry about it." He stood and gathered his bowl. "If you think dinner with my folks will be like being with your mother, don't worry. Mom and Dad aren't ogres." He went to the dishwasher.

His back was to her, but she could easily imagine the wry look in his hazel eyes. He seemed to think Grace and Andrew Duncan were capable of conducting an entire day of conversation without once bringing up marriage or family planning.

But what set of grandparents could do that?

Chapter Seven

Duncan called the Fayette County coroner's office first thing Friday morning. Maddie's autopsy was scheduled for ten. "I'll go to the autopsy if you start the background check," he said to Cavendish. She shook his hand. "Deal."

The lead-gray November sky presaged snow, but no significant accumulation was in the forecast. Not that it meant anything. With the temperatures hovering in the mid-thirties to low forties, snow wouldn't be unusual. In fact, the ski resorts were probably getting the snow-making machines ready to start the season at the end of the month. Maybe he'd take his father, who was an avid skier, out to the slopes. Duncan rarely went himself. Skiing alone wasn't the same, and he simply didn't have the time. In fact, he didn't own skis and would need to rent them. But it'd be nice to spend some one-on-one time with Dad. And it would give his mother time to get to know Sally.

Speaking of Sally, Duncan wondered about her marked lack of enthusiasm for Thanksgiving dinner. What exactly had Noreen said? He'd only met Louise Castle a couple of times, but he knew she wasn't shy about expressing her opinion. And in her mind, Sally had been single and childless for far too long. Which was guaranteed to put Sally's back up. She was too headstrong and independent to stay quiet while someone else planned her life. Even, or maybe especially, if that person was her mother.

His parents were not like that. Yes, they'd been disappointed when his marriage ended without children. So had he. He'd never hidden his desire for a family from Sally, but he only wanted it if she did. Grace and Andrew

38

firmly believed everyone had to choose their own path. His mother would not be asking about wedding dates or planning baby showers.

Somehow, he had to make Sally understand that.

When he arrived in Uniontown, he parked his Jeep on the street in front of the yellow-brick building that housed the morgue, paid for his parking, and went inside. Burns, the county coroner, and the pathologist were already suited up, and Maddie's naked body was on the metal table under the bright lights. It was evident she'd been washed and photographed, and the technicians were ready to start.

"Trooper Duncan," Dr. Rice, the pathologist, said.

"Doc."

"Hey Jim, long time no see." The coroner, Walt Higgins, was a portly man with a cloud of white hair, an open face with a reddish complexion, and a friendly manner. Odd for a man who dealt with dead bodies day in and day out until you knew he was also a funeral home director who often dealt with grieving families. "You want to get close, or are you satisfied with the cheap seats?"

"Walt." Duncan waved. "I'll watch from behind the glass. I don't feel like dealing with the gear today."

"Suit yourself." Higgins looked at Burns. "Let's get started."

Duncan moved to a small viewing room with a Plexiglas window and a speaker so he could hear the ongoing narrative. Outside, the three forensic specialists began their necessary, but gruesome, duties.

"Victim is a Caucasian female, twenty-one years of age. Five foot three inches, one hundred and fifteen pounds. Exterior examination shows no signs of wounds aside from a few minor abrasions on the back." Higgins narrated while Burns made the Y incision and Dr. Rice performed his exam.

Abrasions. Maddie had been lying on a scratchy wool blanket, one you might buy from an Army/Navy surplus store, Duncan thought. Had she thrashed around? Burns said she was a fighter.

Rice's words cut through his thoughts. "No signs of sexual assault. Hymen is not intact. No indication of recent sexual activity."

Maddie was not a virgin, or at least probably not. Duncan knew there'd not been semen, but Rice's observations indicated there were none of the other physical symptoms of intercourse either. At least not right before her death.

"She's in tip-top shape," Higgins said. "I wouldn't be surprised if she was an athlete, given the tone of her muscles."

"Agreed." Rice worked through the organs, weighing them and taking samples. "Her internal physiology is perfect. Lungs are clear, heart is normal, liver is in good condition. She clearly didn't smoke or drink or use recreational drugs."

Burns held up a small cylinder. "She had one of those low-hormone implants in her arm." He held it out to the pathologist.

"I wouldn't be surprised if she made her partners use a condom, then had birth control for herself. Smart cookie. Definitely one of the better-looking corpses I've worked on in a while."

Duncan shook his head. Almost every aspect of his life involved morbid humor, and it didn't bother him in the least, even if he didn't contribute to the conversation. What did that say about him?

"The hyoid bone is not broken, consistent with ligature strangulation. The scarf around her neck was likely what the suspect used." Rice continued. "Petechia also consistent with that finding."

The team continued working, and eventually Higgins indicated Rice could close up the body. Then he waved to Duncan, motioning him to come to the main office. Once he'd shed his autopsy garb and seated himself, he grabbed a Yeti travel mug and clicked open the top. Steam rose from the opening. "Best investment I've ever made," Higgins said. "These damn things keep coffee hot for hours. You should get one."

"What's the verdict?" Duncan asked.

"Cause of death, asphyxiation by strangulation. Manner of death homicide." He leaned back. "Definitely murder."

"Time of death?"

"That's a little trickier. The cold temperature would make the body cool faster, but slow decomposition." He took a tentative sip of coffee. "I don't think she was moved. Livor was fixed and clearly visible in her back, the

40

backs of the legs, etcetera. She appeared to be in full rigor, but it dipped below freezing last night, and Burns said it wasn't all that warm when she was found. However, her stomach was empty."

Duncan looked up from the notes he'd been taking. "Completely?"

"Exactly. Her small intestine was clear as well. You found her when?"

"Around five o'clock."

"Then she didn't eat lunch. Or breakfast, if you want my guess. Not on the day she died."

Duncan clicked his pen. "Then death could have occurred as many as, what, twelve hours earlier?"

"Possibly." Higgins sat forward, and his chair snapped into position. "I won't have the full report until the tox screen comes back. However, there wasn't any alcohol in her blood, and you heard the observations. I don't think she used anything. Maybe a little recreational marijuana. All the young people do these days. But that's likely it. I'm sure Burns will slip you the prelim if you call him Monday." He glanced at Duncan, and the hint of a grin tugged at his lips.

"Thanks, Walt. Sounds like the only thing that's going to nail down time of death is a little old-fashioned shoe-leather work."

Higgins pulled out a form to start his report. "Then I suggest you get at it."

* * *

The decision to take Friday off allowed Sally to spend the night in Confluence. They each kept a spare set of clothes and personal items at the other's home, just for these occasions. Sally used hers a lot more frequently. As she brushed her teeth, she thought maybe she should throw in the towel on the apartment-hunting. Then again, if her mother found out she and Jim were moving in together, it might invite more headaches. Right now, Mom's desire to see Sally settled down was at the baby-flame stage. Announcing their intent to cohabitate would throw gasoline on the fire.

Sally puttered around for the morning. She played with the dogs in the backyard, cleaned the house, and did a little paperwork in preparation for

41

Monday. Then she decided to make a lasagna. It finished baking around noon, and she bent to remove the pan from the oven. Jim had offered to make dinner, but with time on her hands, she might as well do something. Besides, if he didn't want to eat it, the pasta dish could always be frozen for later.

At that exact minute, his landline rang, a shrill electronic tone Sally hated. She looked around for a place to set the hot pan. "Don't suppose either of you guys can help a girl out?" she asked Rizzo and Pixel, who both sat nearby, tongues hanging out as they panted, no doubt wishing with all their canine powers that she'd drop the tasty treat. "Right, no thumbs." She set the food on a wooden cutting board as she used a foot to raise the oven door. Tugging off her mitts, she lunged for the phone. "Duncan residence."

The voice on the other end was a very puzzled-sounding woman. "Um, I'm looking for Jim Duncan. Did I dial the wrong number?"

"This is his house. He's not here at the minute. Can I take a message?"

"Who are you?"

"Oh, sorry. This is Sally Castle. I'm his girlfriend." The phrase still sounded stupid to her ears. Wasn't there a better word to use when you and your partner were both in their late thirties?

"Oh, how wonderful. I'm Grace, Jim's mother. What a pleasure to talk to you."

Maybe Sally should have let the call go to voicemail. "Mrs. Duncan, hi. Jim didn't mention you'd be calling. He had a work thing early this afternoon, and I'm afraid he's not back yet. But I can tell him you called."

"Thank you." Mrs. Duncan paused. "Jim's told me so much about you. I understand you're a lawyer?"

Sally had hoped to avoid this conversation. Not because she disliked Jim's mom, after all, she didn't know the woman, but because she wasn't prepared. As an attorney, there was nothing worse than being unprepared for answering questions. "Yes. I started at the district attorney's office in Allegheny County, then moved to the public defender's office in Fayette County. That's how I met Jim. Now I have my own practice."

"I bet you have a ton of stories. Most of which you aren't allowed to talk about, of course."

"Oh, I have a few."

"Hopefully, you can tell them over Thanksgiving. Andrew and I have been looking forward to meeting you. It's been years since Jim has been in a steady relationship."

Was Sally expected to say something? She didn't know what, so she held her tongue.

Mrs. Duncan hesitated again. "I hate to ask this and sound like the nosy mom..."

Here it comes.

"I hope you're happy with Jim. I mean, we raised him to act a certain way with girls, and I assume a strong woman like yourself wouldn't be with a man who didn't treat her well."

It was not the question Sally had been expecting. "Oh, no worries on that front, Mrs. Duncan."

"Please, call me Grace."

"Grace. Jim is a perfect gentleman, and really, he's one of the best guys I've ever been involved with. In fact—"

"Yes?"

Sally silently reprimanded herself. Grace had wormed her way under Sally's defenses and done it rather quickly. She'd almost gotten Sally to say she could envision a life with her son. Not the direction Sally wanted to go in this call. That was a face-to-face conversation if there ever was one. "I adopted a dog last October, and Jim is keeping him while I look for a dog-friendly apartment."

"I love it." In the background, a door opened, and a man's voice called out. "I'm on the phone, Andrew," Grace said. "Sally, it was wonderful talking. I can't wait to meet you. And your dog. Take care."

Sally said goodbye and hung up the phone. That hadn't been so bad. Maybe she was overreacting, and Grace Duncan, and her husband, would prove to be wonderful dinner companions who didn't pester her to commit to a life Sally hadn't planned on. Grace hadn't come across that way on the phone.

Then again, maybe she was saving it up so she could ask her questions in person.

Chapter Eight

After the autopsy, Duncan drove to the Pennsylvania State Police headquarters in Eighty-Four. When he arrived, he found Cavendish at her desk, a pile of printed pages next to her. "Looks like you've been busy."

"Idle hands are the devil's tools. That's what my mom's aunt used to say." Cavendish pulled out her messy bun, shook her blonde hair, and redid the knot. "I'm kind of surprised you came all the way back here from Uniontown. Didn't you say Sally had taken the day off? I expected you to go spend some time with her."

He hung his jacket on the back of his chair and dragged it over to his partner's computer. "Nah, she's watching the dogs. I'll make it up to her later."

"Uh-huh."

He lifted an eyebrow. "What does that mean?"

"Jim, didn't you tell me you were divorced? And the primary reason your ex left was because she never saw you?"

"Sally's different. She understands."

"Does she?" Cavendish shook her head. "Women don't like to be taken advantage of. She might be okay with it the first two or three times. After that, well, proceed at your own risk."

The statement took him by surprise. Sally had always said it was fine when he needed to bail on plans. Unexpected happenings were part of their jobs. After all, sometimes, he was the one who received those "working late" texts. Had he overdone it?

Cavendish smirked. "Got you thinking, didn't I?"

He decided to make dinner extra special just in case Cavendish was right. For now, there was work to do. "Thanks for the tip." He pointed at the monitor. "What's the 411 on Maddie Tilgher?"

Thankfully, Cavendish followed his unspoken directive. "Madison Abigail Tilgher. Age twenty-one. She's a senior at St. Vincent College, like her parents told us. Majoring in Finance with a minor in Accounting."

"I'm surprised she doesn't volunteer with something more in line with her field of study."

"She does. She's worked with an organization that provides tax and financial services for low-income families in the Latrobe area for the past two years. She's been at the Center for the Developmentally Disabled for a little longer, since the end of her freshman year. Maybe she just really enjoys helping out with people like Noah."

Duncan rubbed his chin. Not the same kind of volunteer work she'd done in high school, but people's interests changed in college. It must have kept her busy. No wonder she'd dropped sports. "Criminal history?"

"Nothing significant. She got picked up her freshman year for a drunk and disorderly after an off-campus party. Bargained it down to community service. Ah ha. She was assigned to the center. Maybe that's when she started and kept it up." Cavendish scrolled down. "Looks like she was also busted in the fall of her sophomore year for possession of a personal amount of marijuana. Other than that, nothing. No speeding tickets, zilch."

Duncan scanned the notes they'd taken at the Tilgher house. "What about this organization she works with? The arts one that is all about playing up the area?"

Cavendish clicked and scrolled. "I think this is it. Laurel Highlands Arts and Entertainment. Yeah, she interns with them as an 'artistic consultant,' whatever the hell that means. Hold on." More clicking and scrolling. "According to their website, the group does video promotions that highlight cultural and natural points of interest in the Laurel Highlands."

"Address and phone number?"

"Right here. Along with the name of the organization's president, Barry

Atwiler. Ugh, dude needs a better photographer and a fashion consultant."

Duncan studied the page. Cavendish was right. Atwiler's dark hair was slicked back, a cold expression on his narrow face. In the picture, he wore a dark suit and tie, but for some reason, all Duncan could think of was a modern-age pimp, not a professional in the arts and advertising field. "Print that." He glanced at his watch. It was only two-thirty, but if he was going to make up his absence to Sally, he needed to hit a grocery store and get home. "We'll call them on Monday morning."

"You got it." Cavendish clicked, and the printer across the room whirred. "I'll see if I can get in touch with him this afternoon. Set something up for early next week. The office is in Brownsville, northwest of Uniontown."

"Sounds like a plan." He stood, grabbed his jacket, and put his chair back. "Did you send in the request for her financials?"

"Already done." Cavendish looked up. "What's your next step?"

"I'm taking your advice and leaving early. I have to find a high-end grocery store."

"Oh?"

He buttoned his sports coat. "The head chef at the finest restaurant in Pittsburgh has nothing on me tonight. After that, well, we'll see where it goes."

A sly grin formed on Cavendish's face. "Jim Duncan, you naughty boy."

"Not yet, Cavendish." He spun his keys. "Not yet."

* * *

Once the kitchen was cleaned up, Sally found herself with time on her hands. She could walk the dogs again. Rizzo would gladly go outside, but Pixel, sprawled out in front of the fire, looked dead to the world. Sally suspected the jingle of the leash would not entice the greyhound to move from his warm, comfy spot.

She'd half-hoped Jim would come home early, knowing she was waiting for him. But she knew that was a fantasy at best. With a new murder case on his hands, there was little chance of an appearance before five. If their places were reversed, and it was Sally with a new client, she wouldn't cut her day short. *It's a good thing I made that lasagna.*

She went to the kitchen. Rizzo trotted after her, and despite looking like he was sound asleep, Pixel sprung to his feet and scrambled into the room. Both canines knew what a trip to the kitchen meant. She fetched her laptop from where she'd left it on the dining room table along with two treats from the doggie cookie jar. She handed each dog his snack, scratched them behind the ears, and returned to the living room. She tossed another log on the fire and curled up on the couch. If Jim was going to be at work all afternoon, she might as well at least pretend to look for an apartment.

But an hour later, she'd added only one candidate to her list, and it wasn't a great option. All of the units in the building shared access to a fenced courtyard, but it was small. She didn't know if Pixel could dodge all the outdoor furniture, and what would the other residents think of his crazy antics? "I love you to death, bud, but you are damned inconvenient sometimes."

Pixel opened one brown eye, blew out a horse breath, and went back to sleep. The hound was one of the laziest creatures on the planet, but he needed exercise. At least two good walks a day and preferably a yard where he could do his daily running, all thirty seconds of it.

She'd put off the decision long enough. She'd tell Jim if the offer to move in was still good, she'd accept. She'd just have to deal with the increased pressure from her mother. "Perhaps if I say no another hundred times, Mom will get the picture and stop asking me about more grandchildren." Probably not.

As far as Jim's parents, well, that would be his problem.

She checked the time on her laptop. It wasn't even two-thirty. Now what was she going to do?

She stared at the crackling flames, the smoldering red bringing to mind the deep auburn of Maddie Tilgher's hair. She had worn clothes that should be way beyond the budget of a middle-class college student. Her manicure had been salon-quality, and the hair color a little too perfect to be natural. A woman only got color that good from a bottle and an expensive one at that.

Perhaps she had a rich boyfriend. Was that who she'd been nervous about when she visited Sally? Had he found out about Maddie's visit to a lawyer, and that's how she wound up strangled in a shabby woodland cabin?

But if that was the case, why had she been in her underwear? Jim said there were no signs of assault, so she must have stripped voluntarily. She wouldn't do that in front of a man who made her nervous, would she?

Sally reopened the laptop. She didn't have the same resources she'd had when she worked as an assistant public defender, but she'd honed her search skills to compensate. As a result, she'd opened accounts with all of the major social media outlets. She didn't post on them, but it allowed her to snoop, especially if the site made all of the content public unless a person deliberately chose to lock it away. Or if people were sloppy with their privacy settings.

Finding accounts for Maddie wasn't hard since the last name was fairly unique, and a lot of big players now frowned on anonymous accounts. The pictures and messages all looked typical of a soon-to-be-twenty-one young woman. Duck-faced selfies, groups of girlfriends at scenic spots around Pittsburgh, and local attractions such as Fallingwater. A couple of shots seemed to have come from a vacation at Virginia Beach, maybe a college Spring Weekend trip. Both girls wore bikinis and clutched plastic drink cups with bar logos on them. Sally zoomed in on a picture from an indoor party. She recognized the red-soled shoes in a couple of shots as Louboutins. Logos from Prada, Gucci, Marc Jacobs, and Helmut Lang peppered her clothing and accessories. These were designers Sally couldn't afford. How in the world did a college student?

The messages were as innocuous as the photos. "Me and Evie. Luv u girl!" "Spring break, baby, yeah!" "Four girls ready to take on the world." A couple were a little snarkier, and some were downright mean, mentioning other users by their handles. "This is fashion, suck it, be-otch." "U only wish u looked this good." Maddie did not indulge in posts about politics, social justice, environmentalism, or weighty matters. There were no pictures of her school work, volunteerism, or the internship. Her life, portrayed in social media, was all about fun, parties, and clothes.

But not boys. None of the photos included any men, young or old. Not Mr. Tilgher, not fellow students, not a single male. Who was the person she'd been afraid of?

Sally clicked into the search bar of a popular picture-based social media site, and her eye caught on another account, two down from "mtilgher0216." The handle was "sexylady216" and the tiny avatar picture looked disturbingly like Maddie. Sally clicked.

The young woman in the photo was more made up, the eyes sultrier, the lips full and pouty. In it, she blew a kiss and winked at the camera. But no doubt it was Maddie. Except for the zero, the same numbers were in the handle. What did they mean? Were they the last four digits of a phone or social security number? "Or a birthday," Sally said. She'd have to ask Jim when he got home.

The account was private. There was no point in requesting permission to follow. With Maddie dead, no one would accept, would they? On impulse, Sally clicked. Then, she went back to the other social media sites. The sexylady216 account existed on every one of them and in every case, the account was private.

Why had Maddie had two social media personas? More importantly, what hadn't she wanted the world to see?

Chapter Nine

D uncan stopped at an upscale grocery on his way home. It was out of his way, but he'd have a much greater chance of finding everything he needed at the bigger store.

Bags in hand, he went through the back door. "Hey, I'm here." A second later, the dogs appeared to sniff the groceries and demand their share of attention. "You two are getting slow." He kicked off his shoes. After he rubbed each dog's head, he moved the bags to the counter and unpacked. He laid the dinner ingredients out on the counter and put a bottle of Chardonnay in the fridge. Pixel and Rizzo danced attention at his elbow.

Sally came in from the front room. "I figured I'd wait until all the excitement was over." She pushed her way through the dogs and wrapped her arms around him. "Hello, stranger."

He cupped her cheek and gave her a long, lingering kiss. "Sorry for being a little late."

"That's okay." She winked. "I have a new man in my life. Two of them, actually."

"Oh really?"

"Yeah. They both have four feet, and they slobber a bit, but a girl can't complain about the attention, especially when she's holding a yummy treat." She looked over the food on the counter. "They don't cook, though. What's on the menu?"

He pointed. "Pan-seared rosemary and garlic chicken, roasted potatoes, asparagus tips, and tiramisu for dessert." He spotted the foil-covered rectangle on the counter. "What is that?"

"I had all this time on my hands, so I made lasagna. But it'll freeze, so don't think you're getting off the hook, not after telling me what you have planned." She took the pasta dish and put it in the freezer. "You're going to make tiramisu right now?"

"I'll admit, I bought that one. But the clerk at the bakery swore it'd be the best we'd ever eaten, or the next one's on her."

Sally moved over to the table and sat. "Did you have a productive day?"

Duncan took off his jacket and tie, draped them over a chair, rolled up his shirtsleeves, and donned a long apron with "Kiss the Chef" printed on it. Sally had bought it for him as a joke gift, but it came in pretty handy. As he prepared the chicken breasts and chopped potatoes, he told her about everything he'd learned about Maddie Tilgher. "On the surface, she appears to be an All-American girl. How and why she ended up in an abandoned cabin wearing nothing but her underwear is beyond me."

"It might have something to do with her alter-ego social media account." Sally described the results of her afternoon research.

He frowned. "We haven't had a chance to start looking into that, but yeah, that doesn't mesh with the picture her parents painted. You said the accounts are private?"

"I sent requests to follow, just in case someone else is monitoring them. I figured it couldn't hurt."

"Let me know if anyone responds. I'll tell the tech guys about it on Monday. They'll be able to get in." He grinned. "Did you really sign up for all of them? Even that crazy one with the videos?"

"Yes, but don't think you'll be seeing posts from me any time soon." Sally drummed her fingers on the tabletop. "What was the name of the group she interned with?"

Duncan was in the middle of peeling onions, but he paused to fetch his notebook. "According to what Cavendish and I found in her employment records, it's called Laurel Highlands Arts and Entertainment." He tossed the notebook on the table and went back to his cooking.

"I'll be right back." Sally left and returned moments later with her laptop. As Duncan seasoned and chopped, he could hear Sally typing behind him, presumably searching for the company. "Find anything?"

"Kind of." She paused. "Jim, are you sure this is the right name? This outfit looks a little sketchy to me. You need a password to get into the site offerings, for heaven's sake."

"Really?" He slid the basket of potatoes into the air fryer and set the timer for twenty minutes. Then he wiped his hands on a towel and went to stand behind Sally. "What do you mean?"

"Look at this." She moused over the screen, which showed an open browser window and a page for Laurel Highlands Arts and Entertainment.

The company hadn't gone big on website design. The images were stationary, and Duncan swore they looked like stock photos of the area. The home page text announced them only as "offering a wide variety of entertainment and visual imagery of the scenic Laurel Highlands." He leaned in. "We did a cursory review of the site earlier, but didn't dig deep. What does it say on the About Us page?"

Sally clicked. "More fluff. 'A forward-thinking, multi-media company, Laurel Highlands Arts and Entertainment provides subscribers with high-quality video, audio, and photographic representations of the Laurel Highlands, including popular attractions such as Fallingwater, historical sites like Fort Necessity, and natural beauty such as the Laurel Caverns.' There's no substance or details."

"What do they mean by subscribers?"

"I suppose they could be a stock art company. You know, one of those outfits that keep a library of photos you can buy to use in your marketing materials." Sally clicked on the Subscription link and whistled. "Two hundred dollars a month? If the imagery they're providing is anything like what's on their website, their customers are getting ripped off."

"You can't preview samples or anything?"

"Nope." Sally went to the Offerings page. "More generic text and a link for subscribers to click and sign in. I get the feeling they aren't just selling pretty pictures of the Laurel Highlands."

Duncan straightened. "Either that or they are super-conservative when it comes to protecting their digital property. They do have some contact information. Cavendish and I will follow up on Monday."

Sally clicked again. "Found it. There's an email address and phone number of the main office in Brownsville. Eww."

"What?"

"Their CEO needs a makeover. Barry Atwiler. What a name."

Duncan returned to the counter. He cut the ends off the asparagus and tossed the stalks in a skillet with some olive oil, garlic, and a sprinkle of salt. "Cavendish and I weren't impressed either. I kinda thought the guy looked like a failed pimp, not an executive."

"That's a good description. Now I really want to see what they're offering and find out if we're right." Sally closed the laptop. Then she got a wine glass and grabbed a bottle of Merlot.

Duncan reached over. "Not tonight. I bought a bottle of Chardonnay. Trust me, it'll go better with the seasoning. But it's not chilled enough yet."

Her answering smile was amused. "If you insist. Are you having beer or wine?"

"Tonight, it's wine. Porter won't go with the meal." He checked the timer, put the chicken breasts in the pan to sear, and opened the fryer to shake the potatoes. "Between this outfit and your social media findings, I don't think I'm going out on a limb by saying Maddie was leading a double life."

"All the signs of her working in the sex industry are there. But was she working in front of or behind the camera? Or was she an escort? There's good money either way."

"I'm sure we'll find out. Cavendish and I will hopefully get her financial background next week." He drizzled olive oil on the chicken. "Maddie's parents claim she was a good student. Monday, I'm going to call St. Vincent to get her academic records."

Sally leaned over and inhaled the fragrant steam. "I hope the school doesn't give you a hard time."

"Why would they?"

"FERPA." She looked at him. "Family Educational Rights and Privacy Act. In general, if the student hasn't signed a waiver, a school cannot disclose information about her educational records. I'm not intimately familiar with the law, but don't be surprised if you need to get a warrant before they'll hand over a transcript."

"Shit." Why did everything have to be so complicated? "Maybe I'll skip the transcript and go straight to the business department. See if I can talk to any of her professors. Her parents said she was majoring in Finance. St. Vincent can't be so big that someone won't know Maddie if we go to the department chair."

"You're probably right." Sally returned to the table, sat, and rested her chin on her fist. "Did she live alone? What about friends? Or a boyfriend? I didn't see any boys in her social media."

"Her father mentioned one girl, Evie Martin. At least he thinks that's her last name."

"That sounds familiar."

"Cavendish and I got Maddie's residence hall room number from her parents. This Evie might know more. Mrs. Tilgher mentioned a boy Maddie had met using a dating app, but no name."

"What app?"

"They didn't know."

"It'll be on her phone."

"I'm sure it is, but we don't have the phone. It wasn't at the scene."

Sally made a face. "Good luck. I wish she'd said more when she visited the office. I'll have to review my notes." She took out plates and silverware. "I hope you weren't planning on having that tiramisu immediately after dinner."

"Why not?"

She set down the dinnerware and sidled up next to him. "Because all these delicious smells are making me hungry. And I don't mean for food."

Chapter Ten

Sally woke Saturday morning to the smell of coffee and bacon. She glanced at the bedside clock. Seven-thirty. Jim had probably been up for two hours, run a mile, and was on his second cup while he made breakfast. Even though his days of working a seven-to-three daylight shift were over, some habits were hard to break. She couldn't complain, though. Jim's tendency to be an early riser meant she never had to wait for the coffee to brew.

After one final cat-like stretch, she got out of bed, grabbed her robe and slippers, and headed downstairs. Rizzo and Pixel were in the kitchen. Their bowls were empty, and Sally was sure they'd had their kibble, but that didn't keep them from fixing Jim with twin brown-eyed stares, trying to convince him they were dying of hunger.

"Morning." She grabbed a mug and the French press and poured herself a cup. "I don't suppose breakfast includes any of that leftover tiramisu, does it?"

Jim grinned. "Hashtag bad breakfast choices."

"Hey, it's got dairy and stuff. It's practically a doughnut."

He pushed over the box. "Have at it."

Several minutes later, after the coffee had worked its magic, Sally licked her fingers clean. "What's the plan for the day? I know you have one."

"I was going to ask if you wanted to go with me to Latrobe." He took his coffee mug to the sink. "My intention was to hunt down this Evie Martin, see what she had to say about Maddie."

"I'm pretty sure your partner would want to be there for that. Plus, I don't think showing up with a defense attorney in tow is a great idea."

"I talked to Cavendish while you were upstairs." He rinsed out his coffee cup. "Turns out her sister's youngest has a birthday party today, and if she misses the festivities, she'll be in the doghouse. She sounded rather jealous of our field trip, to be honest."

"A house full of screaming...how old?"

"Three."

Sally shuddered. "Screaming three-year-olds. I completely understand where she's coming from." For a moment, Sally thought a flash of disappointment crossed his face, but it was gone so fast she was sure she had imagined it.

He leaned against the counter and crossed his arms over his chest. "Did you look up Evie's social media yesterday?"

"No, I concentrated on Maddie."

"Finish your breakfast, and let's take a look."

Sally popped the last bite of her cake in her mouth and washed it down with the remainder of her coffee. "I'll get my laptop. You want to do this in here?"

"Yes. This way, we can both work."

Sally brought her laptop into the kitchen and set it on the table. Jim pulled up a chair next to her, and she took a minute to inhale the scent of him, clean soap, spicy aftershave, and the undefinable element she associated with his presence. Then, she went to the first site and searched for Evie Martin. She tapped the screen. "I've never seen her, but this must be our girl based on her profile. It says she's a student at St. Vincent."

Sally's first thought was that Evie looked a little more "girl next door" than Maddie. She had long brown hair and usually had it swept back in a ponytail or clip. In a picture of the two of them, Evie towered over her friend. "How tall was Maddie?" Sally asked.

Duncan consulted his notes. "Five-foot-three."

"Evie's at least three, maybe four inches taller. And that's not from wearing high-heeled shoes." Sally clicked through several photos. Some were taken against the backdrop of Ohiopyle State Park, Cucumber Falls and the Meadow Run waterslides prominent. Both girls wore practical outdoor clothing. Sally zoomed in. "Looks like Maddie saved the super expensive stuff for another time. Both girls are dressed in similar clothes in these shots."

"Look at the party pics, those right there." Jim pointed at the tiny frames.

It was a holiday get-together of some sort, New Year's Eve, judging from the dates on the photos and the festive regalia. In these photos, Sally could immediately spot the difference in couture. Evie's clothes were nice. Maddie's were runway chic. "Well, Maddie certainly didn't share with her best friend. It's hardly surprising, given the differences in their size, but whatever money Maddie had for shopping, she wasn't giving it to Evie. Except those earrings. Do you see the size of the diamonds on those pendants?"

"I see the rocks, not the size."

"Let me zoom in." Sally did so. The stones in question had to be a couple of carats. "Gifts or a loan? Or are they fakes?"

"Don't know, but if they're real, I'm betting a loan. College kids don't give away jewelry like that." Jim leaned in. "Is there any engraving on the necklace?"

"I don't know." Sally tried to enlarge the picture, but the pixelation obscured the charms. "There might be something, but I really can't tell. You'll have to ask her when you see her." She decreased the resolution to normal size. "The design looks familiar, though. Maybe a 'best friends' piece? And look here, Maddie has a matching necklace."

Jim added to his notes. "I'm not an expert on women's clothes. How much money are we talking here? Hundreds? More?"

"Jim, I doubt I could afford one or two pieces from these designers. Hell, I don't think Lisa, Tanelsa's wife, can lay her hands on stuff like this and she's a fashion buyer. I wouldn't be surprised if it were worth thousands if you put it all together: clothes, jewelry, and shoes."

"I don't get it. Her family is middle-class. She goes to college on scholarship." He rubbed his chin. "Is this stuff real or knock-offs?"

"Hard to tell from the pictures." Sally clicked through a few more. "If they are fake, they're very high quality, which can also be expensive. You said the clothes you found at the scene were designer?"

"They had the labels, but I don't know how to tell if they're the genuine article. The techs didn't say anything about them being imitation." He paused. "The underwear wasn't cheap, either. Not from Victoria's Secret. But it looked like silk and lace to me."

Sally navigated to another site and searched again for Evie. It was more of the same. Evie was a pretty young woman whose clothes were not bought at a thrift store, but she wasn't in Maddie's class. "She never looks jealous."

"Come again?"

"Evie." Sally nodded at the screen. "I don't see any evidence she envied her friend's things. Why?"

"Maybe she has a heart of gold."

"Could be she knows the pieces aren't real." Sally looked over at him. "Or something about how Maddie bought them that lowers their value - at least in Evie's eyes."

"Like maybe if you have to turn tricks to afford fancy clothes, it isn't worth it?"

"Exactly." Sally stared at the computer screen.

"We'll be searching her dorm room today. It'll be interesting to see if we find anything."

Sally was slightly surprised it hadn't been done already, but she also knew there must be a good reason for the delay. Probably something involving the paperwork. She pursed her lips. Maddie had come to her for help. She wasn't a client, but Sally felt she owed the young woman.

Jim broke through her thoughts. "I know that look. You're wondering if you can justify going to the college based on the fact Maddie Tilgher came to you for advice."

"Do you blame me?"

"Not at all." He gathered up his things and stood.

"Where are you going?"

"To take the boys for a walk. We won't get back from Latrobe for a couple of hours, so I'll give them some exercise now. That gives you enough time to shower and get dressed." He grabbed his coat and the leashes and led both dogs to the front door.

Chapter Eleven

A fter Duncan returned from his walk with Rizzo and Pixel and made sure they had fresh water, he'd still had to wait for Sally to finish her shower and get dressed. They arrived at the St. Vincent campus by eleven o'clock.

"Are you certain Jenny is okay with this?" Sally asked as she got out of the Jeep.

"Yes, I already told you it's fine." He briefly thought of the look of horror on Sally's face when he'd mentioned the party. What had that been about? He'd meant to follow up, but they'd gotten so involved in discussing Maddie he'd forgotten to go back to the topic. *Later.* Right now, he had other things to focus on. He consulted the map of the campus he'd printed off the school website. He hoped the delay in getting the warrant, caused by a new judge's fastidious questioning of the application, hadn't cost them too much.

"What did you tell her?" Sally asked.

"I said Maddie had come to your office, so naturally you were curious. All Cavendish said was, 'Be careful and let me know how it goes.' I think she knows you well enough that she figured if you didn't come with me, you'd take it upon yourself to visit the college. Which wouldn't be wrong." He pointed. "This way."

The St. Vincent campus would be pretty when all the trees had leaves. Even now, there was a kind of austere attraction to the piles of dry foliage, barren branches, and red brick buildings. Duncan had been here once before, during the Steelers' annual training camp. Of course, there hadn't been any students around at that time. He looked at the fresh-faced young people, many of them bundled up, but just as many with bare fingers tapping away on phones. "God, they all look like babies," he said under his breath.

Sally had evidently heard him, because she laughed. "You sound like an old man."

"Well, look at them. Tell me you don't feel the same."

"No comment." She stopped and studied the surroundings. "Where is this dormitory?"

"I think we took a wrong turn somewhere." He called out to one of the passing groups of students. "Excuse me. We're looking for Rooney Hall. Can you give us directions?"

A young man, desperately in need of a haircut, pointed. "Down that way on the left. You'll see the sign." He looked over Duncan and Sally. "Did you lose your kid?"

Sally snorted as she suppressed a fit of giggles.

"No, we're looking for a student, Evie Martin. You don't happen to know her, do you?"

"Sorry, bruh." The student jogged away to catch up with his friends.

Duncan stared after him, then turned to Sally. "What the hell is a bruh?"

"I think it's the modern version of bro."

He shook his head. *Really?* "Do I look like a *bruh* to you?"

"Yep, you are definitely an old man." She grabbed his arm. "Come on."

They continued in the direction the student had given them and eventually came to Rooney Hall. It was a rectangular building made of the same brick as others they'd seen on campus. Some of the windows were covered with shades or curtains. Others were bare to let in the November sunlight. Duncan observed male and female students entering and exiting and gathered the dorm offered co-ed living. Hopefully not on the same floor. He studied the building.

"What's up?" Sally asked.

"I'm wondering about the living arrangements. I see both girls and guys coming out of that place."

She consulted the map. "It says here the building offers suite-style and apartment living for upperclassmen of both genders. The bathrooms are probably inside the living quarters, so I guess it's possible they have both men and women on the same floor."

"Things have definitely changed. There's no way they would have allowed mixed living when I was in college."

She pushed him to the door. "A lot has changed in almost twenty years. I don't even remember suites being a big thing when I was in school. What room are we looking for?"

He consulted his notes from the discussion with the Tilghers. "Room 219."

They climbed the stairs, scanned the numbers, and made their way to the room. Open doors revealed students lounging. He could easily identify the female resident rooms from the male, simply by the style of decorating. He reached their destination and knocked.

The door opened to reveal the young woman from the photos. Evie Martin was barefoot, but topped Sally by about an inch. Her light-brown hair was pulled back in a messy knot. She wore a black sweatshirt and sweatpants emblazoned with the school name and logo. She appraised them through gray eyes that were clear and showed a light of intelligence. "Who called the cops? I don't know who had the weed last night, but it wasn't me."

Duncan pulled the wallet with his ID from the back pocket of his jeans. "No one called me. Trooper Jim Duncan from the Pennsylvania State Police. This is Sally Castle."

"I don't think you're a cop," Evie said, turning that frank gaze on Sally.

Sally held out her driver's license. "No, I'm a defense attorney."

"I'm telling you, I have no freaking idea who was smoking. I was in my room all last night with my boyfriend. We were eating pizza and watching a movie." Evie crossed her arms over her chest.

"Are you Evie Martin?" Duncan asked and put away his ID.

"Yeah, why?" she asked in a wary tone.

"You roomed with Maddie Tilgher, is that correct?"

"Mads isn't here. She's in Pittsburgh, some trip with the company she interns for."

Whatever Maddie had been up to, she hadn't let her friend in on the secret.

Either that, or Evie was covering for her. "I'm sorry to be the one to tell you this, Miss Martin, but Maddie is dead."

Evie blinked, her gray eyes wide with disbelief. "What kind of sick joke is this? She's in Pittsburgh. She texted me Wednesday night that the trip had been extended and she'd be back tomorrow."

Sally stepped forward. "Miss Martin, is there somewhere we can sit?"

"You can have a seat in the living room. Belle and Monica, that's the other two who live here, are at brunch. They should be back soon."

"It would be better if it were somewhere with a little privacy."

"I'm not going anywhere with you people. Not until you explain yourselves. I have the text right here." Evie stepped away and came back with a smartphone in a sparkly blue case. On the back was a picture of her and Maddie, mugging for the camera. "Look." She unlocked the phone, tapped it, and thrust it at Duncan.

It was a text from "Mads" timestamped seven-o-six on Wednesday night. *Got held up. Be back Sunday. Lend me ur psych notes? XOXO* He showed it to Sally, then gave the device back to Evie. "Miss Martin, I think Ms. Castle is right. This would be better if we could sit and talk somewhere more private."

* * *

Jim insisted they wait for a uniformed trooper to show up to stand guard outside the apartment before they left. While he and Sally waited for Evie to get her coat, they held a whispered conversation. "Don't you want to talk to the other two?" she asked.

"Yes, but I want to get Evie on her own first." He looked around. "I didn't see any pictures of Belle or Monica in the socials, did you?"

"No."

"That tells me Maddie wasn't as close to them. Evie's going to be a better source."

"Point."

Evie returned wearing a white puffer jacket. "You don't need to leave a guard at the door," Evie said. "Belle and Monica won't touch anything."

"It's standard procedure," Jim said, voice mild.

As soon as the trooper showed, they left the dorm. Evie sped up, so she walked a few paces ahead of them. She wasted no time pulling out her phone and making a call. Unlike so many people on cell phones, Evie kept her voice down so she couldn't be heard.

Sally took the opportunity to study Evie's body language. She showed surprise and disbelief, but also a vague overtone of apprehension. Who was she talking to?

"What are you thinking?" Jim asked.

Sally noticed the way Evie fidgeted with the zipper of her jacket with the hand not holding the phone. "I think she's definitely taken off guard, and she believed her friend was in the city. But I don't know. There's something about her that tells me Evie isn't completely shocked."

"You picked up on that, too, huh."

Sally stuffed her hands in her pockets. "I wonder if she always suspected Maddie's stories weren't entirely on the up-and-up, and this is corroboration."

"I guess we'll find out. I'd like to know who she's on the phone with and what's so secret she doesn't want us to hear it."

No surprise that his thoughts mirrored hers. "I have the exact same questions. Good thing we waited for the second trooper."

Jim raised an eyebrow. "This isn't my first rodeo."

Evie took them to a café-style place in the student center and bought a bottle of juice and a granola bar. "Hope you don't mind. I'm feeling in need of some carbs."

"No, go right ahead." Sally looked around. She wasn't going to admit this to Jim, but the college students did indeed look on the young side. Did some of the guys even shave yet? "Who'd you call while we walked over?"

"Oh, just letting my study group know I might be late. Come on, we'll grab a table." Evie went over to one in the corner and sat.

No way that was about a study group, Sally thought. Evie wouldn't have needed to hide a conversation like that. She'd thought Jim was being a little pedantic in insisting they wait for another trooper to watch the apartment. Not now.

Jim positioned his chair so his back wasn't completely to the room before sitting. He took out a notepad and pen. "When did Maddie leave for Pittsburgh?"

Sally took the place next to him and focused on Evie.

Evie slugged back some juice and wiped her mouth with the back of her hand. "Wednesday morning. It was some conference, or so she said. Originally, she was supposed to be back later that day, but then I got the text I showed you. I was a little surprised. She is, I mean was, so anal about being in class, but I figured this was unavoidable." She paused. "Are you sure Maddie's dead?"

Jim nodded. "Quite sure. I'm very sorry."

Evie sagged a bit, and her gray eyes filled with tears. "Damn it."

Sally leaned forward. "Excuse me for saying this, but you don't seem shocked. It's almost like you half-expected her to get into trouble, maybe not this, but something. Did you have reason to think Maddie might be living a risky lifestyle?"

"Risky, as in she could end up dead? No." She picked at the label on the bottle. "But Maddie...it's hard to describe."

Sally folded her hands on the tabletop. "Try."

Evie took another drink and a bite of the granola bar. "Mads had great clothes. I mean really great. All designer labels. Not just Ralph Lauren. You can buy that in any good department store. She had things you'd have to get online or in New York City. I knew her family didn't have money and that she was here on scholarship. When I asked where she was getting this stuff, she said, 'That's a secret, Evie. Best you don't know too much about it. It might shock you.' She bought me this necklace." Evie fingered the gold chain around her neck. It was the same one she'd worn in the party photo. "It's from Tiffany's. She got a matching one. They're inscribed 'best friends.' Mads said they were eighteen-carat gold. Seriously, who can buy two of those? Whatever she was doing to get cash, it had to be illegal or at least barely legal. At least that's what I thought."

"But you never pushed it?"

"No. I should have, though. She might be alive. I guess I was selfish. See, I couldn't borrow her clothes. We didn't wear the same size, obviously." Evie waved her hand. "I'm four inches taller, and my shoes are way bigger. But Mads let me take things like purses, and I could wear her jewelry whenever I wanted, so I never asked any tough questions and accepted what she told me. Honestly?" She half-laughed. "I was afraid of the answer I'd get if I pinned her down."

Jim looked up. "And that answer would be what?"

Evie stared at him as though he was being dense. "You know."

"No, I don't. Not for certain."

"I thought...well, I thought she was an escort or something." Evie's cheeks flushed, and she fixed her gaze on the granola bar wrapper.

Sally shot a look at Jim. "What made you come to that conclusion?"

Evie shifted in the chair. "The hours she kept. Like I told you, during the week, she was all business. She never missed a class, went to the library on a regular basis, and volunteered at that center for disabled people. But on the weekends, she'd disappear for hours. Sometimes during the day, other times at night. She never answered phone calls or texts while she was gone. We'd go out on Friday or Saturday evening, and around eight or so, I'd ask if she was ready to go to another place, but she'd tell me she had something to do. Then I'd hear her sneak in at three in the morning. She was terrible at it."

Sally tapped the table. Working as a high-end prostitute made sense. And yet, it didn't. Jim was right. A luxury escort didn't meet her customers in a shabby cabin in the woods. At least not unless those customers had fetishes. "Do you know anything about Maddie's internship with this local company?"

"Laurel Highlands Arts? Not a lot." Evie sniffled. "I had a project once and needed some pictures about local history. I joked that she could get me some freebies, and she said I didn't want the kind of pictures the company did. I didn't think anything of it." She wiped her nose with her sweatshirt cuff.

Sally handed her a napkin. "And now?"

"I don't know." Evie blew her nose. "That was another thing Mads didn't talk about much. They had her working all sorts of hours. She didn't seem to have a regular schedule. It struck me as a little odd for an internship, but whatever."

Jim arched an eyebrow. "What about boys?"

Evie wadded up the napkin. "What about them?"

"Did Maddie date? Did she have a steady boyfriend?"

"Oh." Evie bit her lip. "Um, no, I guess not."

Sally perked up. "What do you mean? I'm surprised attractive young women such as you and Maddie had a hard time finding dates."

"Finding dates isn't a problem." Evie rolled her eyes. "But finding a good relationship is a whole other thing. College guys aren't *there* in terms of maturity, if you get my meaning. No disrespect." This last was directed at Jim.

His answering smile was faint. "None taken. I remember being in my early twenties. We heard from Maddie's parents there was someone in her life recently."

"Yes and no." Evie shifted in her chair. "It was a stupid dare. We'd each been striking out in the boyfriend area, so we downloaded this dating app. This was before I met the guy I'm dating now." She paused. "It lets the woman choose whether to meet. There was an end-of-year party last spring, and we didn't want to go without dates. We jokingly said the app couldn't be much worse than the people we met on campus, so why not?"

"Let me guess," Sally said. "It was worse."

"At least as bad. Turns out, guys lie online, just like in real life. I know, shocker." Evie blushed. "At least we were smart enough to meet the match before the party. I struck out. Mads went on one date, and he *seemed* normal, but then he got weird."

Girls lie, too. "In what way?"

"Possessive. I mean, it was one freaking date, right?" Now that the conversation had shifted from Maddie's nocturnal habits, Evie seemed more at ease. "They met for coffee, and it went well enough that they decided to go to a movie. But after that, Mads said that this guy wasn't such a great catch. He wouldn't stop calling and texting her, though. She blocked his number, and he still found a way around it. Creepy. Eventually, she threatened to go to the cops. I think that stopped him for a little while, but he'd started up again when fall semester began. She was going to see someone in Uniontown this week to try and get some help."

"I think that might have been me," Sally said.

"Really?" Evie raised her eyebrows. "What is it you do again?"

"I'm a criminal defense attorney."

"Were you able to help her?"

"No. She left before we discussed any details." Sally didn't offer any further information. Maddie might not have gotten to the client stage, but that didn't mean Sally felt comfortable talking specifics with just anyone, even Maddie's roommate. After all, it didn't sound like Maddie had taken her friend into her confidence.

"What was the name of the guy?" Jim asked.

Evie frowned. "His first name is Zach. I know that much. I don't remember his last name. I think it might have started with an F."

"Zach as in Zachary?"

"I think so, yeah. He definitely spelled it with a 'ch.' I remember that."

"What was the name of the app you used?" Sally asked.

Evie's blush deepened. "Buzz. It's all bumblebee and flower-themed. Stupid, huh?"

"Dating is hard these days." Sally glanced at Jim. "One last question. Did Maddie ever talk about someone named Noah Freeman?"

"Oh yeah." Evie nodded. "He was some guy from the center where Mads volunteered. She thought he was sweet, but he's younger, and he has autism or something. She mentioned once that she was afraid he'd fixated on her, so she was trying to get him to notice other girls."

"Was it working?"

"Unfortunately, no. Noah only had eyes for Mads. He made crafts for her and stuff. Kid things. Like I said, really sweet, but definitely not the right guy."

Jim scanned his notes. "Did he ever contact Maddie outside the center? Phone calls, texts, emails?"

Evie's expression morphed into confusion. "Oh, nothing like that. At least not that she ever mentioned to me. How would he even have gotten her phone number? I don't think she gave it to him. He'd have had to steal it from the center or something, and I don't think he's smart enough to do that."

Sally could tell Jim shared her thoughts. Being autistic does not make you unintelligent or incapable of deception. She'd have to meet Noah Freeman and see for herself if he was a viable suspect.

"One last thing," Jim said. "When was the last time you saw Maddie?"

Evie thought. "I don't think I saw her after breakfast on Wednesday. Yeah, that was it. She left on this trip while I was in class and was supposed to be home after dinner. But like I said, she texted me that afternoon and said she'd been delayed and I wouldn't see her until tomorrow."

"Evie, thank you for talking to us." Jim handed her a business card. "If you think of anything else that might help, please call me. My work number and cell phone are listed, and you can use either one."

The young woman took the card. "No problem. Mads could be a real pain, but we've been friends since freshman year. Are you really sure it was her? I mean, maybe you've got the wrong person. Mistaken identity happens."

Sally squeezed Evie's forearm. "No mistake. Here." She took out one of her own business cards. "This is my number. In case you can't reach Trooper Duncan or you're uncomfortable calling him."

Evie took the card. "What about her stuff?"

"I have a search warrant to go through it. Then I'm sure the college will make arrangements for someone to come and collect it." Jim took out his phone. "Head over to the dorm. We'll be right behind you."

Chapter Twelve

On the way back from the café, Evie once again walked faster, leaving Duncan and Sally to trail behind her as they made their way back to Rooney Hall. "Thoughts?" he asked.

Sally considered a moment. "She's in shock a bit. I think she's being mostly truthful. She didn't know the whole deal with what Maddie was up to or where the money came from, but she suspects more than what she's saying. Yes, I know." She held up a hand. "She already said she thought Maddie was working in the sex industry, and she might not have detailed knowledge. But I get the idea it went a little beyond vague feelings."

"I think you're right." He jammed his hands in his jacket pockets. "It'll be interesting to see what's in the room."

Unfortunately, since Latrobe was in Westmoreland County, the trooper who showed up to assist was out of Troop A. Duncan would have preferred to work with McAllister. Being closer in age to Maddie Tilgher, she might have had insights he or Sally would miss. But the middle-aged man who had arrived would have to do.

Evie slung her backpack over her shoulder. "I have a tutoring session in five minutes. Do you need me to stay?"

"No, go on," Duncan replied. "If we have more questions, we'll catch you later."

She bolted from the apartment.

Sally's gaze lingered after her. "Is she afraid of what we'll find or just uncomfortable going through her dead friend's things?"

"Could be both." Duncan held out his hand. "Here's a pair of gloves. I would prefer if you didn't move anything around, but I won't try to keep you from looking. I know better. But don't mess up the chain of evidence, got it?"

Sally snapped a faux salute. "Yes, sir." She took the gloves, tugged them on, and went to the bathroom to begin her inspection.

The uniformed trooper Laughlin looked around. "God, I didn't take this much crap when I went to college. Where do we start?"

"I know exactly what you mean." Duncan waved. "Let's do the bedroom first."

Maddie's room was a study in purple. Everything from the bedclothes to the desk accessories was some shade of violet. Duncan inspected the sheets and comforter. He judged them to be a cut above the cheapest set available, but not the most expensive, either. The pens, desk blotter, storage caddy, and other paraphernalia could easily have been bought at Target. He flipped open the black laptop on the desk. The lock screen was a psychedelic pattern in shades of purple. Cracking the password would be a job for the tech guys.

He bagged the laptop. An extra-long charging cable, also purple, was plugged into a power strip. Maddie's phone was absent. Duncan was sure when he found it, it would be in a purple case. "Where the hell did she leave it?"

Laughlin didn't turn around. "Leave what?"

"Her phone. It wasn't at the scene. There's a cable here, but no phone."

"That's odd. Young people don't go anywhere without their devices these days."

"Exactly." Duncan opened the desk drawers. "Keep your eyes peeled."

The drawers offered nothing but a collection of old daily calendar pages, folders, a ream of standard white printer paper, and a hodgepodge collection of rubber bands, paper clips, and binder clips. He thumbed through a planner with a purple vinyl cover. All of the notations appeared to be related to academics. Class times, professor contact info, and assignment dates. "She had a standing appointment every weekday at eleven in the morning with a Doctor Travers. Whoever that is."

"Check the faculty page of the school website," said Laughlin. "Could be her advisor. She was a clotheshorse, wasn't she?"

"Everything we found at the scene was high-end fashion."

"Yeah, well, her closet isn't any different. My eldest is a financial advisor up in Pittsburgh, and she isn't dressing in duds like these." He expertly ran his hands over the clothes and checked the pockets of the coats. "Loose change, wrappers, no phone."

Duncan bagged the planner. He picked up a framed four-by-six photo of Evie and Maddie. They were atop Mount Washington in Pittsburgh, based on the view of the skyline. The wind tousled their hair, and their cheeks were pink, but they weren't wearing coats. Late fall, maybe? Evie looked much like she did earlier, leading Duncan to believe the picture was recent. "Hey Sally, come here a moment, will you?"

She appeared. "What's up?"

"What are the shoes with the red soles?"

"Louboutins. Tanelsa has a pair."

He held out the frame. "Maddie is wearing them in this picture. Don't suppose you recognize anything else?"

She scrutinized it. "I *think* Maddie is wearing diamond earrings, or something that is catching the light and sparkling, anyway. That's the Prada logo on her purse."

"What, the thing that looks barely big enough to carry a lipstick? Is that what they're calling a purse these days?" He held out his hand. "If it has a logo, does that mean it's real?"

"Not necessarily. High-quality knock-offs have logos. You have to look closer to spot the forgery. And high-quality fake stuff is expensive in its own right." She gave back the photo. "Lisa explained it all to me once. That's who you should talk to for this. She'll be able to tell you if Maddie's items are real."

"You find anything in the bathroom?"

"Maddie's taste in perfume and bath accessories was not on par with her clothes. I found nothing in there that I can't get at a good department store. A bottle of vitamins and one of no-name ibuprofen. No prescription drugs of any kind, including birth control."

"We found an implant on her at the autopsy."

"That explains that." Sally played with the phone charging cord. "If Maddie texted her friend, and the phone wasn't there when you found the body, then her killer took it."

"Or she lost it, or a third party removed it from the scene and locked the door on the way out." Duncan looked over at Laughlin. "What's in the closet?"

"More shit than I've seen in twenty years. And since that covers a good amount of time living with four women, including my wife, that's saying something." Laughlin took down a box. "Here's a bunch of photographs. Some cheap ones, like you'd get at one of those mall kiosks. A handful of three-by-fives."

Sally took it and sat on the floor, where she shuffled through them. "Interesting."

Duncan looked up from his search of the last desk drawer. "What?"

"These pictures." Sally spread them out. "A lot of them are date stamped. Look. These are from three years ago, so Maddie would have been a freshman."

He crouched down. "What about them?"

She pointed. "This is the kind of clothing I'd expect a college student from a middle-class family to wear. Now look at these."

He studied the dates. "Hard to tell in the photos, but the general look is more polished. I start to see the difference, what, eighteen months ago or so?"

"Middle of her sophomore year." Sally selected several of the photos. "Take these into evidence. Whatever Maddie was into, porn or prostitution, it started then."

"We aren't positive she was a sex worker."

Sally gave him a flat stare.

"I'm simply pointing out there are other illicit ways of earning a lot of money." Duncan dropped the pictures into a bag, sealed it, and filled out the information. "It could be she met a very generous boyfriend."

"I suppose." She cast her gaze over the room. "Anyone coming in here wouldn't be able to tell Maddie Tilgher from a thousand other college kids." She stood.

"I think that's the point."

Laughlin finished his search. "You want me to go take a look at the common area rooms?"

"Yes," Duncan said. "I'll join you when I finish in here."

The older trooper nodded and left.

Sally ran a gloved finger over the desk. "Haven't you looked everywhere?"

"Not quite." Duncan stepped over to the bed. "When I was a kid, if I wanted to keep something from my parents, I hid it under my mattress."

"That worked?"

"No, because my mother was smart. Mrs. Tilgher isn't here. What are the odds Maddie used the same trick to keep stuff out of sight of her roommate?" He pulled back the bedding and lifted the mattress.

"I suppose it's a common trick. Might as well look."

In the center of the frame was a deep red book. Based on the silver text on the cover, it was a planner. Now, what would Maddie think was sensitive enough to hide under her mattress?

"Grab that," he said to Sally. She did, and he lowered the bed. Then he took the book and flipped it open. It was, in fact, a weekly desk diary. Each two-page spread contained boxes for seven days, laid out with lines on the half-hour. On various dates, Maddie had drawn blocks that had the names of local points of interest: Fallingwater, Ohiopyle, Fort Necessity, and others. The blocks had been shaded in.

"Appointments at those places?" Sally asked as she stood next to him and read. "But the times, wow. Who goes to Fort Necessity at eight o'clock on a Sunday night?"

"That's what I'd like to know." Duncan dropped the book into an evidence bag. What had Maddie been doing at those times?

* * *

While Jim and Trooper Laughlin completed the search of Maddie's apartment, Sally wandered through the rest of Rooney Hall, looking for people who knew the young woman. She quickly determined Maddie had a reputation for being friendly, a little flirtatious, and a bit outrageous at times. No one had anything negative to say until Sally spoke to a young man who lived in the third-floor apartment directly above Maddie and Evie's.

"She was a bitch," he said as he leaned in his doorway. Brown curly hair tufted out from underneath his baseball cap, which was backwards. His Bearcats T-shirt looked like he'd picked it up from the carpet that morning. The faint sour odor off his clothes confirmed it.

Sally took half a step backward. "Why do you say that?"

"She lives right downstairs. Every Saturday night, I host a video game get-together for my bros. Seems like every week, that bitch is up here screaming at us about the noise. She's even called security. Can you believe that?" His tone of voice made it pretty obvious he expected Sally to be on his side.

How could she be up here complaining and out at the same time? Sally suspected the young man was exaggerating. "Well, how loud are these parties and how late? I mean, if she's trying to sleep at three in the morning, I can see where a lot of noise would be more than a little irritating."

He scoffed. "She's not trying to sleep. Not in the 'getting rest' sense of the word anyway."

"How do you know?"

"I've seen her." He smirked. "She comes in real late sometimes, not looking nearly so put together as she did when she left. Oh yeah, I saw that, too." His expression deepened. "I'll tell you another thing, she can talk some shit. Things you wouldn't expect a nice girl to say. Acts that I didn't think were anatomically possible, if you know what I mean."

Sally did not consider herself a prude, and she'd heard a lot from clients in her years at the public defender. But the tone of his voice and the gleam in his eye made her skin crawl. "I get the picture." She paused. "When was the last time this happened?"

He yelled behind him. "Bro! Did the red-headed witch call security on us last week?"

A mumbled response came from within the apartment.

He faced Sally. "Last Saturday, around seven. Hell, quiet hours don't start until eleven on the weekends."

Sally took out her phone and made a note. "She was an attractive young woman. Did you ever come on to her?"

He snorted. "Hell no. Well-dressed or not, I don't have time for a skank like that. Look, I gotta go." He slammed his door.

Sally stared at the tarnished brass numbers. Why on earth would he say something like that? She raised her hand to knock.

"I wouldn't bother," said a female voice behind Sally.

She turned to see a young woman dressed in the ubiquitous college uniform of sweatshirt and pajama pants. "Oh?"

"Connor is a jackass. He likes to talk about how he had this girlfriend from Philly and how she was hotter than any girl here." She tossed her head. "Personally, I think he's full of shit."

"Got it. Say, did you know Maddie Tilgher?"

"Not more than anyone else on the floor. She seemed okay."

"Why would Connor call her names like that?"

"I told you, he's a jerk." The student glanced at her watch, a big square thing that was probably the latest model of whatever wearable was hot that fall. "Sorry, I gotta go. If you're looking for info on Maddie, try her roommate, Evie. Those two are tight." She wandered off.

Great suggestion. Except Evie hadn't exactly been a fountain of information.

Undeterred, Sally continued to roam the halls and ask questions. But aside from Connor, no one had much to say. Wherever Maddie's close friends had lived, it wasn't in Rooney Hall. No one could corroborate Connor's accusations. No one could remember the last time they'd seen the young woman with the dark red hair.

Just like she'd vanished from Sally's office, Maddie had disappeared last Wednesday. The sad part was that no one, aside from Evie, sounded like they cared.

Chapter Thirteen

While Duncan finished his search of Maddie's apartment, Belle and Monica, the other two roommates, returned. Neither of them had much to say.

"She was fine," said Belle.

"Didn't you know her?" Duncan asked.

Belle shrugged. "I'm better friends with Evie. But Maddie was cool. A little secretive, but cool."

"Secretive how?"

"Dunno." Another shrug. "Sometimes she was really outgoing, and other times, she was really vague and shit. She'd say she couldn't go somewhere, but wouldn't give a real explanation of why."

Duncan turned to Monica. "What about you?"

"I barely knew her." The young woman glanced at her friend. "Belle told me she was with a group looking for a fourth in a suite and asked if I was interested. As far as I know, Maddie was okay. I didn't talk to her much."

These two weren't going to be a lot of help; that was clear. The warrant hadn't extended to the other living spaces, but his gut told him that aside from the weekly calendar under the mattress, there was nothing else to find. It didn't appear that Maddie had trusted her friend enough to ask her to keep something secret. Sally had taken off to wander around the rest of Rooney Hall. Duncan called Cavendish. "How's the birthday party?"

"You seen one, you've seen them all. Kids, cake, too much sugar, crying, and little party favors that get broken thirty seconds after the kids get them." The murmur of speech and background classical music came over the line.

"Frankly, I'm about to fall asleep, and if one more old woman asks when I'm going to get married and start a family, I'm gonna stab her."

Just like Sally's situation, Duncan thought. What was it about mothers and grandmothers that made them pry into the lives of younger women, be they relatives or not? "Try not to get into trouble. I don't need to bail my partner out of jail."

"I'll behave myself. How has your morning gone?"

Duncan brought her up to speed, including the find of the pictures and the hidden planner.

"Well, that's weird. One, the appointments, and two, why hide it?"

"That's what I thought."

"What does Sally say?"

"She thinks however Maddie was getting her clothes, it started around the middle of her sophomore year. Both of us think the planner has something to do with whatever the victim was into, but we aren't sure if those are code words for clients or something else."

"Hmm." Cavendish paused. "This roommate, Evie. She doesn't know anything more about Laurel Highland Arts or whatever their name is?"

"The internship? No. I find it very suspicious that Maddie didn't want Evie to see the photos. If this so-called internship was legit, I would think Maddie would want to showcase her work."

"Good point. We need to do a deep dive into this place on Monday and visit Mr. Atwiler."

"Duly noted." Duncan looked up and saw Sally approaching. "I'll call you later if we turn up anything else. Remember, no killing grandmas."

Cavendish muttered some unintelligible words and ended the call.

Duncan slipped his phone into his pocket. "We're done here. Where'd you go?"

"I walked around and tried to find out if anyone had any useful information."

"And?"

She told him about Connor, the possibly unhelpful upstairs neighbor.

"Interesting that the other student you spoke to put a damper on Connor, but didn't offer anything else." He looked around. "I remember dorm life a lot differently. Whether you were friends with someone or not, you knew about them. At least something. This isn't a large school."

"No." Sally tilted her head.

"You're plotting something, I can tell."

"Would you agree that we're at a dead end here? At least for now?"

"Yes." He waved around the apartment. "I sent Laughlin back to patrol. I think we found the most important thing, that day planner. We might get something off Maddie's laptop, but we need to break the password."

"There are two people who we could talk to."

"Who?"

"Noah Freeman and his mother."

Duncan rolled the idea around in his head. It was certainly a possibility. Noah had said precious little the day they'd found Maddie's body, but Sue Hepworth had been fairly resistant to more questioning of her son. "What makes you think we'd get any further?"

"Maybe we could catch him at the center when he's away from his mother."

"No way. Yes, he's nineteen and an adult. Technically. But there's no way we'd stay out of trouble if we questioned him without a parent. Not an autistic person. I have no desire to find myself in a disciplinary hearing." He held up a hand. "I know. You don't have a boss, but think it through. If Noah was your client, what would you say if you found out a cop had questioned him without counsel or a responsible adult present?"

"I'd be furious." She tapped her chin. "But didn't Evie say Noah had an attachment to Maddie? Isn't that worth following up on?"

It was, and under other circumstances, he'd do it in a heartbeat. "Fine. We'll go to the center. But if Noah is there, we can't talk to him without his mother's permission."

* * *

The Center for the Developmentally Disabled was in Mount Pleasant, approximately a thirty-minute drive from Latrobe. "I wonder why Noah comes here." Sally mused as she stared out the window of the Jeep. The countryside had the sere, dead look of the in-between time of the fall. After the blaze of colorful foliage, but before the blanket of snow that marked winter and the beginning of ski season.

"What do you mean? They probably have great programs. Or maybe he's been coming here for a long time." Duncan turned into a parking lot with fresh asphalt and crisp lines, and parked as close to the door as he could get.

"That may be, but look at the distance." Sally got out of the Jeep and held out her phone.

Duncan made sure the doors were locked, rounded the back of the vehicle, and looked. "I see what you're getting at. This is at least a forty-five-minute drive from Noah's house." Surely, Sue Hepworth could have found a more convenient resource for her son.

Inside, the overall decor combined for a sea of soothing pastels. Vases containing flowers occupied various surfaces. Duncan was pretty sure they were fake, based on the presence of tulips and lilies, blooms that even he knew were wildly out of season for the area. Framed artwork, probably done by center clients, hung on the walls.

He went to the reception desk, where a perky-looking young woman was focused on her computer monitor. He waited a few seconds, then cleared his throat when she didn't look up.

She lifted her head and removed two tiny wireless earbuds from her ears, which had been hidden by her long brown hair. "Oh, sorry. Welcome to CDD. How may I help you?"

He held out his ID and introduced himself and Sally. "We'd like to speak to either a director or a senior employee of some kind."

"Oh." She gave him a hesitant look. "May I ask what this is about?"

"I'd prefer not to get into detail at this very moment, but it's about one of your volunteers. Maddie Tilgher."

"Is she in trouble?"

Duncan glanced at Sally, who shrugged and moved off to inspect some framed prints. "Ms. Tilgher was found dead a couple days ago. Murdered. We're trying to compile as much background information about her as possible."

The young woman gasped. "Oh my God. Um, right. God, that's incredible. I mean, she was just here earlier this week. Wow."

Duncan removed his notebook. "Did you talk to her?"

"Of course, well, sort of. I mean, I saw her, said hello, and we chatted a bit. I know she's a senior at St. Vincent. I graduated from Seton Hill last spring. She asked about job searching, life after college, stuff like that."

"What did you think of Maddie?" He checked her nameplate. "Ms. Abbot?"

"Think of her?" Abbot twisted her fingers together. "She was a good person, I guess. She had a bubbly personality. She got along with just about all our clients."

"I understand she's been volunteering here for a while. Do you know why?"

"No, sorry. I only started a few months ago. I got a degree in creative writing from Seton Hill, so it's a thin job market. I'm thinking I should have listened to my parents and at least minored in something more practical." She shrugged.

"Do you know Noah Freeman?"

"Not really. Look, let me call Liz. She's our assistant director. She'll probably be more helpful than me." Abbot got up and excused herself.

Duncan wandered over to Sally. "See anything interesting?"

"Yes." She pointed. "This is by Noah Freeman. Check out the subject."

Noah wasn't Michelangelo, not by a long shot. While the face of the young woman in the picture was crude, based on the long red hair, knee-high boots, and the fact that the figure was clearly supposed to be short, there was no doubt who Noah had drawn. Maddie Tilgher. "He liked her enough to make a picture of her. I wonder if this is the only one he did."

A small cough interrupted them. Duncan turned to see a woman in her early thirties with short ash-brown hair. Her makeup was minimal, and her clothing practical: jeans, a fleece jacket over a turtleneck, and short boots. "Are you Liz?"

She held out a hand. "Liz Jackson. I'm the assistant director. I understand you're interested in Maddie."

"Yes." Duncan looked around. "Is there somewhere private we can talk? I'd hate to disrupt things or upset anybody who happened to overhear us."

"This way." Jackson led them to a room with a table, a few chairs, and a box of fake greenery in the window. "Chelsea tells me Maddie is dead. How did it happen?"

"She was murdered. I can't talk about the exact details of an ongoing investigation, you understand." He sat. Sally wordlessly took the chair next to him.

Jackson nodded and seated herself. "No leaks to the public. Got it. I read detective novels." She ran a hand through her hair. "So sad."

"Was Maddie a long-time volunteer?" Sally asked.

"She's been here, what, a year or two? That's long for a college student. I think it was originally a community service sentence for some minor infraction, but she seemed to enjoy the work. At least she stuck around long after the legal commitment was fulfilled."

"Was she a good volunteer?" Duncan leaned forward. "I mean, did you ever have any problems with her or her work?"

"Not until recently." Jackson folded her hands. "She never missed a day without informing us in advance. She was pleasant and tried to get along with all the clients."

"Tried?"

"You have to understand, Trooper, our clients are all along the spectrum of behavioral and cognitive disability. Some are very high-functioning and are only here for the socialization. Others have severe problems, and some can be downright unmanageable. Maddie did her best to get along with all of them."

"Did she play favorites?" Sally asked. "We've heard that she may have had a special relationship with Noah Freeman."

"Ah, Noah." Jackson's knowing smile implied she knew exactly what the question meant. "Noah is a long-time client. For all his abilities, he's also one of our more…difficult ones. Well, that's unfair. Noah himself is mostly an agreeable young man."

"What do you mean?" Sally asked.

"His mother can be a little demanding."

Having seen Sue Hepworth in action, Duncan believed it. "He lives quite a distance away. It's a little surprising he's one of your clients."

"Noah has been with us since he was five. They used to live in Mount Pleasant, but moved about a year ago. Ms. Hepworth didn't want to disrupt his schedule, so she continued to bring him." Jackson tilted her head. "What does this have to do with Maddie?"

"Noah is the one who found the body," Duncan said. "Some people have told us Maddie had a special relationship with him. His mother denies it. What would you say?"

For the first time, Jackson looked uncomfortable. "It wasn't entirely Maddie's fault. She was a very pretty young woman. Noah might have read more into her friendliness than he should have. Lord knows she tried to keep him centered, right down to pairing him up with other girls for activities. But he always came around to her. I saw you looking at his drawing in the lobby."

Duncan glanced at Sally. "He was infatuated. How did Maddie react?"

"She told him she was flattered, but she didn't like him that way, and it wouldn't be appropriate for them to be together. Noah became very agitated."

Sally leaned forward. "How so?"

Jackson fidgeted. "It wasn't pretty. He was throwing things, yelling, shaking his fists. I'd never seen him act that way. It took two of our aides to calm him down, and we had to ask Maddie to leave. She and I talked about it, and that's when I suggested maybe it was better if she stopped volunteering completely."

"I thought you just said she was good with your clients." Sally folded her hands. "Were there other incidents? With young men other than Noah?"

"No, and yes, she was, but...."

Duncan waited. "Yes?" he finally asked. "You mentioned you didn't have problems with her until recently. I take it this was one of them."

"There were two issues. One, she had become inappropriately involved with Noah."

"I thought you said she wasn't interested in him?"

Jackson waved her hand. "Not romantically. I learned she was looking into Noah's background. It was more than a volunteer should do. Heck, it would have been out of line for a staff member. All about his parents and where he came from. He didn't understand, but it was almost work for a private investigator, not a young woman donating her time."

Sally drummed her fingers on the table. "Why? I mean, is there something wrong with Ms. Hepworth?"

"I don't know." Jackson shrugged.

Duncan made a note. "What was the other thing?"

Jackson shifted in her chair. "It was pretty clear to me that Maddie had something going on, something in her private life. I'm sure others have told you, and no doubt you noticed yourself, her clothes were far too expensive for a young woman of her age and economic class. She'd get texts and go off to the bathroom. Someone called her once, and she went ballistic, told whoever it was never to call her at that number, especially when she said she was unavailable."

"She didn't tell you who it was?"

"No. I asked, but she said it wouldn't happen again, and it was nothing I had to worry about." Jackson looked at Duncan straight in the eye. "She was bullshitting me, I was certain. Whatever she was up to, I was concerned for her, and moreover, I worried it would negatively impact everyone here."

Chapter Fourteen

Sally stood in the parking lot by the Jeep, staring at the Center for the Developmentally Disabled. Jim was still inside, following up on other questions he had about Maddie, her behavior, and any relationships she might have had. Sally didn't want to be present for that. In fact, it was most likely better she wasn't.

Noah, despite all the people who described him as gentle, sounded like he had a violent temper and deep feelings for Maddie. How deep? Sally understood Maddie's unwillingness to get involved in a personal relationship with him. One, it *would* be inappropriate considering her status as a center volunteer, and two, Maddie wouldn't have wanted to start a relationship with a developmentally challenged young man. It was a hard truth, but there it was.

Sally also knew how Jim would have to proceed. Now that he knew about the incident, he'd have to follow up with Noah, and the young man would have to be added to the suspect list. Having autism did not make you incapable of killing someone, whether you called it murder or manslaughter. Had Noah Freeman been the person Maddie had in mind when she visited Sally?

That idea felt wrong. It would have been fairly easy for Maddie to remove herself from the situation without legal assistance. She could volunteer on days or at times when Noah wasn't present. It was unlikely he could drive or knew where to find her, even if he'd discovered her phone number. No, Sally's common sense told her Noah wasn't the person who had Maddie so worried.

Then again, why had Maddie been investigating Noah's parent?

A gust of wind made Sally shiver and turn up her coat collar. Where was Jim? She should have asked for his keys so she could get in the Jeep.

The guy Evie had talked about…Zach something…he was more of a possibility. But getting the records from the dating app would be hard. Those companies were notoriously reluctant to give up subscriber information without a court order. And sometimes even with one.

She leaned on the Jeep, took out her phone, and searched for Buzz. The top result was the Buzz app, "a new way to date for the twenty-first century." She put her phone in landscape orientation to better see the web pages. The app looked like it would appeal to young people with its colorful, bubbly aesthetic. Not as traditional, and it seemed to be trying for a more "fun" experience than established online dating outlets. Sally kept reading. Evie had mentioned something about Buzz putting the woman in charge. How did that work?

Sally tapped and scrolled. According to the description, both men and women created accounts and put up a "seed profile" describing their likes, dislikes, and desires. Men could indicate their interest in a date by tagging a woman's profile. The woman could then weed through the respondents, or look at a "flower catalog," then they tagged a profile with a bee on a flower to set up a date. Those she wasn't interested in were marked with a bee sting.

Sally mentally rolled her eyes at the corniness of the terminology, but it must connect with singles in their twenties. The Buzz site boasted over 100,000 subscribers and claimed to add more every day. Not for the first time in the last few months, she thanked her lucky stars she'd gotten together with Jim. How could anybody find a real relationship amid all the gimmicks?

She dropped her phone in her purse. Maybe they'd find a login for the Buzz website on Maddie's laptop. It would be better if they could find the phone, which would have the app and associated records. Where was the damn thing?

Jim came out of the building, and Sally straightened up. "Finally. What else did you learn?"

"Get in." He slid into the Jeep and started the engine. "Sorry, that took longer than I thought it would. I didn't even learn enough to make it worth the time."

Sally fastened her seatbelt. "But you got something?"

"Not beyond what you heard from Liz Jackson." He blew on his hands and bumped the heater up a couple notches. "A lot of people knew who Maddie was, but they weren't friends. She didn't invite confidences. I had to be careful talking to the clients, but I got the impression that most of them were in the same boat. They know her name and face, but there aren't any real connections here."

"Except for Noah."

"Except for him, yes." Jim leaned back and closed his eyes.

"You're going to have to talk to him again. Especially since we know he can be violent."

"Thank you, Sherlock."

She paused. "I want to be there."

He didn't look at her. "Of course you do." He opened his eyes and fixed her with a firm stare. "You also know why I can't have my girlfriend present when I question a witness in a murder investigation. If he ends up being charged, any decent defense attorney would shred his statement. You know you would."

She hated it, but he was right. "What if I wasn't part of the interrogation? I'd just be a silent observer."

He arched an eyebrow.

"I'd even stay in another room. Somewhere I could hear what was happening, but I wouldn't interfere."

He put the Jeep in drive. "I'll think about it."

* * *

About an hour later, they pulled into the driveway at the Hepworth home. Sally had spent the entire journey thinking through what she wanted to say and, more importantly, what she wanted to know. However, she needed to stay out of Jim's way. After all, he had the legally permissible reason to be here. He was investigating a murder. She was tagging along because of her personal commitment to Maddie, but Sue Hepworth could easily turn her away.

Jim rapped on the front door. "Remember, you stay quiet. In fact, you go to the kitchen. I'll talk to the kid in the TV room. You'll be able to hear everything."

She covered her frustration. She knew it was as good as she was going to get, seeing as Jim was right and she shouldn't technically be present at all. "I'll be a fly on the wall, a quiet snoop."

He sighed. "I appreciate your cooperation, but I think you're a little more than a snoop. A young woman comes to you for help, splits, and turns up dead two days later? I don't know many attorneys who wouldn't be interested in the whys of that one. Never mind a person with your cat-like curiosity."

"True, but as the saying goes, look what happened to the cat." Comments like that were one reason why she loved him. He could have told her to wait in the car, and he'd report back. But he respected her enough to let her listen in. "I promise I won't interrupt you."

Sue Hepworth answered the door. "Trooper Duncan, right? Can I help you?"

Jim nodded. "I have a few more questions for Noah, and I thought it would be better if you were present."

"You should have called first. We might have been out."

Sally was willing to bet the woman would have come up with a reason not to be home had she been warned of their arrival.

Jim had to have the same thought, but only said, "I was in the area and decided to run that risk."

Sue's gaze cut to Sally. "Who is this?"

Jim made the introductions. "Maddie Tilgher sought out Ms. Castle's assistance in the days before her death. I was talking to her before we arrived."

Sally maintained a straight face. Talk about skirting the facts. Nothing

Jim said was a lie, but it wasn't the whole truth, either.

Sue gripped the door. "Isn't that illegal? Breach of confidence between lawyer and client or something?"

Sally stepped forward. "Ms. Tilgher and I never got to that point." She tried to look over Sue's shoulder. "Can I wait in your kitchen? It's cold out here, and I hate to use up Trooper Duncan's gas by making him keep his Jeep running. I'm sure you've seen the prices at the pump lately."

The other woman paused for a long second. "Noah is watching TV. He's not been himself since he found that girl. You can ask your questions, but I'm not sure it'll help." She shot Sally a suspicious look. "I suppose you can wait in the kitchen. I'll make you a cup of tea or coffee if you want one." Her tone of voice told Sally not to want a drink.

"Thanks, but I don't want to be a bother."

"I appreciate your time." Jim motioned for Sally to enter the house and followed her. "Which way?"

"Here." Sue led them to a comfortably-decorated room with overstuffed furniture and a thick-piled dark brown carpet. A large flat-screen television was mounted on the wall. Noah sat on the floor, transfixed by the images on the screen, some sort of nature program, by the looks of it. "The kitchen is through that door."

Sally took the unspoken directive and went to the room. The decor was not brand-spanking new, but not old either, with solid-surface counter tops, blond-wood cabinetry, and appliances she guessed were less than ten years old. She took a seat at the table. By positioning her chair, she could not only hear the conversation from the next room, but see most of the action as well.

Sue returned to her son's side. "Noah, honey? The police officer is here to see you. You remember Trooper Duncan, don't you?"

Noah glanced at Jim and returned his attention to the TV. "I don't want to talk to him."

Sue crouched down. "Sweetie, it'll be okay. Just a couple of minutes. I'll be right here."

Jim got down on the floor. "Hi, Noah. How are you?"

It seemed Noah was going to ignore Jim completely, but the autistic young man finally looked at him. "You found Maddie."

"That's right." Jim shifted to a more comfortable position. "You found her, really. I brought her home. You were very helpful that day. I hoped you could give me a little bit more assistance by talking to me."

Noah didn't answer. Sue bit her lip, but nodded for Jim to continue.

Sally watched the scene in front of her. Noah seemed distant, uncaring. Was that normal for autistic people? The mention of Maddie's name didn't appear to faze him. Sue, on the other hand, was a coiled spring, quivering with suppressed energy. Why?

"Noah, tell me. Did you like Maddie?" Jim asked. "I heard she worked at the place where you hang out during the week."

More silence from the young man.

"I talked to Ms. Jackson earlier. You know her, right? She said you and Maddie were friends."

Sue paled, but didn't say anything.

Noah gave a slow nod.

"Maddie was awfully pretty. I saw a picture you drew of her last spring." Jim looked directly at Noah, who kept his eyes averted.

Sally focused on the boy's body language. He'd tensed as Jim spoke, his hands curled into fists on his lap, the knuckles white. What Jim was saying was getting to him.

"You can tell me. It's okay." Jim's voice was calm, inviting Noah's response. "Did you think of Maddie as more than a friend?"

No answer, but Noah's body tensed. Sally hoped Jim saw the same thing and trod carefully.

Jim paused. "Ms. Jackson said you argued, though. With Maddie. Can you tell me a little about that?"

Without warning, Noah lashed out with his left fist, catching Jim on the forehead. "Get out! Get out! Maddie is a good person, and she loves me! Get out!" He scrambled forward.

Sue grabbed her son. "Trooper, you'd better leave."

Jim rolled out of the way and got to his feet. "I'm sorry to disturb you. I'll be going."

"Don't you talk about Maddie like that," Noah said, still fighting to get around his mother.

"Trooper, please, just go." Sue focused on her son. "It's okay, Noah. No one is going to hurt you."

Jim shot a look toward the kitchen. Then he turned and left the room. Sue followed him, maybe to make sure he really went out. She had apparently forgotten there had been another person with him when he arrived. Noah went back to watching TV.

Sally left her post in the kitchen and moved to sit on the chair in the corner closest to Noah. "Hey, it's okay. He's gone. He didn't mean anything, I promise. His job is to ask a lot of questions, and I know it can be a bit much sometimes."

Sue re-entered the room and started to speak, voice low but thick with suppressed anger. "Ms. Castle, I really don't think—"

"Noah, look at me, please?" Sally ignored the other woman and devoted all her attention to Noah. He faced her, expression fierce. "Maddie came to me to talk about something that was bothering her. But she left before I could do anything. I'd want to help her now. I know you'd like that, too."

His breathing, which had been coming in heaving puffs, slowed. "You were Maddie's friend?"

"Not exactly, but she came to see me one day. I wish I'd had the opportunity to know her better. Why don't you help me with that, huh?" She motioned at Sue to move aside.

She hesitated, but took a seat on the couch.

"Maddie loved me." Noah said the words with the simple certainty of a child. Not the passionate declaration of a lover. But who knew what he thought?

"I'm sure she did. But Ms. Jackson did tell us you fought with her. Why would you do that?" Sally rested her arms on her knees.

Noah focused on her, ignoring his mother. "They made her say she didn't want to be with me. She said she wouldn't come to the center to see me anymore. I had to make her understand that I love her, too. That's why I drew her picture for Valentine's Day."

"It was lovely." Sally snuck a look at Sue, whose gaze was fixed on Noah, arms tightly crossed. "What did your mom say?"

"Mom thought Maddie was too old for me. But it was only by a couple of years." His wide-eyed gaze held Sally's. "I couldn't let her leave. You understand, right?"

"What do you mean by leave?"

Noah shrugged. "Leave the center. She told me she wasn't going to be there anymore. I wanted her to stay."

Sally paused and again glanced at Sue. Had she not been wearing long sleeves, she would have jammed her fingernails right through her skin. Her expression was calm, but her gaze now had fear mixed with her previous anger. Fear of what Noah had said? Or what he might say?

It was clear he had made some sort of connection to the young volunteer. His feelings had not been reciprocated, not in the way he believed. It was possible Maddie had understood and tried to break it gently to Noah, with disastrous results.

But could Noah have turned into a murderer? Why would he have taken Maddie to that cabin? Even more to the point, why would Maddie have gone? A sophisticated young woman would not get sexually involved with a boy like Noah. Unless she was a mean-spirited witch, playing with Noah's emotions. Nothing Sally had learned pointed to that. Complaining about a noisy upstairs neighbor didn't make you an awful person.

Plus, Maddie might not have been romantically interested in Noah, but the talk with Liz Jackson made it clear Maddie had been interested in *something* about him.

Sue cleared her throat. "Ms. Castle, please, I really do think you need to go."

She knows something. More accurately, Noah saw or did something, and his mother doesn't want it coming out. Without any legal standing, Sally couldn't force the conversation. Jim had to have picked up on the same vibe, though. He wouldn't let it drop. "Okay." Sally stood. "Noah, thank you very much. I think this will help Maddie a lot."

Noah returned to staring at the television and didn't respond.

Sue hissed in her ear. "I think that's quite enough." She led Sally back to the front of the house. "I appreciate that you feel obligated to help figure out what happened to that girl. But neither you nor Trooper Duncan should come here again, and I forbid you in particular to speak to my son."

"Ms. Hepworth, I'm sorry if we caused Noah distress." Sally shouldered her purse and faced the other woman. "I will certainly heed your wishes. However, regarding Trooper Duncan and his partner, they're conducting a murder investigation. If they need to talk to Noah, they will. You may be able to influence the conditions under which that happens, but he's a valuable witness. You can't simply forbid the police from doing their job."

"That little bitch." Sue yanked open the door. "I never should have let her be around Noah. She caused me a lot of trouble with her *volunteer* work, and she's still making my life miserable."

Sally went out to the porch, the venom in the woman's words clear. Maddie had screwed *her*? Noah's feelings, Sally could understand, but the mother's? It didn't make sense. "I'm not sure I see how Maddie would have had an impact on you."

"I don't appreciate you, or the police, coming here and upsetting my son, Ms. Castle," Sue said.

"I told you, I understand how you feel, but you must see—"

"I don't have to see anything. I've been very patient, and Noah has answered enough questions. I'd appreciate it if you'd leave us alone from now on." With that, Sue shut the door.

Chapter Fifteen

D uncan loitered by the Jeep, waiting for Sally to come out. He rubbed his forehead where Noah had struck him. Not hard enough to raise a lump, but the blow left a red mark. He hadn't meant to upset the kid. But the reaction was interesting. He'd talk it over with Cavendish on Monday, and they could decide how to proceed.

Sally came out of the house, and Duncan caught Sue Hepworth's final words before she slammed the door. "Sounds like that went well," he said as Sally approached.

"It was definitely an experience." Sally got into the Jeep.

Duncan climbed in, started it, and pulled away. "What'd I miss?"

Sally described the entire interview, including Hepworth's final ultimatum.

"She does know that's not how it works, right? She tells me 'You can't talk to my son' and I meekly crawl away?" Jim asked.

"I warned her of that, yes." Sally stared out of the window. "There's something fishy about her."

"She's a protective parent. I've encountered a lot of them on the job." He glanced at her. "Considering her son is disabled, she's probably more of a worrywart than most."

"That's not it." Sally seemed to struggle with what to say. Unusual for her. "She's actively trying to keep Noah out of the picture. As if she's afraid of what he might say or do, not just that he'll get upset."

Duncan hadn't gotten that vibe the first time he'd interviewed Hepworth. Of course, she'd been distraught. Anything odd in her behavior he'd chalked up to panic, then overwhelming relief. This second time, even though he'd had his attention on Noah, he could tell Hepworth had been on pins and needles. "You were watching from the kitchen. What stood out to you?"

"I kept my eyes on her while you spoke to Noah. She was a bomb ready to explode."

"She was concerned Noah would get agitated."

"I think it's more than that." She twisted in the seat to face him. "I've seen this in interviews with clients before. They'll be listening to someone else speak, and the tension just radiates from them because they are afraid of what the other person might say. Invariably, I corner them afterward, when it's just us, and the truth comes out. They thought the other person was going to say something that put them on the spot. Sue Hepworth acted the same way. If you hadn't been so focused on Noah, you'd have noticed it, too."

Duncan took a moment to digest this fact. Another thing for him and Cavendish to do on Monday. Build up Hepworth's personal history. "What about her and Maddie? Maddie and Noah? Did he say anything about that?"

"Oh, Noah is clearly in love with Maddie." Sally waved her hand in dismissal. "Or what he thinks is love. Remember, he probably has the emotional maturity of a much younger person. I also am pretty sure he was convinced she loved him. He mistook her kindness for romance. I know his mother says he's incapable of that kind of thing, but you and I both know that's bullshit. So does Liz Jackson. I'm quite sure that's one reason why she didn't want Maddie around Noah any longer."

"Agreed." He noted a sign for Wharton Furnace. The name brought back the case with Colin Rafferty and Aaron Trafford from the previous fall. He gripped the wheel tighter, remembering the showdown with Trafford. It had been over a year, but funny how a name brought back the memory instantly. He wrenched his mind off the past. "Does Hepworth not like the fact her son loved Maddie because she doesn't want to admit he's a grown man with feelings, not a little boy? Or did she not approve of Maddie?"

If Sally noticed his moment of stress, she didn't mention it. "Maybe a little of both. I'm not a mom, but I know Reen has talked about how she's not ready for her kids to be dating, even though they're years away from it. You know, the whole 'Jimmy and Sally, sitting in a tree' thing kids do in elementary school." She paused. "But remember. Liz Jackson was going to ask Maddie to stop volunteering because she thought Maddie would be trouble. Both in relation to Noah and her personal life."

Duncan shot her a look. "You think Hepworth's maternal instincts felt the same?"

"I do." Sally went back to staring out at the Fort Necessity National Battlefield as they zipped past.

"You said Noah's infatuation with Maddie was one reason Sue didn't like her. What's the other?"

"I'm not sure. But I'll bet money it also had to do with her son."

"You think Noah is who Maddie meant when she came to see you?"

"No." She gave a quick headshake. "That was someone else, I'm sure of it. She had other troubles, and they must have been pretty serious."

"You think?"

Sally faced him. "Why else do you seek out a criminal defense lawyer?

* * *

Sunday evening, Sally stood on Jim's back porch, hands stuffed deep in the pockets of one of his fleece-lined flannel camp shirts, which she'd thrown on to ward off the evening chill. Pixel and Rizzo raced around the yard in what had become part of their daily routine. Pixel won, of course. Both dogs appeared to be having the time of their lives. It would last until Pixel, the sprinter, ran out of gas and flopped on the ground, tongue hanging out of his mouth while he panted. Then Rizzo would act a bit puzzled, as he always did.

For the moment, Sally admired the athleticism of the greyhound, the flexing and extending of his muscles, how he flew over the ground, and the glossy black of his coat as it reflected the last rays of the November sun. How different he looked from the emaciated, cowering animal that Jim rescued from a murder house at the end of the summer. Rizzo galloped behind his canine friend, golden fur flying, but always a step or three behind. Pixel made sure of that.

Once the races were over, Sally led the dogs inside, where they attacked their water dishes. Jim stood at the sink, finishing the dinner cleanup. He turned his head, arms buried in soapy water. "Who won?"

"Pixel. I swear, it looks like he slows down a pace on occasion, just enough to let Rizzo think he has a chance, and then he pours it on." The hound came over, water dripping from his muzzle, and she rubbed his ears. "You big meanie."

"He's got you in the sprints, doofus," Jim said to his dog. "But you'd kill him in an endurance event."

Rizzo lapped up his water, completely unconcerned with the human conversation.

Jim shook soap suds from his hands and grabbed a towel. "You ready to go?"

"Yeah, I suppose I should. I have to work tomorrow." She took off the shirt and hung it on the back of a chair.

"Tell you what. How about I come to Uniontown for dinner after my shift? You've done a lot of driving to Confluence lately."

"About that." Sally ran her hand over the shirt.

"Yes?" Jim's tone was wary, as though he waited for the shoe to drop.

"You know I've been looking for apartments. I haven't had a lot of luck. Nothing I can afford has enough space for Pixel, and I can't ask you to board him forever." She chanced a look at his face, which wore a polite, but puzzled expression. "Last summer, you offered to let me move in. I'd like to take you up on that, if it's still on the table, that is."

As she spoke, Jim's face cleared. He took two steps across the kitchen, swept her up in his arms, and gave her a kiss that sent little thrills of excitement right down to her toes.

After a couple seconds, he pulled back. "Does that answer your question?"

Chapter Sixteen

Monday morning, Sally arrived at her office around eight-thirty. Tanelsa had not yet arrived. Sally checked her phone. No message. Usually, if her partner was running late, she'd call or text. Hopefully, nothing was wrong.

Sally's mother had called the previous evening, asking about Thanksgiving plans, and had gone straight to the topic Sally most wanted to avoid when she said she'd be spending the day with Jim and his parents.

"If you two have picked a date, I need to know," Louise Castle said.

"We haven't, Mom. Relax."

"I don't know what's holding you up." Louise sniffed. "You know, at your age, your sister had—"

"Yes, I've heard this all before." But Louise kept going as though she hadn't heard her youngest daughter's response. By the time Sally hung up the phone, all the nice, relaxed sense of the day had evaporated.

God, please give me strength. She couldn't bear the thought of spending an entire day parrying Grace Duncan's questions about wedding bells and baby showers. Jim didn't seem to think she would, but in her experience, every grandmother wanted one thing: more grandchildren. Come to think of it, Jim had once mentioned starting a family. Maybe they should have talked about that before she took the step of moving in with him.

She got a cup of coffee and glanced at the clock, which read eight forty. Where the heck was Tanelsa? If she didn't show her face by nine, Sally would call and make sure everything was all right.

In the meantime, she opened her laptop. Time to find out what was up with this online dating site, beyond what she had seen on her phone.

The Buzz site did have a login. Sally kept a throwaway email address for these kinds of things, places where you had to create an account to get beyond the fluffy marketing content of the public pages. She signed up, gave a bogus phone number, and opted out of text notifications. Then she started browsing.

It didn't take long to determine the site was kitschy, but appeared otherwise harmless. She had to set up a bare-bones profile to start seeing other users' information, then she clicked through the "flower catalog." The pictures were all of younger people, none older than thirty-five. The site said you had to be at least twenty-one to register, but there was no validation when creating your account. It would be easy to put in a bogus birth date. That's what Maddie and Evie must have done. At least Sally didn't see any pictures of girls who were obviously in their teens. The men all looked to be clean-cut types. Although using a fake picture was even easier than a phony date. *I am such a cynic.*

The site mentioned same-sex matches in the marketing copy, but most of the requests were for straight relationships, with a couple of lesbian postings scattered around. She didn't see any "male seeking male" asks, which made sense if the site was geared to putting the decision-making in the hands of the female subscribers. Gay or straight, there was nothing kinky about the listings. Most of the descriptions were along the lines of "Thirty-something single woman seeking like-aged man for steady relationship. Must like classic movies, alternative rock, and the outdoors. Non-smoker only. Animal-lover a plus." Evie and Maddie hadn't gone over the edge in their foray into online dating.

The bell above the door alerted her to someone entering the office. She looked up to see a slightly flustered Tanelsa, her normally sleek hair escaping the twist she habitually wore, her jacket rumpled, and her shoes not quite the usual perfect match to her outfit. She clutched a go-cup of Starbucks in her hand, a smear of red on the lid where she'd taken a drink.

"There you are," Sally said. "I was getting worried."

"Sorry I'm late. Lisa and I were…discussing something." Tanelsa threw her leather briefcase onto her desk, flipped open the cup, and took a deep gulp. She turned to face Sally. "What are you looking at?"

Sally evaluated her partner with a critical eye. "T? Looks like you got a hole in your chin."

"What?"

"Check your shirt." Sally tapped her breast. "Unless that's some kind of new abstract pattern the fashion industry is rolling out this year, I'd say you spilled your coffee. I hope you don't have a court date or a client meeting."

Tanelsa muttered an oath and practically slammed down the cup, causing a little liquid to slosh out of the lid. "Be right back." She went to the wardrobe in the corner, grabbed one of the spare shirts inside, and disappeared into the bathroom.

Discussion, my ass. They argued about something, and Tanelsa didn't like it. Sally rarely saw the other woman out of sorts. Whatever the topic of the fight had been, it must have been a doozy.

Tanelsa returned a couple minutes later wearing a fresh white silk shirt under her charcoal gray jacket, the soiled one in her hand. "Thanks for that. I don't have any appointments this morning, but I'd have been mortified if someone walked through the door and saw me with coffee down my front." She folded the dirty laundry and stuck it in a drawer. "Speaking of appointments, what have you got scheduled today? I was going to cruise over to the courthouse and see if I could drum up some business."

Sally did not miss the fact that Tanelsa didn't mention her wife again. Instead of pushing, Sally took a page from Jim's book and let it slide. Tanelsa would talk when and if she was ready. "Don't mention it. As for my docket, it's clear."

"Still? You closed that one with the teenage shoplifter before we moved. I can understand taking moving week off, but we're settled now. Shouldn't you be looking for, how shall I put this, a paying client?"

Sally averted her eyes. "I'm working on it." Tanelsa was absolutely correct, but Sally wouldn't be able to focus on a new case until she'd found out a little more about the one that got away.

"Famous last words. Now that I'm cleaned up, tell me what you're up to."

Tanelsa perched on the edge of her desk and took a sip of coffee, much more collected than she'd been when she entered.

"Remember the redhead who came to the office last week? The one who rabbited before I could get any real information out of her?"

"I do."

"Her name was Maddie Tilgher. She turned up two days later, murdered."

Tanelsa set down the cup. "Get out. I saw something in the paper over the weekend, but they hadn't released the name of the victim. What happened?"

Sally brought her partner up to date on everything she knew, including the conversation with Evie Martin, the search of Maddie's dorm room, her volunteer work, the fishy internship, and Maddie's research into Noah Freeman, along with his exaggerated notion of their relationship.

"You think she came to you about Freeman? Maybe she was afraid of him. It sounds like he has a temper, even if he's autistic. That might be more dangerous, to be honest. Maybe he lashes out, like he did with Jim."

"It's possible, but I don't think so. Don't ask me why, it just doesn't fit. Strangling someone is not the same as hitting them in anger."

"Huh." Tanelsa emptied her cup and threw it in the trash. "Then who? Is it related to the internship? Or this online creep the roommate mentioned?"

"That's what I'm looking up now." Sally beckoned. "I'm on the Buzz website. Be warned, it's a little cartoonish."

Tanelsa dragged her chair over to Sally's desk, sat, and skimmed the web page. "You've got to be kidding me. Are people this desperate for a date?"

"They must be. The Buzz advertising boasts over a hundred thousand subscribers. I'm trying to get a sense of what they're about."

Tanelsa read. "This isn't Maddie's profile."

"No, it's mine."

"Oh, Sally."

"Relax. I have a junk email for this stuff." Sally clicked to another page. "Obviously, I can't hack into Maddie's account. It's illegal, and I don't have the skills. Messages are private. All I see are the public postings."

"Isn't there anything on her phone? There's no way this outfit doesn't have an app."

"There probably is, but Maddie's is missing."

"How convenient." Tanelsa sat back. "What's the minimum age to join?"

"Twenty-one, but it'd be child's play to fake a birthday."

Tanelsa murmured in agreement. "Did you search for her profile? What does it say?"

"All I've done so far is general research. I was about to check when you walked in."

Tanelsa rolled her wrist. "So stop yammering and do it."

It took Sally a couple of tries to locate Maddie. She had listed it under "Madison A. Tilgher" and given her location as Pittsburgh, not Latrobe. But if Tanelsa had been expecting an outrageous posting, she was disappointed. "Soon-to-be college graduate seeks man under thirty for a steady relationship," Sally read. "Must not smoke. Moderate drinker, okay. Should love animals, the outdoors, and Thai food. College degree preferred, but if you are a great conversationalist, education is negotiable."

She sat back.

"That might be the most boring online dating profile ever." Tanelsa scrolled down the page. "Her photos are pretty straitlaced, too."

Sally had to agree. The headshot Maddie had used was not professionally done, but something her roommate might have taken. The picture screamed "wholesome," right down to the stuffed St. Vincent's mascot in the background. All the other images Maddie had used were also sedate. She'd skipped the vacation bikini shots and party candids in favor of one of her with her family dog and another of her standing near the Ohiopyle Falls overlook. "Nice girls can end up with stalkers, you know."

"Too true." Tanelsa clicked around. "So where do you go to say you're interested? You know, like the copy says."

"Um, maybe here?" Sally went to an area titled Contact. "Yeah, here it is, look. So, a guy browses the gallery. If he sees a woman he's interested in, he leaves a comment here. If she's open to meeting, she 'plants a flower,' as they say and sets up a date."

"What was this guy's name?"

"Zach, spelled with an H. Don't know the last name." Sally slowly scrolled down the list. Maddie had attracted a fair amount of attention, but nothing after July of the past summer. "Interesting. Looks like she switched her profile to inactive right around Independence Day."

Tanelsa pointed. "That one. I think he's our guy."

Zach Fabery had tagged Maddie's profile in May. He looked harmless enough. His wavy dark blond hair was a touch long and curled over his ears. He had dark brown eyes that crinkled at the corners, an aquiline nose, and a charming smile of dazzling white teeth.

"Go to his profile," Tanelsa said.

Sally complied. Zach's listing was almost as bland as Maddie's. He professed to be a dog lover, a Steelers fan, and said his favorite memory was the summer he biked the Great Allegheny Passage. In the photos, he came off as the guy next door, hugging his chocolate Labrador, roughhousing with another guy over a football, and biking part of the GAP trail. His listed birthday was two years older than Maddie's, and he claimed to have a degree in marketing from Pitt.

"He doesn't look like a goofball."

Sally opened another browser tab and went to the site she used to start background checks. "They never do."

Chapter Seventeen

Two things arrived at Duncan's desk at nine o'clock. "I have the report from the Crime Scene Unit and some financial records," said the messenger. "Who wants what?"

Duncan reached out his hand. "I'll take the forensic report. The numbers are all yours, Cavendish."

"Oh, goodie." She accepted the manila envelope with a word of thanks for the departing delivery man.

Duncan slit open his own package. "You're better with figures than I am."

"Not all figures," she said with a coy smile. "How did dinner go?"

"It was just fine, thank you very much." He resolved not to look at his partner, knowing her expression would persist whether he gave details or not. Cavendish should know by now he wasn't a kiss-and-tell guy. Instead, he focused on the report from the CS techs.

As expected, the cabin was a mess. They'd found bits of debris, moldering leaf remains, and a healthy amount of dust. No blood, even though Burns had speculated the assailant had been scratched up pretty badly during the fight. Maybe the actor had cleaned up, although getting rid of bloodstains was harder than most people thought. The CS report didn't say anything about signs that someone had tried erasing their presence. Especially when Duncan got to the paragraph about fingerprints. "Holy hell."

Cavendish didn't lift her head. "What?"

"They found multiple sets of usable prints at the scene." He counted. "A total of six. The victim and five sets of unknowns. That doesn't include any of the ones that were too indistinct, but I'm gonna guess some of those are from the same people."

That made his partner sit up. "Was she having a freaking party in there?"

"Sure seems that way." He read the narrative. "The decedent's prints were in multiple places. That makes sense. There were four sets, including hers, on the door. One set over in the corner." He consulted the photos. "That would be where we saw those circular marks."

"Let me see that shot again." She took the picture. "From the pattern, I'd say someone set up a tripod. Something of that nature. Look, the marks make a triangle." She handed it back.

Cavendish was right. Duncan laid aside the picture and continued. "Another unique set was on the outside of the window, the one I used to get in. Those are different from the ones in the corner and those on the door, but are on the cot. The cot itself yielded four sets, the victim's plus three."

"You think the killer is in that set of three unknowns on the bed?"

"That would make sense." Duncan returned to studying the photos. "If the fifth or sixth person had gone over there, they'd have left prints."

"Or wiped away the others if they tried to get rid of their own."

"That's what I'm thinking." He flipped the pages of the report, but there was nothing else notable. "I cannot believe they couldn't match any of these other five."

"It happens." Cavendish paused. "How sure are you that the kid didn't enter? The autistic boy who found her? Didn't he say he saw her through the window? Those might be his."

"Before I saw this, I would have said pretty sure. Now, not so much, seeing as the outside prints match the ones on the cot. You're right about those probably belonging to Noah." He returned to the description of the fingerprints. "They think the padlock was wiped clean."

"Clear as mud. Sounds like we need to get prints from Ms. Hepworth and her son for elimination. She's gonna love that."

"Tell me about it." Five sets of unknown prints? Finding multiples wasn't unusual, but most of the time some of them had at least one match. He pulled out a piece of paper and made a list:

- Door: Victim, #1, #2, #3,
- Corner: #5
- Window: #1
- Cot: Victim, #1, #2, #4

The rest of the forensic report was unremarkable, except that Maddie's clothing was verified as genuine designer fashion. Older, but well-cared-for pieces. That was also puzzling. If Maddie had money, why was she not buying new stuff? "Anything interesting in the financials?"

"Yes and no."

He pushed his chair over. "Like how?"

"Here." She laid out the pages. "Maddie had two bank accounts."

"That we found."

Cavendish dipped her head in agreement. "This one is obviously where she kept her major income. Look at the deposits."

Duncan let out a low whistle. "She was bringing in some cash. That tells me she was either dealing drugs or working in porn, and we've seen no evidence of the former. It's too much for her to be hooking. She'd have to be sleeping with," he counted on his fingers, "I can't do the math quickly, but a lot of guys per day."

"Agreed. You can see she transferred money into this account here, which is where she must have had her debit card and made payments." Cavendish tapped the column of numbers. "I thought Maddie had a scholarship."

"That's what everybody said." He went to his notes from the conversation with the Tilghers. "According to her parents, it was worth twenty grand a year."

"Well, starting the second semester of her sophomore year, there are several payments to St. Vincent."

"Tuition?" Duncan rolled back to his desk and brought up the school's website. "Okay, tuition and fees for this year is estimated at a little over thirty-six thousand. That leaves her sixteen grand short. It's too much. To cover tuition plus the clothes?"

"She could be getting other aid. If I'm reading this right, cash to St.t

Vincent is under ten thousand for the academic year."

"Something to ask the school. You put in the paperwork, right?"

"I did."

"I still don't think she'd make enough working as a prostitute or escort. Not in this area. My bet is on drugs or porn." Duncan looked at the calculations. "If she gets other aid that takes a chunk out of the remaining sixteen—"

"Which she probably does, if she was as good of a student as people say. Her parents told us she also had loans."

"Then it might work." He twirled his pen. "Mom and Dad couldn't foot the remainder of the bill, so she started working another angle?"

"Could be. Here's a few more. She sent some back to her folks. It adds up to about two thousand dollars." She handed over a page. "And there are a lot of payments to some websites. What the hell is New4Me.com?"

Duncan typed the name into the search bar of the browser. "Second-hand clothing sales. What else?"

Instead of reading the names, Cavendish passed him some sheets. Every website was pretty much the same. Second-hand retailers of designer goods. Clothing, shoes, purses, and accessories. But it was clear the New4Me site was her favorite. "That's why her clothing was older."

Cavendish looked up. "Come again?"

"The forensic report." Duncan scrabbled around until he found what he was looking for. "Here. The items of clothing, shoes, and accessories recovered from the cabin were all authentic, but several years old." He flicked the paper with his fingers. "If she's buying second-hand, that makes sense."

"It also helps explain why a twenty-something college student can afford this stuff." Cavendish leaned back. "She's not paying retail."

"Still a pretty penny, I'd bet." He needed someone who could explain how this worked. Tanelsa Parson's wife worked in the fashion industry. Sally said the woman could help him. "Okay, we know where the money is going."

"Tuition, back home, and clothes." Cavendish ticked off the items on her fingers. "We have to lock down exactly where the cash is coming from.

There's a conversation I am not looking forward to having. Can you imagine being told that your all-American daughter is dabbling in the seamier side of life?"

"No, and I don't want to." Duncan rubbed his chin and studied the reports. Maybe Sally was right in not being enthusiastic about kids.

* * *

The first thing Sally needed to do was verify Zach's identity with Evie Martin. She called the young woman. "Would you please do me a favor?"

"I guess. If I can."

"This should be easy. Go to the Buzz app, search for Zach Fabery, and tell me if he's the guy Maddie dated and broke up with."

There was a pause, presumably while Evie did her search. "That's him. Mads was over the moon after the first date. He was older, he had a degree. After the second, she cooled, and after the third, she ended it."

Sally grabbed a legal pad and pen. "What happened?"

"She never got specific, but she told me he was weird." The emphasis in Evie's voice put quotes around "weird."

"Like how?"

"Just asking questions that were way out there for a guy you hardly knew. Did she have male friends? What did she think of her male professors? If he and Mads were dating, would she continue to talk to other guys? That kind of thing."

Read "possessive" and "controlling." Sally thanked Evie and ended the call. Then she told all this to Tanelsa. "Let's see what we can find on this guy."

Tanelsa had moved to her own desk while Sally talked to Evie. "Already on it. I'm checking social media. Why don't you handle the legal end?"

Sally pulled up the site they used for criminal background checks. But she came up empty for Zach Fabery. Given Evie's description of him, she half-expected to find a sexual harassment charge or worse. But the guy was clean. "You find anything?"

"Yes and no. Come over and look at this."

Sally crossed the room and bent over to look at Tanelsa's screen.

"His social media is pretty hum-drum. I mean, here are more pictures of his dog. This is him on some trail, a couple of obligatory 'beers with the guys' shots. Standard stuff, right?"

"Nothing I'd find out of the ordinary for a young man less than ten years out of college."

"But look at some of his comments on *other* people's posts, especially the women."

Sally skimmed over the messages. At first blush, he was only compliment-ing people. Maybe not in the way men forty years ago talked, but aside from updates to language, it was harmless. Until she read closer. Sometimes he made three or four comments on a picture, each one a little more grasping in tone. A couple of times, she swore he'd carried on a previous unwanted conversation with the person. "Sweet face, but cold heart. Why'd you block my number? Sorry about last night. Just pick up the phone, and I'll explain." She straightened. "I'm definitely getting a not-that-great feeling from these."

"I know, right? It's like whatever he did, the woman cut him off, and he won't go away. You don't block somebody's phone number after one bad date, do you?"

"Not unless it's a truly horrific episode." Sally rubbed a knot out of her lower back. "Get those names. Did you find anything about him after college?"

"Here." Tanelsa switched over to a site for professionals. Zach had over a hundred connections, mostly to marketing directors at various companies in Pennsylvania. "According to this, he works as a marketing manager for a small retailer up in Pittsburgh. Zach does all their press, including managing their social media presence."

"What kind of retailer?" Sally walked back to her desk.

"Outdoor Adventurer. Hold on." Tanelsa tapped a few keys. "They do clothing and equipment for outdoor enthusiasts. Camping, biking, stand-up paddle boarding, boating, you name it. The store is in Shadyside, on Walnut Street." She clicked, and the printer whirred to life. She reached over and grabbed the sheet. "Address and phone number. However, I gotta ask. What's this got to do with us? Madison Tilgher wasn't our client."

Sally took the sheet. "No, but maybe she should have been."

Chapter Eighteen

Duncan shrugged into his sports jacket. "I think we should go over to the Hepworth residence and get them to come in so we can get prints. She's going to go ballistic, but if Noah was around the cabin, we need to rule him out. And they'll help us with the background check on her."

"Or the kid is lying, and he did more than look in a window." Cavendish's desk phone rang. "Criminal Investigation, Cavendish. Uh-huh. Yeah, sure. Say, ten minutes? Okay." She hung up.

"I get the feeling we're going to make a stop first."

"That was the techies. They got into Maddie's laptop."

They headed for the IT department, where they found the technician, Andy, talking on the phone. When he saw them, he said goodbye and hung up. "Nice to see you again, Duncan."

"Likewise." He introduced his partner.

"You two are here about the Tilgher computer, right?"

"That's the one," Cavendish said.

He pulled out a slim laptop in a purple hardshell case. The outside was adorned with a variety of stickers, some from St. Vincent.

Duncan recognized others from the second-hand retail websites listed in Maddie's bank records. "What did you find?"

"For starters, your victim had three email accounts." Andy opened the lid and clicked on the email client. "As a side note, I love users like her. The ones who never delete anything. She has over a thousand emails in this inbox and it's just her school account. Makes my job so much simpler."

Note to self: Clear out email inbox and deleted items folder. Not that a computer whiz couldn't retrieve the information, but there was no sense in making it easier.

"So. As I said, three accounts." The tech tapped the screen.

Cavendish pulled over a chair, turned it around, and straddled the seat. "There's nothing unusual about that."

Duncan had to agree. "I've got two myself, work and personal."

"No, there isn't, but let me finish." Andy scrolled through the list. "This is her college account. Pretty boring stuff, a few back-and-forth conversations with professors, some friends, some correspondence with organizations that I think are campus clubs. However, if you go back, way, way, back, there's a thread with the bursar's office I think you'll find interesting." He clicked on an email.

Duncan bent and read. "This is to inform you that your account is past due. If you need to discuss payment plans, please contact our office. If you cannot pay your bill and have decided to withdraw from St. Vincent, please contact the Registrar." He looked at the date. "This was sent when Maddie was a sophomore, a week after the second semester started."

Cavendish leaned on the chair back. "Doesn't that almost coincide with when we think Maddie started working this mystery job? What you saw in the pictures?"

"Pretty sure." Duncan consulted his notes. "Here it is. Based on the photographs we found, we're guessing the cash started rolling in around March of that year."

"Which is corroborated by her bank statements. The second account was opened in February." Cavendish drummed her fingers on the chair. "When did she start that internship?"

"I'll have to double-check, but I'm pretty sure it was mid-February." Duncan turned back to Andy. "Anything further on the tuition situation? I don't suppose they mention dollar amounts."

"Maddie replied that she was working on something, arranged a deferral, and then at the end of March, I see the confirmation from the bursar that the account is paid in full." Andy opened the email. "No numbers, just that it's taken care of."

Duncan turned to a blank page and sketched a timeline. "Do we have any further info on the so-called internship?"

Cavendish shook out her hair before tying it back again. "No, but it's on our list of things to do. Call Barry Atwiler."

"I think that needs to move up in priority. We can call him from the road." He clapped Andy on the shoulder. "That it?"

"Hardly. Over here is her second email account, what I'm pretty sure is a personal one." He switched to a web browser. "The address is Gmail, madison.a.tilgher, so I think she was setting this up for use after school, you know, as she started applying for jobs and whatnot. But she also used it to correspond with her parents. Check this from the end of her sophomore year." Andy pivoted the laptop.

Again, Duncan bent to read. "Well, that's interesting."

"What?" Cavendish asked.

"Mrs. Tilgher inquired if there was anything outstanding on that semester's tuition. Maddie says no and goes on to say, 'I've got things covered from now on. You just concentrate on getting well.' In the next email, Mrs. Tilgher thanks her and says, 'I'm so sorry we couldn't give you the money this spring. Things have been so tight. And you were so generous, sending some to us. That must be some second job you've got. I hope your work isn't interfering with school.'"

"What does Maddie say to that?"

Duncan reached over Andy's shoulder to click the next message in the thread. "She says no problem, 'You and Dad have always taken care of me. Now I get to pay it back. Don't worry, I've got a new gig.' Then a lot of emojis." He scrolled some more. "I don't see anything else on the subject. No wait, here's one from the fall. This time from Dad. 'Thank you for the money, sweetie. I can't deny it was helpful. Mom is really hurting after that last round of chemo. But you shouldn't have to take care of us.' Then another response from Maddie along the same vein as the previous one."

Cavendish bit her lip. "That fits with what I remember from the bank records. Mom gets sick, they can't pay tuition. Maddie takes a secret job, either porn or drugs, to pay the school bills and sends some back to her folks. Plus, she gets to spend a little on herself."

Duncan thought back to the contents of the dorm apartment. "I can't say as I approve of her methods, but jeez, it's hard to knock her motivations. This is a young woman who did everything they tell you to do to succeed in life. She worked really hard in high school, went to a solid college on a decent scholarship, and life dealt her a bum hand."

Cavendish stood and replaced the chair. "Now we just have to pin down the details."

Andy held up a finger. "I think I can help with that." He clicked over to another web browser tab. "The third email account. This one is another webmail client. This account is almost exclusively correspondence with a man named Barry, address batwiler2."

Duncan exchanged a look with his partner. "The head of the Laurel Highlands Entertainment outfit where Maddie was interning."

Andy laughed. "Oh man, if this is what they call an internship these days, sign me up."

Duncan's stomach tightened. "What are you talking about?"

In response, the tech pushed over the laptop. This time, both troopers leaned in to look at the screen. Many of the emails had photo attachments. In them, Maddie reclined in provocative poses. The surroundings were a mix of indoor and outdoor locations.

"Someone forgot to bring her wardrobe," Cavendish said in a deadpan voice.

Duncan pointed. "That's near Fallingwater."

"Are you sure?"

"Positive." He opened message after message. "That's the wall at Fort Necessity, there in the background."

She tapped an email. "This is one with a video. Open it."

He did, watched five seconds, and shut it. "Well, in their advertising copy, Laurel Highlands Entertainment does claim to feature local landmarks and scenery. I'm not sure that's exactly what most people would think of, though."

"How can doing that on the bare ground be comfortable?"

He shuddered. "No wonder the subscription fees were so high."

"You think she's getting a flat rate or a percentage?"

"No idea, but we're gonna ask." He pushed the laptop back to Andy. "Do you think those are finished products?"

Andy shook his head. "I've looked at the stills. I think they're proofs. In the email they're attached to, this guy, Barry, asks for her input."

"Those appointments in the book," Cavendish said. "They aren't code names for customers. They're shooting locales. How the hell did they pull that off without anyone seeing them?"

Duncan thought back to the notations. "Some of them, they'd be able to find a spot off the beaten path. But I'll venture a guess that they weren't photographing at peak hours. They most likely visited the location to determine when the tourists were there and scope out an appropriate place away from the security cameras. They came back to do the shoot after hours. Probably brought lighting equipment with them. It's something to ask when we talk to Mr. Atwiler."

"I guess Maddie Tilgher isn't the first young woman to use porn to pay her bills."

Andy pulled the email client back up. "She was getting out. Or at least she wanted to. There's an exchange between her and Barry, dated only a couple weeks ago, where she says this is her last session. Here." He clicked. "It says, 'Barry, I told you. I'm out. I'll do one more shoot for you, and that's it. And this time, you'd better provide better heating. But I mean it. After this, I'm done. It's time for me to start focusing on life after college.' It makes me think the scene where you found her was supposed to be her last job."

"Any response from Atwiler?" Duncan asked.

"Oh, sure. It goes on for a couple emails, him trying to get her to stay, says she's one of the company's most popular models, and she turns him down. Repeatedly. But the last one is interesting. Maddie says if he doesn't honor the terms of her contract, which seems to have an escape clause, she'll make it known that not only is he a horrible person to work for, she'll blow the top off his secret deal."

Cavendish looked up. "A secret deal, huh? What does Atwiler say?"

"That if she does, he'll wring her neck." Andy pointed at the screen again. "Wasn't the victim strangled?"

Duncan went in for another read. If the scene had been Maddie's last job, there'd been a photo crew there, which would explain why there were so many sets of fingerprints. "Is that all?"

"No, click over to the browser history." Andy pulled up another chair. "Are you familiar with Buzz?"

Duncan looked to Cavendish, who shook her head. "No, what's that?" he asked.

Andy reached over to type. "It's an online dating app. This one lets women choose the dates." He used a wireless mouse to highlight a whole section of the history. "It was in her top five most frequented websites."

Duncan thought back to the conversation with Evie Martin. "Her roommate said something about it. She claimed it was a dare and not serious."

"Well, your victim spent a lot of time on it for it to be just a fling. Look at this." He circled the pointer around a group of visits. "All these correspond to a conversation with one other member, a guy named Zach Fabery."

Duncan consulted his notes. "That could be the one Evie mentioned."

Cavendish looked over their shoulders. "What did they say?"

"Here." Andy reached to the printer. "I printed off the thread. Whether or not there's more on the victim's phone, I don't know, but I figured this was good enough to get you started."

Cavendish took the pages. "Typical. Starts off mister nice guy, she says it's not going to work, he gets pissy. What is it with guys under thirty?" She handed the printouts to Duncan.

"They're under thirty." He leafed through the pages.

"You couldn't pay me to use one of those sites."

Duncan grinned. "Should I have Andy look for your profile?"

Before Cavendish could answer, the tech typed. "Nothing."

Cavendish slapped her partner on the shoulder. "I told you. Okay, wise guy. Search for Sally Castle."

Duncan scoffed. "Sally isn't going to be on some kooky dating site."

Andy turned the laptop. "Really?"

Not possible. But there was no mistaking the picture or the profile. He stared, speechless.

Cavendish hooted with laughter. "Wouldn't I like to be a fly on the wall at dinner tonight! Is your cooking that bad?"

"Knock it off." *Sally, you got some 'splaining to do.* He turned back to the laptop and spotted an icon on the desktop labeled Find. "Hey, what's that?" He hovered the pointer over it.

Andy peered at the laptop. "Oh, this manufacturer allows you to group all your devices under a single account. That way if you lose your phone, you can look for it with your computer and vice versa."

"Is the range limited?"

"No. As long as the devices are connected to the internet, it works. And they need to be powered on and have the service enabled, of course."

Duncan clicked the icon. A screen popped up, and a blue dot zoomed in and out of focus, finally landing on a spot. "I'll be damned." According to the map, the phone was at 29787 Stoney Point Road.

Sue Hepworth's house.

Chapter Nineteen

Sally didn't have any difficulty finding a phone number and address for Zach. She tried calling, but had to leave a voicemail. His address was also in Shadyside, not that far from the store where he worked. When she called his employer, the young woman who answered said Zach wasn't in the store that day. "I think he's off getting pictures for our next social media campaign. Can I take a message?"

"If you've got a minute, I'd like to ask you a couple of questions."

"Uh, who are you?"

"My name is Sally Castle. I'm a defense attorney down in Uniontown."

The clerk's voice became hesitant. "Is Zach in trouble? I don't think I should say anything until I talk to him."

If only Sally's conscience would permit her to lie about her identity. But that was out of the question. "Not that I know of. I'm investigating another case, and his name came up. I'm just trying to gather a few facts." Whether or not that led to Zach getting into hot water was another matter.

"I still don't think I should say anything."

"Are you afraid of something?" A thought occurred to her. "Are you scared of Zach?"

"No." The girl drew the word out. "It feels funny, like I'm talking about him behind his back."

"Nothing you say to me will get to him, I promise. He'll never know we had this conversation."

The young woman hesitated. "I can hang up, right?"

"Absolutely."

"What do you want to know?"

"General things. How long have you worked with him?" Sally grabbed a legal pad and pen.

"I've only been at the store a couple of months. To be honest, I don't see him that often. I work the floor, and he's usually in the office. I only talk to him when he's getting info for a campaign or something."

"When you do see him, is he easy to work with?"

There was another pause, but when the sales clerk answered, her voice sounded more relaxed. "He's okay. Funny. Really cute, but he's too old for me. I'm only twenty-two, and he's, like, gotta be almost thirty or something. But he's super nice and knows a lot about the company and the products, and stuff."

She was three years off in her estimate of Zach's age, but Sally didn't correct her. "How so? I mean, does he help you out or do things for you?"

"He moved some heavy boxes for me one day. And he's given me compliments, like on my hair or if I look particularly good. Just the other day, he said how the color of my shirt really made my eyes look great."

"Has he ever said or done anything that made you uncomfortable? Or maybe made one of the other female employees feel that way?"

Instantly, the young woman's voice became guarded. "I don't see what that has to do with anything. Look, I've got to go. I have customers." She hung up.

Sally replaced the receiver. It could be the clerk simply didn't want to get a co-worker in trouble. Or she could be a young woman who'd received unwanted attention, and the topic made her uncomfortable. The #MeToo movement had changed a lot of things about workplace harassment, but many victims were still hesitant to speak out, especially against someone in authority. Or who they felt was in that position.

Tanelsa looked up. "What'd she say? I assume it was a she from the way you were talking."

Sally relayed the conversation. "Does the Outdoor Adventurer website list corporate contacts?"

"Hold on." Tanelsa tapped a few keys. "Just the store address and phone number. Looks like the company president and CEO is a guy named Don Rearick. But yeah, the store is the only point of contact." She looked over. "You want me to call?"

Sally played with a pen. There might be more than one employee answering the phone, but if the same one answered, there was little chance she'd connect Sally to the front office. "Please. Ask for Rearick, see if you can set up a meeting for today around lunch."

"You got it." Tanelsa dialed and asked for the Outdoor Adventurer CEO. "He's in a meeting? Yes, I'd like to leave a message. Please have him call Castle & Parson at this number." She rattled off the main office number. "We're defense attorneys in Uniontown, and we need to speak to him about one of his employees. If possible, we'd like to meet with him today. Yes, it's important. No, I can't say anything more, not in a message. Yes, thank you." She hung up. "Mr. Rearick is in a meeting with a supplier and will return our call at his earliest convenience."

It was a line Sally had heard before. Maybe this time it would even be true.

* * *

After Duncan and Cavendish left Andy, they debated about the next move. "Atwiler or Hepworth?" Cavendish asked.

Duncan spun the keys to an unmarked Ford Interceptor on his finger. "Stick to the plan and go talk to Sue Hepworth. But let's call Atwiler, see if we can set up a meeting for later today."

"Think she knows about the phone?" Cavendish looked up the number for Laurel Highlands Entertainment and dialed.

"Might be why she's been so squirrelly."

Cavendish wound up leaving a message for Atwiler, so the troopers headed off to the Hepworth residence. When they pulled into the driveway, the same older-model brown Ford Taurus they'd seen on the day of Noah's disappearance was parked in the open garage. "Looks like she's home," Cavendish said.

Duncan got out, straightened his jacket, and took a fresh look at the property. The house wasn't palatial, just a solid Colonial, most likely built twenty years ago or more. Either Noah was good at yard work, or Hepworth paid for a lawn service, because the grass was neat and devoid of leaves. The flower beds had been prepped for winter, and the bushes carefully wrapped in burlap. Did Noah's father help pay for any of it? Duncan went to the front door and knocked. When he didn't get a response, he did it again, this time a bit louder.

Moments later, Sue Hepworth, a pencil tucked behind her ear, answered. "Can't you read? No sol—oh, it's you." Her eyes narrowed, and her mouth puckered. "I told you, through Ms. Castle, to leave us alone. Do you have a warrant? Where is it? Are you going to arrest Noah for assaulting a police officer or something?"

Duncan forced down a sigh. "Ms. Hepworth, this is a murder investigation. We would like to ask him, and you, a few additional questions. We'd also like you to come to the nearest station so we can get fingerprints from both of you. For elimination purposes."

Hepworth gripped the door. "We weren't in the cabin. We told you that last time."

Cavendish stepped forward. "We've discovered new information that puts your claim in doubt."

"What new information?" Hepworth's words dripped scorn.

"The fact the victim's phone is in your house. Since you failed to mention any visit Maddie Tilgher made to your residence, we can only conclude that Noah, or you, was inside the cabin and removed it. Thus, the need for fingerprints."

Hepworth's grip on the door turned white-knuckled. "That's a damned lie. We never went near that girl."

Cavendish opened her mouth to respond, but Duncan held up a hand. "Ms. Hepworth, technology doesn't usually lie. We've traced a signal to Maddie's phone, and it's coming from this house." He paused. "You may have a perfectly good explanation for all of this, including why you didn't mention it the last time we talked. There are two ways this can go. The easy way is you let Trooper Cavendish and I in, we talk, retrieve the phone, go do the fingerprinting, and we'll be on our way."

Hepworth narrowed her eyes. "What's the hard way?"

"We'll leave, go get a warrant, and we'll have the same conversation, including the fingerprinting, but we'll do it at the nearest State Police barracks. There's no difference, except location." He waited, wondering how this would play out. For Noah's sake, Duncan hoped they could conduct the interview here. It would be far less traumatic if the encounter happened in the familiar confines of the family house.

Hepworth didn't move. "Maybe I should call a lawyer first."

Duncan could practically feel the waves of frustration coming from his partner, but he admired her ability to stay calm. "That is entirely your right. However, at this moment, we're only talking. If we get to a point where I am no longer able to legally proceed until Noah, or you, obtain representation, I'll tell you. You have my word."

The woman stood rock still, maybe examining his words for a trap or loophole. Then she stepped back and opened the door. "Fine, come in. But I warn you, I won't wait for your procedural rules to kick in. The minute I don't like this conversation, I'll stop it and call an attorney."

Duncan motioned to Cavendish and stepped through the door. "Yes, ma'am."

Chapter Twenty

Don Rearick called about a half-hour after Tanelsa left her message. It took some persuading on Sally's part, but since he was already in the Laurel Highlands for a meeting with a local outdoor adventure company to discuss business, he was willing to meet her in Uniontown at ten-thirty. "I have to be in Ohiopyle by noon, though," he said.

"I doubt this will take more than thirty minutes, and I appreciate you squeezing me in."

Unfortunately, it was too early for Dex's, which didn't open until eleven, but Sally arrived at a Panera a few minutes before the agreed-upon time. She ordered a bagel sandwich and a coffee, then grabbed a table for two.

Less than five minutes after she sat, a man walked in, stopped, and looked around. He appeared to be in his mid-forties, maybe six feet tall, with a full head of brown hair generously dosed with silver. His face had the rugged, sun-browned look of someone who spent a lot of time outdoors. Even though he was wearing business attire, he would look right at home in outdoor sporting gear.

Sally waved. "Mr. Rearick? Over here."

He turned to the sound of her voice. "Ms. Castle. Let me get my order in."

"No hurry."

He came to the table a few minutes later, carrying a toasted bagel smeared with cream cheese and a steaming cup of coffee. He put down the food and held out his hand. "Don Rearick. I wish I could say it's a pleasure to meet you."

Not a great way to start things off. Sally shook. His hand was callused and his grip firm. "Sally Castle. Thank you for talking to me on such short notice."

"Glad to." He sat, took a bite of the bagel, chewed, and swallowed. "Who did you say you were representing again?"

"No one. I'm gathering some background information."

"On Zach."

"Yes, but I assure you, it's not in relation to any case I'm currently litigating. This is truly a casual conversation."

Don took a bite of his bagel. After a moment he said, "Zach's a great guy. He does all our social media, our PR campaigns, ads in magazines, all that jazz. You know, the stuff that I can't make heads or tails of." He chuckled. "Ask me what kind of craft is best for a whitewater rafting beginner, and I'll talk for hours. Ask me about the best way to publicize our business, well, I'm all thumbs. Figuratively speaking."

"I completely understand. The two skills rarely go together." She took out a pad and pen. "Don't be alarmed. The notes are merely for my own information. When did Zach start working for you?"

"Let me see." Don blew on his coffee and took a sip. "Right before the season started this year, maybe March or April? Sometime in the spring. The young woman who'd previously had the job left for bigger pastures, and I wanted someone in place before things really ramped up. Zach was a godsend."

"He does a good job, then?"

Don narrowed his eyes. "Yes." He took another bite. "I don't really understand all the metrics, but our social media engagement is way up, and our brand recognition is much better. We just had our most successful summer season ever, and money is a measurement I do understand. Right now, we're gearing up for winter, and I'm eager to see what he comes up with."

"You don't just handle summer recreation?"

"No, we're a year-round operation. Boats, swimsuits, paddle boards, all that stuff, and now we're switching over to skiing, snowboarding, even snowshoes. Gear and packages. That's why I'm down here. We have an opportunity to partner with a group that offers whitewater tours next summer." He paused. "You're asking a lot of questions about one guy for 'background research.' I gotta ask, research into what?"

"General information for my own knowledge." Sally pretended to check her notes. "Are all your employees male?"

The light in Don's eyes hardened. "What does that have to do with anything?"

"I'll take that as a no. Have any of the women ever said anything about Zach?"

His expression became guarded. "I don't think I like where this is going."

"I told you, there isn't any pending litigation." She paused. "I'm simply looking to get a sense of how he interacts with his co-workers. Do they like him? Is he standoffish or overbearing, that sort of thing? Have you ever had to address his conduct at work?"

Don carefully wrapped the remaining half of his bagel. "I don't think I want to continue. Feel free to contact my office again, but next time, please make an appointment and make sure you have all the necessary supporting information." He turned and stalked out of the restaurant.

Sally leaned back and tapped her pen on the table. She hadn't gotten the answers she wanted, not verbally, but it didn't matter.

Don Rearick's refusal to talk was all the answer she needed.

Chapter Twenty-One

Duncan and Cavendish followed Sue Hepworth to the back of her house. "Before we talk to Noah," Duncan said, "do you have Maddie's phone?"

Hepworth threw him a dirty look. "Why in heaven's name would I have that? She's never been in my house. I told you before. I didn't associate with her outside of the center. So no, Trooper, I don't have her damn phone."

Duncan raised an eyebrow.

"Do you work from home, Ms. Hepworth?" Cavendish asked, maybe in an attempt to keep the meeting from ending before it began.

"Yes, I do freelance editing for academic publications." She didn't elaborate. "Noah will be most comfortable if you talk to him in the family room. He likes to have the TV in the background."

"I understand that," Duncan said. "But I don't want him to be distracted. If we can use your kitchen table, that would be better."

She gave him a side-eye glance, but shrugged and went to the kitchen. "Have a seat. I'll get him."

The two troopers sat. "Do you want to talk, and I'll scribe?" Cavendish asked. "After all, you've spoken to him before. He might respond better to you."

"I don't know about that. The last time, he nearly punched me in the eye." Duncan unbuttoned his jacket. "But sure, I'm good with that approach."

Less than a minute later, Hepworth led her son into the kitchen. "I'll be right here, Noah. Don't worry. You aren't in trouble."

That was debatable. Somehow, Maddie's phone had ended up in the

Hepworth home, but Duncan let the comment pass. "Hello, Noah. Do you remember me?"

The young man sat on the other side of the table from the two troopers. "You were here before. With the other lady. And you were there when I found Maddie."

"That's me." He gestured at Cavendish. "This is a friend of mine, Jenny. We'd like to ask you a few more questions about that day."

Noah picked at the placemat in front of him. "Okay."

"Why don't you tell me what happened that morning?" Duncan asked. "Start at the very beginning."

Hepworth laid a hand on Noah's shoulder. "We've already told you about that."

Duncan hoped it wouldn't become necessary to remove the mother from the situation. "I'd like to hear it in Noah's words." He waited.

Noah glanced at his mother, then looked at Duncan. "I had breakfast early. After that, I went to watch TV, like I always do. But the show was a repeat, and I got bored, so I left."

"Yeah, repeats are pretty dull. Where'd you go?"

"At first, just through the woods."

"Then down to the dock, right?" Hepworth said.

"Ms. Hepworth." Cavendish looked up. "We understand your concern for your son. But Trooper Duncan is talking to Noah, not you. When we have a question for you, we'll ask it."

Rebuked, Hepworth sat back, a scowl on her face.

Duncan kept his gaze on Noah. "You went through the woods, you said. Do you know when this was?"

"Early. I left when Animal Adventures was on, and that's every weekday from eight to nine," Noah said. The way he spoke sounded like he'd memorized a TV announcement, which he probably had.

"Okay. You're in the woods a little after eight, but before nine o'clock in the morning. What did you do?"

"I wandered around. Then I saw the cabin. I looked in the window, and that's when I saw Maddie."

Out of the corner of his eye, Duncan saw Noah's mother twitch. *Not the story she gave McAllister that day.* "Did you touch the window?"

"Yes, I pressed my fingers against it to see better."

That would be the set of prints labeled #1. "Was she moving?"

"No, I thought she was asleep." Noah continued worrying the edge of the placemat. "She was on the bed. So I went in and tried to wake her. Me and Maddie are friends."

Prints #1 had been on the cot, Duncan remembered. "You went inside? Wasn't the door locked?"

"Nope. It was closed, but I opened it. Maddie didn't answer, so that's when I went for Mom to bring her to the cabin."

Duncan glanced at Hepworth, whose scowl had disappeared, replaced by an expressionless mask. "Did she come?"

"Yes. We went back." Noah's voice was matter-of-fact, as though he stumbled across dead young women in cabins all the time.

"While you were there, did you try to find out if Maddie had a pulse, or if she was breathing?"

"Not the first time," Noah replied. "When we were there the second time, Mom got upset. She said something had happened to Maddie, and we needed to get out. I wanted to stay, but she made me leave."

"Noah." Duncan leaned forward. "Did you take anything from the cabin? Maddie's cell phone?"

The young man's cheeks colored. "Yes. It was on the floor. It has Maddie's picture on it, and the case is her favorite color, purple. I picked it up when Mom wasn't looking and put it in my pocket."

Hepworth sat straight up. "Noah! How could you—"

Duncan held up a hand. "Then what happened?"

Noah looked up. "We left. Mom found the lock on the ground and put it on the door. She wiped it with her shirt. Then she made me come home." He twisted in his chair. "But I didn't want to! If Maddie was in trouble, I wanted to help her. I went back to the cabin, but I couldn't get in. I was angry at Mom, so that's when I went and hid at the dock."

Duncan turned to Hepworth. "Which is when you called us and Trooper

McAllister showed up. Why did you lie about where Noah had been?"

The woman refused to look at him. "I didn't want him to get into trouble. The girl was dead when we got there. You'd have found her eventually. I didn't see any reason for us to get involved."

"Except you'd trampled all over a crime scene," said Cavendish in a dry voice. "Then you wiped the padlock, not only destroying your prints but any others that were there."

"Well, excuse me for trying to protect my family." Hepworth slapped the table, got up, and stormed to the sink. "I know Noah looks like a grown man to you, but mentally he's a boy. He didn't need to be mixed up in a murder scene."

Noah glanced frantically from Duncan to his mother. "Someone killed Maddie? Why? Who?"

Duncan laid a hand on his arm to calm him, hoping the gesture didn't provoke another violent outbreak. "That's what we're trying to figure out. You're helping a lot with that." Duncan transferred his gaze to Hepworth. "Noah, what I need now is for you to get Maddie's phone and give it to me. Please?"

"But it was hers. It has her picture on it. Can't I keep it?" The young man's voice trembled.

"I'll tell you what. I'll see what I can do about sending you a copy of that picture for your own, all right?" Duncan glanced at Cavendish. "But right now, it's very important I have the phone because it might help me figure out who killed your friend."

Noah hesitated. "Okay." He looked at his mother, who jerked her head in a nod. He got up and left the kitchen.

Cavendish stood. "Ms. Hepworth, as soon as Noah returns, we'll need you to follow us to the nearest police station so we can get your fingerprints. Or we can drive you. It's your choice."

"Whatever for?" Hepworth asked, voice harsh. "You can't possibly believe either Noah or I had anything to do with that girl's death. Besides, I cleaned the padlock, or have you forgotten already?"

Duncan could tell his partner was fighting back a retort, so he said, "Did you touch anything in the cabin? Maybe the door?"

"Yes. No. Possibly. I don't know."

"Did you wipe anything down other than the lock?"

She blinked. "No."

"Then you probably left prints elsewhere. We identified several distinct sets. This will help us determine if yours are among them."

"I am curious about something else, Ms. Hepworth." Cavendish crossed her arms. "Why do you hate Maddie Tilgher so much?"

"I didn't hate her. Dislike, yes, but hate is the wrong word."

"No, I think it's right."

"Why do you say that?"

Cavendish tilted her head. "We've been talking for twenty minutes. Maddie has come up multiple times, and you never use her name. She's always 'that girl.' The way you speak about someone says a lot about what you think of them."

Duncan stood. It was a good point, one he'd talk to Cavendish about later. "I'd like to leave as soon as Noah returns. I promise we'll try to take as little of your time as possible."

Hepworth didn't answer. She didn't need to. Her glare said it all.

Chapter Twenty-Two

Sally returned to the office after her meeting with Don Rearick filled with fresh determination. An alleged stalker like Zach Fabery didn't get to his late twenties without a complaint or criminal charge in his history. Yet when she looked, she'd found absolutely nothing. He didn't even have a sealed juvenile record. That only meant she'd have to look harder.

Inside, she hung up her coat. "Rearick wasn't willing to talk to me about Zach. No surprise there. Rearick probably thought I was ready to file a lawsuit against him or his company. Where would you find a history of complaints against a young man for sexual harassment? I mean, besides his criminal history." She turned to face Tanelsa, who sat at her desk transfixed by her computer screen, her expression slightly sick. "T? What's wrong?" She hurried over to her partner's desk.

"I paid the $200 for a month-long subscription." Tanelsa's normally vibrant voice was a mere whisper. "Dear God, Sally. This is sick."

Sally turned the laptop and put her hand over her mouth. "Soft porn" was a generous description for what Laurel Highlands Entertainment sold. Some of the images went way beyond that. She clicked to play a video clip, but didn't get past the thirty-second mark. "Did you find any shots of Maddie?"

Tanelsa nodded. "Quite a few. She's been doing this for a while. Only one video that I saw, thankfully. Sally, some of her photos have the highest user ratings."

"She was popular." Sally steeled herself and clicked through the galleries and recognized a fair number of the surroundings. She remembered the appointment book she and Jim had found. *I don't even want to think about the logistics.* "Well, that confirms where she was getting the money. At least some of it."

"You think the cops know about her side hustle? If it was a *side* job. This might have been her main source of income."

Sally scoffed. "Of course they do. Jim confiscated her laptop when we were at the college. The tech division has to have cracked it like an egg." She took a deep breath and went back to the video. It had a "picnic in the woods" look, and Sally was fairly certain it had been shot somewhere along the Youghiogheny River. She thought she saw a faint mist that might have come from whitewater rapids, or maybe even Ohiopyle Falls, in the distance. "Who's her co-star?"

He was handsome, in a slick sort of way. Dark wavy hair that looked windswept and had probably been meticulously styled pre-shooting. Broad shoulders, narrow waist, well-defined abs. His eyes were dark, but looked deep blue, not brown, in some of the close-ups. And he was young, no more than thirty.

"According to the opening credits, his name is Will Longfellow. I don't think he's related to the poet." Tanelsa fast-forwarded through the video. "Even I can admit he's a handsome devil. But I get a creepy feeling from him, even from some stills I found, never mind how he comes off in the video."

Sally watched the high-speed motion. "Is he in anything else with Maddie?"

"No. Like I said, she only has this one video, and the stills are her on her own."

"Wait!" Sally put her hand on Tanelsa's shoulder. "Back up and slow it down."

"Uh, you sure want to see this in real time?"

"Just that part."

Tanelsa complied, and Sally leaned in. Supposedly, this was a couple out for a picnic along the river. But there was no mistaking the twist of pain in Maddie's face as Will gripped her arms, nor the slightly malicious look of pleasure on his. "I know they are supposedly acting," she put air quotes around the word, "but does that look like Maddie's enjoying any part of this?"

Tanelsa rewound and watched again. "This isn't my normal entertainment fare, but I'd have to say no."

They endured the scene to the end. Maddie smiled, but Sally could see the hurt and fear in her eyes. Whatever that had been, it hadn't been part of the script.

* * *

Duncan and Cavendish looked after the taillights of the brown Ford as it pulled away. Hepworth had lost no time grabbing her son and driving off after the fingerprinting was completed. She hadn't even said anything, she just led Noah to the car, practically pushed him in, and pulled out as quickly as she legally could from the parking lot of the police station. "Guess she didn't want to go out for coffee afterward," Cavendish said.

Duncan lifted an eyebrow. "Did you think she would?"

"No." Cavendish headed for their state-issued sedan. "What are the chances their prints match some of the ones at the scene?"

"Seeing as Noah admitted touching the window, I'd say one hundred percent." He tossed her the keys. "But that still leaves three sets of unknowns."

"My money is on whoever was there to shoot the pictures. Or video, or whatever they had planned."

Duncan's phone pinged with Sally's text tone. *You need to see Maddie's work with Laurel Highlands Entertainment. Come to the office.*

"What is it?"

He slipped his phone into his pocket. "Sally wants to show us something. Head over to Uniontown." He gave Cavendish the address.

They pulled up in front of the building slightly before noon and went inside. Sally and Tanelsa wore matching unsettled expressions.

"This doesn't look good," Duncan said as he looked at the pair of attorneys.

Sally didn't waste time on chitchat. "Have you seen any photos of Maddie from Laurel Highlands Entertainment?"

"Some. And a video. Enough to know what she was up to." He glanced at Cavendish, who nodded. "She needed money for tuition, and we think her family was short. Her mother had some health issues, and Maddie sent cash payments to her folks. Between the two, we're assuming she wasn't working for Starbucks."

Tanelsa coughed. "More like the kind of amounts you make in porn?"

Again, Duncan shared a look with his partner. This time, Cavendish answered. "Yes. How'd you learn that?"

Sally handed a closed laptop to Duncan. "Tanelsa forked over the subscription fee for Laurel Highlands Entertainment."

"Was that wise?"

Tanelsa shrugged. "I used a dummy email and a PayPal account that I've since emptied and closed."

"I don't know if you'll get the money back. I'm pretty sure that's not a reimbursable expense," Cavendish said.

"I'm not worried about the money. I'm worried about *that*." Tanelsa pointed. "And I don't mean the laptop, although I'm gonna have to find the cyber equivalent of bleach to make sure it's clean."

Sally's eyes were deep green and somber. "Take a look."

Duncan opened the lid. Cavendish stood next to him. "Oh my…" she whispered. "The video in her email was *not* like that."

Duncan gritted his teeth so hard it hurt. "Can you download this stuff?"

Tanelsa nodded. "We only saw the one live-action shoot."

"The one we have looked like a first take of something different." Duncan set down the computer. "Cavendish, there should be a flash drive—"

"Yeah, I got it." She left.

Sally picked up a few sheets of paper from her desk. "Two things. The man in the video. His name is Will Longfellow. I didn't think that was a real name. I tried to look him up in the databases I subscribe to, but I didn't find anything. There aren't any records in that name in any government source I have access to or the DMV. So I can't tell you anything else."

Duncan took the papers.

"After I saw that video, I did some research on Laurel Highlands Entertainment. They were drowning in red ink. Until about four months ago. I didn't have time to track the cash, but there was a deposit of fifty grand in the company bank account."

"Don't worry, we'll find out who he is."

Cavendish returned with a flash drive in her hand. "Who *who* is?" She plugged it into the laptop and copied the files.

"This guy." Duncan tapped the screen, which showed Longfellow's frozen image. He took out his phone and snapped a picture. "Will Longfellow."

"I don't even want to know." Cavendish glanced at Sally. "Do you want me to go back to HQ and hunt him down? I can take an Uber or you can drop me off."

"Nope." Duncan spun the keyring on his finger. "We're gonna squeeze Mr. Longfellow's real name out of his producer."

Chapter Twenty-Three

Duncan and Cavendish left Castle & Parson and headed to their car. "Who's driving?" Cavendish said. "You or me?"

He watched the traffic go down East Main Street. He'd already known what Maddie had been up to. He had hoped Sally wouldn't find out, only to spare her the sadness of knowing.

"Earth to Jim Duncan."

He snapped back to attention. "Sorry." He opened the car door. "I'll drive. But we need to grab some food. I'm starving. Meanwhile, get on the horn and get someone working on financials for Laurel Highlands Entertainment." He told Cavendish what Sally found.

Cavendish dialed. "That's a nice chunk of change. Loan? Or did Atwiler pick up a silent investor?"

After hitting the drive-through, Duncan pulled up the address for Laurel Highlands Entertainment on his phone's map application. When they arrived, he could see the offices were plain to the point of austere. The building was in a semi-empty strip mall. The only other businesses were a nail salon and a laundromat. All the other places had signs in the windows advertising availability. Laurel Highlands Entertainment's small lobby held three metal chairs with cloth seats. A young male receptionist sat behind a tall, Formica-topped dividing wall. The white paint had a yellowish tinge, as though it had endured years of cigarette smoke and never been cleaned. Even the imitation potted plant drooped.

Duncan walked up to the front desk and showed his badge. After introducing himself and Cavendish, he said, "We'd like to speak to Barry

Atwiler."

"What's this about?" the young man said in a high-pitched voice.

"Business." Duncan studied his face, which bore the scars from adolescent acne. "Is he in?"

"He eats lunch from noon to one." The receptionist licked his lips, and a sheen of sweat broke out on his forehead. "I, uh, I think today he had an appointment afterward, so I'm not sure when he'll be back."

Cavendish leaned on the cheap counter. "Where does he normally eat?"

"I'm not telling you that." The words said bravado, but the quaver in his voice betrayed his nerves.

"Look." Duncan fixed his gaze on the man's face. "We have time. We can wait over there in those chairs until Mr. Atwiler returns, or you can tell us where to find him."

"Who said he's coming back?"

"I see an overcoat on the coat tree in the corner. I suppose it might be yours, but it looks too expensive for a receptionist. Your boss might be able to get away without it as long as the sun is out, but he'll want it tonight. Or tomorrow morning." Duncan paused. "Where is he?"

The receptionist swallowed. "Mandarin, the Chinese place at the end of the mall. Don't tell him I said anything."

"We won't." Cavendish tapped the counter.

They left and headed down the string of empty storefronts until they reached Mandarin. A small neon sign glowed in the front window, but otherwise, the restaurant was a hole in the wall, probably known to, and supported by, locals. They entered.

"Table for two?" The smiling host grabbed two menus.

"No thanks. We're looking for Mr. Atwiler." Duncan scanned the dining room.

Cavendish nudged him. "In the corner."

They made their way over to Barry Atwiler, who sat by himself at a secluded table. Up close, he looked more like a businessman down on his luck than the slick image portrayed by the photo on the website. His thinning hair, held back with a lot of product, couldn't quite hide his scalp, and the lapels of his jacket shone more from age than design.

"Excuse me, are you Barry Atwiler?" Duncan asked.

Atwiler didn't look up from his bowl of noodles. "Who wants to know?"

The troopers held out their badges. "Pennsylvania State Police," said Cavendish.

Atwiler lifted his head, eyes narrowed in suspicion. "Who told you I was here?"

"No one." Duncan sat in the chair facing him. "We heard you were at lunch, and we decided to cruise the stores here, just in case we saw you."

"Which we did." Cavendish took the remaining chair.

"I'm not doing anything illegal," Atwiler said, his voice nasal.

Interesting statement. Eating was definitely not against the law. Porn was technically not illegal, and they'd seen no evidence that Laurel Highlands Entertainment was engaged in anything involving children. But the CEO had not asked what they wanted or why they'd come. He'd jumped straight to protesting his innocence. "We didn't say you were," Duncan replied. "We have some questions about one of your models."

"Who?"

"Maddie Tilgher," Cavendish said.

Duncan watched the filmmaker's face, which remained smooth. "What about her?"

"She's dead."

Still no reaction. "I'm sorry to hear that, but what's it got to do with me?"

Duncan picked up a fortune cookie and studied it. "She didn't die of natural causes, Mr. Atwiler." He put down the cellophane-wrapped package. "She was murdered. Strangled, as a matter of fact. We think it was at one of your shooting locations."

That got a reaction, albeit a small one. Atwiler's face paled, and he lifted his eyebrows. "What makes you think that?"

Cavendish crossed her arms across her chest. "Stop playing games. We know what business Laurel Highlands Entertainment is in. We have email correspondence between you and the victim, so we know she worked for you. Evidence at the scene suggests someone had a tripod. Shall I go on?"

Atwiler delayed and slurped up more noodles. He pushed the bowl aside. "Okay, fine. Maddie was one of my models. One of my most popular, as a matter of fact."

"What kind of work did she do?" Duncan asked.

"Stills, mostly. Posed images at various locations throughout the area."

"Including historic spots like Fort Necessity and Fallingwater."

Atwiler's answering smile was thin. "It is our specialty. If you've read our website, and I bet you have, you know that."

"She didn't do videos?" Cavendish asked.

"Just two, one of which never made it to release. She didn't like the more physical side of the work." Atwiler's shoulders rose and fell. "I told her she could double her income with live action, but she didn't listen."

Cavendish's expression didn't change. "Maybe because she had to work with people like Will Longfellow. By the way, what's his real name?"

"I don't have to answer that."

"No, you don't. But we'll find out anyway. Why don't you save us the time? Unless you want us to get a court order and come back. We might end up interrupting another meal."

"His name is Will Brackin." Atwiler's answer smile was oily and knowing. "He is another very popular star. His videos are some of my top sellers. He's a young, handsome guy. Who wouldn't want to work with him?

"A girl who didn't like getting manhandled?" Cavendish asked, voice deadpan.

Duncan held up a hand to stop her. "It sounds like you knew Maddie quite well."

"If you want to believe that, go ahead," Atwiler said.

"When was the last time you saw her? On a job, that is."

The producer sipped from a glass of water. "Last week. Wednesday, I think it was. Yeah, that afternoon."

"Near Dunlap Creek Lake?"

"I don't remember. I'd have to check the book."

Duncan watched the man. He was acting way too casually. "Were you there?"

"I don't make a habit of visiting the sets."

Cavendish didn't budge. "Then where were you?"

Atwiler barely glanced at her. "I'd have to look at my calendar. I'm a busy man, Trooper. I have a lot of meetings."

A smiling waiter came over. "Would you like to order? Special today, sesame chicken."

Duncan waved him off. "We're good, thanks." He turned back to Atwiler. "I understand Maddie was getting out of the business."

"Who told you that?" Atwiler sat back.

"She did. It's in her emails to you. She was doing one last job, and she was quitting."

Atwiler didn't blink. "She was under contract."

"She was going to exercise her escape clause," Cavendish said. "And you weren't too happy about it. She threatened to say what a lousy producer you were, dishonest and untrustworthy. What did you say again?" She looked at Duncan and back to the porn director. "Oh, yeah. You threatened to wring her neck. That was two days before we found her, strangled. Funny coincidence, huh?"

Again, Atwiler's face was calm, but he squinted at Cavendish. "And that's all it is, coincidence. A figure of speech." He stood and threw some money down on the table. "As lovely as this conversation is, I have places to be. The fact is, you're fishing. You can't prove I was at the cabin and a couple of heated emails mean nothing."

Cavendish smirked. "Who said anything about a cabin?"

Atwiler flushed a deep brick red. "If you want to talk again, I suggest you make an appointment. Have a good day." He walked away.

Duncan raised a hand. "What's the secret deal?"

Atwiler turned around. "I beg your pardon?"

"Maddie threatened to blow the lid off your secret deal. I'm wondering what it is."

"I do many deals, Trooper. I keep a lot of them on the down-low. In this business, you protect anything that has to do with your intellectual property." The producer smoothed his jacket. "There aren't any other companies in the area that do exactly what I do, use local sites. I wouldn't want to give them a leg up. Now, if you'll excuse me." He left.

Duncan remained sitting, staring at the half-empty water glass.

"He's right, you know. He'll provide proof he was miles away from the area, and we'll have squat." Cavendish leaned forward. "What are you thinking?"

Duncan took out a handkerchief and picked up the glass. "Mr. Atwiler may have unwittingly given us his fingerprints."

* * *

After the troopers departed, Tanelsa sat back and looked at Sally. "Are you sure that was the right thing to do?"

"Yes." Once upon a time, Sally would have chased down Will Longfellow on her own, but not anymore. The guy was a creep. He may have a record, and, at least in her mind, he could be a killer. Such an individual was best left to the police. She went back to her desk.

"Then we're done?"

"I didn't say that." Sally took out the notes she'd made from the weekend, when she'd visited St. Vincent. "Maddie's roommate was cagey when we talked to her last Saturday." She told Tanelsa about the hushed phone call Evie had made. "Maybe if the police aren't hovering, she'll open up to me."

"If you say so." Tanelsa consulted her calendar. "I have a prospective client meeting at two. Can you handle this girl on your own?"

"Pretty sure I got this." Sally found Evie's phone number and dialed. Hopefully, the young woman wasn't one of those who let unknown calls go to voicemail. Sally was fairly sure her message wouldn't be returned this time.

Evie picked up after three rings. "Hello? Who is this?"

"Ms. Martin, this is Sally Castle. We met last Saturday. I was with a member of the State Police."

"I remember you." The tone of her voice said it was a memory she'd rather repress.

"I need to speak with you again about Maddie."

142

"Now's not a good time. I have a big paper due right before Thanksgiving break. It's a third of my grade. Besides, I don't have anything more to tell you."

"If you talk to me, I think you'll discover that you do." Sally paused. "Ms. Martin, this is important, or I wouldn't be asking. You said you and Maddie were close. Do you want to help your friend or not?"

The silence spun out and except for the sound of breathing, Evie Martin might have ended the call. "Okay," she finally said. "I'll be in the same place at two o'clock. I'll wait ten minutes. But after that, I'm leaving, and I won't want to hear from you again."

Sally consulted the clock. It was only twenty to one, plenty of time to get to Latrobe. "I'll be there."

Chapter Twenty-Four

Duncan took fifteen minutes to explain to the restaurant owner why lifting fingerprints from the abandoned glass was not a violation of anything. He wasn't sure the man understood, but eventually was allowed to complete the task and leave. They returned to HQ, where Duncan immediately took the prints to the lab for analysis and comparison against those from the murder scene.

"If they are a match, do you want to go back to Atwiler immediately or try to pin down the remaining two sets?" Cavendish asked.

"Ask me when we get the results."

She glanced at her watch. "I need to make a quick call to the DA, make sure we're set for that deposition next week. Want anything from the vending machine?"

Duncan pulled out his wallet and handed her a five. "Would you get me a Coke? Grab something for yourself if you want it. And while you do that, I'll get started on Brackin's background."

"Thanks. Be back as soon as I can." She took the bill and left.

At his desk, Duncan slung his coat over the back of his chair, rolled up his sleeves, and put in the necessary requests for Brackin's financials. After that, he ran William Brackin's name in NLETS. But while Duncan was able to determine Brackin lived in Mount Lebanon, in the upscale Virginia Manor area, there was nothing else to be found. He did not have any wants or warrants. Without fingerprints to check in AFIS, he had no idea whether Brackin had any convictions. Duncan pulled up the address to look at the street-view pictures. He could just see a sports car in Brackin's garage. The houses were on the larger end, lots of stone with neatly manicured yards. He could tell some of the lots were generously sized, with plenty of mature trees and shrubbery. *How the hell does he afford to live here?*

However popular Brackin was in porn, he didn't make the kind of money to afford this lifestyle. In Duncan's experience, the most common way to Easy Street was drugs. If that was the case, he might be on the radar of the Pittsburgh Narcotics division. Who did he know up there? He picked up the phone and dialed.

After a couple of rings, a hearty male voice answered. "Dave Thompson."

"Dave, it's Jim Duncan."

"Jim, long time no talk! You still patrolling the back roads of Fayette County?"

"Still here, but not on patrol." Duncan brought his friend up to date on his move to the Criminal Investigation section. "Listen, got a favor to ask you."

"I didn't think you'd call just to shoot the shit. What do you need?"

"Has the name William Brackin ever turned up in any of your travels through Pittsburgh's drug scene?"

"Lives in Mount Lebanon, calls himself a freelance model, actually does porn? That Brackin?"

"The very same."

Thompson chuckled. "Oh yeah, we've had our eyes on him for a long time. Slippery cuss. We've never been able to nail him. Picked him up a few times, but he always slithers away, and all we're left with is some poor homeless person he convinced to take the heat for him."

"Convinced?"

"Tricked, bribed, threatened, call it what you will."

Duncan mulled this over. "You keep a record of your arrests, right?"

"Damn straight."

"Mind giving me the view from 10,000 feet? What's this guy been up to for the last decade?"

Thompson paused, and when he spoke, his voice was cautious. "What's your interest in Brackin?"

"I'm investigating the murder of a college girl from St. Vincent, and his name popped up as a known associate."

"Murder?" Another beat of silence. "Hold on."

Duncan waited, presumably while Thompson looked for whatever he had. When he came back on the line, he said, "Okay, I'll scan what I've got in my book and send it to you. But keep it close to your vest. Give me your email."

Duncan complied, and Thompson said he'd send the material as soon as he could. True to his word, the email arrived about half an hour later, and Duncan printed the attachment. It made for intriguing reading.

Cavendish returned ten minutes after that and set a bottle on his desk. "You got the last non-diet one in the machine. Here's your change." She laid the money next to the bottle. "What have you found?"

"Thanks again." He unscrewed the bottle top. "NLETS came up empty, so I called a friend of mine up in Pittsburgh. Turns out their Narcotics guys have been watching Mr. Brackin for a while. He's an interesting character. He's been arrested for simple assault, two counts of harassment, and possession of heroin with intent, but no convictions. Not enough evidence to pursue prosecution. In addition, he's been on the scene at three other drug arrests. But always released without charges."

Cavendish sat. "He needs better friends."

"Maybe. But I bet he's got a great attorney. Here's what I think. Brackin is a dealer. The cops roll up, and someone else literally ends up holding the bag for him. He gets away clean, just a guy in the wrong place at the wrong time. I wager even if the others try to roll on him, his lawyer can keep him out of it."

"The Teflon drug dealer?"

"Something like that." He pushed a printout across the desks and took a drink. "Look at the other name on the bust from ten years ago."

"They've been tracking him that long, and he's still conviction-free? That's not a great lawyer. That's a fabulous one." She read, then looked up. "Janice Hepworth? Is she related to Sue?"

"Sister. Once I saw the name, I did some digging. Funny, Sue never mentioned a sibling. Of course, based on Janice's record, they probably don't talk much."

"Long?"

"As your arm."

Cavendish re-read the report. "Isn't Mount Lebanon a rather upscale neighborhood?"

"Parts of it. If you pull up the address online, you can see pictures."

She set down the sheet of paper and did so. "He's unmarried, right?"

"Based on everything I found, yes." Duncan paused and took another swig of soda. "On the background info, his occupation is a freelance photography and videography model."

"No way is he affording that house on a porn star's salary. Hell, not even as a local talent for cleaner work. Maybe if he was in New York or LA. Maybe." She peered at the screen. "Is that a Mustang in the garage?"

"According to the DMV, it's brand new. Zoom way in and you'll see from the back bumper it's a Shelby GT500." He set down the bottle. "If you're not a car fanatic, let me tell you that is a very expensive ride."

Cavendish sat back. "Fancy house, pretty car, and he's dodged how many drug charges?"

"Four that we know of."

"You're right. Mr. Brackin has very good friends who are willing to take the heat in his place." She pulled a pack of mints from her desk drawer and took one out. "You said he has a minor assault arrest?"

"At a bar in Pittsburgh's South Side. But he doesn't have anything else on his sheet. Every time he's been arrested, the charges were dropped when the witnesses didn't want to testify." He caught his partner's gaze. "I think we need to talk to all of them. Before we corner Mr. Brackin."

"Why do I think I'll need something stronger than a breath mint when we're done?"

* * *

Sally's estimate of how long it would take to get to the meeting with Evie was a bit off. She arrived at St. Vincent almost exactly at two, but she forgot to figure in the time it would take to walk from the main visitor's parking lot to the café. Even so, she entered the building only five minutes late and hoped Evie had honored the full ten-minute grace period.

She had. She sat by a wall, hands wrapped around a cardboard cup with a lid. Steam escaped from the hole. Her face was a mask of apprehension, but held a trace of determination as well. Whatever she hadn't said on Saturday scared her a little. With luck, she would overcome that fear and talk now.

Sally sat down across from her. "Thanks for agreeing to meet me."

"Do you want anything to drink first?" Evie asked. "The coffee's pretty good. Not upscale standard, but definitely a step above what you get at a grocery store."

"No, I'm fine." Normally, Sally would get a beverage to be sociable, but she sensed Evie's skittishness. Sally didn't need the young woman to bolt like her friend had. "I'm going to record our conversation, if you don't mind." She laid a small device on the table.

Evie immediately pulled back. "Hold on, you didn't say anything about that."

Sally reassured her. "It's for my use only. The only other person who might hear it is my law partner. If I record, I'm free to concentrate on you. If you insist, I won't, but I'll have to take some kind of notes. Otherwise, I might not remember everything, and I'll end up calling you again."

Evie bit her lip, eyeing the recorder as though it was a dead animal. "I guess it's okay, but you gotta promise. No one but your partner hears it."

"You have my word." How she'd communicate any information relevant to the murder investigation, if needed, to Jim was a question she'd deal with later. "Why are you so afraid?"

"I saw him once. The guy Mads was working for." Evie took a sip of her coffee. "He barely said anything, but he scared the crap out of me. She told me later that the less I remembered of him, the better."

"You saw Barry Atwiler?"

"I didn't know his name. Mads just said he was the guy in charge."

Atwiler's picture on the website didn't look threatening, but that didn't mean anything. "Let's back up a bit. Did you know about the work Maddie was doing?"

Evie wouldn't lift her gaze from the table. "Yes. One time, her phone rang while she was in the shower. She left it in the kitchen, and I answered it. We did that for each other a lot. I guess the guy thought I was her because he started spouting off stuff about the next shoot, and the conditions, and how late he expected the evening to be. All sorts of stuff. I finally broke in and said I wasn't who he was looking for."

"Was he mad?"

"No. I expected him to be. But he acted like it was funny." Evie took a gulp of coffee, even though it still appeared hot. Maybe she needed the caffeine hit to steel her nerves. "He asked if I wanted a job and if so, I should send a headshot."

"Did Maddie know you talked to her boss?"

"She came into the kitchen and heard the end of the conversation. She was pissed. But also scared. She grabbed the phone and went to our room, but I could hear her yelling at the guy, how he was never to call that number, no matter what."

"Did she get angry with you?"

"No. She said she was sorry I had to hear that, and the guy wouldn't call again."

"Did she tell you what she was up to? Did you ask?"

Evie half-laughed. "She didn't have to. I could tell from the little bit of conversation I had with him that Mads was into porn. I tried to talk her out of it. Said there were better ways of getting money, but she told me it was only temporary."

Sally drummed her fingers on the table. "Do you know what she needed the money for?"

"School." Evie stared out of the window. "Her mom was diagnosed with leukemia in the fall of our sophomore year. Mads said it was pretty bad. With all the medical costs, her folks weren't gonna have enough to pay tuition. Plus, they needed money themselves. When I found out what she was doing, I asked why she didn't just take a loan. She said that was her plan when this opportunity came up. Why go into debt when she could have cash?"

"Being in the sex industry wasn't going to look great on a resumé. Did she know that?"

"She did all the work under a stage name." Evie glanced at Sally. "She thought no one would ever tie it back to her. And I think she enjoyed being able to buy nice clothes, even if she was shopping second-hand. It wasn't like her parents could afford that kind of stuff when she was in high school."

The attitude only demonstrated how little young people understood how much damage those kinds of photos could do to them later in life, Sally thought. Those images would be tied to Maddie Tilgher forever, no matter what name she worked under. "Why'd Mr. Atwiler come to campus?"

"He said Maddie wasn't answering her phone." The young woman picked at her cup. "He had a change to the schedule, and if she wasn't going to take his calls, he'd have to visit her in person to make sure she got the information."

"Think carefully." Sally leaned on the table. "Was she afraid of him? I mean, when he showed up."

"Afraid?" Evie's forehead creased as she thought. "I didn't think so at the time. Mostly, she was angry. Like super angry. I always knew when Mads was about to lose it because she'd get real quiet. That's how she was with this Atwiler guy. But thinking about it now…." She looked at Sally. "I think she was a little scared. Maybe not of him, exactly, but what would happen if anyone found out about him."

Sally ran this information through her mind. Maddie could have been looking to keep Atwiler at a distance, but then why do one more shoot for him? "I think I told you this, but before Maddie died, she came to me and hinted there was a man she wanted legal protection from. Can you think of anyone she'd be afraid of?"

Evie scrunched her face. "Well, I already mentioned Zach. I'm not sure Mads would feel she'd need protection from him, though. I mean, the guy was weird and creepy, but not threatening, if you know what I mean. She was short, but she was feisty. Not many people intimidated her."

"I'll be looking into him. Anyone else?"

Evie stared over Sally's shoulder. "There was only one person she ever seemed scared of. He was incredibly handsome, like movie star gorgeous. But arrogant. He showed up one day with two dozen roses for her and said something about how she was the most beautiful woman he'd seen in a long time, and he couldn't wait to work with her again, and he'd even like to get to know her better, which wasn't something he often did with costars, blah, blah, blah. His car was amazing."

The physical description fit Will Longfellow. "You noticed the car?"

"Hard not to. It was a Mustang, brand new, cherry red. The license plate said 'HotStuf.' I'm not sure if it was talking about the driver or the car, but both were pretty hot."

Sally made a note of the plate. "What did Maddie say?"

"She turned white as a sheet. She swore at him and said if she ever saw him again, she'd call the cops, and she wouldn't work with him if he was the last person on earth. I'd never heard her use words like that, but the look in her eyes was scary." Evie brought her gaze to Sally's face. "You know, in nature shows, how animals freeze when they see a predator, like they hope they won't be seen or something?"

"Yes."

"That's exactly how she looked. I'd never seen her act like that before. She must have been really scared." Evie caught her lip between her teeth. "Then he said something weird."

"What?"

"She, Maddie, didn't know as much as she thought, and there were some things she should keep her nose out of. 'Don't go messing with things you shouldn't be involved with. You might find more than you bargained for. Your role is in front of the camera.' Something like that."

The car registration should give Sally a name and address for Will Longfellow. After that, she'd need to find a safe method of talking to him. "One final question. On the day I was here with Trooper Duncan, he was the police officer you talked to, you made two phone calls. One on the way over here and one on the way back. You seemed awfully anxious we not hear those calls. Who were you talking to?"

Evie's head drooped. "I called Belle. I knew Maddie had a book for her appointments. I'd seen the book once, but I also knew she hid it. I asked Belle to look for it and put it in a safe place, somewhere it wouldn't be seen, but Belle couldn't find it either. Maddie wasn't a horrible person. She wasn't. I didn't want you to think of her as cheap or...dirty." Evie brushed her hand over her eyes. "I guess I was stupid, huh?"

"You wanted to protect your friend, I understand."

Evie stared at her hands and flexed them, like she was thinking. "There's something else."

Sally waited.

"Two weeks ago, a woman came to campus. I saw her with Mads in front of the building."

"What did she look like?"

"She was, I dunno, older. Not old-old, maybe the same age you are or close. Her clothes were nice, nothing fancy. She had short brown hair."

"Did Maddie know her?"

Evie tilted her head. "I think so. Mads said something about calling as soon as she had details, and they hugged. You wouldn't do that to a stranger, right?"

"I wouldn't think so." Sally drummed her fingers on the table. "Did Maddie tell you this woman's name?"

"No, she didn't say anything to me, but I heard the woman's first name because we had the windows open. After they hugged, Mads said, 'Don't worry, Janice. It'll be fine.'"

Sally said nothing. All she could do was stare at the young woman across the table.

Chapter Twenty-Five

Sally returned to her car. She wanted to continue searching for details on Zach Fabery and William Brackin as soon as she got back to the office. But Tanelsa was right. They needed to spend time with real clients who were able to pay. Tanelsa had been very understanding so far, but if Sally continued what could only be called a personal mission, her partner would get perturbed, to say the least. And rightly so.

On the other hand, dropping the case didn't feel right either. Maybe Tanelsa would be willing to compromise.

As soon as Sally started the engine, her phone rang. "Yeah, T. I'm on my way back. Did you get any good leads from the courthouse this morning?"

"No, but you need to get back here as soon as possible," Tanelsa said, her voice low and oddly restrained.

"Why? What's happened?"

Tanelsa paused. "Sue Hepworth walked in the door ten minutes ago with Noah in tow. You need to hear what she has to say."

*＊＊

Duncan and Cavendish didn't have a lot of luck with their phone calls. The bar owner didn't remember the fight on Brackin's arrest record, but said it was most likely an altercation between two drunks. "That's usually the case. Sometimes there's a woman involved," he said. "The date you're asking about was a weekend, and there's no way I'm going to remember details months later. It feels like we have one or two of those kind of dust-ups every

Saturday."

The women involved in Brackin's harassment charges didn't offer much information, either. One hung up as soon as Duncan identified himself. The other said, "I don't want to talk about it," before ending her call.

Cavendish scrolled as she stared at her computer screen. "Maybe I should have called them."

"You might be right. But I also got the feeling anyone who said she was from the police was going to get shut down." He rubbed his face. "What are you staring at?"

"While you were on the phone, I decided to do a little more digging on Noah Freeman. Most of it we already know. Lives with his mother, nineteen, no job. He did graduate from high school a year ago. No criminal record."

Duncan hadn't been thinking about the autistic boy and his mother, content to let those two stay on the back burner until he did a little more work with his three prime suspects, Atwiler, Fabery, and Brackin. "Sounds pretty dull."

"On the surface, yes."

"What do you mean by that?"

Cavendish looked up. "You wondered why Noah had a different last name than Hepworth, right?"

"Yeah. I mean, it was a minor point, but I did think about it."

She beckoned to him. "I think I just found out the reason."

* * *

Sally broke the speed limit a couple of times on her way from Latrobe to Uniontown and arrived at the office shortly before three-thirty. Sue Hepworth, Noah, and Tanelsa were all clustered in the main office. Tanelsa had gotten a bottle of Coke for the young man. She and Sue both held cups of coffee.

"You're back. Good. You can tell me about your trip later." Tanelsa indicated Sally should pull a seat over to the group. "Ms. Hepworth has some…interesting information to share with you."

Sally dragged her chair over to Tanelsa's desk and sat. "First off, Ms. Hepworth, it's good to see you again. I didn't think I was high on your list of favorite people."

"You weren't. Still aren't, to be honest." Sue took a sip of coffee. The tremor in her hands was evident.

"Then why are you here?"

"I'm hoping you can help us. Me. Noah. Your partner says you might."

Sally glanced at Tanelsa, who didn't move. "Help with what?"

"I think Noah is going to need a lawyer, and soon."

That didn't make any sense. When Jim had been here earlier, he hadn't given any hint that Noah Freeman was a serious suspect in Maddie's murder. Was Sue referring to something else? "I'm not sure I understand you. Why do you think that?"

"The police were at my house earlier today. They know Noah and I were at the scene of that girl's death." Sue set her cup on Tanelsa's desk. "They took our fingerprints. Plus, Noah removed her phone from the cabin. I didn't know about that. If I had, I would have wiped it off and told him to put it back."

None of that was good, but it still didn't explain Sue's presence or her obvious agitation. "I see. You think the police consider Noah a suspect? What about you?"

She sighed. "I don't matter. I only want to protect Noah. You see." She folded her hands in her lap. "Does Noah have to be present while we do this? I'd rather speak to you privately first."

Tanelsa stood. "Noah, why don't you and I go talk? Let your mom and Ms. Castle have a chat." She held out her hand. Wordlessly, Noah got up, and she led him from the main office.

As soon as they were gone, Sally said, "What do you have to say that you don't want Noah to hear?"

Sue sighed. "Our relationship. It's a lot more complicated than it seems."

Sally waited.

The woman focused on her hands, then looked up. "Noah isn't really my son."

Chapter Twenty-Six

Sally stared at the woman who sat across from her. "What do you mean Noah isn't your son? Does he know that? He calls you Mom."

Sue twisted her fingers together. Gone was the belligerent mother determined to keep her boy out of a bad situation. Sue's hair was a bit disheveled, her face worn and stamped with exhaustion. "We don't talk about it at home. It's a long story."

Tanelsa had taken Noah to the conference room. Sally could hear the lively chatter. Whatever Tanelsa was doing, it had Noah enthralled.

"I have time," Sally said. "Although, before you start, there is one major point I'm curious about."

"What's that?" Sue asked.

"Why come to me? There are other lawyers in town."

The older woman blew out a breath. "When the police showed up, found the Tilgher girl's phone with Noah, and hauled us both in for fingerprinting, I knew I needed to get some help."

"For you."

Sue waved a hand. "I'm not worried about me. Noah needs someone on his side. He'll get himself into trouble. He's a good boy, Ms. Castle. People don't understand him, because of the autism, but he wouldn't harm a soul."

Except Sally had seen Noah's temper and how it could become physical. This wasn't the time to push that point. "That still doesn't explain how you ended up in my office. There are lots of good attorneys in the area you could have gone to."

"I can't afford them." Sue rubbed a finger, as though trying to remove imaginary ink. "He doesn't qualify for the public defender, either. The secretary at the office down at the courthouse said to come see you, that you and your partner were more open to hard-luck cases."

Dear old Doris. The longtime secretary in the public defender's office had been crushed when Sally left and nearly in tears when Tanelsa followed her. Of course, Doris would push clients their way. And she was right. People who needed assistance and didn't qualify for a court-appointed lawyer, but couldn't afford a private one, were exactly the people they wanted to help. "Fair enough. Why don't you explain the situation, and we'll go from there?" She studied her prospective client.

Sue took a deep breath. "Noah is my sister's son. My younger sister. Her name is Janice."

"How much younger?"

"Three years. Janice...she has problems. She started with drugs and alcohol in high school. She dropped out. Of course, that meant she couldn't get a job, not a good one. Then, she got pregnant when she was nineteen. My mother and I begged her to stop using and drinking, but of course, she wouldn't listen."

"Noah had Fetal Alcohol Syndrome?"

"He dodged that bullet. But I'm convinced that's what led to his autism. I can't prove it, but I'm sure I'm right." Sue paused to pick up her coffee cup and take a sip.

Sally didn't look up as she wrote. "Did Janice know who Noah's father was?"

"Some guy named Todd Freeman. Not that he gave a shit. Janice insisted Noah have his last name, so she could try to get child support. But Freeman split about a month after Noah was born. None of us have ever seen him."

"How long have you been caring for Noah?"

"Since the day he came home." Sue ran her finger around the rim of the cup. "Janice didn't have the first clue about mothering, and she had no interest in learning. She just wanted someone to take care of her kid so she could go on partying. Mom and I split the responsibility until I got a decent job, then I took over."

Sally lifted her head. "Why didn't you adopt him?" Sally asked. "Or change his name?"

That sparked a reaction. Sue bit her lip. "I tried," she said, voice full of bitterness. "First, they told me I wasn't a good candidate because I wasn't married. I got a sympathetic lawyer, but even she said it was a tough row to hoe. The courts don't like taking kids away from their mothers. He already had a social security card when he came home from the hospital. I decided it was common enough for kids to have different names from their mothers that I wouldn't rock the boat. Besides, I never claimed I was his mother. Other people assumed I was, and I never corrected them."

A sin of omission, then. Sue was right. It was not uncommon for mothers and children to have different last names these days, so no wonder no one ever raised a fuss. "But Janice doesn't sound like she was a fit parent."

"She always cleaned herself up in time to make a good impression." Sue scoffed. "I'd say something about getting the court involved and she'd swear she was off the drugs, she got a job, and she'd even keep it up for a couple of months. But she always went back to her old ways. I tried to get her to agree to let me adopt him, especially after it became clear he had special needs, but she refused. She said she loved her son." She gave a derisive laugh. "What she loved was the extra public assistance money she got for having a child."

"What happened?"

"I took him. Janice had disappeared, as usual, and had been gone for a couple days. By this point, Mom had died. Before Janice came back, I packed up his things and moved."

Sally fixed her with a stern gaze. "You kidnapped him."

"I didn't!" Sue squirmed. "I took him out of a negative situation."

Sally put down her pen. "You removed a child from his home without his custodial parent's knowledge or consent. I'd have to look up the statute to get the exact wording, but that sounds a lot like kidnapping to me. Even if it did happen, what, over fifteen years ago?"

There was silence for nearly a minute, then Sue set her cup back on the desk. "Yeah? Well, his mother never reported him missing, thank you very much. I'm quite sure she kept on drawing the money for him, but as far as she was concerned, it was one less thing to worry about. Trust me, Ms. Castle. I know my sister. Even before her difficulties, she was lazy, always looking for the easy route. I have zero problems believing that she saw this as a perfect situation. Noah was off her hands; she still got the same money from welfare, and she could go on her merry way."

Sally held her breath for a moment at the outburst. True, she'd never seen herself with kids. But if she had one, she was sure she'd try to be a good mother. If someone had taken her child, she'd certainly report it. It didn't sound like Janice Hepworth was cut from the same cloth. "All right. The Pennsylvania statute of limitations on kidnapping is only five years, so that's long past and not even something we have to worry about. And Noah wouldn't be in trouble for that anyway." She went to a fresh sheet. "Why do you think he needs representation? Did the police tell you he's a suspect in Maddie's death?"

"No, but if they don't consider him one yet, they will soon." All the anger left Sue's voice. The only thing left was desperation.

"There's more to Noah's relationship with Maddie, isn't there?"

"He was obsessed with her. No, wait. Let me finish." She looked over her shoulder. "Your partner has Noah entertained?"

"I hear a lot of laughter, so I'll say yes."

"Good." She paused. "When Maddie first showed up at the center, Noah was entranced by her. She was young, pretty, and no one he knew had hair that color. At first, I didn't think anything of it. But then it was Maddie this, and Maddie that, on and on. The day he announced they were getting married, I just about lost it."

"Wait, they were *engaged*?"

"No." Sue shook her head. "That's Noah for you. I'm fairly sure Maddie was never anything but nice to him. But the more she tried to get him interested in other girls, the more he clung to her. I'll give her that much, the girl did try." She balled up her hands into fists. "I *told* her. Leave it alone. He'll forget it. He always does. But no, she pushed and teased. I could have killed her." Realizing what she said, she clapped her hand over her mouth.

"Not literally. I didn't mean that the way it sounded."

Sally dismissed the words with a wave. "Don't worry. People often get carried away in the heat of the moment. I know what you meant." Even Jim wouldn't take a statement like that seriously. At least, she hoped he wouldn't. "How did Noah react when he learned Maddie was leaving the center?"

"You know about that?"

"I spoke to Liz Jackson. She said she'd told Maddie to stop volunteering. How did Noah take it?"

"He was furious." Sue's voice dropped to a whisper. "I've never seen him so angry. He-he overturned tables and chairs and threw art supplies. He threatened to tear up her picture, the one he drew. He said he wouldn't let her leave. He'd make her stay. It was…not good." She took a big breath.

"And then what happened?" Sally's instinct told her there was more.

"Maddie came to me and said she knew about me. That I wasn't Noah's real mom. I would have been able to blow that off, except she said it in front of Noah."

"Let me guess, he didn't handle it well.

"To put it mildly. It was the first time I'd ever seen him angry with her. He told her to stop lying about me; she needed to stop saying that, or he'd make her. *That's* what I think the police will find out about. When they do, it'll get added to the fact that he took her phone…his fingerprints at that cabin, and they'll charge him with murder. I'm telling you, Ms. Castle, he *didn't do it*. He lashes out at things, not people."

Except he'd punched Jim in the eye, Sally thought. But still. Rampaging through the activities room at the center, or lashing out wildly, was not the same as deliberately strangling a person. "Ms. Hepworth, has Noah been charged with a crime?"

"Not yet."

"But you expect him to be?"

"It wouldn't surprise me."

Sally rubbed her chin. "I'm not sure what you expect from me here. Normally, we don't get involved until charges are filed."

Sue hesitated. "I want you to do whatever you can to keep him from being arrested. If that means doing a full investigation, don't worry. I'll pay you for your time and work."

"Ms. Hepworth, I think you'd be better off with a private investigator. This just isn't work we usually do."

"I don't know any of those. I do know you. Despite the conditions we met under, I think you'll do your best to protect my son."

Sally thought it over. "All right. We'll do what we can." Another thought occurred to her. "You realize, Ms. Hepworth, that if I agree to represent Noah, I don't know if I can represent you as well. That's something I have to discuss with my partner and make sure I wouldn't be violating any standards from the ethics board."

"I don't care about me, Ms. Castle." Sue's eyes shone. "But I will do anything, *anything*, to protect my son."

Chapter Twenty-Seven

Duncan sat at his desk, staring at the background information on Noah Freeman. "How did Sue Hepworth end up with custody of Noah?"

"I'm not sure she ever had it, not legally," Cavendish replied. "It doesn't look like she formally adopted him."

He paged through his notebook. "Everyone refers to Sue as Noah's mom. *He* calls her mom."

"I know. But she's not. At least according to the law. That might also explain why she's so squirrelly about him. She doesn't want anything upsetting the apple cart on the lie they've been living. People might ask uncomfortable questions, like we are right now. At least Sue's a blood relative."

Duncan mulled this over. "Where can we find her? Janice."

Cavendish shook her head. "She's a ghost. She has a record, mostly for possession, the worst being a five-year sentence for a heroin charge. She was paroled after eighteen months for good behavior. Looks like she lived with a Bernadette Hepworth until about fifteen years ago. Then she bounced around. I called her last known residence, but the guy who answered said she's been gone for over a year. He didn't even know she had a kid."

"Got a phone number for Bernadette?"

"We won't be able to contact her unless you believe in mediums. She died right before Janice left."

Fifteen years would be when Noah was four. Duncan paged through his notes. He was sure Sue Hepworth had made mention of Noah's childhood.

"What about the father?"

"Name on the birth certificate is Todd Freeman. I haven't looked for him yet."

Duncan put that on their list of tasks. "Janice had to have a mailing address to get benefits."

Cavendish scrolled. "A lot of that is paid out electronically, like a reloadable card. But she did have a post office box in Pittsburgh. I'd have to do a little more research to confirm this, but I think Bernadette is Janice and Sue's mother. My guess is Janice lived with her mom until Bernadette died. She's been moving around ever since, thus the mailbox. Somehow, Sue ended up with Noah."

"Get Janice's bank records." He pulled up the search screen on his computer. "I'll find Freeman."

It didn't take long to figure out that Todd Freeman had left the area a long time ago. His last arrest was ten years ago in Pittsburgh for possession and disorderly conduct. There wasn't a record of his death, so he must have moved, but determining where would take more effort. Duncan was fairly certain he'd had little, if anything, to do with Noah. Given Freeman's criminal history, it was doubtful he'd ever paid child support, if that's why Janice had given her baby his father's last name.

He picked up his phone and dialed Sue Hepworth's number. When she didn't answer at home, he tried her cell, but got her voicemail. He didn't bother to leave a message either time.

While Cavendish worked, he reviewed his material from both conversations with Hepworth. She'd frequently referred to herself as Noah's mother. Liz Jackson had done the same. If Hepworth had been left holding the bag, or the baby, when Janice disappeared, why weren't there formal adoption papers?

"Request's in for Janice's financials," Cavendish said. "Penny for your thoughts."

He shared his questions with her. "Why don't you adopt a child you've taken responsibility for?"

"Biological parents won't agree, maybe you can't afford to slog through the legalities?"

"I can't find any evidence that she tried." He sat up straight. "We need to find Janice. If there's no death certificate, there's a good chance she's around somewhere. Do we have anything from Maddie's phone yet?"

"Are you kidding? We only handed it over at noon, that was less than three hours ago." Cavendish pawed through the clutter on her desk. "We don't even have the records from her carrier yet."

"Damn it." Why was everything so slow? "I'll call Andy and see if he can put a rush on it. Did Noah take that phone because it belonged to a girl he liked, or was it something else?"

"Or did Sue take it, and she's fobbing it off on Noah?"

"She's so protective of him, I have a hard time believing she'd do that. I find it more likely she picked up the phone, and Noah took it from *her*, without Sue's knowledge."

Cavendish put her feet up on her desk. "Looks like we have some time on our hands. What do you want to do while we wait?"

Duncan picked up the keys to their state car. "How do you feel about a drive to Pittsburgh?"

* * *

After Sue and Noah left, Sally related the entire story to her partner.

Tanelsa stared at her, eyes wide and mouth slightly open. "She kidnapped her nephew, raised him as her son, and you accepted her as a client?"

"No, I accepted Noah as a client, not his mother." Sally straightened her desk and avoided making eye contact.

"His aunt."

"Oh, come off it, T." Sally ceased fussing and now met Tanelsa's gaze. "It's true Sue Hepworth isn't Noah's biological or adoptive mother. But run the details through your head again and tell me she hasn't been more of a mother to that boy than anyone else. I dare you." Why did Tanelsa's statement make her so angry? Sally had never thought she had great maternal instincts, one of the reasons she shied away from having her own kids or even talking

164

about the possibility. But even she understood more went into mothering than genetics.

Tanelsa held up her palms. "Okay, point taken. I talked to him while you and Ms. Hepworth were chatting. He was definitely in love with that girl."

"I know."

"I said I'd heard she wasn't going to be a volunteer at the center and how that made him feel. Know what he said?"

Sally didn't want to hear it, but she knew it was important. "What?"

"That he wouldn't let that happen. And when I asked how he'd manage that, he said, and I quote, I'd hold her down if I had to, end quote."

Sally slumped in her chair. "Maddie had also told him Sue wasn't his mother." She told Tanelsa about Noah's reaction.

"I don't care what everyone thinks. The boy has anger issues."

"I know." But every time Noah lost his temper, it was reactionary. Strangling someone was such a deliberate action. One that took determination. But if Noah had been really angry, who knew what he might have done? Sue could have found him after the fact. No wonder she'd be eager to clean up the scene.

No, Sally didn't buy it. If Maddie had been stabbed, or shot, or even bashed over the head, she'd consider Noah a viable suspect. Those were all spur-of-the-moment crimes, where the damage was done in a flash. But to wrap his hands around a girl's neck and squeeze for five minutes? It wasn't in him. At least Sally didn't think so. The location and Maddie's unclothed body were all wrong, too. "He hasn't been charged with anything, yet. Let's not get ahead of ourselves."

Tanelsa picked up a pen and a piece of paper. "She must really love that boy. Sue Hepworth. First, she commits a felony when he was little, now she probably tampered with a crime scene. Gotta say, you pick some doozies for clients."

Thinking over the past few, Sally had to agree. But this one struck a chord with her, one she hadn't expected. She didn't know how much DNA Sue and Noah shared. But sometimes, the family you chose was closer than the family you were born into.

Chapter Twenty-Eight

I t turned out to be too late in the day for Duncan to make the drive to Pittsburgh. He called both phone numbers he had for Brackin, landline and cell, but didn't get an answer on either. He and Cavendish split the tasks of building profiles for Brackin and Zach Fabery, and locating Janice Hepworth. Duncan took the guys, and Cavendish set about locating Noah's biological mother. Listening to his partner curse in frustration, Duncan concluded he'd taken the easier task.

Around four, Cavendish threw down a pen. "I give up. This woman vanished, poof, gone."

"People don't go poof. What have you found?"

"I've got a pretty good handle on her up to about the time we think her sister left with Noah. Janice didn't finish high school, and she never went back for a GED. She held a string of minimum-wage jobs, broken up by long periods of unemployment. She collected benefits, like SNAP, for Noah."

"Did she ever enroll him in CHIP?" Pennsylvania's health care system for children would go right along with the food benefits provided by SNAP.

"He was covered as an infant, but that ended when he was five."

"Sue might have listed him as a dependent on her insurance, which would make sense if she started passing him off as her son." Duncan paused. "What else?"

"The erratic employment would have covered Noah's young childhood. Within a couple months of his fourth birthday, Janice fell off the grid, well, sort of. I only have the one address for her I told you about before. But that post office box was rented for her at the same time, so she probably used

166

that to get all her mail, and she drifted around in terms of where she lived."

"Does she still get the benefits?"

Cavendish consulted her screen. "No. Looks like she stopped around four years ago. The rental on her post office box ended at that time as well."

Duncan made a note. "What about a marriage or death certificate?"

"None filed in any county in southwestern Pennsylvania."

"Anything in NLETS?" If Janice had a record for terrorism or connections to drugs, the system would have the information.

"Nothing."

She could have moved out of state. "Tomorrow, let's visit and see what they can tell us at the post office. We can expand our record search to Ohio, West Virginia, and Maryland, if necessary."

"Fine." Cavendish undid her hair and ran her hands through it. "Please tell me you had more luck."

"I think I did." He handed her several printouts. "First up, Zach Fabery. On the surface, there's nothing to him. He has an apartment in Shadyside. He works in Shadyside, where he's the marketing coordinator at a store specializing in outdoor equipment, activities, and whatnot. He pays his taxes, drives a three-year-old Chevy Trax, and has no criminal record. The worst I can find is that he's a bit…awkward when it comes to his personal postings on social media."

Cavendish read. "Define awkward."

"From his postings and the responses, it seems like he doesn't understand no, means, well, no."

She looked up. "But you said he doesn't have a record."

"Correct, which only means no one has filed a complaint. But he definitely has a history of pushing women a little too far. Seems to me, he gets more attached to them than they do to him, and he can't seem to shrug off the rejection and move on."

"Maybe Maddie was the last straw. He meets her on the dating app, she breaks it off, and he snaps."

"If we'd found her in his apartment, her dorm room, or a hotel room, I'd have an easier time buying that than her being in a run-down cabin."

Cavendish pointed at him. "You said he works at an outdoors company. I'll bet you lunch if we talk to his boss; he has a habit of doing the same thing to his female co-workers as he does online."

"Which is why I want to interview Don Rearick, who is the company CEO." One of these days, Duncan's research would result in suspects falling off the list, not clinging to it like flies on sticky tape. "Next up, Will Brackin. Talk about a charmer. You saw his record, his house, and his car. He graduated from the performing arts high school in Pittsburgh and has a degree in theater arts from a college in Ohio."

"That's definitely not a recipe for a high-end house and car."

"Surprisingly, he has a very small social media footprint, but in the stuff he does post, it sure looks like he's living the good life. I can't wait to see this guy's financials. I've also asked for his phone records. I want to see if he was in touch with the victim outside work."

Cavendish tied back her hair once again. "What about the people we think took the fall for him?"

"One dead, one in jail out west, and one on probation, now living in the Hill District."

Cavendish's phone rang. "Cavendish. They do? Interesting. Thanks." She hung up. "That was forensics. Barry Atwiler's prints match one of the unidentified sets at the scene. So much for not going on set."

"Which ones?" Duncan took out his chart.

"On the door. The ones you have marked as number three, if I remember."

He looked at his chart, which, after he added Atwiler's name, now read:

- Door: Victim, Noah, Sue, Atwiler,
- Corner: #5
- Window: Noah
- Cot: Victim, Noah, Sue, #4

Duncan glanced at the clock. It was about four fifteen. Plenty of time to interview Barry Atwiler again.

* * *

Sally decided to leave the office a bit early and drive back to the Center for the Developmentally Disabled, where she could hopefully catch Liz Jackson and learn more about the relationship between Noah, Maddie, and Sue.

"I'm not sure I should be talking to you," Liz said, motioning Sally to take a battered chair in the cramped director's office.

She set her briefcase on the floor next to her. "I agreed to represent Noah in any legal action. I'm here as his attorney, and my only goal is to help him."

"Sounds like he isn't facing charges at the moment." Liz sat in a wheeled desk chair, showing more than one duct tape repair in the upholstery.

"Not yet." Sally crossed her legs. "But his mother is worried."

Liz rolled her eyes. "Ms. Hepworth is always worried."

"I take it you think she's overreacting." Did Liz know Sue's secret? It didn't seem so.

"A lot of times, yes." Liz sat back and intertwined her fingers over her stomach. "I get mothers with special needs children. The world is a rough place for a so-called normal child. Bullying is a real thing. There's more pressure on kids to perform in school than there ever was. The internet is full of people with less-than-admirable intentions, never mind crazies who nab kids from parks."

Reason number 943 why I don't want kids. Sally was well aware of all the threats. And it wasn't just psychos who grabbed kids. Sometimes it was well-intentioned relatives. "Why did Ms. Hepworth bother you?"

"There's a limit." Liz tapped her thumbs together. "These kids need to learn to be as self-sufficient as they can. Strong. I've found if you over-coddle them, it actually hurts them in the long run. This isn't Victoriana, when they believed people with cognitive disabilities couldn't function and had to be shoved into institutions for life. Many of our clients have jobs. They go to school; they participate in the same kinds of activities you and I do, such as swimming or hiking. Ms. Hepworth, however, was determined Noah would not be like that."

"What do you mean?"

"Take education. Noah finished high school, true. But I believe he did cyber-school for the last two years. Something about her worrying over the types of kids he'd encounter in the classroom. He doesn't have a job, although he'd be more than capable of working as a bagger in a grocery store, or a stock boy in a big-box store. Even when he was here, she fussed over who he spent time with, how much, and whether someone was supervising."

"And that included volunteers, right? You mentioned Maddie the last time I was here."

"Maddie had a special gift with Noah, that's for sure." Liz offered a small smile tinged with a little sadness. "When Noah would have one of his tantrums, Maddie could calm him down like no one else. He related to her. When he wouldn't talk to any other staff member, he'd talk to Maddie."

"What did they speak about?"

"Anything, everything. How the Steelers or the Penguins were doing. Why the Pirates suck. How Noah wished his mother would let him learn to ski. Maddie shared stories about being in college, like the funny things her roommates would say, or how bad the food was in the dining hall."

Now was the time. "Were you ever concerned about the relationship between Noah and his mother? I mean beyond her being slightly overprotective."

Liz furrowed her forehead. "I'm not sure what you mean?"

How could Sally phrase the question without spilling Sue's story? "Were you ever concerned that there was a hidden history, or were there things that might have been red flags in the typical mother-son dynamics?"

"You mean abuse?"

"Anything."

Liz chewed her lip. "Not really. Yes, she was over the top when it came to protecting him. It felt, to me, like she held the world at arm's length, but I figured that was because she didn't want him hurt. But what mother doesn't do that, at least to some extent, right? Especially when a young man likes a girl. My own mom never thought anyone my brother brought home was good enough for him, at least while he was in high school. Ms. Hepworth was pretty much the same."

CHAPTER TWENTY-EIGHT

Sally would come back to Maddie in a moment. "Did Noah often have a temper?"

"I wouldn't say often." Liz paused. "It usually became a problem when he really wanted something and he couldn't have it. He'd strike out at people, throw things, even swear. That's when we'd call for Maddie, if she was here."

"How did Ms. Hepworth feel about that?"

"She didn't like it, that's a fact." Liz's blunt tone didn't leave room for doubts. "She thought Maddie was too close to Noah. She would graduate college, leave, and Noah would be stranded. Ms. Hepworth thought Noah was forming an unhealthy attachment to the girl."

"That he was in love with her?"

Liz shrugged. "If you want to put it that way, yes. That's the other thing about people with cognitive issues. They often have a hard time dealing with disappointment. For example, if you loved a man who didn't love you back, it might be disheartening. Eventually, however, provided you have the right resources, support, and a good mental attitude, you'd get over it and move on. For those like Noah, that process is much more difficult. But Ms. Hepworth took it to extremes, especially lately."

"What do you mean?"

"She came to the center to pick Noah up one afternoon a few weeks ago and found him and Maddie talking to each other. They were in the common area, but away from the other clients. It seemed like they were having a private conversation. Ms. Hepworth went ballistic. She said we were never to let Noah be alone with anyone, especially Maddie Tilgher, or she'd find another center."

Under normal circumstances, it would be the actions of a stereotypical, overly protective parent. But after what Sally had learned this morning, maybe Sue wasn't trying to control Noah as much as she was terrified of what he might say and that someone would figure out what she'd done. The statute of limitations on kidnapping might be up, but that didn't mean there couldn't be serious consequences for past actions. "How did Maddie react?"

"Now that you mention it, Maddie shrugged it off." Liz turned thoughtful. "I apologized to her afterward, and she said something like how it would all be okay because secrets didn't stay hidden forever. I assumed she was talking about something Noah had confided to her, maybe something he'd done that was against the rules. But then I found she'd been looking into Noah's personal life. Where he was born, his early childhood, things like that. I told her it was unprofessional."

It was a perfect segue. "It sounds like Maddie was a great volunteer. Yet the last time I was here, you told me you were going to ask her to leave."

"She was a great worker, and that's why I put off my decision as long as I did, including counseling her about the violation of Noah's privacy instead of dismissing her on the spot." Liz brushed a strand of hair out of her eyes. "In the beginning, Maddie was one of the most, if not *the* most, reliable volunteers I had. If she was going to miss a scheduled day, she told me well in advance. She was fun and interactive. Lately, however, that had changed. She was often late. She'd taken to checking her phone when she ought to have been paying attention to clients. That was bad enough, but she had a couple visitors recently that were definitely over the line."

"Who?"

"One was an older man. I'd say fifty or thereabouts. He said he was Maddie's internship supervisor, but she did *not* talk to him like someone in that sort of position."

"How many times was he here? Did you hear their conversation?"

"Only once and some of it, yes. He said he needed her to work and she retorted that she'd told him she wasn't available and he'd have to get someone else. Then he mentioned how she was best suited, and she told him it didn't matter, she wasn't doing that kind of job anymore and he'd have to find another actress. And how he better never come here again, or she'd go public with what she knew."

The visitor had to be Barry Atwiler. The work must have been another photo shoot, but it sounded like Maddie turned it down. Maybe another video job with Will Brackin? That was the only time Sally had detected any sort of discomfort in Maddie's expression in the pictures. Had she been going to turn Atwiler in to the police, perhaps for enabling abuse and rape? An accusation like that would ruin him, personally and professionally. "Who was the second?"

"A much younger guy. He looked sweet, but acted a little pathetic. He never got beyond the reception area. He begged for another chance, and Maddie told him she was sorry, but it was over, and he needed to move on. She spoke to me afterward, and I asked if everything was okay. She said it was fine, just a guy who couldn't take a hint. That's when I told her it seemed her personal life was getting in the way of her volunteer work. It was disrupting things for the clients, and maybe she should give up her post, especially seeing as how she was going to graduate next semester, and she probably had a lot to focus on for that."

"What did she say?"

Liz frowned. "She begged me not to let her go and said she loved being here. 'This is the only good spot in my life right now, Ms. Jackson. I can make a difference here. Please don't make me leave.' I thought it was odd."

"How so?"

"She was a smart, pretty young woman with a promising future. I would have thought her life was full of good things."

Since the rest of Maddie's life had involved trying to quit the porn industry, a potentially abusive co-star, and a dating-app hookup who wouldn't go away, Sally didn't agree with Liz Jackson's assumption.

Chapter Twenty-Nine

Duncan and Cavendish headed to the offices of Laurel Highlands Arts and Entertainment. "You think he'll still be there?" Cavendish asked as they parked in the nearly deserted lot. Only one other car was there, a silver BMW.

Duncan ran the plates. "Well, his car is. If our idea is right about how they do the photo shoots, he may be in the office prepping for tonight's job."

The door was unlocked, so the troopers entered the office. The lobby was empty, the receptionist's desk unoccupied, and the lights off. But they clearly heard voices from the back. "I don't want any problems with this, got it?" Atwiler's voice.

A young woman responded. "Yes, sir." Another model? Or an office worker like the one who had manned the front desk on the last visit?

"Good. Are you set with the photography equipment?"

A laconic male voice said, "Of course. Keep your shirt on. As long as the subjects are there, we'll be fine. You're letting what happened to the Tilgher girl get to you."

Duncan looked back at Cavendish. The photographer, at least Duncan assumed that was who the speaker was, seemed to be implying Atwiler knew more about Maddie's death than the man had claimed.

The scrape of a chair across the floor. "She was one of my most popular models. Why do the good ones have to be trouble?" Atwiler said, grumbling.

"No clue," the other man replied, "but stop bitching. As long as the cops don't know anything for sure, you can't be tied to her. Other than the fact she worked for you."

Cavendish tapped Duncan on the shoulder and nodded in the direction of the voices. The meaning of the gesture was clear: *That's our cue.*

Duncan loosened the Glock in his holster and strode forward. He found the group in a small room. Atwiler stood at the head of the table, studying a piece of paper. Over in the corner, a scruffy man in his thirties with a ponytail checked a variety of camera lenses and lighting equipment. Between them, a young woman hovered, like she was waiting to be given a task.

"Evening, everyone." Duncan entered the room. "Hope you don't mind us showing ourselves in."

Atwiler clenched his fist, crumpling the paper. "What the hell are you doing here? We're closed."

Cavendish took up a position near the doorway. "Then you should lock up and hang a sign."

Atwiler whirled to the young woman, who flinched. "Don't you know anything? When I say close up, I mean turn off the lights and lock the goddamn front door!"

She squeaked.

"Don't just stand there. Go take care of it before anyone else comes in. Dumb bitch. Don't forget, you can be replaced."

She scurried out of the room. Judging by the way Atwiler spoke, she wasn't a model.

Duncan heard Cavendish's low growl and saw her eyebrows bunch. He spoke before she let fly something that could jeopardize the situation. "No need to treat the young lady that way, Mr. Atwiler. In fact, I'm going to have to insist you don't."

Atwiler sneered. "You can't arrest me for snarling at my own staff."

"You're coming dangerously close to a minor assault charge," Cavendish said. "And we *can* arrest you for that."

Atwiler frowned, as though he couldn't quite figure out what she meant. "I didn't touch her."

"Assault isn't always physical."

He waved her off. "I'm sorry, but we're closed for the day. You'll have to come back tomorrow."

"Except we're already here." Duncan crossed his arms. "We have a couple of questions, and then we'll be out of your hair."

"Speaking of charges, I should file one for harassment," Atwiler said. "I know you don't approve of my business, but it's legal. I'm not photographing kiddies. All of my models are adults and signed a contract of their own volition."

"I'm glad you brought that up." Duncan removed a pen and notebook from his pocket. "One of the things I'm curious about is how your operation works."

"Oh come on. You aren't that naïve."

"No, not that. I mean, what's your contract structure? Do your workers get to choose their jobs? How do they get paid, by the hour or by the gig?"

Atwiler glanced at his photographer, who shrugged. "Boilerplate contract pays each person a flat fee per job. Plus royalties."

"How do you calculate royalties on smut?" Cavendish asked.

"They get a percentage based on the number of downloads," Atwiler answered, but kept his eyes on Duncan. "More downloads, more money. Videos earn more than stills."

That might account for some of Maddie's income, Duncan thought. If she was as popular as Atwiler claimed, she might get better-than-average money. "Did Maddie do videos?" He knew about the one. Had there been more?

"Only one. I knew she needed the cash, so I suggested it. But after that, she said no more. Her loss." Atwiler shrugged.

Did you not pay attention? Duncan had seen the look of fear in the young woman's eyes. Hard to believe the producer hadn't. "How do people end their contracts?"

"Easiest way is to let them expire. They do include an escape clause, but it's a pain in the ass."

"Did Maddie try to use hers?"

Atwiler paused. "We talked. I told her it would be difficult. Much better to just let it roll."

Cavendish didn't move, but when she spoke, her voice was hard. "I don't think you just *talked*. I think you argued. We've seen her emails, Mr. Atwiler. You didn't want to let her go. She threatened to smear your professional reputation. How'd that make you feel? Angry? I bet it did. Of course, you work in a shitty industry, so I'm not sure having a good rep is something to brag about."

"Tell me Hugh Hefner doesn't have people who respect him. And I told you. My deals are proprietary." Atwiler glanced at Cavendish and obviously saw something he liked, because he let his gaze travel up and down her body. "You've got a good figure, Trooper. Ever consider a side gig?"

Duncan put out a hand, just in case she lunged at the filmmaker, but she didn't move.

"Not that one," she said in a deadpan voice. "You couldn't afford me."

The comment didn't seem to faze Atwiler. "If that's all, I need to get ready."

"You haven't answered my questions."

"No, I wouldn't appreciate being slandered in front of my peers."

"What about the secret deal she mentioned?"

"I told you. My deals are proprietary information. You want to know about them? Get a warrant. Is that all?"

"Just a couple more things." Duncan pretended to consult his notes. "You use some pretty famous landmarks in your work. How'd you get their permission?"

The other man smirked. "Who said I did? Trust me. I'm not going to tell you all my secrets, but I have my ways. *Without* trespassing, if you were thinking of going there."

"I wasn't. Maddie's last job. Tell me what happened."

"How should I know?"

"Because your fingerprints are at the scene," Cavendish said.

Atwiler's reaction was almost comical. His eyes widened, then narrowed. He flicked his gaze back and forth between the police officers. "How do you know that?"

She threw his words back at him. "We have our ways."

At that moment, the photographer broke in. "Give it up, Barry. Tell them what they want to know, and let's get this show on the road."

Atwiler ran a hand through his greasy hair. "The theme for the shoot was 'rustic romance,' that's why we used the cabin. It was the closest thing to a frontier-like setting. Maddie did the pictures. At the end, I said I'd be in touch about her next session. She said she was finished."

Now we're getting somewhere. "What happened?"

"She'd put her clothes back on."

"Is that all?"

"We argued, okay?"

"Screamed like Boston fish wives," the photographer said.

Atwiler threw him a withering glance. "Maddie said I'd better let her out, or else she'd make sure every model in the area knew I didn't honor my contracts. She'd do her best to make sure I didn't get another decent girl for months. I told her to stop being a bitch."

"Did she say anything else?" Duncan asked. He didn't believe the "proprietary information" claim about this deal. The more Atwiler refused to discuss it, the more suspicious it sounded. *Maddie knew something about it, though.* "What else?"

The other man paused. "I may have told her she'd regret it if she did. But I meant she'd never work in the industry again. Not that I'd kill her."

"Is that all?"

"Yes. She was alive when I left. Ask him." Atwiler pointed at his photographer.

The pony-tailed man nodded, hands in the pockets of his worn denim jacket. "She was breathing when we left."

"That statement could be taken a number of ways," Duncan said.

The photographer shrugged. "I meant she was alive and well."

This man's prints could be the set in the corner, based on the marks on the floor they thought could be from a tripod. "What's your name?"

"Clarence Jones."

"We'll need you to come in so we can take fingerprints for elimination purposes."

"No need, I was there." Jones brushed hair off his forehead. "I did all of

Maddie's shoots. She was a nice girl with a good figure. I'll miss working with her. She told me her plans a while ago. I tried to convince her to get to the end of her contract, but no dice."

"You didn't argue with her?"

"Hey, not my life. I wished her well and said if she ever wanted back in, I'd give her a recommendation."

Cavendish had not stirred from her spot by the door. "What did you mean earlier? When you said your boss was letting Maddie get to him."

"When did I say that?"

She snorted. "Right before we walked into the room. We heard you talking. You definitely mentioned Maddie and that everything would be fine 'as long as the cops don't know anything.' Know what?"

Jones didn't flinch. "You're attaching too much meaning to my words. I meant that Maddie and he only had a professional relationship. There's nothing else to know."

Duncan very much doubted that was the case, but he'd rather interrogate Jones on his own, after learning about the man's background. "We still need your fingerprints. Come to the State Police headquarters on Route 40 down in Eighty Four at one."

For a moment, it seemed like Jones was going to object, but he sighed. "If you insist."

Duncan turned back to Atwiler. "Last question. When did Maddie's contract expire?"

"March of next year," he replied. "They usually have a twelve-month duration."

That lined up perfectly with their hypothesis. If Maddie had first signed in March of her sophomore year, she'd be on her second one. "Thank you for your time, Mr. Atwiler," Duncan said.

"No problem." Atwiler's voice oozed sarcasm. "Please. If you need any more information, come back."

"Don't worry." Cavendish eyed him with scorn. "We will."

Duncan stopped at the door. "You deposited fifty grand in your business account last spring. Where'd you get so much at once?" It was a shot in the dark. That fifty thousand came from somewhere. Duncan couldn't shake the feeling that the "secret deal" Maddie referenced and the cash were related.

Atwiler licked his lips. "None of your damn business."

"Suit yourself." He went back to the car.

Cavendish followed. "Did you really expect him to say anything?"

"Nope." He started the engine. "But if he thinks we can't find out, he doesn't watch a lot of TV. They do get some things right."

Chapter Thirty

That evening, Sally stood in front of her stove, staring at the covered pot of quick-cook risotto, replaying the interview with Sue Hepworth. The woman had insisted she didn't want representation for herself. Her sole concern was Noah. Why? What had she not said?

Sally and Tanelsa had talked by phone after Sally left Liz Jackson and headed back to Uniontown. During the time Tanelsa had entertained him earlier, Noah hadn't said anything noteworthy and hadn't displayed any of the temper he had with Jim or that Liz Jackson said he could fall into. Tanelsa's verdict had been firm. "No way that boy choked Maddie to death. That's too deliberate, and I don't think his mind works that way." After Sally shared the summary of her interview with Liz, Tanelsa agreed

Sue Hepworth looked like a better suspect than her son.

And yet Sue had been adamant. Noah was the one who needed a lawyer.

The scent of burning rice brought Sally back to reality. Muttering curses under her breath, she snapped off the flame under the pot and checked the salmon under the broiler. It was perfect. She set the oven to keep the fish warm and noted the time. Mondays were always dinner at her place and it was a couple minutes past six. Jim would arrive soon.

He came through the door as she finished setting the table. "Something smells good." He kissed her.

"I think the risotto might be a little burnt on the bottom, but hopefully not. Grab a beer, have a seat, and I'll bring everything to the table."

Minutes later, they were seated, full plates in front of them. "I was thinking." Jim shook out his napkin. "I know your lease doesn't expire until March, and that's over three months away. But maybe you can talk to your landlord about subletting or whether he'll let you out early. Either way, what do you think about moving some of your stuff to my place now? Especially anything heavy. It'll be easier to do it before there's a foot of snow on the ground."

Oh, shit. She hadn't thought about her decision to move in with Jim before she'd accepted Noah as a client. "Yeah, about that."

He set down his beer bottle. "Don't tell me you're having second thoughts."

"Oh, no. That's not it. It's only that I'm going to have to wait a bit before we start the whole moving process for professional reasons."

"What do you mean?"

She might as well tell him. The fact she represented Noah wasn't privileged, and she remembered all too well the last time she'd withheld information like that from Jim. It hadn't been pretty. He'd find out from other sources, especially if Noah did end up being charged. "Sue Hepworth came to see us this afternoon."

"And?"

"I've agreed to take Noah Freeman on as a client." She waited for his response.

Characteristically, Jim took a few moments to process her statement. "He hasn't been charged with anything."

"I know that."

"Then why would he need legal representation from a criminal defense attorney?"

"You know I can't tell you." She pushed risotto around on her plate. "Can I ask you something?"

"I might not answer."

"I can respect that." She laid down the fork. "Does my client need to worry about being charged? Do I?"

Jim sat back and stalled by taking a swig of beer. "The investigation is still ongoing."

She had half-expected the answer, but secretly hoped for more. "Is there *anything* you can tell me? If I was a reporter, and asked if there were any new leads in the Tilgher case, what would you tell me?"

"To contact the PR flak." He gave a tight grin. "Before I say anything else, you've been on top of this one from the get-go. Why?"

"It's just…I can't help thinking that if I'd handled it differently, better, when Maddie came to see me, she might still be alive." Sally picked up her fork and stabbed a piece of broccoli. "I should have asked Tanelsa to bring me a pad, or found something else to write on. Anything but leave Maddie alone. I could tell she was upset."

"Hey." Jim reached across and squeezed her free hand. "Stop beating yourself up. Even if you'd done things exactly like that, Maddie still could have wound up dead in that cabin. You have no way of knowing. Turns out she had a lot going on in her life."

"So I've learned." She looked into his eyes. "Look, I've done this enough to know an investigator doesn't look at every suspect in the same way. Some are serious candidates; some are on the fringe. All I want to know is where you put Noah Freeman on that spectrum. If you can't tell me, I suppose that's an answer in itself."

Jim withdrew his hand and sat back. His hazel eyes darkened.

Sally could tell he was debating with himself. She stayed quiet.

"Okay, this stays between you and me. Not you, me, and Tanelsa, Just the two of us, got it?"

She nodded.

"I haven't been able to strike Freeman from the list, but honestly? He's at the bottom of it. We know the real name of Will Longfellow."

"Who is he?"

"Nope, not telling you that. But he's got an interesting history, one that makes us want to talk to him. We know Barry Atwiler and his photographer were at the cabin."

"How? Did you match their prints to the scene?"

"No comment." Jim lifted an eyebrow, his classic "confirmation without saying a word" response. "We're tracking the money you found." He gave her the high-level details of the email exchange between Maddie and Atwiler, including her threats to expose some deal. "Naturally, he refused to talk about it."

"Is he being obstinate, or does he have something to hide?"

"We don't know. Yet. Zach Fabery, of the dating app, is still hanging around, too. There are details we need to follow up on with him and at his place of employment."

"I talked to Zach's boss. I didn't get much." Sally told him about her conversation with Don Rearick, owner of Outdoor Adventurer. "So good luck. Of course, the fact he shut me down makes me suspicious."

"That's because you're cynical."

She threw a napkin at him. "Tell me you wouldn't think the exact same thing."

He batted it away. "I would, but that's because I'm cut from the same cloth, especially after years of interviewees lying to me and trying to lead me down the garden path."

She paused as she ate a few more bites of fish. "But there's nothing you can share about Sue Hepworth or Noah?"

Jim's expressionless mask returned, and he took time before responding. "If you're his lawyer, I'm sure you know as much, or even more, than I do."

Sally again thought of Sue's visit to her office. *The police will know soon enough.* Had Jim and his partner learned about Sue's real relationship to Noah and his abduction, if you could call it that? If not today, it had to happen soon. "Thank you. I appreciate your honesty and the fact you told me as much as you can."

"I wish I could tell you more. I do." He forked up another bite of salmon. "Just so I understand the situation surrounding your living arrangements. You still intend to move to Confluence, right?"

"Of course. But I need to take care of my client. I'm pretty sure you and Jenny are good enough that you'll have a suspect in custody long before my lease ends, and everything will be fine."

Jim stared at her, fork held in front of his mouth, eyes thoughtful. "What if that suspect turns out to be Noah Freeman?"

"I'll cross that bridge when I come to it." The planks might crumble beneath her as she scrambled to safety, though.

Chapter Thirty-One

D uncan got to work the next day at eight-thirty, and found Cavendish already seated at her desk. "Good news." She waved a sheaf of paper at him. "Records from Maddie Tilgher's cell phone carrier. And we have financials on Laurel Highlands Entertainment."

"Do we have anything from the device to go with the carrier information?" He hung his jacket on his chair and sat.

"No, but maybe this afternoon. I started going through the numbers listed."

"Hold that for a minute." Duncan picked up the numbers from Atwiler's porn company. "Have you looked at these financials?"

"No, I dove right into the phone records. What's up?"

"Laurel Highlands Entertainment isn't so much bleeding as hemorrhaging. Tanelsa Parson told us the monthly subscription was two-hundred, right?"

Cavendish pursed her lips. "That sounds familiar."

Duncan skimmed down the columns of numbers. "Even with paying his so-called talent peanuts, Atwiler was barely breaking even. Right up until this spring." He highlighted a row. "Here's the deposit Sally told us about. Looks like it was cash."

"How would Atwiler have suddenly come up with fifty large in cash?"

"No clue, but I wonder if that's enough to get a warrant for his emails and phone records. I'll check." Duncan pulled out an affidavit form and started writing as fast as he could. "I'd bet if Maddie agreed to another contract, it would have been for less money. Before that deposit, there were a few bounced payments, too. I'd have to dig to see who got stiffed."

Cavendish held out her hand. "Maddie?"

He paused, writing long enough to hand her the page. "Maybe. All I have here are numbers of payments that were refused. We'd have to match them." He looked up. "Could be that's what Maddie was complaining about. Not the work, but Atwiler's crappy cash flow, especially if she was one of the ones not getting paid."

Cavendish drummed her fingers on the desk. "If that's what she intended to spread around, it might negatively affect his ability to recruit new models, which would mean even more financial woes. I've been wondering what the upside for him was in killing her. I mean, why would he kill one of his most popular stars, right?"

"We know Maddie threatened to expose a deal Atwiler had in the works, too."

Cavendish picked up a rubber band and played with it. "She knew where this money came from and it wasn't good. But as long as she got what she wanted, she'd keep her mouth shut."

"Rather than run the risk, Atwiler killed her." Duncan finished the affidavit. "Let's find a judge and fast-track that."

"You got it."

He set aside the paperwork. "Before we do, though, what have you found out from the wireless carrier?"

"There are lots of calls and texts to and from her parents here. That's not really surprising. There are also a fair number of messages to Evie Martin."

"Also not a shocker." Duncan noted the information as Cavendish spoke. "What else?"

"It looks like there is a double-handful of calls to a local 724 number." She read it off.

Duncan did a reverse lookup. "That's Atwiler's cell."

"Which makes sense. They didn't communicate via text, only voice calls. I'm guessing she didn't want a record on her phone in case someone unlocked it and read her messages." Cavendish highlighted the rows, using a different color for each recipient. "There are three incoming calls, each lasting less than a minute from a 412 number. Sorry, the first two are short.

The third one went for a little over twenty minutes." She rattled off another number.

"Well, well, well." He looked at his partner. "Will Brackin. Two straight to voicemail and one conversation?"

"The plot thickens." She grabbed a fourth highlighter. "How about 724-555-9786? There are a number of texts from and to that one, but it also looks like she blocked it a few months ago."

He did another search. "Zach Fabery."

"Okay, that fits if she had her dates earlier this year. Could be she cut him off when he wouldn't go away."

Duncan stared at the screen. "But he must have stayed in contact. At least he did if he was the one Maddie was nervous about when she sought help last week."

Cavendish thought a moment. "There are so many messaging apps now. We can't know the answer to that until we get the report on her actual phone."

"Is that all?"

"Oh no. There are a number of calls to a 740 number. A lot of them. Look." She held up a page where over half of the numbers had been highlighted in green.

Duncan typed. "That's an Ohio area code." He entered the rest of the digits. "That one is registered to a Robert Montgomery. Who the hell is he?"

"No clue. But Maddie talked to him a lot. Mostly over the last three months."

Of course, the search on Robert Montgomery, even limiting it to the part of the state covered by the three-digit code, turned up over two dozen hits. Without more details, they could spend days down that rabbit hole.

He made a note to talk to the Tilghers and Evie. They might know more. "Anything else?"

"I saved the best for last." Cavendish held out a sheet of paper, a wicked grin on her face. "This number looked familiar, so I double-checked it to make sure I was right."

He took the sheet. "Talk about intriguing." Over the last two months,

Maddie had made several calls to Sue Hepworth, none lasting less than ten minutes.

* * *

Sally sat at her desk, trying to proofread a brief from Tanelsa, but her heart wasn't in it. She kept replaying the scene at dinner last night. She and Jim hadn't talked about business after her announcement that she'd taken Noah Freeman's case. She hadn't expected Jim to elaborate on his suspicions, or lack thereof, regarding the young man, and she certainly hadn't thought Jim would share any evidence. In fact, after she affirmed her intention to move to Confluence, Jim hadn't said much of anything on either topic. Maybe that was his way of letting her know he understood and accepted her decisions.

Of course, it could have meant he was furious and didn't trust himself to talk.

Stop it, Sally scolded herself. They were past that stage. If he had truly had an issue with anything, he'd tell her. Would he be disappointed things couldn't move as fast as he wanted? Sure. But that was all.

On cue, her phone sounded a text alert, the one associated with him. *Forgot to ask last night. Do you like sweet potatoes or yams for Thanksgiving?* She chuckled and typed *Neither, but thanks for asking.* She watched the three dots, indicating he was responding. *Sweet potatoes it is.* The message was accompanied by a winking emoji. She tossed the phone on her desk. Clearly, her recent professional choices weren't an issue that would destroy their relationship.

Uncapping a red pen, she picked up the brief and glanced at the time. It was almost nine o'clock, and Tanelsa wasn't in yet. This made the second day in a row her partner was late without contact beforehand. She counted the red marks on the sheet in front of her. What was up with that woman?

Sally returned to her reading and at nine-fifteen, Tanelsa rushed into the office. "Sorry, sorry. I promise I'm not making a habit of this." She dropped her briefcase and purse on her desk and went to hang her coat in the closet.

Sally took a moment to study her partner. Her hair wasn't as sleek as it usually was and her earrings didn't match her outfit. Strike that, one earring. Her right lobe was naked. Her skirt was creased, and the blouse looked like it needed another trip through the steam iron.

Tanelsa settled herself at her desk. "Anything big happen before I got here?"

"Not a peep." Sally tilted her head. "What's the problem?"

"Nothing. No problem. Things just got away from me this morning." Tanelsa focused on her monitor.

"T, cut the crap and stop insulting my intelligence."

"There isn't any. Crap, there is."

"Bullshit. Let's examine the evidence against that statement. Exhibit A, this is the second day in a row you've been late without an explanation. You're never late. Exhibit B, your clothes look like you pulled them out of the laundry without stopping to press them. Exhibit C, yesterday your shoes didn't match, and today you're missing an earring."

Tanelsa's hands went to her ears.

"And finally, Exhibit D." Sally held up the sheet, which had so many red marks a casual observer might have thought they were the result of a nasty paper cut.

"Everybody makes mistakes." Tanelsa's face took on a defensive expression.

"Absolutely. So do you. But I know your work. You make, oh, four of these silly goofs a year." Sally shook the paper. "There are four in a single paragraph. Spare me the protestations of innocence and tell me what the hell is going on with you. And then we'll figure out how I can help. I'm your friend, Tanelsa, not just your partner. I'm concerned."

Tanelsa sagged back and rubbed her face. Her arms fell to her sides. "The thing is, I'm not sure you can do anything about this."

"Try me."

"All right." Tanelsa closed her eyes. "Lisa wants to have a baby."

The words brought Sally up short. She'd been expecting a personal problem, but not that one. "Well, I'm not going to claim I know a lot about the process, but if that's what you want, I'm sure it can be done. IVF and all that."

"That's just it. *I* don't want it at all. Lisa does."

"Oh." Sally fell silent. What more was there to say?

Tanelsa continued. "When I came out, my mom didn't know how to take it. She made her peace with the reality of a lesbian daughter eventually, but at one point, she told me, 'I guess I'll have to rely on your sister for grandchildren.' I remember that very clearly."

Ouch. "Didn't you take girlfriends to meet your family? I mean, before Lisa?"

"A couple of times." Tanelsa's smile was tinged with regret. "Mom always referred to them as my 'friends.' As long as she could pretend I wasn't in a romantic relationship with any of them, she was good. It was okay for *me* to be gay, but to be intimately involved with another woman was a level she couldn't go to. At least my brother and sister were cool, but Mom? Forget it."

"Has she met Lisa? I mean, she was at your wedding, right?"

"Yes, she's met Lisa. That was another level of crazy. To admit that her daughter was not only gay but in a mixed-race relationship? No way." The smile disappeared. "She didn't come to the wedding. She claimed she had pneumonia and sent her regrets."

Double-ouch. "I'm so sorry."

Tanelsa waved away the words. "I came to grips with it ages ago. I mean, it still smarts a little. Sometimes Lisa and I go to my sister's for holidays. Mom is there, and she's polite, but she's never acknowledged Lisa as my wife. It is what it is, I guess. I hate that phrase, but there you go."

Sally mulled over the situation. This was shaky ground for her. She'd never had a friend in this position, but she decided to move on as though Tanelsa and Lisa were any heterosexual couple. After all, conflicts about having kids happened in straight relationships, too. Look at her. "Well, that truly sucks. But, and I apologize if I'm being dense, how does this impact you and Lisa having a baby?"

"It's background." Tanelsa ran her hands through her hair. "Like any couple, Lisa and I had The Talk before our marriage about the big ticket items. Those would be money and kids. Because that's smart, right?"

Sally was pretty sure it was still true that squabbles in those two areas led to a large number of divorces, and she nodded.

"At the time, we agreed. No kids. We were both professionals. We loved our jobs, and raising a family didn't fit well into either career path. Plus, although it's getting better, kids from same-sex parents still get a lot of crap. And in my case, I didn't have a great opinion of the world even if that weren't true. I mean, look at what we deal with every day in court. Is this a world where I want to raise a child? Hell no."

Now this, Sally could relate to, since it was almost exactly her reason for not wanting to have a family. She loved her job. She had just enough time to take care of a dog, and even that required a change in her living arrangements. Where in her day would she be able to give a baby the attention she deserved? Putting a child in daycare for eight or more hours a day, especially considering her work schedule and Jim's, wasn't fair, nor was continually relying on relatives. No, if a couple didn't have time to devote to parenting, wasn't the responsible decision to choose not to have kids?

And Tanelsa was right. Society wasn't entirely made up of muggers, sex offenders, and drug dealers. But Sally saw too much of that side of life to think being a parent was a good idea. Maddie Tilgher wasn't a relative, and Sally believed what happened to her was sickening. How would Sally react if it was her daughter found like that? "Sounds like you agreed, at least at the time," Sally said. "What happened?"

"Lisa turned thirty-five." Tanelsa scowled. "All of a sudden, she thinks she's missing out on a vital piece of womanhood. She's approaching mid-life, and I think she's freaking out and believes having a baby would help."

"This may be a personal question, but who would carry this kid? I mean, who would get pregnant?"

"Oh, she's willing to do that."

"Then she's the one who'd give up her career?"

"That's the best part." Tanelsa looked at the ceiling. "She says she'd go back to work because we need both incomes. Since she travels for her job, and I don't, I could be the person responsible for childcare while she's away."

She finally looked at Sally. "Can you just imagine? Sorry, Sally. I can't make that court appointment this afternoon. I have to pick up Janie from daycare. Oops, can't come into the office today. Janie's got a fever." Her face flushed, and her voice carried an unmistakable note of bitterness. "As though *my* career is more flexible or family-friendly or...whatever."

Something else Sally could relate to. Who would stay home when her child was sick? She could hardly ask Jim not to investigate a crime or testify in court so he could watch the baby, nor could she tell a client they'd have to postpone a hearing because she had to stay home with her son or daughter. There were plenty of lawyers who made it work, but Sally was quite sure she didn't have the patience to be one of them. "That's what you've been arguing about."

Tanelsa nodded. "Lisa came home Friday afternoon from a doctor's appointment with a sheaf of pamphlets about IVF and said she wanted to start as soon as possible. We've been bickering all weekend. It's gotten so bad, last night I slept in the guest room."

Sally looked at the red-spotted pages in front of her. What was their schedule like this week? She pulled up her calendar on the computer. Two court appearances, two meetings with the District Attorney's office, and not much else. "T, if you want to take some time off and get a handle on this, I've got things covered here. Unless Noah Freeman gets arrested today, I don't expect to have to do a lot. You need to get on the same page with Lisa."

"That is exactly what I *don't* want to do, Sally. I'm an equal partner in this firm. That means I do my share of the work."

"Hey, everybody has personal emergencies. Even when you don't have kids. I said earlier, I'm not just your partner. I'm your friend. If you need some time off, I'll be okay."

Tanelsa cocked her head. "And if Noah Freeman *is* arrested?"

Sally lowered her gaze to the marked-up pages on her desk. "I'll figure it out."

Chapter Thirty-Two

After going through the wireless carrier records, Duncan and Cavendish came up with a plan of attack. They needed to interview Will Brackin, Don Rearick and Zach Fabery. They also needed to find out who the hell Robert Montgomery was. The order of events was up for debate.

Cavendish swept up the loose paper on her desk. "That last one is going to be the toughest task."

"Don't remind me." Duncan's phone rang. "Yeah, Andy."

"I got the preliminary report on the contents of the Tilgher girl's phone. You want me to email it?"

"Please." He hung up and looked at Cavendish. "We'll have the information from Maddie's phone shortly."

It took five minutes for the report to arrive. Duncan printed it as soon as it did. Then he picked up the paper and went back to his desk. "You ready to do this?"

"Yup." Cavendish picked up a pen. "Shoot."

"Maddie's contacts include a host of people, but not Atwiler, Brackin, or Fabery."

"I'm not surprised about the first two. Especially if she was trying to keep her extracurricular activities secret. Are we sure she didn't have a second phone?"

"Not that we've found. I asked the Pittsburgh police to search her home, and they didn't find one either. The Pittsburgh folks asked her parents, but given that they didn't know anything about Laurel Highlands

Entertainment's real business, it's not surprising they didn't produce one."

Cavendish circled the numbers. "Now Fabery, she might have had a contact for. They did date."

"But not for long." Duncan scanned the pages. "She may well have had one, but deleted it after the breakup. We'd have to get a court order for her cloud backups, if they exist, to find out. I'm not sure it's that important."

"Hmm, you might be right. No contact for Robert Montgomery?"

"Nope."

"That doesn't make any sense to me."

He looked up. "Why do you say that?"

"She called that number a lot, comparatively speaking, over the last few months." She counted. "At least a dozen times. Some of the conversations went on for quite a while. Now, if you only call someone once or twice, I can see not putting them in your phone. But this often? Why keep dialing the number?"

"She could have kept going back to her recent call list."

"Possible, but I still think there'd be a name. This is a frequent contact. She'd want to know at a glance who it was if there was an incoming call or text. She'd want to make that number a favorite, not scroll through a list of past calls." Cavendish shook out her hair and redid her bun.

Duncan picked up his phone. "Hold on." He dialed the number for the Tilghers, and Mrs. Tilgher answered. She had never heard the name Robert Montgomery. Duncan re-examined the report. "There isn't anybody in her Contact list with an Ohio area code."

"What about her text history on the device?"

He flipped pages. "Nothing to that number. Does that not match the phone company records?"

She checked. "Looks like only phone calls, no texts. Could be another situation where Maddie didn't want a written record." She looked up. "Should we call Montgomery now? See what he says."

"Not yet. Let's see what we can find on him. I hate flying blind." He ran his finger down the page. "No contact for Sue Hepworth, either."

"That one I can believe. They weren't exactly best friends."

"But Maddie did call her."

"Oh yeah. Again, only phone calls, no texts." Cavendish set aside the phone records. "What's in her email app?"

Duncan went to the relevant section. "She only had her school and personal email delivered to her phone. Not the address she used to communicate with Atwiler. There's nothing on the phone that we didn't already get from the laptop."

"All right. Look at the Buzz app."

Duncan searched until he found the information he wanted. "Again, this pretty much matches what we saw on the computer. From what I can tell, the app makes it easier to connect and swipe, but doesn't offer any additional messaging functionality."

"So much for that." She leaned back. "What about other apps, especially ones that do messages?"

He grabbed a highlighter and circled a section. "She had a couple. Looks like she used them with friends. But this one here, this seems to be how she communicated with Atwiler. It's one of those apps where the message is supposedly deleted after you view it, but there are several unread ones here. All of them are the same theme. Atwiler offered her another photo job, at a higher rate. Then there's a few more where he threatened to blackball her or worse if she tried a smear campaign. She must have been able to see a preview for these. I can't believe she didn't check for days."

"She may have gotten a notification, seen the message was from him, and ignored it. What I can't understand is why she didn't get rid of the app."

"Me neither, unless she kept it so she could take a screenshot of incoming messages and keep them for some future use." He read. "He messaged her the day of the murder."

"What'd he say?"

Duncan read. "We'll talk after the shoot, but I suggest you keep your nose out of things that don't concern you. Where I get money for my business is my, well, business." He looked up.

"Mr. Atwiler didn't mention that before. Think that could be related to whatever the photographer was talking about?"

He looked at his watch. "We'll ask him this afternoon."

Cavendish stood and stretched. "Is that all?"

Duncan paged through the report. "We were right about Fabery messaging her in ways other than text. There's a chat history on one of her social media apps. Back and forth about how she doesn't think it'll work, him begging, her telling him to get lost. His last message is 'I'm desperate here. One more chance, that's all I want.' But that was two months ago. Nothing after that. He either gave up, or she blocked him."

"While that's not great, it doesn't scream 'murder' at me either. More like he's pathetic." She twisted once more and sat. "That thing isn't exactly a treasure trove."

Duncan had to agree. There weren't any incriminating messages, no explosive reveals in the apps. Had Maddie been careful enough to delete anything she wanted to keep secret? This was just the preliminary report, Andy had said. Maybe he'd have more once he retrieved any information he could from servers that didn't exist on the phone. Just then, Duncan's computer sounded the arrival of another email. It was from Andy. Then another. Each one contained a series of photo attachments. Duncan opened the first set. *These were in albums in her photos*, Andy had written. "Cavendish, look at this. She did take pictures."

She got up and rounded the desk. "Well, hot damn."

The first set of photos was a collection of screen captures from the messaging app, the one where messages were supposedly deleted. Several were from Atwiler, clearly responses to threats from Maddie. "Do it, and I'll wipe the floor with you," was the nicest.

"I'd say that went a little beyond disagreeing," said Cavendish. "What's in the others?"

He opened the second email. It was another set of screen grabs, this time from Brackin. Fewer, but pointed. "Stop being a baby. It didn't hurt that much," Duncan read. "You can't call it rape or assault if it was a job, sweetheart."

"Lovely," Cavendish murmured. "He sounds like a real peach to work with."

"Agreed, but look at this one." He pointed. "Janice is a liar. I had nothing to do with her, whatever she says. And she's probably lying about her kid, too."

"Holy hell." Cavendish exhaled, the words barely audible.

There might not be a record of it anywhere, but Maddie had not only found Janice Hepworth, she'd talked to her.

* * *

Tanelsa shrugged into her coat. "Are you sure you'll be okay?"

"I'm positive," Sally said. "I got a call earlier that this afternoon's court appearance has been postponed. You've got most of the brief for tomorrow's hearing done, and we don't meet with the DA until Thursday morning. Go home."

Tanelsa picked up her purse and briefcase. "I don't like leaving you like this."

"Tanelsa, I don't know much about kids or same-sex relationship challenges. But I do know this." Sally leaned on her chair. "If you and Lisa don't hash this out and come to an agreement, it'll eat away at your marriage. Where's Lisa?"

"At the apartment. She doesn't leave for her next trip until Monday. She's doing a little virtual work before that."

"Then go to her." Sally had learned the hard way about the importance of open communication. She and Jim had survived, but she didn't want to see anyone else go through the same thing, not if she had the power to help.

"If you insist." Tanelsa took a couple steps toward the door. "But if you need me, call, promise?"

"I promise." Sally made a shooing motion. "Now get out of here."

As soon as her partner left, Sally refreshed her coffee and returned to her desk. First up was a search of the DMV database. The vanity plate HotStuf would be easy to track. Sure enough, a minute later, Sally had the name and address of the registered owner, Will Brackin of Mount Lebanon. Another minute of searching yielded his phone number.

Sally subscribed to Tracers, TLO, the service from Transunion, and IRBsearch, the same databases that were used by private investigators, skip tracers, and bail bondsmen, which provided a wealth of information on people, including criminal history. She typed in William Brackin and sipped while she waited for the computer to return results.

"Gotcha," she said as the records popped up on the screen. Brackin's rap sheet was short, but interesting. Simple assault, harassment, and a possession with intent to deliver drugs charge. The last one had been dropped.

Next, she searched for Janice Hepworth's history. Hers was much longer, although the charges were not as serious, mostly for possession without intent. Except one. She'd served time on a PWID charge for heroin.

Sally went back to Brackin's record. The charge that had been dropped was also for heroin possession and had occurred on the exact same day and time as Janice's.

What were the odds?

Sally wrote the names on her legal pad and drew a line between them. Over the line she wrote *Connected?* Then she put Maddie's name under Janice's with another line. Those two were definitely tied together. As an afterthought, she wrote *Noah* with lines to both Janice and Maddie.

She sat back. Could Will Brackin have known Janice Hepworth? It sure seemed that it was possible, at least on the surface.

Sally picked up her phone. After a moment's hesitation, she called Aislyn McAllister.

"Hey, Sally, what's up?"

"I need clarification on a hypothetical situation."

Aislyn's voice turned suspicious. "How hypothetical?"

"Very. This has absolutely nothing to do with a case I'm handling or an open investigation in the PSP. It's more a question of procedure."

"Why don't you call Boss?"

Sally smiled at the younger trooper's nickname for Jim. "He's up to his armpits with a murder. I don't want to bother him." *I've done that enough already.*

"Okay, well, as long as you promise this has nothing to do with anything active, sure. What do you want to know?"

Sally breathed a small sigh of relief. "Here's the scenario. Person A hands a bag containing heroin to Person B. The bag has enough heroin to warrant a possession with intent to distribute charge. The two are arrested together. At the station, Person A claims to have no knowledge of the contents of the bag, a fact that is corroborated by Person B. Is that enough to get Person A's charge dropped?"

Aislyn mumbled over the line.

"I'm sorry? I didn't hear you."

"Nothing, just repeating the facts." Aislyn waited a moment. "The statement of Person A, that he was ignorant, wouldn't be enough. Even if Person B swears on a stack of Bibles that it was all her fault, that wouldn't get the charges dropped. There still would have been an investigation. I take it Person A got out of it somehow?"

"Yes."

"Well, someone, either the DA or Narcotics or another investigating party, would have to have come up with a reason not to go ahead and prosecute." The squawk of a radio sounded in the background. "Is that all? I gotta go."

"Yes, thank you." Sally set down her phone and studied her notes. How had Will Brackin gotten out of his charge?

Only one way to find out.

Chapter Thirty-Three

An hour later, Cavendish navigated the streets of Mount Lebanon. "I'd forgotten how nice the houses are up here."

Duncan gazed out of the passenger window, taking in the yards freckled with leaves, and houses behind stately trees which would provide great shade in the summer. "Which only makes me even more suspicious about how a single guy, who works as a freelance model, can afford to live here. This is the street."

She turned. "We're looking for 7629?"

"Should be up here on your left."

Brackin's house was not the biggest on the block, but hardly the smallest. Two pillars flanked the shiny black front door. The garage door was up, and the red Mustang was inside.

"Looks like he's home." Cavendish parked the unmarked Ford and shut off the engine. "Good cop, bad cop?" she asked as they walked toward the door.

"Bad cop, bad cop." Duncan knocked.

They didn't wait long. Brackin, dressed in black sweatpants and a Steelers jersey, opened the door. He held a bottle of sports drink and looked completely unfazed by the presence of two strangers on his front step. "Can I help you?"

Duncan held out his badge. "Are you Will Brackin?"

"In the flesh."

"We'd like to speak to you regarding a young woman named Maddie Tilgher."

"Who's she?"

Cavendish answered, voice stony. "Someone you worked with."

Brackin thought a moment, shrugged, and pushed the door open. "Come in."

There was a small entry space that was tiled, with a bench where visitors could sit and remove their shoes. A row of pegs on the wall held a couple of jackets, one leather and one a winter puffer style. A pair of boots was underneath the bench. "Do you want anything to drink?" Brackin asked.

"No, we're good." Duncan took in the decor. It was ultra-modern and undoubtedly pricey, all glass, chrome, and leather. He followed Brackin into a sitting room where a glossy black marble fireplace surround dominated the space. Cavendish followed.

Brackin flung himself on a black couch. "Have a seat."

"We'd rather stand," Cavendish said.

Brackin pushed his hair back, leaving it artfully tousled. "Who's this girl you claim I worked with?"

Duncan didn't buy the porn star's act. But he decided to play along for now. "This is her." He held out a photograph of Maddie.

"Oh, Suzie Nightingale. Yeah, I know her. Only worked with her once. What kind of trouble has she gotten herself into?"

"What makes you say that?" Cavendish took out a notepad.

The actor smirked. "Two state cops show up asking about her, she's in trouble."

Duncan crossed his arms. "When was the last time you saw her?"

"Beats me. Like I said, we only worked together the one time." Brackin gulped from his bottle.

"Don't you keep in contact with your coworkers?"

"Hell no. At least not ones I do a single job with."

Cavendish took up the questioning. "Would you say Maddie enjoyed the time you worked together?"

An expression of supreme arrogance marred Brackin's features. "Who wouldn't enjoy working with me? I mean, come on, I make this couch look good."

"Someone who didn't appreciate being raped in the name of acting, even if it was a porno," she replied, no expression on her face.

The words wiped the sneer from Brackin's face. "Who told you that?"

"No one," said Duncan. "We've seen your work."

"Whatever she said was a freaking lie," Brackin replied, voice low. "She was told the terms of the job. That little bitch has no right coming back now and accusing me of rape. She agreed to the sex. Period. It's hardly my problem if she doesn't like how I work."

The two troopers exchanged a look. Brackin talked about Maddie like he didn't know she was dead. Truth or another act? Duncan didn't enlighten him. "You said you haven't been in touch with her. At all. No interactions after that one job."

"Nope," Brackin said, voice flat.

"That's funny. See, there's a whole collection of screenshots showing you, and she had a rather heated conversation a month ago. I think it might have been a discussion of that work engagement."

"Prove it."

"I will, Mr. Brackin. Or rather, the DA will, if this ever comes to trial."

Brackin shot to his feet. "I didn't rape her."

"Who said rape?" Cavendish hooked her thumbs over her belt. "She's dead."

The actor's eyes widened a fraction. "What?"

"Murdered, as a matter of fact," Duncan added. "At the scene of another photo shoot for Laurel Highlands Entertainment. Are you still going to tell us you haven't talked to her?"

Brackin stepped back and ran a hand through his hair. This time, the result was not a stylized look. "I might have exchanged a few messages with her. Not texts. We don't use those. We're supposed to communicate via a specific app, so—"

"The messages disappear without leaving a record. Right." It never ceased to amaze Duncan how ignorant people could be about the internet. "She took pictures. Nothing on the web ever disappears. You should know that."

Brackin set his bottle on the glass-topped coffee table and paced. "Look," he said. "It was one lousy job. All right, I did know Suzie's real name. She was upset about that video. She accused me of sexually molesting her, and I said exactly what I told you. It was a job, end of story. She agreed to it, dammit!"

"Did she tell you to stop?" Cavendish's voice was scathing. "Because if she did, and you refused, it could be argued that it *was* rape, job or not."

Brackin muttered under his breath.

"Who's Janice?" Duncan asked.

The other man froze. "Who?"

"You talked about her with Maddie in your last conversation. You called Janice a liar. Who is she?"

Brackin averted his gaze. "Just a skank I knew once."

"It couldn't be Janice Hepworth, could it?"

"I don't know her last name."

Duncan looked at his partner, who maintained a stony expression. She didn't believe the porn actor any more than Duncan did. He decided to try a new line of questions. "You have an awfully nice house, Mr. Brackin. And an extremely expensive car. I find it hard to believe you can afford that on a freelancer's salary, even if you are in the porn industry."

Brackin studied the carpet. "I have investments. They've done pretty well."

Duncan pressed. "What kind of investments? Janice Hepworth has a history of drug arrests. Was she a runner for you? Maybe someone you used as a scapegoat? Janice took the heat when the cops showed up and allowed you to walk away?"

No response.

A thought occurred to Duncan. "How closely do you work with Barry Atwiler?"

Brackin hesitated. "I'm one of his actors. Sometimes I do photo shoots, but I'm more of an action guy."

"Are you a partner?"

Next to him, Cavendish tensed.

"A partner? Whatever makes you say that?" Brackin rolled his eyes.

Duncan spread his hands. "He needed money. You have money. All of a sudden, so does he. It makes me curious."

"I enjoy my work with Laurel Highlands, don't get me wrong. But it's not a good long-term money-making opportunity."

Cavendish shifted her stance. "When was the last time you talked to Janice, Mr. Brackin? Do you know where she's living these days?"

Brackin looked from Duncan to his partner. "I don't appreciate being made to feel like a suspect. Get out of my house."

"Why? We're just talking."

"Screw you, I know how it goes. I say out, you get out. Or arrest me, read me my rights, and I'll call my lawyer."

Duncan studied the man in front of him. Arrogant, yes, and definitely angry, but was that fear under the surface? "We're going. But I advise you to get that attorney ready. I've got a funny feeling you're going to need him."

The troopers left. Cavendish opened the driver's door, but didn't get in the car. "He knows the drill? That makes it sound like he's had visits from the cops before and more than once. What do you think?"

Duncan stared at the house. "I think we need to find Janice Hepworth. And get a warrant for Will Brackin's bank records."

Chapter Thirty-Four

At noon, Sally stopped working, got up from her desk, and stretched, feeling the bones in her back pop. After today, she'd need to book an appointment with a chiropractor to get all the kinks out of her neck and spine.

But at least now she had a somewhat decent overview of what had happened to Janice Hepworth, from her high school years, through Noah's birth, up until she disappeared. She had served her time and, when paroled, had gone to a rehab clinic outside Pittsburgh. After her parole was up, she must have left the city, maybe even southwestern Pennsylvania. This all would have been slightly less than ten years ago. Noah would have been barely middle-school age. Sue had long since left their childhood home. Their mother, Bernadette, had died. Sally wondered if Janice had attended the funeral or attempted to find her sister and her son.

Sally dialed Sue's number. "When was the last time you saw Janice? Or spoke to her?" she asked when Sue picked up.

"I didn't really talk to her after I left with Noah."

"Are you telling me you haven't seen or heard from her in fifteen years?"

Sue's exhaled breath over the phone was loud. "Well, no. We did speak briefly at Mom's grave once. I'd gone there to lay flowers on Mother's Day. This was maybe six or seven years ago. More than five, less than ten. Janice looked ill. She said she was clean and sober, but I had my doubts."

"Was Noah with you?"

"No, he was at a youth group event at our church."

"Did she ask about him?"

There was a long pause, and when Sue spoke, she sounded reluctant. "Yes. She asked how he was doing in school and if he was happy. I told her he was fine. She wanted to know if he ever talked about her, and I told her the truth, which was no. She said, 'I can't say I'm surprised. I wasn't exactly around when he was little.' Then she told me she was going away, said to take care of him, and I haven't seen or heard from her since. I swear."

"I believe you." Janice's rehab might have changed her and made her realize that Noah was better off with the mother he had known since babyhood, even if that woman wasn't his so-called "real" mom.

"Have you…have you heard anything else from the police? Are they going to charge Noah? You can't let that happen, Ms. Castle. All we have is each other." Sue's voice caught on the last sentence.

"I'm not privy to the details of the police investigation, but I'm not worried about an imminent arrest. I'll be in touch with you when I know more." Sally ended the call.

She returned to her desk and expanded her search, but to no avail. The Division of Vital Records did not have a death certificate for Janice Hepworth. None of the counties in the western half of the state had marriage certificates. Had she gone east to Philly, losing herself in the sprawling metropolitan area? Had she left Pennsylvania entirely?

Sally's gaze went back to Will Brackin's record. The timing of his arrest and Janice's bothered her. She made another phone call.

"Will Brackin."

"Mr. Brackin, my name is Sally Castle. I'm a defense attorney down in Fayette County. I'd like to speak to you regarding an old arrest of yours, a PWID charge from several years ago."

"What the hell? Why is everybody so interested in that non-event today?"

Her grip on the phone tightened. "I'm sorry, what are you talking about?"

"First the cops, now you."

Jim must be traveling the same, or a similar, path in his search for Janice Hepworth. "What I'm really hoping you can help me with is locating a missing woman."

He muttered, then said, "Fine. You can come to my house, and we'll talk."

Alone in a house with a potential murderer? No way. "Do you mind if we meet somewhere more public? A coffee shop or something?"

"Are you afraid of me?" He laughed, but it wasn't a sound that inspired mirth.

A frisson of fear went down Sally's back, but she kept her mouth shut.

"There's a Starbucks where we can meet." He gave the address. "When do you want to get together?"

Sally glanced at the clock. It was nearly twelve-thirty. "How about two-thirty this afternoon?" That should give her plenty of time to arrive early and claim the higher ground.

"See you then." He clicked off.

She swept up the paper, littering her desk. Evie had definitely heard the name Janice. The woman she'd seen fit Janice's age and general description. After so many years, what had happened to bring her back? And why would Maddie be involved?

* * *

Since Duncan and Cavendish were already in Pittsburgh, they decided to stop at Outdoor Adventurer in Shadyside and talk to Zach Fabery, Don Rearick, or both. Even in the middle of the day on Tuesday, the trendy business area of Walnut Street was jammed, all of the stores doing a brisk pre-Thanksgiving business. The third time Duncan stood aside to allow young people more engrossed in screens than their surroundings walk by, he uttered an uncharacteristic oath.

"What's got you so grouchy?" Cavendish asked.

"I hate the city," he replied through clenched teeth. "It's too crowded, too cluttered, and nobody watches where the hell they're going." He dodged yet another knot of millennials, phones in hand, bags on their arms, and taking up far more space on the sidewalk than they needed to.

Cavendish chuckled. "You're such a country boy. Here we are."

Outdoor Adventurer was hardly less crowded than the sidewalk. "Hi there." A chipper young woman in a fleece pullover with the store logo approached. "Can I help you find something?"

Duncan and Cavendish held out their badge wallets. Duncan slipped his back in his pocket. "Not something, someone."

"Who?"

"Zach Fabery." Cavendish put her badge away. "Or Don Rearick. If both of them are here, even better."

The sales associate, whose name tag read Emily, wilted a bit. "Mr. Rearick isn't here. What's this about?"

"We're not at liberty to give details." Duncan studied her. "We just have a couple questions."

Emily shot a glance at the back of the store. "Zach's not normally here. If you leave a number, I'll tell him you visited."

Duncan had not missed the giveaway look. Fabery was in the back office.

"Let me ask you something, Emily. Woman to woman." Cavendish took a step closer and lowered her voice. "What do you think of Zach?"

Emily's cheeks pinked. "Oh, I don't know. I mean, I guess he's okay." She lowered her gaze to the floor.

"That doesn't sound like a ringing endorsement."

"I shouldn't say anything."

"I understand. You don't want to get a co-worker in trouble. And my partner here, well, he's a guy, and he might not understand, right?"

Emily nodded.

Duncan took half a step away and tried to look nonchalant. *Since when am I not understanding?* He knew Cavendish was playing up to the younger woman, but her words still grated his nerves a bit.

Cavendish leaned in. "Emily, you can talk to me. I see this all the time. He makes you uncomfortable. Just a little bit, right? I promise, no one is gonna know you said anything. We're trying to get a read on Zach. We'd appreciate any help you can give us."

Duncan moved another step away, giving the women space to talk, but was still able to hear.

The young woman twisted her fingers and snuck a look around the showroom. "Zach's...he's kind of a dork with girls, if you know what I mean."

"No, not quite," Cavendish said.

"I think he's asked every girl here out at least three times, and that's the problem," Emily replied. "Some of us said no the first time because he's just not our type. Plus, dating a guy you work with? Awkward. I think Marla went out with him once. She said he was too intense. Like there aren't a thousand other girls in the city. But he's so pushy."

"Does he ever say or do anything that makes you feel threatened?"

"I shouldn't say anything."

Cavendish lowered her voice even more and injected a double-helping of the sympathetic tone she often used with female interviewees. "Emily, in my line of work, an answer like that means he has. If that's the case, you need to speak up before someone gets hurt."

Emily's gaze darted around the showroom. "I've never felt threatened." She bit her lip. "But definitely uncomfortable. I know Mr. Rearick has talked to him a couple times. And when Marla wouldn't go out with him again? Zach really lost it. He wasn't violent or anything, but he was way too upset for one date. Some of us," she hedged closer to Cavendish, "we wonder if he shouldn't be on meds. There's definitely something wrong with him."

"I see." Cavendish looked toward the back. "He's in the office, isn't he?"

Emily fidgeted. "I don't want him coming back to me."

"I'm not going to tell him we spoke." Cavendish looked at Duncan, nodded toward the back, and walked off.

Duncan followed, pausing only long enough to give Emily a reassuring smile. "Let me guess, it's my turn?" It made sense. She'd handled the hesitant young woman. Now it was time for guy to guy.

"I'll be right behind you."

They found Zach at a desk, working on what looked like a photo display. His laptop was attached to a large flat-screen monitor, and he dragged different pictures of happy-faced models in outdoor settings back and forth. "Look, I don't know who told you I was here, but I'm really busy. If I don't get this layout finished this afternoon, we aren't going to hit our milestone for the winter ad campaign." He didn't look up from the computer as he spoke.

"I'm pretty sure you can spare us some time," Duncan said.

"Who are you?"

"Troopers Duncan and Cavendish, Pennsylvania State Police."

That got the younger man's attention. "I didn't do anything."

"Now, that's a very interesting statement, Mr. Fabery." Duncan waved at the one chair in the office and indicated Cavendish should sit. "We didn't say you did. Do you have a guilty conscience?"

"That's not it." Fabery's cheeks flushed. "When the cops turn up at my job, what else am I supposed to think?"

"Do you know a young woman named Maddie Tilgher?"

"Yeah, we went out a couple of times. We met through Buzz. That's—"

"A dating app, we know. How many dates?"

"Um, three, maybe four? She...it didn't work." Fabery's voice was flat.

Duncan didn't move. "We've heard you didn't take it well. Is that true?"

"I was disappointed. I didn't think she gave me a good enough chance. But I guess that's how it goes."

"You kept messaging her. You sounded pretty desperate to keep things going."

"Talk to Maddie, okay? Yes, I tried to get her to change her mind, but she got awfully snotty at the end. She blocked my messages and my phone number. She cut me off without an explanation, and I spent good money on those dinners. We didn't go to Burger King."

"That'll be hard, seeing as she's dead." Duncan watched for the impact of the words.

The blood drained from Fabery's thin face. "She's...what...how...no way."

"Yes, way," said Cavendish from her corner.

The pallor of the young man's face wasn't feigned, and his shock struck Duncan as real. "When was the last time you spoke to Maddie?"

"I don't know." Fabery sat back. "September, maybe? I went to St. Vincent to see her when she got back to school. I thought maybe we could try again."

"What'd she say?"

210

The younger man's response was mumbled in embarrassment. "That if I ever showed up on campus again, she'd get security to haul me off." Then he looked up. "I don't know why she didn't tell me the truth. She'd found another guy. I saw him, big bunch of flowers in his hand, driving a flashy car. She should have said something and not made me feel like a loser."

Cavendish sat forward. "This other guy, what did he look like?"

Fabery blinked. "Tall, blond, I guess girls would find him handsome. He looked like a douche to me. I think Maddie must have known him from her job."

Brackin. Duncan snagged on the words. "You knew about her work?"

The flush crept back into Fabery's cheeks. "Yeah, I, uh, found out by accident. Look, I didn't care. But you'd think a girl in that business would be a little more relaxed, you know? That her standards wouldn't be so high. Of course, if she had guys like Mr. Fancy Car, I guess I didn't have a chance."

Out of the corner of his eye, Duncan saw Cavendish's lips thin into lines. He could guess what she was thinking, because he had the same thoughts. Just because a young woman worked in the sex industry didn't mean she deserved unwanted attention. "Then Maddie and this guy, they were friendly?"

"I don't know," Fabery said in a disinterested voice. "I left. That was the last time I saw or spoke to her."

"You never visited her at work? Picked her up afterward?"

"No. Like I said, I found out after she'd ditched me."

"How did it make you feel?" Cavendish sat back. "Being dumped for a guy like that? Or learning that the girl you liked was a porn model?"

"I didn't—" He caught himself. "I didn't care."

"One last question, Mr. Fabery," Duncan said. "Where were you last Wednesday?"

Fabery studied his desk calendar. "I was in the Laurel Highlands. I went to Ohiopyle, Seven Springs, and Hidden Valley. I was getting images for the winter social media ads."

"You were there all day?"

"Yes."

"When did you get back to Pittsburgh?"

Fabery looked confused. "I don't know. Later. I mean it had been dark for at least an hour, so what, seven? I didn't look at the time."

Cavendish dragged her finger up the wall. "Can anyone confirm that?"

Fabery stood, hands shaking. "Do I need to provide an alibi or something? I didn't kill her. If she'd rather sleep with some overly handsome jerk than date me, fine. Women, you're all the same." He looked at Cavendish and snorted. "Why do you always go after the losers? I'm healthy, I've got a good job, and I'm not a troll. Why do you all treat me like I'm crap?"

Duncan opened the office door. "Thanks for your time."

Cavendish strode out, but paused in the doorway. "You want more success with dating, Mr. Fabery? Here's a tip. Learn to read the room. No means no."

Chapter Thirty-Five

D uncan and Cavendish arrived back at headquarters just in time to see Clarence Jones, the Laurel Highlands Entertainment photographer, enter the Criminal Investigation department. "Mr. Jones, thank you for being cooperative and coming down," Duncan held out his hand. "Can we get you anything to drink?"

"Nah, I'm not thirsty." Jones held up his hands. "I expected to be scrubbing fingerprint ink off for days. Guess you guys have gone high-tech with the scanner. I thought the gadgety stuff was all on TV."

"We do have some toys." Duncan checked with the secretary to see what rooms were available. As he turned around, he saw Aislyn McAllister dressed in civvies. "What are you doing here?"

She held up a folder. "Came to see you, Boss. I think you should have this."

He held up a finger to Cavendish and faced McAllister to take the paper. "I'm about to conduct an interview. Can it wait, or can you tell me quickly?"

"You can do it later, but definitely make some time to read." She pointed. "Sally called me earlier asking some procedural questions. She said it was a hypothetical situation, but the scenario was a little too specific to be purely her imagination. I called in a favor and got some info. What you have in your hand concerns the arrest of one William Brackin for PWID, heroin. The charges were dropped. The DA decided there wasn't enough evidence to proceed to trial."

Duncan raised an eyebrow. He hadn't mentioned Brackin to his former trainee. "And?"

She gave a lopsided grin. "He was arrested in the company of a woman named Janice Hepworth. Same name as the missing boy from the day we found Maddie's body. Thought you'd be interested."

"I know this already."

"Ah, but what you hold is a first-hand account of the Pittsburgh patrol officer who made the collar. Do you know *that?*"

Not for the first time, he thought McAllister would have a hell of a career in the PSP if she kept up this level of work. "You did this on your day off?"

"Tommy-boy is working, and I had time to kill. Might as well make myself useful." She turned and walked away, wiggling her fingers in the air. "Toodles."

As much as Duncan wanted to sit down and read the file, he had to deal with Jones first. He entered the interview room, where Cavendish was getting the process rolling. "At thirteen-thirty-four, Trooper Duncan entered the room," she said for the benefit of the recording. "Mr. Jones and I just finished recording his name and address. He told me he's worked for Barry Atwiler for almost ten years."

"Is that right, Mr. Jones? Or should I call you Clarence?" Duncan asked.

The photographer winced. "I wish you wouldn't. My grandpap strong-armed my mother into naming me after him. Jones, or Jonesie, is fine."

"Got it." Duncan looked at the interview sheet. Clarence Arnold Jones. No wonder the man preferred to go by his last name. "You said you knew Maddie Tilgher. What was she like?"

Jones sat back, a smile tinged with sadness on his face. "She was a pistol. Smart, pretty, the whole package. We would talk during the shoot, so I knew all about how she was working for tuition money, her mother's illness, and she never planned to make a career out of porn. She was a business major, she said. Her experiences made her want to get involved with helping students understand finances so they could get the money they needed for college without going into too much debt or being forced to do what she'd had to do. She had a great sense of humor, too. I mean, the official pictures all have that sultry look, but I took a lot of goofy ones for her."

"Do you have them?" Cavendish held out a hand.

"Gave them all to her," Jones said, "except this one." He pulled a five-by-seven glossy out of his inside jacket pocket and slid it across the table. In it, Maddie, fully clothed, and Jones mugged for the camera, clearly enjoying themselves. They were outside, somewhere in the Laurel Highlands during the summer, trees in full leaf and bushes of mountain laurel in the background.

"You liked her." Cavendish pushed the picture back.

"Damn straight." Jones put the picture back in his pocket. "She was good people. You don't come across many like her in this business."

A thought occurred to Duncan. "What about the video shoot with her and Will Brackin? Did you do that?"

Jones's expression darkened. "I did, but I almost left. That asshole Brackin, he was overdoing it. If I've told Atwiler once to get rid of him, I've said it a dozen times. Brackin may be good-looking, but he's a classless jerk. It's like Brackin's got something on him. Atwiler, I mean."

Something worth fifty thousand dollars? "Why didn't you stop the shoot?"

"I tried." Jones licked his lips. "Atwiler told me to get behind the camera and shut my mouth, or he'd get another videographer on scene. I knew he would, so I stayed. At least if the situation got even worse, I'd be there to help Maddie. I tried to talk to her when we were done, but she brushed it off. I could tell she was upset. She only did one more video, even though Atwiler pressured her to get into that side of the business. And she wouldn't work with that jerkwad Brackin."

Cavendish leaned on the table. "We found a rough-cut video in her email. Who was that with?"

"Let me think." He paused. "Oh yeah, Tyler. He goes by the last name of Nighthawk. I don't know his real name. His style is a lot softer than Brackin's. He and Maddie talked about how she wanted to do it before the shoot. Fancy that, communicating with your co-star."

Cavendish tapped a pen on the table. "Do you think Brackin could have hurt her? I mean away from the, uh, professional scene."

"Like would he come to that cabin and strangle her?" Jones shook his head. "I want to say no. Not that he wouldn't do something in the heat of

215

the moment or in the course of a shoot. But there'd have to be something serious going on for him to drive out there and catch her alone."

Duncan thought again of the connection between Brackin and Janice Hepworth. What had Maddie said that made him call Janice a liar? "What was the argument between her and Atwiler?" Duncan asked.

Jones's answer was blunt. "Maddie wanted out. This was her senior year of college. She had enough cash for fall and spring tuition. Her contract expires this coming March. She wanted to use her escape clause before the holidays."

Cavendish sat back in her chair. "Atwiler didn't want to let her."

"Barry Atwiler is a cheap bastard. And mean to boot." Jones scowled. "He wasn't lying when he said Maddie's pictures were popular. He wanted to hang on to her until the last minute, and I wouldn't have put it past him to try and pressure her into signing another contract. He made a fair amount of money off her."

Duncan thought about the calendar. "Maddie insisted?"

"I told her to just wait it out. Another four months wouldn't make that much of a difference. Atwiler was talking about a big holiday-themed shoot, and she wasn't interested. Wanted to spend the time with her folks." Jones stared at the wall, then turned back to the troopers. "I told him to let her go. She'd done enough, and he didn't need her. But it was like trying to mediate between a rock and a brick wall. Neither of them wanted to listen."

Duncan sensed the man wasn't finished and waited.

Sure enough, Jones continued. "Technically, what Maddie wanted to do was perfectly legal, and yes, Atwiler was in the wrong. Violation of contract, as they say. If Maddie'd just gone ahead and canceled her contract, he'd have griped for a while, but really, there wasn't much he could do. But then she said she knew his secret, and he'd regret it if he stood in her way. She'd do her best to make sure no one would work for him. Well, he couldn't have that. He doesn't have much of a reputation in the business, but he'd go broke if he couldn't get talent." He paused. "He's going belly up now, you probably know that. I know he hasn't been able to pay people on time, including Maddie. Lots of the models were honked off about it. Maddie was just the most vocal. For Atwiler, it became less about keeping her and more about making her shut up."

Jones's story made Duncan want to see Brackin's financials more than ever. "What did Atwiler do?"

"Do? Nothing. Say? Well, that's different. He threatened to make sure everybody knew what Maddie'd been up to with him for the past two years. She said she didn't care. I think that was a lie, but she sure sold it. Atwiler told her to be careful. If she insisted on playing that game, he'd make her sorry." He looked at the troopers. "I don't think he meant anything physical. He's a coward. He talks big, but when it comes down to it, all he has are words. That day in the cabin? There was a big old wolf spider on the floor when we went in. Atwiler bolted. Maddie was the one who scooped it up and threw it outside. Now I ask you. Would a man who can't deal with a spider have the balls to strangle a girl?"

Maybe not, but Duncan wasn't going to say that. "What do you mean he *was* going broke?"

Jones leaned back and set one foot on the knee of the opposite leg. "He spent months cutting corners and saving pennies. Then, all of a sudden, he's flush with cash. Tells me to price out new equipment, says he's going to look into more exclusive locations. I said the equipment would cost, and he waved it off. When I asked where he got the money, he said he had a new investor who would foot the bill."

Cavendish leaned in. "Did he say who the investor was?"

"Nope. Quite honestly, I had a strong suspicion I didn't want to know, so I didn't ask too many questions."

"You thought it was illegal?"

The photographer thought a moment. "I wasn't sure it was entirely on the up and up. I figured it was best I stick to taking pictures and leave the business details to him. What do they call it? Plausible deniability."

Duncan made a note. "The day of the shoot, who was there?"

"Maddie, of course." Jones counted off on his fingers. "Me, Atwiler, and the girl who was there the night you came to the office. Gemma. She's props, costumes, such as they are, and a general gofer."

And the owner of the last set of fingerprints, Duncan surmised. He shared a look with Cavendish.

"Who left first?" she asked. "After the shoot?"

"Gemma," Jones replied. "She left before we were done, since the last few shots were just Maddie nude on the cot. Atwiler did a bum's rush as soon as things were finished. These digital kits don't take as long to break down, so I offered to drive Maddie back, but she said she was meeting someone nearby and she'd get a ride to school. When I left, she was texting."

Meeting someone? Duncan straightened in his seat. "Did she say who?"

"Naw. I figured it was a friend. She was only half-dressed. It must have been someone she was comfortable seeing."

"Meaning, while she was in her underwear."

Jones blinked in confusion. "Don't know what you're talking about. She had jeans and a shirt on when I left, although the shirt wasn't buttoned up yet."

The two troopers exchanged a wordless communication. Maddie had been undressed when she was found. Was that the killer's work? Why?

"You said she was sending texts," Cavendish broke in. "I don't suppose she said who?"

"No idea. But it must have been some exchange because Maddie's thumbs were flying." Jones paused. "Look, Barry Atwiler is a weasel. But I swear, Maddie was alive and breathing when he left. I suppose he coulda doubled back, but he seemed pretty keen to get out. Is that all?"

"One more question," Cavendish said. "When you left the cabin, did you see anyone else in the vicinity?"

Jones frowned in thought. "No, no, I'm pretty sure no one was around. Just us."

Duncan held out his hand. "Thank you again, Mr. Jones. We appreciate your cooperation."

Cavendish spoke to the recorder. "Interview concluded at fourteen-thirty-three."

Chapter Thirty-Six

Sally sat in the Starbucks where Will Brackin had agreed to meet and looked at the clock on the wall, which read two-forty-five. He was fifteen minutes late. According to Google Maps, the coffee shop wasn't that far from his house, not enough that he could be caught in traffic. Where was he?

It was not impossible that he'd decided to blow her off. Hardly worth getting mad over. If that was the case, she'd be a little miffed, especially considering she'd driven over an hour to get there, but based on everything she knew, Will didn't have a great character. She decided she'd wait until three and then cruise by his house. If his car was in the garage, she'd know he was home and, for whatever reason, had changed his mind about the meeting. What she'd do next, she wasn't sure. Stomping up to the door, ringing the bell, and demanding he talk to her was not in the cards.

At the top of the hour, Sally stood, shouldered her purse, and left. She got in her Camry and drove to the address she had for Brackin. Even from half a block away, she saw flashing red and blue lights. Was that why he hadn't shown? Could he not get around the knot of official vehicles clogging the street? But if that was the case, why hadn't he called?

But as Sally got closer, she realized the police cars weren't merely blocking his driveway. They were in it, along with a white van marked with the logo for the Allegheny County Medical Examiner's office. *Holy shit.*

She pulled her Camry to the side of the street across from the house and parked. She checked for traffic, then hurried across. "Excuse me," she said to a man in a Tyvek bunny suit. "Who's in charge here?"

"Detectives Mason and Billingsley," he said. "Who are you?"

She took out a business card and handed it over. "Could you let one of them know I'm here? I'd like to speak to them, please."

The CS tech took the card and went inside. A minute or so later, a tall Black man in a suit came out of the front door and looked around. When he spotted Sally, he crossed the yard. "Detective Carl Billingsley," he said, holding out his hand. "Are you Ms. Sally Castle?"

"Yes. I had a meeting scheduled for earlier this afternoon with the man who lives here. When he didn't show, I came over. What happened?"

The detective hesitated. "Mr. Brackin is dead." He took out a notepad and pen and clicked the latter. "What were you seeing him about?"

"Can you tell me if he died of natural causes, or was it something else?"

Billingsley eyed her. "He was murdered. Someone hit him in the back of the head with a brass fireplace poker."

Sally stepped back and studied the house. It was pricey, she could tell that much. All of the houses on the block had to be in the six-figure range, if not higher. Will Brackin had been an actor for a two-bit porn operation. What else had he been into? She thought of that arrest for heroin possession. The drug trade would pay for all of this and the red Mustang she could see in the garage. He'd been killed hours after she called about Janice Hepworth. That couldn't be a coincidence.

She realized the detective was talking. "I'm sorry, I zoned out. What did you say?"

"I asked why you were getting together with the victim?"

"It's about a client of mine. Without going into specifics, I believe Mr. Brackin may have information regarding the young man's biological mother. She's been missing for some years, and I'm trying to locate her."

"What's her name?"

She paused. "Janice Hepworth. According to her criminal record, she was arrested in Pittsburgh for possession of heroin with intent to sell. There is a similar charge on Mr. Brackin's history, although it was dropped. The two events occurred so close together, I wondered if there was a connection."

Billingsley wrote this down. "Why does that affect your client?"

"I'm sorry, Detective. I can't say more without violating attorney-client privilege."

"Of course." Billingsley's dark eyes held her in place. "Had you ever met Mr. Brackin before?"

"No. We spoke on the phone this morning. That was the first time I'd talked to him."

"What else do you know about him?"

Even if the two Mount Lebanon detectives didn't know now, they would soon. "He calls himself a freelance model and actor, but he does a lot of work with an outfit called Laurel Highlands Entertainment. They make pornography, videos, and pictures. After seeing all this?" Sally gestured at the house, garage, and car. "I'm no dummy, Detective. I'm sure he was into something else. Given his past history, probably something drug-related. But that's speculation on my part. I have no proof."

"Hmm." Billingsley narrowed his eyes. "And aside from a possible connection with Janice Hepworth, does Mr. Brackin have any relationship with your client?"

Was he connected to Noah? How? Yes, he may have known Janice, but was there something else? Sally didn't know, but to be safe, she couldn't say anything. "I'm sorry, Detective—"

"I know, I know." His lips puckered, like he'd bitten a lemon. "Attorney-client privilege."

* * *

After the interview with Jones, Cavendish offered to run out for sandwiches. Duncan asked for a turkey and Swiss on marble rye and went back to his desk.

Maddie had been in her underwear when she died. Given what he'd learned and what Jones had said, it was unlikely she would have stripped for her soon-to-be-ex boss. But if that was the case, who undressed her? No way had she hung out in the cabin for hours so scantily dressed on her own volition. She'd told Jones she was meeting someone. Her killer? No, that didn't make sense. Except for Noah, Maddie didn't trust anyone on the list of suspects. Duncan believed her relationship with Noah had been platonic. Which meant if Maddie had taken her clothes off again, she'd been with someone she felt comfortable with.

Duncan wasn't sure of much, but he was confident Maddie would not have chosen that ramshackle cabin for a date.

Wait. Jones said Maddie had been texting. Duncan pawed through the papers on his desk until he found what he was looking for. But there was no record of a text message sent from Maddie's phone on Wednesday evening. In fact, there were no records after one o'clock that afternoon, period. "Son of a bitch," he said.

At that moment, Cavendish walked up and dropped a paper bag on his desk. "What?"

He told her about the phone company records. "But Jones swears she was texting."

Cavendish unwrapped her sandwich. "Depending on the type of message, it might have been sent as data. Those wouldn't show on a phone bill."

"What the hell are you talking about? A text is a text."

"You see—" Cavendish broke off. "All you need to know is that SMS messages are recorded by the phone company. Data messages aren't. Have you checked the laptop?"

"The phone and laptop were synced. I'm sure it's gone."

"If I delete a data message conversation from my phone, it doesn't automatically delete it from my computer." She took a bite. "Maybe Maddie's is the same."

Duncan ignored the fact his partner spoke while she chewed and shuffled around until he found the laptop records. "Got it. Between Monday and Wednesday of last week, there are a few messages to the number we now know belongs to Robert Montgomery. No contact information on the computer, either. Just the number."

"That makes sense. Contacts deleted from one place would be removed from the other. What do the messages say?"

"The first three are nothing, just 'I'll call you tonight' or stuff like that.

But this last one is interesting." He read. "Meet me Friday on the road near Dunlap Creek Lake and I'll take you to Noah. Don't worry, he'll love you." He looked up. "And a few crossed fingers and heart emojis after that. That sounds like she was talking to Janice. Who else would Maddie be introducing Noah to?"

Cavendish licked mayonnaise from her finger. "Maybe this Robert Montgomery character is Noah's father."

"No, his father is Todd Freeman."

"Could be he changed his name and is back in the area and wants to reconnect with his son."

Duncan drummed his fingers on his desk. "I think it's time we gave Mr. Montgomery a call."

"Want me to do it?"

His phone buzzed. "Hold on a second." He checked and saw a text from his dad. *Arrived early, see you at your place for dinner.* He made a note to call or text Sally to let her know. If she walked into his house tonight and saw his parents there ahead of schedule, she'd feel ambushed.

"Problem?" Cavendish asked.

"It's my mom and dad. They came for Thanksgiving and got in earlier than planned."

"Do you have to go pick them up at the airport or something?"

"No, they planned to get a rental car before. Dad didn't say anything about needing a ride." He picked up the file from McAllister. "This is Brackin's arrest record, that heroin charge that was dropped." He skimmed through the pages. "The DA declined to prosecute. Not enough evidence." He slapped the folder down and pushed it over to Cavendish. "Look who he was arrested with."

She held her sandwich with one hand, a gob of egg salad threatening to fall out. "Janice Hepworth."

"Give me that Ohio number." Duncan picked up his phone.

Cavendish read it off, and he dialed. After several rings, the call went to voicemail. "Mr. Montgomery, this is Trooper Jim Duncan of the Pennsylvania State Police. I need you to call me on a matter of some urgency."

He rattled off his number and hung up. "I'm calling Brackin. He's gonna talk to us, and I don't care if it's with his lawyer."

After three rings, a woman answered Brackin's phone. "Who is this?"

The voice startled Duncan into silence for a moment. Then he said, "Who is *this*?"

"I asked first."

"My name is Jim Duncan. I'm a trooper with the Pennsylvania State Police Criminal Investigation section. I'm calling to speak to Will Brackin. Is he there?"

"Oh, he's here all right," the woman's voice drawled. "Trooper Duncan, this is Detective Felicia Mason from the Mount Lebanon police. I'm sorry to tell you, but Mr. Brackin is dead."

"Dead, how? Natural causes, drug overdose, suicide?"

"None of the above." There was a beat. "Brass-handled fireplace poker to the back of the head. We're still doing our canvass, but so far, no leads. No sign of forced entry into the house, either. Why did you want to talk to Mr. Brackin?"

"I needed to talk to him about a woman he was arrested with ten years ago. Her name is Janice Hepworth."

"Hold on." Mason covered the phone and spoke to someone, presumably her partner. "Funny thing. A woman was here earlier, wanting to talk to the victim about her. Who is she? Janice, I mean."

It had to be Sally. What was she doing at Brackin's? "She's connected to a murder I'm investigating down here in Fayette County."

"Well, now. Since Ms. Hepworth's name has come up in relation to two murders, I think I'd really like to talk to her as well. Where is she?"

"That's the question." Duncan agreed to let Mason know if he found Janice and hung up. "Dial Montgomery's number again."

Cavendish complied. She put her phone on speaker and set it down so both of them could listen.

Just as the phone would have gone to voice mail, a woman picked up. "Hello? Who is this?" Her voice was mellow, but reserved.

Duncan looked at his partner, who pointed at herself. "This is Trooper

Jenny Cavendish with the Pennsylvania State Police. Is this Mrs. Robert Montgomery?"

"Yes. I'm at a loss as to why you're calling me, though."

"Mrs. Montgomery, your number, or rather your husband's number, is listed multiple times in the phone records of a murder victim in a case currently under investigation. Is this your phone or your husband's?"

"It's mine. He keeps the records in his name for privacy reasons. Can you tell me what the victim's name is?"

"A young woman by the name of Maddie Tilgher."

Silence, then a soft exhalation. "That's why she didn't show."

Duncan's heart leaped. He grabbed a paper and wrote *Ask her first name* and handed it to Cavendish.

She nodded. "Mrs. Montgomery, what is your first name?"

Again, there was no answer. If he hadn't heard breathing, Duncan would've sworn the woman had hung up.

"Mrs. Montgomery, are you still there?" Cavendish asked.

"Yes. I was thinking about poor Maddie. I knew her. I was going to meet her. You see," she took a deep breath, "my name used to be Janice Hepworth."

Chapter Thirty-Seven

Sally drove back to Fayette County in a fog. What did she know? Will Brackin was out of the picture. Well, maybe. It could be he killed Maddie, and someone else, for unrelated reasons, killed him. That house and car, he had to be involved with some kind of illegal racket. With his history, drugs made perfect sense. He wasn't some white-collar accountant involved with embezzlement or some other kind of corporate crime.

If that was the case, and he'd been killed over a bad deal, his death didn't concern her or Noah's situation. It was still frustrating, though. One possible avenue of finding Janice Hepworth was closed, and she'd been so sure Will would have been able to tell her something.

Why did it matter so much? She'd been hired to defend Noah from any murder charges that might be made in the death of Maddie Tilgher. Finding Janice had nothing to do with that, did it? Sally's job was to make sure Noah's rights were protected if he ended up in police custody. And although so much was still a black hole, she was quite certain the autistic young man was not a murderer.

Was it because she wanted to see a mother and son reunited? Or at least she could let the son know what happened to his mom? But he didn't seem to care. Sue was his mother, the one who'd taken him to doctor visits, nursed him through any childhood illness, supported him through school, and put him at the center of her life. He didn't seem to be bothered by Janice's absence, so why should Sally worry?

Except for the niggling instinct that told her Sue had not been entirely honest. Sally believed she'd cared for her infant nephew and taken him from a drug-addicted mother who was in no state to be responsible for him. Janice's criminal history spoke for itself. But didn't people change? Didn't a mother deserve to know her son?

Liz Jackson's words rang in Sally's mind. "Ms. Hepworth is always worried." Mothers did that. It was their job. God knew Sally had seen Noreen fuss over her kids enough. And yet, Sally could see a difference. At least she thought she did. Noreen let her kids be kids. She might intervene to keep them from serious injury, but little hurts, small fights with classmates? She stayed out of those. And she didn't try to control who they saw and when. It didn't sound like Sue had acted the same way.

The hands-free phone system in the car rang, interrupting her thoughts. The number on the screen was Noreen's. "Yeah, Reen. What's up?"

"I need a favor. Eddie's running a fever, and I have to take him to urgent care. Craig is still out of town. Can you come watch Amanda and Tim for me?"

"Sorry. I would, but I'm still working."

"Come on, Sally. I could use the help. Can't you forward your calls or something and work from here?"

"I'm not even in Uniontown, and it would take me at least an hour to get to your house. I'm sure you don't want to wait that long. Also, I'm on my way to meet with my client's mother. Maybe you can ask Jonathon." Their older brother was not only closer, but his wife would be more than happy to take Noreen's kids because they could play with their two.

"I did. He has an office dinner tonight, and his kids are already with a sitter. And please don't ask me to call Mom. I already have and got an earful about how she's not unpaid childcare." She sighed. "I'll have to take all three of them. You know, kids don't only get sick when it's convenient. Sometimes work has to wait." Noreen hung up.

Sally pushed the "end" button on her steering wheel. "This is why I don't want kids." She was too attached to her life, her independence. It wasn't just her job. She loved the ability to go where she wanted when she wanted. She had a dog now, but kenneling Pixel was simply a part of the budget.

Children put restrictions around all that, ones Sally didn't want to deal with. If she got sick, she could crawl back into bed guilt-free.

No, she knew her limits. Caring for an animal was about all she felt qualified to do.

She loved her nieces and nephews, she truly did. Could she have made helping Noreen work out? Possibly. She could have called Sue or met with her first thing tomorrow. But ever since Sally had opened her own practice, these kinds of calls from Noreen had become more frequent. She had to draw the line somewhere, didn't she?

Then again, if Sally didn't want offspring of her own, why did she feel so damn maternal toward Noah?

Maddie appeared to have gone to a lot of trouble to find Janice and reunite mother and son. Why?

Sally headed to Sue's house. Her brown Ford was in the driveway when Sally arrived shortly after four-thirty. The car was in desperate need of a wash. As she walked past, she heard the faint ticking of the engine. The Ford had been driven recently. Most likely, Sue had just gotten home from picking up Noah.

Sally rang the doorbell, and a flustered Sue answered. "Oh, Ms. Castle, I wasn't expecting you."

"May I come in? I won't stay long."

Sue glanced over her shoulder. "I guess. Come on back." She pushed the door open and immediately headed for the kitchen.

The house was silent. "Where's Noah? Out for a walk or something?" Sally asked as she set her purse down on the kitchen island.

"Oh, he's still at the center. I won't leave to pick him up for another half an hour." Sue's hair straggled over her forehead, and she pushed it back.

"You look a bit overworked." Sally reached toward her.

The other woman's shoulders twitched. "It's nothing. Just work stuff. I'd offer you something to drink, but as I said, I'm leaving soon to pick up Noah. It's been a long day. I think I'll see if he wants to go out for pizza. I sure hope so because I don't feel much like cooking." She grimaced.

"Work giving you problems?"

228

"Yeah, it's…just one of those things. A big end-of-year deadline is coming and people are trying to get everything they should have done in June completed before December. I've been staring at my computer screen all day."

Yet the car engine had been warm. At least Sally was sure she'd heard the sound of it cooling. "The reason I stopped was to ask you about Janice."

"What about her?"

"As I'm working on what a defense might be for Noah, I've learned Maddie had spent a lot of time looking for her. In fact, I'm pretty sure they were in contact."

Sue's gaze turned wary. "What makes you say that?"

"Maddie's roommate at college saw her with a brown-haired woman, and Evie, that's the roommate's name, is pretty sure Maddie called the woman Janice." Sally looked at Sue, who definitely had the air of a hunted animal about her. "Your sister had brown hair, right?"

"When it was natural, yes. But she was always dying it, mostly crazy colors, sometimes pure black." Sue scoffed. "Why would Maddie be trying to find a drug addict? She had no business prying into our lives."

"You're very sure Janice is still an addict, aren't you?"

"I know my sister, Ms. Castle." The nervousness was still there, but a tone of disgust had entered Sue's voice. "Leopards don't change their spots."

Sally thought a moment, then gambled. "Ms. Hepworth, you've talked to your sister recently, haven't you? Did she say she wanted to see Noah? Are you worried she'll take him away from you? I can tell something is bothering you beyond what you told me yesterday."

"As if." Sue turned away. "Noah doesn't even know Janice. She's nothing to him. If she turned up right now, he wouldn't say two words to her." She faced Sally. "I told you, I'm the only mother he's ever known and the only one that matters. Tell me, Ms. Castle, do you have kids?"

"No."

"Then you don't know what I'm talking about. A mother, a good mother, sacrifices everything for her children. Whether they're of her body or not. Tell me, do you think you could do that? Put aside everything for their sake?"

Sally thought of the call from Noreen and how Sally had chosen to put her job first. She couldn't make that sacrifice.

Chapter Thirty-Eight

The sun was low in the sky when Sally pulled into Jim's driveway. The chill air was dry with the dusty scent of fallen leaves, which crackled underfoot as she made her way to the front. Odd that she didn't hear the dogs.

Inside, she kicked off her shoes on the mat by the door and unbuttoned her coat. "I'm here."

Pixel and Rizzo raced out of the kitchen to greet her. But as soon as they failed to find treats, they scampered back to where they'd come from.

Sally breathed deeply. Fresh bread and stew? No wonder the dogs had abandoned her.

Jim appeared in the doorway. "Hey, right on time. Did you see my text?"

"No, I had do not disturb on."

"No problem. Turns out—"

"Jim, we need to talk." She hung her coat on the tree.

"Okay, but first—"

"No, now, before we get distracted. This is really important, and I've put it off long enough." She steeled herself. "I don't want kids. It's nothing against children. I love your niece and nephew, and all of my own. But that's not how I planned my life, and that isn't going to change because we're together." She caught a flicker of movement out of the corner of her eye. Probably Rizzo and Pixel. She stayed focused on Jim's face.

"Can we discuss this later? I don't think this is the best time."

"It's the perfect time." She stared into his hazel eyes, which darkened as she spoke. "I'm about to move in with you. Before we do that, take this next step, we need to be on the same page on some important topics. Money, I'm not terribly worried about. We've been together long enough that I think we're pretty close in our opinions on that."

He put his hands on her shoulders. "I get it. I do. But please. We'll talk about this later. I promise."

Why didn't he get it? Later would put her in the same position as Tanelsa, starting her day with arguments and furious texts that distracted her from her responsibilities. "Jim, this is really important to me. I love you, but I don't want to let you live with false expectations. I want you to know my thoughts and reasoning. We need to get this hashed out before your folks get here, and I get bombarded with questions about grandchildren, and things get awkward."

Steps sounded behind him, and a woman said, "Is there a problem? Jim, is this Sally? Bring her into the kitchen so we can say hello, have dinner, and get to know each other like civilized people."

Sally's stomach sank.

Jim moved aside to reveal an older woman. She had silver hair and wore jeans and a fisherman's sweater. There was a warm smile on her face, and her dark eyes crinkled at the corners.

Jim held out his arm. "Sally, I want you to meet my mom, Grace. Mom and Dad came into town a little early. He's out picking up some wine for dinner. Mom, this is Sally."

Terrific. And their first impression of Sally was her saying how much she didn't want kids. Just what she hadn't wanted.

* * *

Duncan could tell Sally was mortified. His mother did not mention the conversation while they ate, but she must have overheard it. In fact, his parents talked about all sorts of other topics, asking questions about Sally's law practice, her time in the public defender's office, things she liked to do in her downtime, and how she'd met their son. Sally answered, her voice casual, but she kept shooting glances at him that clearly said she believed she'd put her foot in her mouth and was off kilter because of it.

The way she'd come bursting into the house, determined to discuss future family plans, said she hadn't expected company. He'd gotten the automatic response indicating she was driving, but he'd thought she'd check messages before she arrived. Or at least before she came inside.

After they finished eating, Grace stood up and gathered dishes.

"Leave it, Mom," Duncan said. "Why don't you and Dad take a glass of wine and go sit in front of the fire? Sally and I will handle the cleanup."

"Oh, I couldn't. I'm your mother, not a guest."

"It's fine. Sally and I have a routine. Go."

Andrew Duncan took his wife's hand. "Come on, hon. The kids want to talk." He pulled her into the living room.

Sally didn't look up as she stacked dirty plates. "Well, that was embarrassing. What a way to introduce myself."

"How can you say that?" Duncan grabbed the silverware. "They love you. I can tell. Relax."

"Why didn't you tell me they were here? I thought they weren't coming until the day before Thanksgiving. I feel like I've been set up." She turned and went to open the dishwasher.

"Yes, that was the original plan. It was a surprise to me, too. But you can't say I didn't tell you. I sent you a text. It's not my fault you didn't check for messages before you arrived."

She paused and did a slow blink. "I was distracted." She blushed. "My fault. I'm sorry for snapping at you."

"You're forgiven." He loaded the forks and knives into the basket.

"We do need to talk, though. About kids. And soon." She gave him what he was sure was a bare-bones version of the tension between Tanelsa and her wife. "I don't want us in the same situation."

He straightened and brushed away a strand of hair that was stuck to her cheek. "We will. I promise. But not tonight. Or at least not while my parents are here. Can we wait until they've left for their hotel?"

"Yes. I agree. We don't need an audience. Aside from the dogs." She went to get the glasses from the table.

"Where were you coming from before you got here?"

"Seeing Sue." She told him about her visit.

"Warm car, huh?" Where had Hepworth been? It could have been something innocent, like a trip to the grocery store.

It could have been a visit to see Will Brackin. Why? If she had visited, was it because he was a known associate of her sister's or something else?

He brought his gaze back to Sally. "What were you doing in Pittsburgh? Was that the distraction? If you can tell me, that is."

"I was going to meet Will Brackin." She glanced at him. "Don't look at me like that. We were going to be in a public place."

"This about Noah's case?

"Only in that it relates to Maddie." She told him about the statement from Evie Martin and how she'd seen Maddie with a woman named Janice. "I checked for his criminal history through my databases."

It was beyond frustrating that she had more information about Brackin's arrest record than he did.

She must have understood his thoughts, because she gave him an apologetic grin. "I won't get into detail, but it struck me as too coincidental that he and Janice both were arrested for heroin possession on the same day, so I wanted to see what he knew about Janice. And whether it involved Maddie."

"I did manage to find out they were caught in the same bust." He leaned on the counter top and told her about his call to his friend in Pittsburgh Narcotics.

"It's lawyers like that who give defense attorneys a bad name. Unfortunately, it was a wasted trip. Brackin is dead." She scrutinized his face. "You already knew that."

Damn her powers of observation. "I wanted to speak to him. Instead, I got a very nice detective from Mount Lebanon."

"Nice to know I wasn't barking up the wrong tree." She grabbed a wet cloth and wiped down the table. "Of course, the Mount Lebanon cops wouldn't tell me much, so I have no idea how Maddie fits in to the whole thing. She was a child ten years ago. I suppose the only person who can tell us is Janice, and I have no idea where she is." She turned and threw the cloth into the sink. After she took one look at him, she said, "You found her."

He shifted. "No comment."

"Jim, saying that is as good as a confirmation, you know that."

"You can take it that way if you like, but I didn't say anything." He took her arm. "Let's go talk to my parents now. They're going to start thinking we're having an argument." He steered her into the living room.

* * *

The realization that Jim had found Janice Hepworth distracted Sally from her discomfort. All the questions she'd planned to ask Brackin could be put to Janice. Not only that, Sally could find out first-hand why Maddie had been in contact. There was only one small problem. Jim would not be able to tell her and she couldn't worm it out of him. Neither option was ethical or moral. But if he couldn't tell her where Janice was, maybe he could give some hints about how Sally could go about finding her.

Not for the first time, Sally cursed the complications involved in dating a cop. If only she didn't love Jim as much as she loved being a lawyer.

At least one thing seemed to be easier than she feared. Meeting Grace and Andrew Duncan. Jim and his father were so alike it was as if she was talking to the same man from two different points in time. Grace, with her ebullient laugh and gentle, yet insightful, personality, proved equally easy to converse with. During dinner, marriage, family, or grandchildren hadn't been mentioned once. The elder Duncans were eager to know about her work and more interested in her history with Jim than in peppering her with questions about the future. What a difference from a dinner with Sally's mother.

After the meal, Grace took a seat on the floor in front of the fire, where Pixel flopped in front of her in his "flat as a flounder" position. She stroked his side, and the dog's pink tongue lolled out of his mouth, eyes closed, in a state of total bliss. "He's beautiful, Sally. Jim tells us he's a rescue."

"Yes. He found Pixel at the scene of a murder this past summer. I adopted him last month. Jim's been keeping him for me." Sally sipped her wine. "There's plenty of literature that says greyhounds live happily in apartments, but I'm sure he's much more satisfied with a yard to run in and a buddy to keep him company than being alone and confined in my place. Even if I was allowed to have him there, which I'm not." She looked out of the corner of her eye at Jim, who nodded. "I plan to move here. I have to get a few things in order, first."

"Jim told us," Andrew said, swirling the glass of whiskey in his hand. Father and son shared the same preferences for alcohol. "Too bad you won't be able to carpool. He says you've started a private practice in Uniontown. Sounds like a lot of work."

"It is, but it's work I like so that makes it easier."

"Do your paths often cross? I mean, are your clients ever the target of Jim's investigations? The Laurel Highlands is a big place, but it must happen from time to time. I would imagine that would be complicated."

Jim's response was unintelligible, and he took a drink.

Sally elbowed him. "Occasionally. We work around it."

Grace scratched Pixel behind the ear. "I'm glad to hear that. Communication is so important to a relationship. Take Andrew and I. We agreed before we got married on two kids. So when my parents started in on when were we going to have a third, after our daughter was born, we had a united front." She looked Sally square in the eye.

Grace hadn't asked a question, but the statement begged for an answer. "I agree," Sally said. "My law partner and her wife are going through something similar right now. I guess they did have an agreement, but things have changed."

"Such is life." Grace ran her hand over Pixel's side. "It's never easy, is it? I remember I had a friend in college, she absolutely did not want children. Had nothing to do with her career plans, although she had big ones. She simply didn't fancy motherhood. Too confining." She laughed. "Oh, the time she spent justifying her choices to other people. Such a shame." The older woman's gaze was too knowing.

Right then, any doubt Sally had about having been overheard earlier vanished. But Grace's words and, more than that, her demeanor, sent an implicit message of support. Whatever happened in the future between Sally and Jim on the family-planning front, they wouldn't have to endure guilt-inducing ploys from his parents. She lifted her wine glass. "I concur, Mrs. Duncan. Life is too short to spend it trying to please other people. People whose opinions may not matter, that is."

"I told you during dinner. Call me Grace."

Sally shot another look at Jim, who arched an eyebrow. She looked back to his mother. "It would be my pleasure."

Chapter Thirty-Nine

Duncan arrived at headquarters the next morning with his thoughts firmly entrenched on last night. Not on Sally's meeting his parents. He'd been sure the event would be as anticlimactic as it had been and that Sally's fears of unrealistic expectations were unfounded. Why she'd insisted on believing otherwise was beyond him.

Then again, he'd met Sally's mother.

He'd known for a while that Sally did not want a family. True, he'd always envisioned it for himself. Then again, when he'd married the first time, he thought it would be for life.

He was used to things not turning out as he expected.

What occupied pride of place in his list of worries at the moment was Janice Hepworth. His parents hadn't left until almost ten the previous night, which hadn't given Sally and him a lot of time for discussion. Sally hadn't pressed for details, for which he was grateful. At the same time, she now knew that Noah's mother had been found. It was only a matter of time before she tracked Janice down, whether the goal was a reunion with her son or an interrogation about what might have led to Maddie's death.

His mind went back to Sue. She'd driven somewhere in her car. Why was she hiding it?

He went to get a second cup of coffee. When he returned, Cavendish was at her desk. "I saw your coat. Should have known you'd be seeking extra fortification." She nodded at his mug. "When is Janice arriving?"

He set down his mug and consulted his notes. "Nine this morning. She said it would take her an hour to get here from Steubenville." He looked up.

"What was the name of that Mount Lebanon detective?"

"The one we talked to? Felicia Mason. Do you want me to call and let her know we found Janice?"

"Not until after we talk to her. If it turns out she can prove she was somewhere other than Mount Lebanon when Brackin was killed, we can let Mason know and save her the legwork."

"And if she doesn't have an alibi? It sounds like she's cleaned herself up. If she and Brackin were arrested together, he may have been a threat to whatever life she's built."

"I know. But regardless, we need to know why she was in contact with Maddie. My gut says it has to do with Noah, and Brackin didn't have anything to do with it."

Cavendish rolled a ballpoint between her thumb and fingers. "Unless he was the guy Maddie was concerned about. She could've been looking for dirt to bolster her case against him. Just because someone bashed him over the head doesn't take him out of the picture for her death."

"True. Any movement on Atwiler's phone records?"

She scoffed. "After a day? You must be joking."

Duncan checked the clock. "Get on the horn to Mount Lebanon. Ask Mason what she's got from the scene and if she has any information regarding Brackin's whereabouts for the time we think Maddie was killed."

"Wednesday night to Thursday morning of last week, right?"

"Yes."

"On it." She picked up the phone.

Duncan picked up an envelope on his desk and opened it. Inside was the forensic accountant's analysis of Atwiler's business. "Huh."

Cavendish hung up. "What?"

"Remember the photographer, Jones? He said Atwiler got an infusion of cash from a new investor. Here." He handed over the report. "He was right. Laurel Highlands Entertainment has been on the ropes for a while. All of a sudden, bam. There's a deposit of fifty grand."

Cavendish gave a low whistle. "It confirms the information from Sally, too. Where'd it come from?"

"They're still looking. It'll be hard to trace because it looks like a cash deposit, but the bean counters are going to give it a try." He rolled an idea around in his mind. "Let's work the money backward. Mason must have requested financial background on her victim. Ask her. Maybe that'll give us a clue."

"You really think Brackin was involved?"

"I think it's highly possible."

Another trooper came up to Duncan. "Your nine o'clock interview is here. I gave her a cup of coffee, and she's waiting for you in room two."

* * *

It was Sally's turn to be a little late to the office. When she arrived, the lights were on, and Tanelsa was seated at her desk, as impeccably dressed as she usually was. "You're looking more put together," Sally said as she hung up her coat. "I take it things are better?"

"Yes. Thanks for making me go home."

Sally got herself a cup of coffee from the kitchenette in the back and returned to the main office. "Did you solve anything?"

"Sort of." Tanelsa grinned. "Lisa talked about her thoughts. I shared mine, and at the end of the discussion, we agreed to get two cats."

"Cats?" Sally giggled.

"You heard me right. It's a trial of sorts. See, we figure with our crazy work schedules, if we can't manage animals, we shouldn't have kids. Dogs might have been a better choice, but Lisa is allergic and I can't stand small dogs. If I get one, I want something like Pixel or Rizzo, you know? Not a floof of a thing that looks like it belongs on the end of a mop."

"That's harsh. Some of those poodle mixes are adorable."

"And expensive. We compromised on cats." Tanelsa tapped the folded newspaper in front of her. "Will Brackin's murder made the news."

"I'm sure it did. Mount Lebanon is a nice area. A murder itself is newsworthy, but the killing of a guy who could potentially be a drug dealer? Even bigger."

"Not potentially." Tanelsa got up and brought the paper to Sally. "According to this, heroin and prescription-strength opioids were found in his basement. But aside from that, the cops are pretty mum on other details."

Sally scanned the story. "I'd expect them to be."

"What does this mean for us?"

"I thought about that last night, and my answer is not much. Our concern is Noah Freeman. His mother told us to do whatever we could to keep him out of jail if and when he's charged with Maddie's murder, which included doing whatever investigative work was necessary. I don't think he's any closer to that than he was yesterday."

"Is that what Jim says?"

"Sort of." Sally blew on the top of her coffee. "He said they have leads and are still investigating. That tells me they don't have enough to charge Noah. But neither has he been officially cleared. What we need to focus on is what our strategy would be if he's taken into custody. I think our digging has turned up enough that we can construct a solid defense for him. There are certainly plenty of other suspects to raise reasonable doubt."

"You think Maddie knew about Brackin's drug business and threatened him?"

"It's a good possibility."

Tanelsa leaned on the edge of her desk. "Means, motive, opportunity. The DA is going to argue Noah has all three. He was angry at Maddie for leaving the center, maybe for spurning him. And if he came across her in that cabin, half-naked, and she told him 'no' again, he might have lost it."

"Right. He could also have found out about Janice. In his mind, Sue is his mother. He may not have seen Maddie's motives for bringing Janice into his life as innocent."

"She threatened his mom."

Sally went to the whiteboard they'd hung on the far wall and began writing the facts. "That's motive. Opportunity. He was in that cabin. Remember, Sue told us he had her phone and the cops have his prints."

"That leaves means." Tanelsa tilted her head. "We can argue all we want that strangling isn't something he'd do. He's a full-grown man, more than capable of it, and that's what the prosecution is going to say. Maddie's scarf, the murder weapon, was right there. He was at the center until five, but I got a copy of the autopsy. Time of death could be as early as Wednesday evening. He'd have been home and Sue said he roams those woods all the time. It's impossible to say he wasn't there."

"And impossible to prove he was. You're right. It's something we have to deal with. But I think we can argue that if he was to kill someone, he'd blurt it out, not try and hide it." Sally wrote all this down. "Noah isn't the only person who checks these boxes, and that's where we can introduce doubt."

Tanelsa picked up another dry-erase marker. "Barry Atwiler was there. He was angry at Maddie. If you ask me, she knew exactly where that money came from, and I bet it wouldn't be good for him if it came to light."

Sally mentally reviewed their information. "I agree. After talking to Brackin, I'm suspicious. Let's do a little more work there and see if we can connect the two more closely than employer and employee."

Tanelsa scribbled a to-do note on the board. "We don't know if Zach Fabery was on the scene, but he's certainly strong enough to throttle a girl as small as Maddie, and he might have been stalking her. Same for Will Brackin." She stepped back.

"If we say Brackin could have killed Maddie, who killed him?"

"Don't know, don't care."

"You're right." Sally studied the board. "I hate to say this, but we can't ignore Sue."

Tanelsa bit her lip. "I don't like it, but you're right. Maddie reintroducing Janice into their lives might have hurt Sue more than Noah."

"And she's hiding something." Sally told her about the warm car and Sue's claim she'd been home all day.

Tanelsa did so and scanned the board. "Lots of alternative suspects there."

"Which is all we need." Sally heard the door chimes jingle. "That should be Noah and his mother. I called them last night and asked if they'd come in to talk."

Moments later, the young man and Sue appeared in the doorway. "Good morning," she said. "This is embarrassing, but I can't stay. A client called with an emergency, and I have to meet with him. Can we reschedule?"

Sally put her marker on the tray. "No need. Will your client situation take all morning?"

"No, probably no more than an hour, but I hate to leave Noah alone." Sue glanced at her son, who was examining the leaves of a potted plant in the corner.

"Don't worry, Ms. Hepworth. We'll take care of him," Tanelsa said. "Noah and I are buds, right?"

He looked over at Tanelsa, smiled, and went back to the plant.

"We're not going to be discussing anything you haven't already heard," Sally said. "We'll save any new questions for when you get back."

Sue didn't seem reassured. "I don't know. Don't I legally have to be here because of his autism?"

"Noah is an adult. Pennsylvania's code of ethics tells me to treat him like any other client. Any other client would call the shots." She looked at him. "Noah, do you want to meet with Tanelsa and me now while your mom goes to work?"

He didn't look away from the plant and shrugged. "Sure."

Sally steered Sue toward the door. "He'll be fine. Right now, time is on our side. I don't believe the police are any closer to filing charges than they were yesterday. That could change at any moment. I want to stay ahead of the game, and that means no delay. I promise Tanelsa and I will be gentle and take good care of him. Go do your job and come back as soon as you're done. You can even call for updates if that makes you feel better."

Sue walked slowly, but allowed herself to be guided. "If you're sure. You'll just be reviewing?"

"Yes."

"Okay. But do not talk with him about anything we discussed regarding my sister, Ms. Castle. Not without me being present."

"You have my word."

Sue hesitated for one more moment, then left.

Sally returned to the main office. "All right, let's get cracking. Noah, would you like orange juice or a doughnut? Maybe both?"

"I love doughnuts. Mom won't let me have them." Noah left the plant and went to the chair Sally had set for him in front of her desk. As he sat down, he caught sight of the paper, folded over to show Brackin's picture. Noah pointed a finger. "I know him. He's a bad man! He hurt Maddie, she said so."

Sally and Tanelsa looked at each other. "You've seen this guy?" Sally asked.

Noah nodded, his face pale, and flapped his hands. "Yes. Yes." He walked back and forth, clearly agitated. "I saw him with Maddie. She said he's a bad man."

Chapter Forty

D uncan grabbed his notebook and an extra pen and headed to the interview room. He took a minute to examine Janice Montgomery through the window. She didn't look like a streetwise addict anymore. Her brown hair was cut to shoulder length, her nails short but clean. She was dressed conservatively in a light trench coat, turtleneck cable sweater, and gray flannel pants. On the fourth finger of her left hand was a gold band and a modest diamond solitaire ring. In short, she looked like a thousand other women in their mid-thirties.

He entered the room. "Mrs. Montgomery. Sorry to keep you waiting. I'm Trooper Jim Duncan."

"No problem. I haven't been here that long, and your colleague was nice enough to offer something to drink."

He seated himself across from her. "First, I want to thank you for coming in. It's not a short drive from Ohio."

She waved it off. "Not a particularly long one, either. I have vacation to burn."

"Where do you work?"

"I'm the secretary at my husband's firm. He's a commercial plumber. I answer the phones, schedule jobs, keep the files straight, handle the bookkeeping, that sort of thing."

"How long have you been there?"

"Ten years, give or take. After I completed my parole here in Pittsburgh, including a stint in rehab, I needed a fresh start. I moved to Ohio, worked a few minimum-wage jobs, and got my GED. After that, I took classes at a local community college and got my current position." She kept her gaze on him, eyes clear. "Robert and I started dating six months after I started, and we married about a year after that."

"He owned the company back then?"

"No, he worked for his father. Dad retired a year ago and left everything in Robert's hands."

Duncan consulted his timeline. "When you left for Ohio, that would have been what, when Noah was roughly nine?"

"Yes." She took a deep breath. "I was a real mess back then. I got pregnant when I was still in high school. I could say that's why I dropped out, but honestly, it wasn't the reason. It was an excuse. I started getting into trouble when I was in middle school. It drove my sister and my mother nuts. Fortunately for Noah, his aunt and grandmother were there for him because I sure wasn't."

"You were never involved with his upbringing?"

"Only when convenient." She took a drink. "Sue would make noises about adopting him. I'd pretend to get my head on straight and even get a job. I didn't want to lose the benefits I received as a single mother. Once the threat was over, I'd go back to the street."

He looked up. "Then you were in Pittsburgh when your sister left with him."

"Yes." She picked at the rolled edge of the paper cup. "When Mom died, I saw Sue and Noah at her funeral. She and I argued. She said she had half a mind to take him away, and I told her go ahead. If she wanted to saddle herself with that burden, she could be my guest because I wasn't going to stop living my life."

Duncan raised an eyebrow at her blunt words.

She must have seen it, because she gave him a wry smile. "Mother of the Year material, that was me. I kept a post office box for a while so I could get my benefits mail, moved around from place to place, got arrested with Will, and, like I said, finally decided to clean up."

"Yet you didn't try to get Noah back."

"I wasn't in a position to take care of him, Trooper." Her brown eyes were steady, but held a slightly haunted look. "He was better off with Sue. I knew he had special needs. I had to get my own life in order. How could I manage his at the same time? And by this point, I figured he'd forgotten me."

"We tried to research your financial records, anything to help find you. There wasn't much there."

"I didn't have a bank account, and credit card companies aren't eager to extend offers to addicts." She swirled the coffee. "I was a cash-only operation for years."

He twiddled his pen. "Tell me about the arrest with Brackin."

"That asshole. Pardon my language." She finished the coffee. "I was trying to score. He saw the cops coming, told me to hold the bag, and he'd make it worth my while. So I did. They did find some heroin on him, but I swore up and down it was mine. He didn't know, you know the story. I went to jail and got five years. I never heard what happened to him."

"The charges were dropped. Not enough evidence to prosecute."

"Figures." She worried the edge of the cup some more. "Although, I probably should thank him. That was when I decided I needed to get my head straight. Whatever happened to him, do you know?"

"He's dead." He watched her reaction closely. "Someone killed him."

"You don't say." Her face paled a bit, but that was it. "Over drugs?"

"It happened in Mount Lebanon, so it's not my case. But for the record, where were you yesterday between seven in the morning and two in the afternoon?"

"At work. My husband and three other men can vouch for me." She tossed the cup in the trash. "I know it's a routine question, but why on earth would I kill him now?"

"It looks like you've got a good life. Maybe he threatened that."

"Robert knows all about my past. We don't have any secrets. I had nothing to fear from Will Brackin."

Cavendish entered the room and sat next to Duncan.

He announced her entrance for the recording, then returned to questioning Janice. "How'd you connect with Maddie Tilgher?"

"It was because of Noah." She examined her fingernails. "After I left, I

247

didn't have much to do with him. That's an overstatement. I didn't have any role in his life. I didn't call Sue, I didn't write, I didn't try to find where they were living. Six months ago, I decided it was time."

"Any particular reason?" Cavendish asked.

Janice brushed back her hair. "They did a mother-child tea at my church for Mother's Day. Watching all those kids…I wanted to see my son, find out what kind of young man he'd become. I talked to Robert about it, of course. I knew Noah had issues because of his autism, so my husband and I agreed it would be best if I introduced myself first. Once Noah was comfortable with me, we could let him know he had a step-dad."

"You were going to take him away from Sue?" Duncan asked. Sue wouldn't take kindly to that.

The question made Janice widen her eyes. "Oh God, no. I'm fully aware that Sue has been more of a mother to him than I ever was, or maybe ever could be. I'd never take that from her. Aside from that, I didn't know if Noah was living on his own, in a halfway house, or if he was still with Sue. No, I just wanted to meet. Get to know him, tell him he had another mother who loved him." She looked from Duncan to Cavendish. "I did, you know. Even when I was screwed up. I left because of it. I loved him so much, I left my son in the care of a woman much better suited to motherhood than I was. No, Trooper. I didn't want to take him anywhere. But I did want him to know I was around. I doubt Sue has talked much about me, not that I blame her."

Duncan was used to people lying. But the bald words and open emotion in Janice's face said she was being truthful. Considering the fact that Noah referred to Sue as "mom" and she called him "her son," Duncan was sure Janice was right about her sister's attitude. "Was Maddie going to help you with that?"

"Yes." Janice picked at her cuticles. "I traced Sue to where she lives now and learned that Noah was a regular at the Center for the Developmentally Disabled. I came to the center to look things over and figure out the best way to introduce myself. Maddie saw me outside. We struck up a conversation, and I told her who I was and what had happened. Well, not all of it, but enough. She was sympathetic. She said she worked with Noah a lot and was sure he'd love to meet me. But she was also pretty certain Sue would not approve. Maddie told me that Sue had never claimed to be Noah's mom, but she'd never corrected anybody's assumptions, either. And she was terribly protective of Noah."

"What was the plan?"

"Maddie said she wasn't Sue's favorite person at the center, but she'd talk to her and try to get her to agree to let Noah meet me. If that didn't work, Maddie would talk to the center director, Liz Jackson, and see if she'd mediate."

Cavendish paged through her notebook. "When was the last time you talked to Maddie?"

"Let me see, last Wednesday? No, maybe it was Tuesday. It was earlier in the week, I do know that. She said she'd struck out once with Sue, but she was going to try again. I met with Maddie a couple of weeks ago while she was at school. She thought getting together at a neutral site, like a restaurant or something like that, would be easier on him for a first meet. The idea was she'd convince Sue to bring him, and we could have lunch or something. I guess Sue turned her down. But Maddie was determined. When we talked last week, she said she was going to see Sue and make another pitch. She said we'd meet on Wednesday and make plans to see him." Janice spread her hands on the table. "She never called to confirm, and she didn't pick up when I tried to get in touch. I thought something had happened to make her change her mind."

Duncan exchanged a look with his partner. He faced Janice. "One last question, Mrs. Montgomery. Did you ever speak to your sister about this plan?"

"No." Again, that clear-eyed look. "But I know Maddie told Sue I was back in the area, that she'd met me, and not only did I want to meet Noah, I deserved to. She and I talked about it on the phone. According to her, Sue was pretty upset, convinced it would completely ruin Noah's life and destroy him emotionally if he even knew I existed."

Duncan had always ascribed Sue's extreme concern over Noah to behavior typical of a parent with a special-needs child. But the information from Janice threw everything into a different light. "Thank you for coming in to talk with us, Mrs. Montgomery," he said, extending his hand. "You've been very helpful."

* * *

It took a couple of doughnuts and a can of Coke, but Sally settled her young client in a chair, and he stopped his hand-flapping. "How're you doing, Noah?" she asked. "Are you feeling better?"

He shot her a quick glance. "Yes." He took a large bite of the frosted treat and washed it down with a swallow of cola.

Tanelsa leaned in to whisper in Sally's ear. "His mother is gonna kill us if we sugar him up."

"She doesn't need to know," Sally said in an undertone. She waited until Noah had devoured the pastry and handed him a napkin so he could wipe his sticky fingers. "Noah, can we talk about the man? Would that be okay? It'll help Maddie."

He rubbed his fingers with the napkin, shredding it. "Okay," he replied, eyes wary.

"Good." She hitched her chair closer. "Where did you see him?"

"At the center," Noah said, balling the paper scraps in his hand.

"Was he inside or outside?"

Beside Sally, Tanelsa took notes. She'd positioned her chair a little further back so as not to interrupt the rapport between the other two.

Noah didn't take his gaze from the table. "Outside. Maddie and I were taking a walk. He was at the door. He said he needed to talk to Maddie. She didn't like him being there. I could tell."

"You said Maddie was angry. What did she say? Do you remember?"

"She told him to go away. He shouldn't be there. But he laughed. I didn't like him when he laughed. It didn't sound nice."

"I'm sure it didn't." Sally kept her voice calm. "What happened then?"

"He grabbed her. Maddie didn't like that. She pulled away, but he did it again. I yelled at him. I was going to hit him, but Maddie told me not to, so I didn't."

"Noah, this is very important. Did the man say anything, and do you remember what it was?"

Noah frowned, deep creases popping up on his forehead. "Not all of it. Something about a woman named Janice. He also said Maddie shouldn't ask questions about him and his business, and just do her job. I didn't understand. Maddie always does her job. She's nice. I wanted her to stay at the center, but Mom said she had to leave. That made me sad."

"I know you were." Sally patted his arm. "You've done a super job, Noah. Why don't you drink your Coke, and I'm going to talk to Tanelsa for a bit, all right?"

Noah nodded, happy again as he grasped the can of soda.

Sally and Tanelsa moved to the far corner of the room. "Brackin knew Maddie had been in contact with Janice," Sally said, keeping her voice low so Noah couldn't hear. Not that he seemed to be paying attention. He was examining the cup full of multi-colored pens Sally kept on her desk.

Tanelsa glanced at him. "I don't know why that's important, though. Did he know Janice was Noah's mom? Or did he know Maddie had found out about his drug activities from Janice and go to the police?"

"Either? Both? Something different?"

Tanelsa rolled her eyes. "Real helpful."

Sally studied the autistic young man, who had grabbed a bright purple pen and was drawing on her desk blotter. She had to talk to Jim.

Chapter Forty-One

Back in the bullpen, Cavendish handed Duncan a sheet of paper. "What is this?" he asked as he read it.

Cavendish sat. "I spoke with Detective Mason in Mount Lebanon. Those are my notes."

As he read, he picked up a pen and clicked it open and closed, more to have something to do with his free hand than because he intended to write. "Why did Brackin call Barry Atwiler the day before his death? And at ten at night?"

"That's the sixty-four-million-dollar question, isn't it? And it wasn't a short conversation, either."

According to Mason's information, the two had talked for over twenty minutes. They could have been talking business, maybe where to set up the next shoot. But that felt off. Wouldn't a call like that take place during the day?

Or had they been discussing the shared problem of Maddie Tilgher?

Duncan put down the pen. "Wasn't there some communication between Brackin and Maddie about Janice?"

Cavendish searched the paperwork they had. "Here it is. It was a text. 'Janice is a liar.' From Brackin to Maddie." She leaned back. "How about this? Maddie knows about Brackin and his history from Janice. He's been harassing her, showing up at campus, and her volunteer work. She's learned about his deal with Atwiler. She says if he doesn't leave her alone, she'll blab about his deal. That has the bonus of getting her out of her contract with Atwiler. He silences her."

"Talk about dangerous. It's a good idea, except Brackin wasn't at that cabin." He tapped his desk. "But Atwiler was." An idea struck him. "Maddie didn't confront *Brackin* with the deal, she told Atwiler."

"Let me out of my contract, or I'll talk. And he killed her to shut her up."

"It fits. Flash to the present. Brackin has another bundle to 'invest,' but this time, Atwiler says no way."

"This time, it's Brackin who makes the threat, and Atwiler acts." She nodded. "Good theory. I'll call Mason."

He set down the notes. "Did she say anything else about their forensic findings?"

"They don't have a lot. No one saw a car. There aren't any traffic cams on the street. She's checking to see if the neighbors have cameras that might have picked something up." She dialed. "Too bad Brackin didn't have one of those video-camera-enabled doorbells." She dialed her phone.

That would be too convenient. Duncan heard Cavendish talking, but he returned his attention to the details of the phone call between the alleged drug dealer and the porn producer. Twenty minutes. The call had taken place in the middle of the night. He checked the number. It belonged to Laurel Highlands Entertainment. He wondered what Atwiler would say when confronted with this fact.

"Thanks," Cavendish said as she hung up the phone. "Nothing substantial from the Mustang, but Mason told me they have one partial print off the poker they believe was the murder weapon."

"Does it match anything?"

"Funny you should ask." She pointed at the sheet in his hands. "It's a thirty-five percent match for Barry Atwiler."

* * *

Sally went back over to sit next to Noah. "Why don't we talk about something else for a little bit. Tell me about the day you found Maddie. What were you doing in the woods?"

"Walking." Noah didn't look up from his doodling. "I walk in the woods a lot. I like it there."

"How did you find Maddie? Do you go to that cabin often?"

"Not as much as I used to. I liked to hide in there. It was a good place to keep stuff I didn't want Mom to know about. It was my secret."

"Is that how you found Maddie?"

"Yes." He flipped over the sheet of paper and continued drawing.

"And you say your mom doesn't know you go there, to the cabin?"

"No, I told you. It's my hiding place. But she got mad that day because I interrupted her."

Sally looked over at Tanelsa, who looked just as puzzled as Sally felt. "What do you mean?"

"I went there to hide some rocks I found down by the lake. But when I got to the cabin, Mom was there."

This didn't make any sense. "Noah, are we talking about the same day? Last Friday?"

"No, it was Wednesday after dinner."

"You must be thinking of a different day."

"It was Wednesday." Noah studied his drawing and added some purple swirls. "My favorite show is on after dinner. Mom went for a walk, and she hadn't come back, so I thought it would be a good time to hide the rocks. She doesn't like me getting too near the lake because she thinks I'll fall in and drown, so I didn't want her to find my treasure. She was inside the cabin. Maddie was asleep. Mom was really mad, especially after she saw me. I thought it was because she knew I'd been near the lake, but she only said Maddie didn't feel good and was taking a little nap. She had Maddie's phone in her hand. She put the phone down and said we had to leave." He shot Sally a guilty look. "I know I shouldn't have taken the phone. But it has Maddie's picture on it. If she was leaving the center, I needed something to remember her by."

Tanelsa came over and bent down. "He's confused on the days. He has to be."

Sally agreed. "Noah, you're mistaken. You didn't find Maddie until Friday."

He slapped the desk. "It was Wednesday." He grabbed his hair and began to rock.

"Shh, okay, I'm sorry. You're right." But he couldn't be. Regardless, she had to calm him down. "Then what happened on Friday? The day Trooper Duncan came to your house."

"I went to the lake and collected some really pretty things, shiny stones and stuff. I wanted to hide them, so I went to the cabin. But the door was locked. It's never locked. I went to the window, and that's when I saw Maddie. She was sleeping again. But this time, she looked funny. Her face was blue. I tapped the glass, but she didn't wake up. I got scared and ran to where they put the boats in the summer."

That had to be the boat docks where Aislyn had first found him. "That all makes sense. But why did you leave home a second time?" Sally asked.

He stopped rocking, but wouldn't look up. "I had to help Maddie. I had to wake her up. It was cold outside, and she didn't have a coat on." He flapped his hands. "But I couldn't! I couldn't get the door to open. I didn't know what to do."

Tanelsa tugged her sleeve. Sally got up and followed her to the far corner. Once there, Tanelsa angled her body so Noah wouldn't be able to see their faces. "Are you thinking what I'm thinking?" she asked.

"Sue told us the police had found their fingerprints, hers and Noah's. Did she say when she was in that cabin?"

Tanelsa thought. "I don't remember. I don't think so."

"We assumed it was the day Noah found Maddie, and that was what freaked Sue out. She'd found Noah in the same room as a dead body. Sue cleaned up as best she could. Noah grabbed the phone, and they left, locking the door behind them."

"Then we thought Noah had gone back."

"Right." Sally snuck a look around Tanelsa to check on her client, who had gone back to doodling. "But if Noah is right, Sue was there on Wednesday evening."

"When do the cops think Maddie was killed?"

Sally took another look at Noah. "Wednesday, anytime late afternoon to that night."

* * *

Duncan stared at his phone. Sally's call had been unexpected, to say the least. What was so urgent that he had to go to her office right now?

Cavendish waved her hand in front of his face. "Who was that?"

"Sally. She wants to talk to me."

"We can stop in Uniontown on the way to interview Atwiler."

He mentally shook himself. "No. I'll go see Sally. You call Janice."

"And ask what?"

"Whether she ever mentioned her son or her sister to Brackin. And why the two would be in communication. Phone records don't lie."

Cavendish tilted her head. "I thought we liked Atwiler for Maddie's murder?"

Duncan went to the whiteboard covered in case notes. "We do, but we don't have proof yet. What if we're wrong?"

"Maddie wasn't killed because of what she knew?"

Duncan faced his partner. "Oh, no. That part is correct. But what if she knew something completely different?"

Cavendish frowned, but her expression cleared as she followed his line of reasoning. "That Janice was Noah's biological mother."

"And she was going to reunite mother and son, which means he'd learn the truth about Hepworth." Duncan felt the pieces wiggling, but they still didn't quite fit. "Maddie learned about Janice. How, I'm not sure. Maybe from something Sue said, or she visited Noah at home, or possibly Brackin mentioned the surname Hepworth in passing and Maddie did the math. Anyway, she embarks on a quest to find Janice Hepworth. There are sources you can pay to get someone's criminal history."

Cavendish nodded. "She discovers the connection between Janice and Brackin, who Maddie knows from her work with Laurel Highlands Entertainment. She asks him about Janice. Again, Maddie could have threatened him with the past arrest, or she knows about the deal with Atwiler. Either way, she uses it as leverage, weasels out as much as she can about Janice, and manages to track her down. Bonus: she can use the same knowledge to get out of her contract."

"After that, Maddie wants Noah to meet his mother. She approaches Sue, who cuts her off hard. That's why Sue didn't like her. And why she didn't want Noah and Maddie to be together. It had nothing to do with Maddie's so-called inappropriate behavior, that's all bullshit. Sue didn't want Noah to learn about Janice." He dropped into his chair. "I don't understand why, though. Noah loves her."

"It would blow up her world. She's spent nearly twenty years caring for that boy. Could also be she was afraid of the effect it would have on him. Can you imagine learning that the woman you've always believed was your mother wasn't *actually* your mom?" Cavendish leaned on the opposite desk. "We know Sue and Noah were in that cabin. We have their fingerprints. She didn't report finding Maddie's body because she believed we'd make this connection, and she didn't want to make herself a suspect."

"Could be." Duncan stood and grabbed his coat. "Get in touch with Janice. Find out everything you can about the family history. After that, get over to the tech guys and find out if they've managed to get Maddie's cloud backup. See if it tells us anything we don't already know." He headed for the door.

Chapter Forty-Two

Sally looked up at the sound of the door chimes. Noah, supplied with a stack of paper and a selection of colored pens, hummed tunelessly from his seat at the table in the corner. "Ready to do this?" she asked Tanelsa.

"As I'll ever be." Tanelsa stood and tugged her jacket into place.

Jim entered the office, hair a little windblown, fat drops of water on the shoulders of his dark gray wool overcoat. "I came as soon as I could."

Sally rounded her desk, hand outstretched. "Trooper Duncan. I'm glad you could spare some of your time."

If Jim was surprised at her formal tone, he didn't show it. "Ms. Castle, Ms. Parson." He nodded at Tanelsa. "Your message indicated it was important." He noticed Noah in the corner, and he looked back at Sally.

"It is." She wanted to keep this meeting formal. Thankfully, his response to her greeting indicated he understood that. "Before we start, would you like something to drink? We have coffee, tea, water, or a couple cans of soda."

"No, thank you. I just need a place to hang my coat." He took off the overcoat.

Tanelsa came forward, hand outstretched. "I'll take it. Please, have a seat at the table."

Jim tipped his head, asking a nonverbal question, to where Noah sat.

Sally led Jim over and sat next to Noah. "I called you this morning because my client, Noah Freeman, has some information that relates to the Maddie Tilgher murder and wishes to make a statement."

Tanelsa returned and took a seat on Noah's other side.

Jim removed a notebook from his jacket and sat. "I don't see Ms. Hepworth here. Has she given permission for this interview?"

Tanelsa folded her hands. "Her presence isn't required. Noah is nineteen and an adult. Despite his autism, he's capable of making an informed decision. Pennsylvania's ethical standards and guidance are clear on that. He is our client, and of course, we'll safeguard his interests under the law."

Jim laid his notebook and pen on the table.

Sally cleared her throat. "I want it understood, Trooper, that Noah is meeting with you of his own volition. We," she waved at Tanelsa, "would like some assurance that nothing he says will be used against him in criminal proceedings."

Jim leaned back, his expression indecipherable. "Ms. Castle, I understand your position. However, as I'm sure *you* know, that decision isn't up to me. It's for the prosecutor to make that deal. If you'd rather talk to him first, before any interview with me, I'm willing to wait."

"That won't be necessary." She held his gaze. "We only want to make sure our client gets a fair hearing."

He didn't move, his eyes boring into hers. She knew he was trying to read her mind. Finally, he said, "I hope we have a good enough relationship that you know I won't use whatever I hear to improperly implicate Mr. Freeman in any criminal charges."

Sally looked at Tanelsa, who shrugged. *That's as good as we're gonna get,* the gesture seemed to say. Sally laid her hand on Noah's arm. "Noah, remember what we talked about earlier?"

"About Maddie?" he asked.

"Yes. I'd like you to tell Trooper Duncan what you told me."

For the next twenty minutes, Noah repeated his story. Jim was a good listener. He took copious notes and interrupted only a couple of times to ask clarifying questions, none of which alarmed Sally. As the conversation continued, the knot of tension that had been between her shoulders ever since she'd called Jim relaxed. She'd made the right call bringing him in.

Noah finished his recitation and looked at Sally. "Can I draw some more?"

"Sure thing. Ms. Parson and I are going to talk to Trooper Duncan for a bit." She pulled over the stack of paper and the pens. Then she, Tanelsa, and Jim got up and moved to the other side of the office.

"What do you think?" Tanelsa asked.

Jim scanned his notes. "If it's true, it's an interesting chain of events."

Sally scoffed. "I don't think Noah knows how to lie. Not on this scale."

"You might be right on that." Jim cast a look at the young man in the corner. "I wonder…"

Sally waited, but he didn't finish the sentence, and she knew better than to ask. "Does this eliminate Noah as a suspect?"

Jim returned his attention to her, a faint smile on his face. "He was never that serious of a candidate, you know that."

Tanelsa crossed her arms. "It's still good to hear."

"One thing puzzles me," he said. "Why'd you call me? I'd have thought you'd keep me away from Sue Hepworth at all costs."

She adopted a formal tone of voice. "Our client had information relevant to an open investigation, and we decided he needed to make a formal statement to the police. It's unfortunate that Ms. Hepworth is implicated, but we need to look out for Noah's interests."

Sally leaned on her desk. "I hope what he told you is helpful."

Tanelsa left, presumably to get Jim's coat.

He studied Sally. "I understand why you wanted justice for Maddie Tilgher. But what's up with Freeman? I've never seen you like this."

"Like what?"

"Forgive the word, but almost maternal."

Tanelsa returned in time to hear him and shot her a quizzical glance.

Sally again looked at Noah, happily scribbling away. Maternal? Maybe. What had Sue said…she'd do anything for Noah? Had that included murder? Or had she been acting in her own interests, too scared to let Noah learn the truth? "No, not maternal." She focused on Jim. "Everyone always lauds mothers for sacrificing for their kids, for going to any lengths to protect them. As for me, well, I believe there are lines that shouldn't be crossed. I guess that makes me a pretty crappy candidate for motherhood."

"Not in my book." He squeezed Sally's arm, took his coat from Tanelsa, and left.

* * *

Duncan walked out of the Castle & Parson office, thinking about what he'd heard. Clearly, Sally attached great importance to what her young client had said. She wouldn't have called Duncan otherwise. But although he didn't think the boy was a liar, he couldn't classify him as a completely reliable witness, either. A defense lawyer would shred Noah's testimony in a heartbeat, casting him as a mentally challenged young person who couldn't keep his days straight.

When had Sue Hepworth been in the cabin? Before or after Maddie's death? That was the question. Noah hadn't seen his mother actually commit murder. Her actions could easily be a frantic parent looking to keep her son out of trouble. She might be guilty of tampering with a crime scene, but homicide? Duncan wasn't sure.

His phone buzzed in his pocket. He glanced at the screen and saw Cavendish's name. "Yeah?"

"Where are you?"

"In Uniontown. I just left Sally's office."

"What was so important?"

He relayed the entire interview.

"She was okay with that? Sally?"

He reached his car and leaned on it. "He was making a voluntary witness statement. Of course, she tried to get me to commit to not charging Noah with anything."

"Naturally. But you didn't, right?"

"I love her, but I'm not an idiot. I'm sure she knew it was futile, but she had to ask." A gust of wind made him push off the car and seek shelter inside. "What did you learn from the tech guys?"

"It's too much for the phone. I'm at the Panera over on Matthew. Meet me there. I'll even buy your coffee." She ended the call.

261

Ten minutes later, Duncan entered the restaurant and spotted his partner sitting by the fireplace, two cups on the table. He threaded his way through the seating area, which was thinning out as the lunch crowd headed back to their offices. "Thanks," he said, grabbing the nearest cup. "This mine?"

"Dark roast black." Cavendish popped the top on her own cup, and a tendril of steam wafted out.

Duncan savored the hot liquid, feeling it warm his core. He hadn't realized how cold he was. "Lay it on me."

"I talked to Janice. She remembers telling Brackin about Noah, but that was years ago, when she was a mess. Maddie did ask about him, though. Brackin. According to Janice, Maddie used a combination of one of those family tree websites and public records, including what's available about that heroin arrest, to track her down. Maddie knew Brackin from her work at Laurel Highlands Entertainment and wanted to know if it was the same guy. She asked if he was still dealing. Janice didn't know, but said it wouldn't surprise her."

"Then we were right." Duncan stared at the dancing flames. "Maddie was trying to get rid of him. She might not have been able to get anything to stick, but it would be terribly inconvenient if the cops started digging into Brackin's activities outside Laurel Highlands Entertainment."

"That's an understatement. Given his drug involvement, including what they found in his basement, he would have been looking at serious jail time." Cavendish leaned back. "Of course, that only strengthens his motive. He would have known where Maddie's last shoot was. He could have shown up, waited until everybody left, then killed her. He cleaned the scene before he left, which is why we didn't find his prints."

"No, that doesn't wash. If he'd done that, we wouldn't have found anything. I'm more inclined to think Brackin called Atwiler, told him to get a grip on Maddie and stayed out of it."

Cavendish mulled that over. "Could be."

"Then, Noah stumbles across the dead body. Sue freaks, thinks he'll be blamed, and tries to stage the scene. In the process, he filches Maddie's phone."

CHAPTER FORTY-TWO

"It explains everything the Freeman kid told you."

"But not Brackin's murder." Duncan didn't like loose ends.

"No, but that's Mason's problem, not ours."

A thought popped into his head. "Brackin called Atwiler. You said there's a partial fingerprint that could match him in his house."

Cavendish held up a finger. "It's a low-percentage match. Which means that print is inconclusive. But yes, we can't ignore the phone call. It might have been about Maddie. It could just as easily have nothing to do with her. Just because they both knew the victim doesn't mean everything is connected to her death."

True. "What about Janice? She's another link between Maddie and Brackin."

"Just for giggles, I checked. Janice's alibi for his murder holds up." She took a drink. "She has no motive to kill Maddie. Not if Maddie was trying to arrange a reunion. I also looked into her story. She told us the truth. Her husband knows about her history, the drug use, and convictions. If it's public knowledge, there's no reason to kill Maddie or Brackin to stop them from talking."

He wanted Atwiler to be the murderer. That wouldn't make it so. He pushed on. "What about the tech guys? Anything there?"

"Oh yes." Cavendish's smile was smug. "Okay, so they gave me a lot of tech jargon that we don't care about, but here's the bottom line. Maddie's phone is backed up in the cloud, which is synced to her laptop. Messages are not part of the cloud backup, which is why we found a thread on her laptop and not the phone. Either she deleted it, or someone else did."

"We already know this."

"Be patient." She took another hit of coffee. "What is backed up are contacts, calendar info, notes, and other stuff, as long as you've set it up. That synchronization happens pretty fast. If Maddie deleted a contact off her phone, it would be removed from the cloud and then laptop within minutes, if not sooner."

Duncan knew better than to interrupt, so he said nothing.

"That means the cloud also doesn't have a contact record for the number we now know belongs to Janice."

He waited, but she didn't continue. "So we're screwed," he said. But that couldn't be the case. Cavendish was enjoying herself too much.

She held up a finger, and her eyes sparkled. "*Au contraire, mon frere.* The tech guys told me that while the current backup doesn't have those records, there is an archive available. They got all geeky about how and when an archive is created, but the bottom line is the current archive is dated the afternoon of the day Maddie was killed."

Duncan thought he knew what was coming. "And?"

"It contains contact records for Janice Montgomery and Sue Hepworth." Cavendish winked. "Which means those records were deleted between the date of the most recent archive and when the phone was found."

"In other words, someone deleted something from Maddie's phone, but it doesn't matter, because the tech guys found a backup."

Cavendish stuck her tongue out at him. "Spoilsport."

"Tech details bore me." Duncan understood the implication. He doubted Maddie would have removed that information. Which meant either Sue Hepworth had deleted it when she found Maddie's body or the killer had.

Assuming they weren't the same person. But Atwiler wouldn't care. No, Hepworth had deleted that information. Duncan was sure of it. Maddie would not have allowed that to happen. Now the question was, had she been dead or alive when Hepworth found her?

His phone buzzed in his pocket. "Duncan."

"Trooper Duncan, this is Detective Mason from Mount Lebanon."

He snapped his fingers to get Cavendish's attention. "What can I do for you, Detective?"

Cavendish took out a notepad and mimed writing.

Duncan nodded. Enough people had left Panera that he felt comfortable putting the phone on speaker.

"We're combing through Brackin's financials and correspondence. You knew he worked for Barry Atwiler."

"Yes."

"It went beyond that." A rustle of paper. "We found a thread discussing the financial health of Laurel Highlands Entertainment and Brackin's need to wash some money. A few days later, Brackin made a fifty-thousand dollar withdrawal from an account that is in his mother's name, but we traced to him."

The exact amount of the deposit made to Atwiler's business around the same time. "Brackin laundered money through a porn operation?"

Cavendish stopped writing.

"Pornography is not tasteful, but it's not illegal either," Mason said. "You must have seen the deposit on Atwiler's end."

"We did." Duncan tapped the table. "Since it was cash, we were having trouble tracing it. I think we just did. Thanks for the tip."

"My pleasure." Mason hung up.

Cavendish looked at her notes. "Brackin gives Atwiler the money to wash. Atwiler's business gets a needed financial bump. Maddie finds out and unwisely decides...what?"

"She should have called the cops. I'm betting she tried to use it as leverage with Atwiler to get out of her contract." Duncan rubbed his chin. "But there's only one person who can tell us."

Chapter Forty-Three

Tanelsa stared out of the window, where she'd been since the door closed behind Jim. She didn't turn as she spoke. "Do you think we did the right thing?"

Sally glanced into the conference room, where she'd installed Noah with a giant stack of paper, pens, and a bottle of water. She returned to her desk. "Yes. We were hired to protect Noah. We couldn't withhold information from the police. What if they discovered Sue had been on the spot, then found out Noah knew, and we didn't tell them? At least this way, we can control the story." She glanced at the clock. "Speaking of Sue, where is she? I'd have thought she'd be back by now. It's been way longer than an hour."

"Maybe she got delayed, although I think she would have called us." Tanelsa frowned. "Going back to the previous point, we keep Noah out of jail, but he loses his mother?"

Sally had gone through the same agonizing decision process, but had come to terms with their decision. "There's no absolute proof that Sue killed Maddie. It is a statement that puts Ms. Hepworth at the scene earlier than she said. For whatever reason, she didn't tell us that." Sally picked up the phone. "Let's find out why. And where she is."

But calls to the Hepworth landline and Sue's cell both went unanswered. Sally left messages. Then she massaged her temples. "Strangulation seems so very unlike the woman."

Tanelsa turned, but didn't move from her post. "True. But Maddie was a tiny thing. Ms. Hepworth had at least six inches and fifty pounds on her. That's my guess. She could do it. And she may not have had any other weapons."

Sally stared into space. "Did she think Noah would up and leave once he knew his biological mother?"

"Possibly. Blood is thicker than water, and all that."

"But she and Noah *are* blood relatives. She's not a stranger. She cared for him for nearly twenty years, if you include the time before Janice disappeared."

Tanelsa's slender shoulders moved up and down. "Fear is a strange thing."

"She'd have to know Maddie was in that cabin." *How would she know that? Did she see them arrive? Did Noah tell her?* "Do you think Sue knew about Will Brackin and his connection to Janice?"

"I'm not sure." Tiny creases appeared in Tanelsa's forehead. "What are you thinking?"

"When Maddie came here, she was afraid. She asked about protection from a guy. Could that guy be Brackin?"

Tanelsa said nothing.

Sally struggled to put her thoughts in order. "Maddie finds Janice. Janice must have told her about the heroin arrest and Brackin. Maddie goes to Brackin and threatens to tell the cops about his drug activities if he doesn't lay off."

"You're building a case against Brackin with that line of thinking."

"I know, but...what if Sue *also* knew about that connection? Maybe that's why she chose to strangle Maddie instead of using another method."

"So it would look like a guy?" Tanelsa's voice was doubtful. "That's out there, isn't it?"

"Possibly. I'm spitballing."

"Then Brackin's death is unconnected?"

"I don't know. Never mind. Forget I said anything." To distract herself, Sally picked up a brief for a court appearance later in the week and tried to read. The words swam in front of her eyes. She'd successfully kept her client out of jail. At least, that was the hope. That was her only job. Why couldn't she leave the question of who killed Maddie alone?

* * *

Duncan stared into the dancing gas flames in the Panera fireplace. Next to him, Cavendish talked on her phone. *What am I missing?*

They had fingerprints. All Noah's statement did was confirm his presence at the scene, his mother's, and maybe that they were there a bit earlier than initially thought. Why couldn't he shake the feeling the whole case hinged on the autistic boy?

He pulled out his phone and dialed Hepworth's number. No answer.

If Sue was there on Wednesday, she had to know about the photo shoot. But that was unlikely. Wasn't it? She wasn't connected to Barry Atwiler, and Duncan believed her when she professed ignorance of Maddie's alternate income source. For Sue to be the killer, she had to have known Maddie was in that run-down hut. How? "She went looking for him," he said under his breath. Hepworth had been looking for her son. Had she found Maddie instead?

Cavendish laid down her phone. "What was that?"

"An idea. Who was on the phone?"

"Mason again." She nodded at the device. "The house two doors down from Brackin's has one of those high-tech doorbells. Mason got the video."

"And?"

"At approximately two-thirty on the day Brackin died, a silver Beamer passed the house. It would have been coming away from the murder scene and was going the wrong way to catch a plate. However, Mason kept going back in time to see if there was anything else."

"She saw it again. Did she get a number?"

"Only a partial. However, it matches the registration for Barry Atwiler's BMW, and Mason said the car in the video *could* be the same model."

He crushed his empty coffee cup and stood. "That's it. We're going to see Atwiler."

"I'm right behind you."

* * *

Duncan didn't bother calling in advance. He had a patrol officer swing by Atwiler's residence, but no one was there.

"Laurel Highlands Entertainment?" Cavendish asked.

"Only other logical place."

"Unless he's in the wind."

"Let's hope not."

It seemed to take hours, but thanks to Duncan's generous interpretation of the speed limit, they pulled up in the strip mall parking lot around quarter after two. The silver BMW rested in the same spot it had on their previous visit.

"Got him." Cavendish unsnapped her seat belt.

Before entering, Duncan unsnapped the safety strap on his Glock.

The reception desk was empty. The troopers followed the sound of a voice to the same conference room they'd been in earlier. Atwiler was talking on his cell phone, but he glowered as they entered. "I'll call you back." He stabbed the phone screen to end the call. "What the hell do you want now?"

Duncan decided to get straight to the point. "When did you decide to get into the money laundering business? Porn wasn't lucrative enough, was that it?"

Atwiler blustered. "How…that is total bullshit. I've half a mind to sue the PSP for harassment."

"Cut the crap." Cavendish moved so the troopers flanked the suspect. "We know about the money from Brackin. We know he was into drugs. He gives you cash, you invest it in your slimy, but legal, business, he gets clean money in return. Our only question is, where does Maddie Tilgher come into it?"

The producer glanced from side to side. "You've got nothing."

Duncan adjusted his stance. There was no way Atwiler could escape both troopers. He wasn't in good enough shape. "We have almost everything. Mount Lebanon has your BMW leaving the scene of Brackin's murder. We have your prints at the cabin."

Atwiler scoffed. "I was there for a shoot. I told you, when I left, she was alive. Ask Jones."

"We did." Cavendish watched him. "You could have come back. Did

Maddie try to blackmail you? Say that unless you let her out of her contract, she'd tell the world you were in business with a drug dealer?"

Atwiler clenched the table.

"You picked the wrong scene, Atwiler." Duncan saw beads of sweat on his suspect's forehead and pressed. "That cabin was too remote. Who else would know Maddie was there? Now, if you'd done the deed elsewhere, maybe you'd have had a better chance of getting away."

"Or not," Cavendish said.

Duncan nodded in acknowledgment. "Or did you rely on Maddie's interference with Noah Freeman and Sue Hepworth to cover your act? You must have known about it, right? Maybe Maddie even mentioned how easy it would be to see them after the latest shoot. A built-in patsy."

Atwiler's gaze flicked to the door.

"Oh please, do try and run." Cavendish mocked. "Will Brackin, what happened there? He get greedy? Want more of a return than you promised? Or did he threaten to turn on you? After all, he's been dodging drug charges for years. He must have thought getting out of money laundering would be a piece of cake, especially if he threatened to hand you to us as Maddie's killer."

"You're going down in Pittsburgh and here, Atwiler." Duncan laid a hand on his Glock. "The only question is who gets to try you first."

Atwiler shoved the table toward Cavendish. He tried an awkward move to climb over the table while she staggered, but Duncan snared his ankle. "Get off of me," Atwiler snarled.

Duncan ignored him. He hauled Atwiler to his feet and cuffed him. "Barry Atwiler, you're under arrest for the murders of Maddie Tilgher and Will Brackin."

Cavendish rubbed her thigh where the table had hit it. "And evading arrest. And assaulting a trooper."

Atwiler's expression turned sullen. "I want a lawyer."

Duncan nudged him to the door. "Why did I know you were going to say that?"

Chapter Forty-Four

Sally looked up at the clock on the wall. Three-thirty. Over six hours since Sue said she'd be back. What had happened? "Any answer?"

Tanelsa set down her phone. "Nada. You know, this woman has been so hyper over her son's safety, and now she vanishes. That's weird."

It was. No client meeting could take this long, could it? But if Sue was truly still working, why hadn't she called to say she was running late?

Noah appeared in the doorway. "Where's my mom? I want to go home."

"I know, buddy. She'll be here soon."

His hands flapped. "Home! I want to go home!"

This was the third time Sally had to calm him. With each episode, he became increasingly agitated. "Noah, listen. I know it's been a long day. But I'm sure your mom will be here shortly. Can we get you anything? A snack or something to drink?"

"No!" He banged his fists against the wall. "I want to go home!"

Sally looked over at Tanelsa, who appeared as baffled as Sally felt. Neither of them had enough experience to deal with Noah in this state of mind. Sally rushed to her desk and called the only person who might have an answer for her. "Ms. Jackson, hi. This is Sally Castle."

"What can I do for you?"

"I have a bit of a situation." She told the center director what was going on. "What do I do? I'm afraid he's going to hurt himself. Or one of us."

"First, you must stay calm, you and Ms. Parson." Liz proceeded to give Sally some advice. "I'm surprised you can't get in touch with his mother. She's never unavailable."

"Frankly, I am too. There are some things going on I can't talk about, but I expected to see her before now."

"Try the tips I gave you and cross your fingers she gets there soon. Do you want me to come to your office?"

Sally considered the offer. "No. I would hate for you to make the trip and get here to find out everything's been taken care of."

"Call me if you change your mind or if you need anything else."

Sally ended the call. Skirting Noah, who was now in full meltdown mode, sitting on the floor, fists full of hair, while he rocked and screamed, she made her way to the lights. She turned off all but one, throwing the room into semi-darkness. She scrolled through her phone and chose a calming playlist she used when doing yoga. She placed the device on her desk and sat on the floor facing the boy, but not too close so he wouldn't feel crowded. "Noah? It's okay. Look at me, please."

It took a few minutes, but he stopped yelling and stared at her, breath heavy, hands still buried in his hair.

"Noah, listen to me. I know this is very frustrating for you. We're doing everything we can. Do you understand me?"

"I want to go home," he said, voice cracking.

"I know. But for now, let's go in the back, okay? I have some blankets and pillows. Why don't you lie down and rest, maybe take a little nap? When you wake up, we'll get you home."

His breathing was ragged, but he unclenched his hands and allowed Sally to help him up. Then she led him to the small kitchen area.

Tanelsa came in, her arms full of seat cushions. "This is all we have."

Sally took them. "Get my keys. In the trunk are a couple of fleece blankets. Bring them in."

Tanelsa nodded. While she retrieved the blankets, Sally made the best makeshift bed she could with the cushions. When Tanelsa returned, Sally called to Noah. "I know it's not great, but it's all I can do." From the front, she heard the bells jingle. Someone had come in. *Just my luck. I'll get him settled, and then he'll have to leave.*

He nodded and curled himself onto the pile. Sally covered him with the blankets. She left one small light on over the sink and pulled the door almost closed. Enough to leave him in deep shadows, but not enough to shut him in.

She brushed off her hands. "That's taken care of. Now all we have to do—" She pulled up at the scene in the main office.

Sue stood in the archway, her hair disheveled, the light in her eyes a mix of sadness and desperation. Another woman was in front of her, stock-still, as though frozen in place. Since they stood so close, it was easy to see the family resemblance, although the woman's features were a little softer than Sue's.

Across the room, Tanelsa was also frozen in place, her hands half raised. She shot Sally a warning look.

"What on earth is going on? Sue, is this your sister? She looks like you."

Sue said nothing.

"You know, we've been calling all day, Tanelsa and I. Where have you been?"

"I had to meet Janice, bring her to see you." Sue gripped the other woman with her left hand. Janice shifted, and Sally saw a small knife in Sue's right. "I didn't want this to happen. But you all wouldn't leave things alone. Where's Noah?"

Sally reached out to the strange woman, presumably Janice Hepworth. "Sue, put the knife down. This will *not* solve anything."

"Like hell, it won't." Sue laughed, a nervous sound that nonetheless sent a shiver down Sally's neck. "Now, where's my son?"

The music cut off as Sally's phone buzzed. She made a move toward the desk.

Sue pressed the knife to Janice's side. "Let it go to voicemail."

Janice licked her lips. "Answer it," she said in a tremulous voice. "I'm fine."

Sally addressed her words to Sue. "It could be a client."

"I don't care. Don't touch it." Sue waited until the phone stopped. "Where is he?"

"Listen to me." Sally held up her hands. "You're going to upset him."

"Like you already haven't?" Sue gripped the knife tighter. "For the last time, where is he?"

* * *

Duncan stood in the parking lot of the Uniontown booking center and ran his hand through his hair as he waited for Sally's voicemail message to end. "It's me. Call me back as soon as you get this." Atwiler had not said a word since the arrest. On the way, Duncan had called Detective Mason up in Mount Lebanon to bring her up to speed. *Now, the lawyers can haggle over who gets him first.* "Any problems?" he called as Cavendish exited the building.

She jogged over. "Nope. He's all tucked in. I think I need a shower after sharing so much time with him." She shuddered. "Did you call Sally and let her know we have Maddie's killer?"

"She's not answering."

"She could be in a meeting."

"She wouldn't conduct an interview with another client if Noah was around. She'd have sent me a text if his mother picked him up. As far as Sally knows, Sue is still a potential murderer." It made no sense. Why wouldn't Sally answer? Or why didn't Tanelsa, if she saw his name on the caller ID? He dialed again. This time, the call connected. "Sally, it's me. What—" He broke off.

Voices came over the line. Women's voices. One of them was Sally, but she wasn't talking into the phone, not directly. Had she put him on speaker? He listened. The other voice sounded familiar. Not Tanelsa. Was that Hepworth?

"Sue, for the last time. This isn't going to be good for anyone, including Noah," Sally said.

"I don't care. I want my son, and I want him now." Definitely Hepworth.

A third voice came over the line, soft, but still audible. "*Your* son? He's my son. I may not have seen him for over ten years, but I deserve to know him, don't you think?" Janice Montgomery.

"That's rich," Hepworth said, voice dripping sarcasm. "You weren't half the mother I was. Not even a *quarter* of the mother."

"That's enough," Sally said. "Sue, put that knife down before you hurt someone."

Biting back an oath, Duncan stabbed the mute button. He looked at Cavendish. "Go back inside. Have Uniontown send two units over to Castle & Parson and tell them it's a hostage situation. One assailant armed with a knife, three, maybe four hostages. Can you get a ride?"

"Yes." Cavendish did not ask questions and went to request backup.

Duncan hit the blue lights and the siren as he peeled out of the parking lot. It had been quick thinking on Sally's part, answering the call and putting it on speaker. Hopefully, Hepworth wouldn't notice. At least not until someone got there.

* * *

Sally focused on the woman in front of her. With any luck, some kind of police presence would be there in minutes.

Sue bit her lip. "Are you sure you shut it off?" she finally asked.

"Of course I did." Sally moved a little to block the view of her phone, which she'd left on the desk. She had no idea where Jim was. But he had to have heard the conversation. Now, she had to keep Sue talking long enough for reinforcements to arrive. "Why'd you kill Maddie? You did, didn't you?"

Sue's hand wavered. "Little bitch. She couldn't keep her nose out of things, oh no. Had to find Noah's real mother. Screw that, *I'm* his real mother, the only one he's ever known. She never stopped to think what it would do to him. 'He has the right to know.' Please." Sue drew a ragged breath. "But I didn't kill her. She was dead when I showed up. I owe someone a favor."

"He does have that right, doesn't he?" Tanelsa asked. By unspoken agreement, she and Sally had positioned themselves so they stood to either side of the sisters, forcing Sue to pivot slightly in order to watch both of them. "This is her, isn't it? Janice?"

"I wasn't going to let that red-haired witch ruin Noah's life. He's too fragile. It would destroy him, do you understand me?

Janice cut her eyes to her sister. "Him or you?" She twisted to try and get away, but stopped when Sue lifted the knife to her throat. "I admit it. I was in no position to be a mother back then. You did an amazing thing, and I'm grateful. But he's not a china doll. I'm not trying to take him away from you. I wanted to know him, meet him. I love him."

"You don't know what love is."

"Don't I?" Janice's voice broke. "I knew exactly what I was doing all those years ago. How was I going to raise a child? What could I give him? Nothing. The best thing I could do for him was to leave. I knew you'd take care of him, you and Mom. But things change. I've changed. I want to know my boy."

Tanelsa cleared her throat. "Did you go to your sister, Janice? Did she bring you here?"

"No. I went to the center earlier and spoke to the director. She gave me Ms. Castle's name. I was on my way in to speak with you, to see if you could help me, and Sue caught me outside." Janice waved to the door. "When Sue saw me, she forced me in with her."

"I'm all packed. I came to get Noah." Sue's voice trembled.

Sally kept her gaze on Sue. "How'd you know Maddie was at the lake?"

"I didn't." Sue shook again. "She'd called me earlier. She told me she'd found Janice and was bringing her to the house on Friday to meet Noah. I'd see this was a good thing. I was going to take Noah and leave for the evening, but I couldn't find him. I knew he liked roaming the woods, so I went looking. He was staring through the window of the cabin. When I went over, I saw her, Maddie. She was half-dressed, jeans on, shirt not buttoned, lying on the bed. I went in, and she was dead. She had a scarf tied around her neck. It looked expensive. Something she'd wear." She took a deep breath.

"You were afraid," Sally said.

"I was glad. But then I realized the cops might figure out I was here. Worse, they'd learn that Noah had been there." Sue swallowed. "I tried to fix up a scene. No one would believe she'd get naked in front of an autistic boy, right? I tugged off her jeans and her shirt and dumped her on the cot. I

276

picked up her phone, deleted my contact, Janice's, and any texts I found, just so there wouldn't be any connection between us. Not beyond what they'd know from her volunteering at the Center. Then I took Noah home. It wasn't until later I found he'd swiped the damn phone."

Thoughts whirled in Sally's mind. It hadn't been Sue? But it all made sense. "What about Will Brackin? Did you kill him?"

Tanelsa's eyes widened a fraction.

Sue frowned. "I have no idea who that is." She shifted her hand on the knife and tightened her grip on Janice. "Enough chitchat. Where is Noah? I'm taking him. We're leaving, and this time, you'll never find us."

Janice went still. "Sue, what are you going to do? Kill all of us?"

"I'm not a murderer. Don't you understand? I have to protect him!" Sue pressed the knife against Janice's throat, and a dot of blood appeared. "Where. Is. He?"

Sally held out a hand. "Put down the knife, Sue. You won't get out of Uniontown, much less Fayette County. If you leave even one of us alive and conscious, that person will be on the phone to the police as soon as you leave. They'll radio every law enforcement agency within a fifty-mile radius and give them your license plate, description, and Noah's description. Give up, and we'll work this out."

Police sirens cut the air, and through the windows, Sally saw the flashing red and blue lights. At that point, several things happened. Sue pulled the knife across Janice's throat. Janice fell to the floor.

And Sally screamed.

Chapter Forty-Five

Duncan watched as the ambulance sped away. A Uniontown black and white had already left, carrying Sue to the city booking station, where she'd be charged with attempted murder and maybe interfering with a crime scene. Thanks to Sally's quick thinking, he and Cavendish had heard the entire conversation. By the time they'd arrived, the Uniontown cops had already entered the office and called an ambulance for Janice. Sally stayed with Noah until a representative from social services came to take care of him.

Cavendish came over. "Janice will be okay. It's a pretty long cut to her neck, but shallow. The blood made it look worse. Getting first aid quickly helped." She looked around. "You talked to Sally yet?"

"No. She was giving a statement to the uniforms. I didn't want to intrude."

"Well, let's go inside. It's freaking cold out here." She hustled into the office.

Duncan followed. Sally had finished talking to the officer and stood back as technicians took care of the scene. He waited until she saw him, then beckoned her into the conference room.

She looked a little haggard but otherwise unharmed. "We've got to stop doing this. Meeting at crime scenes, that is."

He resisted the urge to brush aside her hair and kiss her. Too many witnesses. "When I heard your scream...."

"I know." She did not seem to share his caution and pressed her lips against his. "How much of the conversation did you get?"

"The whole thing."

278

"I was terrified Sue would notice, but she was so fixated on us I don't think the thought ever occurred to her. Did she really not kill Maddie and Brackin, or was that a bluff?"

"No bluff." Duncan proceeded to tell Sally everything. "Sex and money. Two of the oldest motives in the history of man."

"Too bad they can't get Brackin for what he did to Maddie." Sally shook her head.

Duncan sat on the conference table. "I don't understand about Hepworth, though. She wouldn't have gone to jail. Over Noah and what happened way back then. I don't know why she panicked."

"Because she thought she was going to lose her son." Sally sat next to him and leaned her head on his shoulder. "There wouldn't have been any legal repercussions, probably. But what if he decided to go off with Janice? Sue's world would have imploded. I think she would rather go to jail than let that happen."

"Yes, this situation is so much better for him. Instead of learning his mom isn't really his mother and took off with him when he was a child, now he has to deal with the fact she held three people hostage at knifepoint and is probably going to prison for that. In addition to tampering with a crime scene."

"I didn't say she made sense. But she was desperate to protect him, to keep him safe, so she did what she thought she had to."

"Crazy." He looked at the bustling technicians. "You'd never do that."

"No, I wouldn't." She sat up. "Jim..."

He laid a finger over her lips. "Later. For now, let's just get you home." He knew what she'd been about to say. They couldn't put the conversation off forever. But this was definitely not the time.

* * *

Two days later, on Thursday evening, Sally parked her Camry in Jim's driveway behind his Jeep. There weren't any other vehicles, so his parents hadn't arrived yet. Thankfully.

Rizzo and Pixel greeted her at the door, both enthusiastically vying for position of "most favored canine." She refused to play favorites and gave each a good scratch behind the ears before heading for the kitchen. Jim had laid place settings for four, uncorked a bottle of Merlot, and set a big bowl of salad in the middle of the table. From the pot on the stove, steam and the smell of braised beef in some kind of herb sauce filled the kitchen. Her stomach rumbled.

Jim gave the contents a stir, then replaced the cover. He set down the spoon and leaned over for a kiss. "What's the news?"

She grabbed the wine bottle and poured herself a glass of the dark red liquid. "Janice is doing well. She'll probably be discharged tomorrow. She got lucky."

"And Noah?"

"Sue's arrest hit him hard, not that he understood everything. He only knows his mother isn't coming, and he can't go home. It's hard on him. However, Janice has seen him a couple of times, and they appear to be getting along. She's taking it nice and slow, which is good. Liz Jackson is helping. I don't know if he'll wind up living with Janice or not, but I think they'll eventually make it work." She sat down. "What will happen to Sue?"

"I don't know. There's no getting around the facts of what she's done. What charges are filed will be up to the DA." He leaned on the counter. "Will a jury relate to the 'desperate mother' story and all that is another matter." He studied her. "How are you?"

"Me? I'm fine."

"Sally, be honest. You've been strangely quiet ever since Tuesday."

Had she? She tried to be normal, but of course, Jim would see right through it. He always did. "I've been doing a lot of thinking."

"About?"

"Motherhood. Families. How I feel about it all." She watched the kitchen lights through the ruby liquid. "Jim, no putting it off. Thanksgiving is next week, and I want us clear on this before then."

He sat. "Clear on what?"

Here goes. "I think I've told you before, I never saw myself as a mother. You know, some little girls play house, where they have babies and households, and all that nonsense. Me, I argued cases before the court. Did you know I once dreamed of being the youngest lawyer to successfully argue a Supreme Court case?"

His lips twitched. "No, but that doesn't surprise me."

"There's the fact that I always saw myself as a career woman. Plus, I like my independence. I can decide to go away for a weekend, and all I have to do is arrange for boarding for Pixel." She set down the glass and looked at him. "I know you want kids. At least, you told me you saw yourself with a family. And it's not that I don't like children—"

"You just don't want your own."

"Exactly." She took a deep breath. "I want us to be on the same page. If they are that important to you, maybe we aren't supposed to be together after all." There. She'd said it. That possibility had kept her up until the wee hours of the morning for days, but it was like she'd told Tanelsa. Without open communication, the relationship would crumble. Better to cut it off now instead of suffering through a slow death. There were other men out there, right? She could find a place for her and Pixel. Maybe the dog was the only man she needed.

Liar.

Jim didn't move for a moment, eyes dark as he thought. Then he reached across the table and took her hands. "Sally, I've never hidden the fact that I'd love to be a dad. I remember playing ball with my father, and I thought how great it would be to do the same someday."

Here it comes.

"But." He kissed her hands. "You can't do that without a woman, and it would have to be the right woman. You are the right one for me. You *get* me. I think it's mutual. Would I love kids? Hell, yes. But there's more to it."

The knot in her chest eased.

"Here's the thing. I want to be with you. Period. If, someday, you change your mind and want kids, hey, I'm all for it. I'll do my part. But I'm not going to pressure you, and neither is my mother. She's kind of big on doing your own thing, if you haven't noticed."

Sally laughed. "We haven't talked much aside from that one dinner, but somehow, I'm not surprised."

He squeezed her hand. "As far as I'm concerned, there is only one problem for Thanksgiving."

"And that is?"

He grinned. "What are you bringing for dessert?"

A Note from the Author

All of the landmarks mentioned in this book are real—Fort Necessity, Fallingwater, etc. I have taken small liberties with geography for the sake of the story. I hope residents and visitors to the Laurel Highlands will forgive me.

Acknowledgements

Wow, ten books. Ten! I remember when one was a pipe dream. There are so many people to thank and I'm afraid I'm going to leave someone out.

A huge thank you to my critique group: the fabulous Annette Dashofy, Jeff Boarts, and Peter WJ Hayes, and critique buddy emeritus, Tamara Girardi. You guys are a big reason I've gotten this far and continue to be able to write novels.

Dru Ann Love, of Dru's Book Musings, has been a fan of Jim and Sally since *Murder Most Scenic*, the collection of short stories I self-published way back in…I don't remember when. Since then, she has done Day in the Life, Twenty Questions, cover reveals and fabulous musings of every book. And she's a wonderful person on top of it all and a dear friend. Thank you, from the bottom of my heart, for everything you do.

Likewise, thank you to Kristopher Zgorski of BOLO Books. When I started this journey, one of the items on my bucket list was a review on the BOLO Books blog. Not only did I get that, I was honored to be invited to be a Composite Sketch subject. Kristopher is another great champion of crime fiction, a great friend, and, along with his partner Michael, one of the people I look forward to seeing at annual conferences.

Thank you to the wonderful women at Level Best Books – Harriette Sackler, Verena Rose, and Shawn Reilly Simmons. They are not only editors, cover artists, and business partners, but good friends, and I treasure you all.

Community is key when writing a book. I would not be here without the love and support from Sisters and Crime and Pennwriters. But it goes further than that. Thank you to the regulars, both in front and behind the curtain, at Jungle Red Writers, Wicked Authors, and Chicks on the Case. I can't start my day without visiting these blogs and checking in with my tribe.

Thank you to all the readers who have embraced Jim, Sally, Aislyn, Burns, and the crew. Without you, there really is no magic. Just me yelling into the void.

Much love to my family, who supports me on this crazy mission. And answers my text messages about the oddest things. Mwah!

Last, but not least, to my husband, Paul. Who knew when you said, "Why don't you take the summer off and finish that novel?" that I'd end up here? Love you.

About the Author

A recovering technical writer, Liz Milliron is the author of The Laurel Highlands Mysteries, set in the scenic Laurel Highlands and The Homefront Mysteries, set in Buffalo NY during the early years of World War II. She is a member of Pennwriters, Sisters in Crime, International Thriller Writers and The Historical Novel Society. She is the current vice-president of the Pittsburgh chapter of Sisters in Crime and is on the National Board as the Education Liaison. Liz splits her time between Pittsburgh and the Laurel Highlands, where she lives with her husband and a very spoiled retired-racer greyhound.

SOCIAL MEDIA HANDLES:
  Facebook: https://facebook.com/LizMilliron
  Instagram: https://instagram.com/LizMilliron
  Newsletter: https://www.subscribe page.com/newsletteridyllic

AUTHOR WEBSITE:
  https://lizmilliron.com

Also by Liz Milliron

The Laurel Highlands Mysteries

Lie Down with Dogs

Harm Not the Earth

Broken Trust

Heaven Has No Rage

Root of All Evil

The Homefront Mysteries

The Truth We Hide

The Lessons We Learn

The Stories We Tell

The Enemy We Don't Know